LOVE DREAMS

LOVE DREAMS

A NOVEL

BY

January Valentine

Printed in the United States of America
Second Edition

ISBN: 978-0984957330
ISBN: 0984957332
ISBN 978-0-9849573-2-3 (ebook)

Library of Congress Control Number 2012932498

Edited by Vic Fortezza, Phaedra Valentine & Joseph Hart
Book Design by Victoria Valentine

Female Cover Image © dpaint
Male Cover Image © gdvcom
Interior Image © Anton Zabielskyi
Used under license from Shutterstock.com

Water Forest Press Books
PO Box 295, Stormville, NY 12582
waterforestpress.com

Love — bittersweet, irrepressible — loosens my limbs
and I tremble.

SAPPHO, To Atthis

TO THE POWER OF LOVE

DON'T EVER UNDERESTIMATE THE MAGIC . . .

ACKNOWLEDGEMENTS

The seed of Love Dreams was planted long ago, never fully developing until 2011, when I pulled out eight original chapters and a skeleton outline, deciding I'd finally bring this story to a close. We went through many revisions, but somewhere along the way, *Love Dreams* blazed a trail of its own, with a physically handicapped hero and an emotionally handicapped heroine sprouting, sharing the spotlight using a unique voice to create a captivating story sizzling with sweet heat.

I'd like to thank several friends for reading the early versions of my manuscript and for cheering me on to the finish line: jacob erin-cilberto, Jill Lapin-Zell, my critique partner Lynda Kaye Frazier, and my beautiful daughter, Phaedra, who never failed to fill in my blanks.

A special thank you to Vic Fortezza and Joseph Hart, who helped smooth out a wrinkled manuscript that was then transformed into the contemporary romance you are about to read.

Thanks and hugs to artist Pameli DelliColli (always there to lend a hand) for her help with enhancing the cover art.

Most of all, to my loving family, who grew to understand a writer's demon, forgiving of my empty place at the dinner table, and much more. Thanks Phae for picking up my slack.

To my parents who showed me that love, kindness and determination make the world go round.

NEW YORK

"**W**hat's her name?"

The responding officer pulls a notepad from his pocket, flipping to the page where he had scrawled, "Sienna Alexander."

The emergency room nurse begins entering information into a computer. "Date of birth?"

"I don't have the exact date, but a neighbor says she's in her early twenties." He rests an arm on the counter separating them.

The nurse stops typing, raising her eyes to stare at the young officer. "Motor vehicle accident?"

"Appears to be a break-in, possibly domestic violence."

"Anyone in custody?"

"Not yet."

"Has next of kin been notified?"

"Neighbor says they're in Canada. The detectives on the case are trying to contact them."

The glass doors slide open and Paramedics rush a young woman down the corridor, slowing only to regard the nurse's nod.

"Take her to Trauma Two." Her gaze catches a cervical brace, slides over a sheet tucked like a deflated cocoon strapped to a gurney.

The Team is waiting, gowned and gloved, ready to spring into action.

Cautiously, she's transferred to an E.R. stretcher. An IV line fastened to a catheter embedded in the top of her hand, covered with sterile tape, momentarily strains as her body is repositioned.

Paramedics step aside, one beginning to report.

"She's been beaten. Was unresponsive when we arrived."

All eyes are on the body lying motionless beneath the white sheet dotted with crimson. An arm appears broken. Her face is bruised and swollen. Blood clings to her mouth and nostrils. Her eyelids are purple, without a lid crease, flush with her brows. Her fingers are also caked with blood.

The Resident lifts her right hand, checking her pulse, inspecting. "Looks like she put up a fight. Three fingernails are snapped off and jagged. Swab the blood. It may not be hers."

A Respiratory Tech administers oxygen and a cardiac monitor is attached.

Blood pressure: 80/60, heart rate: 120, respiratory rate: 18.

As the Resident verbally assesses her condition, a nurse documents the findings on a flow sheet.

"She's breathing on her own," says the doctor.

Respiratory packs up their equipment, rolls the ventilator to the door.

He inspects her arms, legs, "Alert the Orthopedic on call." Gently, he peels up each lid, shining a penlight. Her pupils are reactive, corneas streaked with bright red vessels.

She's moved to Radiology for X-rays and CT scans.

THE FOLLOWING DAY

Her lids do a slow roll, then burrow beneath her brow bones. "Where am I?" she asks the nurse who is replacing her IV bag depleted of glucose and medication.

She rests a hand on her arm and says, "You're in St. Luke's Hospital."

"What happened?"

The nurse's lips tighten. "You had an accident, but you're going to be fine. The doctor will talk to you soon, just rest."

"My head hurts."

"That's expected."

"My arm . . . What happened to me?" Close to hysteria, the pitch of her voice hits her eardrums like a slingshot.

The nurse pats her hand. "I'll be right back, dear. I'm going to find your doctor." She pauses at the doorway. "I'll also let your family know you're awake."

"My family's here?"

His eyes bloat beyond their sockets, then his face goes blank.

She struggles to remember who he is.

She wants to scream, but there isn't enough air left in her lungs. His grip is tighter, fingernails digging into her throat, scraping, puncturing tender flesh. She tries to pry his fingers loose, but he's so strong. Her arm, twisted severely behind her, throbs with pain. The room looks smoky, black shadows are closing in, blocking her vision. She knows she's dying.

Her scream echoes through the corridor. The nurse drops the phone and runs back into the room.

January Valentine

CONNECTICUT

The quest for perfection can drive a mind insane. Although there's always room for improvement, at some point, you need to walk away. Rob Lucas was perfection, or so thought Sienna Alexander. When she tried to walk away, he followed her from Canada to New York, where her nightmare began.

Sienna Alexander waited for the traffic arrow to signal green. She closed the window of her red Corolla, turned up the radio, and sang along with *TNL: "falling from the sky, when I look into your eyes, you can't make me new, maybe make me try, but loving is a place, that always made me cry, it tore out what was best, so I'm hiding all that's left . . ."*

That's exactly what Sienna promised to do — hide what was left of herself. She had hoped to leave tragedy behind when she moved to suburban Connecticut, into one of the few areas she could comfortably afford. It was a beautiful place to live, and safe. She enjoyed the tranquility, but there was a downside. There wasn't much to relieve her mind of the past.

The dampening day bit right through her T-shirt. Shivering, she brushed goose bumps from her arms. If she were at home, she'd slip into a warm shower and wrap herself in a cuddly robe. But she wasn't at home; she was about to do weekly shopping. Frowning, she checked her rearview mirror, then fluffed her windblown hair into place. *Pretty haggard for twenty-eight. But what should I expect? I barely get any sleep! Should probably wear some makeup. Who gives a damn, anyway.*

⌒

"You were a reservist, weren't you, Michael?"

"Yep, Army." He pushed aside a half-eaten turkey club. From an hour in the sun, the dressing looked like dried mustard instead of Thousand Island. "Many moons ago." His dark eyes searched the veranda, then studied the stucco archway leading into the main dining room.

"When you're my age you can talk about how many moons you've seen." Art, the man sitting across the table, laughed. "You're still a kid."

"It's not the number of years that count. It's where they take you that matters."

"Eh, I guess you're right. Did you serve outside the States?"

"Fifteen months in Afghanistan."

"My son's thinking about enlisting in the Army, but he's been talking about the Reserves as an alternative. What do you think?"

"Depends on what he's looking for. Where the hell's our waitress?"

"Everything okay?" Art's suntanned forehead creased. In one polished movement, he lifted his Sox cap and scratched his head, then tugged the brim down to his brows. "You seem edgy."

"Yeah, everything's fine. Just a little preoccupied." Michael pulled two twenties from a wad of cash bound by a silver money clip and dropped them on the glass tabletop. "I'm gonna hang around here a while longer. Tell Gus to keep an eye on things. I'm not sure if I'll get back to the site today."

Michael was built for construction, although not dressed for work. He slid the sleeves of his burgundy polo to his elbows, placed his hands on his lap and laced his fingers.

Art nodded. "You got it, boss."

After paying the lunch check, Michael remained on the veranda of the Plaza Restaurant, beneath a colorful canvas canopy, drinking iced tea from a tall frosted glass. Sunshine glinted off steel handlebars, and spokes of the wheels that rested alongside the wrought iron table where between sips he set down his glass.

With each lowering, he aimed for the same ring of condensation. Lifting, he watched a downpour of droplets splatter, roll, seep back into the circle like kin leaving the nest and returning, sometimes stronger, sometimes damaged, but always finding their place. It was something to do while passing time.

The plaza buzzed with shoppers and business men and women, arriving and departing the forty plus stores in a flurry of organized chaos. On the walkway below, an attractive blonde in a spandex outfit broke out from behind two women pushing toddlers in strollers. Looking up she smiled and waved, then sprinted off, a sequined tote slung over her shoulder, bouncing off her hip. Michael nodded, watching her lean legs pump effortlessly as she faded behind blossoming apple trees framing the road.

The girl was lovely, but there was only one woman who impressed him, put that extra beat into the rhythm of his heart. Although he had only seen her from a distance, he was convinced; any guy in his right mind could fall in love with her, given the opportunity. He found himself wondering about her. *Someone like her could be habit-forming.*

He savored the lemon tea as he would her, should she fall into his arms. *What are the chances of that happening?* A snicker was more of a grunt that stirred his shoulders. Her face stalled in his mind until he drifted back to earth with thoughts of other habits he'd had to break, like jogging in the rain, running on the beach. He stared at the sky, clouds breaking like ocean waves. Taking the boat out on the Sound at dawn, when the water was still and the bass took the bait, was something he missed most. He'd like to take her out on the boat. But then, he'd like to do a lot of things.

Gathering clouds curled like the murky plumes of dust forming above the construction site huddled at the foothills beyond Interstate 95.

ACCIDENTAL RUN IN

Easing her car around the driveway median, Sienna cruised the aisles, searching for a close parking space. She had too much to do on her day off to waste time hiking the plaza. She'd save hiking for another day, a sunny day she'd spend with — spend with no one in particular. Nova Scotia sprang to mind. The trails, the bluff, the ocean she never wanted to leave. Family and friends she had all but abandoned. The parking spot she edged into was as tight as her grip on the wheel.

She had it down to a science. Grocery shopping could be done in less than fifteen minutes if the checkout lines weren't long, and today she was in luck. The lot was full but the stores weren't. When she left the market drizzle filled the air, but she didn't mind. She closed her eyes, tilted her head, and let droplets touch her face. After a moment of heaven she sighed, then focused on the sidewalk and her last stop before heading home. Her sandals nipped her heels as she walked, avoiding puddles as much as she would have liked to avoid Dyson's Cleaners. But doing so would have meant driving twenty miles out of her way. She could handle the owner more easily than rush hour traffic.

"Here you go. One dollar twenty-seven cents, Ms. Alexander." Dyson's hand rested on hers as she balanced her groceries on the cluttered counter.

She jerked away and dropped the change into her purse. He was becoming a real pain in the ass, but she wasn't in the mood to wipe the smirk off his face. Not today.

She whisked her plastic-covered dry cleaning through the air, mouthing, "Dream on pervert," not caring if he lip-read.

Arms filled with groceries, hobo bag slung over a shoulder, she left the store. Her fingers, wound around the wire hangers, were red and beginning to sting.

I can do this . . .

The heel of her sandal snagged the rubber mat outside the door. Her body lurched forward on one leg while her sandal stayed behind.

Oh crap . . . Tell me this isn't happening . . .

As she strangled her packages, her hobo slid from her shoulder scraping her inner arm, then caught at her wrist. The momentum tossed three plump grapefruit out of a bag, up into the air. They hit the ground like mini basketballs. Blood rushed to her head that began to throb. Sure Dyson would pop up at any moment, she could almost hear his throaty laugh as he reminded her he had offered to help her to her car.

"Let me give you a hand." The voice behind her was rugged and smooth. If oozing nectar poured sound, it would have been his voice.

Sienna couldn't catch the grapefruit, but kept her balance as she pulled her sandal free, managing not to twist an ankle as she spun.

His dynamic shoulder span was the first thing to strike before her eyes jumped to his face.

A breeze whipped his hair into loose mocha waves that gathered at his neck. He flicked away strands snagged by his lashes, then simply stared.

She hoped she didn't look as foolish as she felt, and instinctively shifted her gaze. She blinked, then mumbled, "Guess I should have used a cart." Then her glance swept his collar fluttering in the same gust that tousled his hair, making him look touchable with his knit shirt showing off his muscular chest. But touching . . . sex was the last thing on her mind. So were men. Still, she was human, and what was wrong with appreciating beauty? . . . From a distance.

"Need a hand?" He squinted with eyes softer than lamplight sifting through a silken shade.

She couldn't help but admire how a fading stream of sun mixed lustrous mocha with sparkling root beer when he angled his head and offered. But here she was, face to face with a man in a wheelchair, wondering how *he* was going to help *her*.

What's he doing in a wheelchair? For a moment she imagined him with a woman in his arms, gliding across a dance floor, or maybe sauntering down a runway. Fleeting thoughts. She shook them off. Ogling was the old Sienna. She was different now.

While she gaped with indifference, he easily maneuvered, snagging the fruit before it rolled off the curb. His forearms flexed seductively as he scooped it up to his lap. The running shoes and Wrangler jeans he wore were a show of virility, but his legs would not budge. He was back at her side before she realized it would have been nice of her to respond. Nice? Big deal: She could have picked up her own damn fruit.

"Are you going to eat all these things by yourself?" He cocked his head and grinned.

Had her hands been free she'd have slapped them on her hips and struck a pose. "Why? Do you want one?"

"Nah. I just had lunch." Laugh lines curved with his cheeks as he held the fruit out with big hands, then drew back. "Look — why don't you let me have those packages while you organize yourself."

He was too enthusiastic, invading her space, her privacy. And she didn't need some stranger touching her fruit. Determined to keep a bag from slipping through her arms, she shook her head. "No thanks, I'm fine— and why don't you just keep the fruit. I can get more if I need it."

"I don't eat grapefruit. Although these do look kind of appetizing." He squeezed the largest one.

"Fine. Hand them over then." After she spoke, she realized she had no way of taking possession of the grapefruit in question. Why were they squabbling over grapefruit, anyway? She clutched the bags tighter, crushing them in a bear hug, cringing as the wheat bread flattened, the soy milk container threatened to burst from the pressure. *Crap. This is all I need on top of everything else. Massacred groceries pouring all over the sidewalk.* Her jaw clenched.

"You sure about that?" He squinted harder.

She let out an exasperated breath. "Hold on. Let me . . ."

"Drop everything?"

"Ha ha, funny. Could have been worse. You could be picking *me* up off the ground instead of my stuff." Drizzle caught her lashes and slipped into an eye. She blinked away a blur and focused on him, lips pursed, ready to snap his head off if he didn't stop offering his help.

"I wouldn't mind. On a lighter note, you could've dumped *everything* out of your purse instead of just your keychain." He extended his arms. "Give me that stuff, will you? Christ, you're stubborn."

"Excuse me?" That was it. One more word and she'd rip the amusement off his lips with one of her snidest remarks. The fire in her eyes alone should have taken effect by now. What was he, nice or just a glutton for punishment?

"Just trying to keep the traffic moving here." He nodded toward shoppers restraining their annoyance as they stepped off the curb to make their way around his chair, and her feet. "You're causing congestion . . . and about to lose everything . . ."

She followed his eyes, leading hers to the hobo's long brass zipper which hung open, exposing the entire contents. "Shit, shit, shit." When she shoved the groceries and dry cleaning onto his lap to bend for her keys, her wallet fell onto the sidewalk, along with her compact, followed by an avalanche of credit cards, and several wrapped tampons. "You've got to be kidding me . . ."

"I kid you not. This happens to me all the time too."

Does this man do nothing but wisecrack and grin? "How annoying."

"You're not the first person ever to tell me that."

She groaned. "Whatever." Then she snatched her things from the sidewalk, cramming them into her bag.

"You're a regular calamity, aren't you?" He chuckled as his eyes swooped over her.

"I usually have things completely under control," she snapped, lifting her chin and repositioning her shoulder bag to nest against the waistband of her jeans.

"So do I. Think you can manage your purse?" He gathered her packages on his lap. "Where's your car?"

"Get lost," teetered on the tip of her tongue, but when she saw the look on his face she relented, just like the words on her lips which suddenly sealed.

With a tilt of his head, he shot her a grin with only half of his mouth that looked lopsided and funny. So she puckered her lips, scrunching them into something of a smile.

"This way." Her voice was dull as she pointed across the parking lot. "I'm not always this clumsy. I must look like an idiot."

"I never thought that. And by the way, I'd say you look like a kindergarten teacher."

"And you look like you could be a quarterback, so what are you doing in that chair?" almost popped out of her mouth, but she stifled the comment, accidentally biting her tongue at the same time.

Most of the manners her parents had taught her had been wiped away by Rob. Still, she wasn't downright rude. She'd get to her car and get the hell out of here. She hated shopping. It was a waste of time, especially for one person. And how much food did a five-foot-three, one-hundred-five pound female need, anyway?

Tucking her bubble gum between molar and cheek, she said, "Actually, I had thought of becoming one." She'd play his game. "So just how does a kindergarten teacher look?"

She could obviously be hell on wheels. Wheels . . . He refused to feel inferior. What an attitude! Why was he attracted to her again?

"I would have to say," he took a deep breath but avoided her eyes as he pushed forward, "sweet." *Maybe not so sweet. . .* he mumbled under his breath. "I bet the kids would crush on their teacher the first day of school.

"What?"

"Nothing. Just joking."

"Kids drive me nuts." Her voice picked up as much steam as her feet, trying to keep stride with him. "It's not that I don't like them . . . I have enough trouble taking care of myself."

"I can see that."

"What's that supposed to mean?"

"Once more. Kidding."

"You seem to do a lot of that."

"Believe me, it helps."

Her eyes slipped over his face, trailing to the spinning wheels of his chair, his feet looking so out of place on the footrests.

"Some weather, huh?"

"Sure is," she replied, watching the wheels splatter through shallow puddles.

She stopped beside the Corolla's rear door and grabbed the handle. "This is mine," she said, trying to level her eyes without looking down at him.

"Nice car. I used to drive a black one. But that was some time ago. What year is yours? 2007?"

"Eight."

"Ah. Mine was an '07. Body style was the same though. Dependable car. They changed this body in '09. Tenth generation, brought back a more powerful engine, good car." Silly small-talk. He sawed a palm across his sprouting beard, smoothing the start of a frown.

"I appreciate your kindness." Treating him like hired help she destroyed the moment, and quickly transferred her things to the back seat of her car, careful not to brush against him.

Still, as she leaned in to lift the last of her groceries, strands of her hair tickled his cheek then rested on his shoulder, but only for a moment — brief but thrilling as he inhaled her. Her hair smelled of jasmine. Her perfume flooded the air with an enticing oriental scent. He liked the way the fragrances mixed and engulfed him — the way she did. During their first official meeting, he knew he liked everything about her, although he hadn't expected her to be a little klutz with a big attitude.

"Hopefully May will be better . . ."

"What?" With knitted brows she faced him. Her eyes, slanted like a cat's, were shocking blue, and had become impossible to read.

"Less rain . . ."

"Oh — right. Let's hope so." She slid behind the wheel and slammed the door shut. "Thanks again. Can I do anything for you? A lift somewhere?"

For a moment her eyes clung to his. He didn't seem like a bad guy. He couldn't have actually been hitting on her . . . She shouldn't have been so unkind. He had only been trying to help.

"Nope. I've got some things to do around here, but thanks for the offer." His face tightened, pulling his full mouth into a troubled shape.

"Better get going before it starts pouring," she said, thinking of her groceries that would be soaked by the time she carried them into her condo if she didn't beat the storm. Through the open window she studied his face. His sable eyes gripped hers, and she felt there was something he wanted to say — but he remained silent.

Michael sat in the parking lot, in drizzle that had turned to steady rain, looking on as she drove away. Eyes fixed on the shrinking bumper stickers plastered across the Corolla's rear: Save a Life-Adopt a Pet, he smiled. Then he headed in the direction of his cottage, hidden from the plaza by evergreen walls trimmed with oak.

He would not return to work today. He would never be able to concentrate.

He thought about her as he set a kettle of water to boil on the stove, recalling she hadn't worn a wedding ring. Actually, her hands had been jewelry free. But he remembered sparkling stud earrings peeking from beneath her long blonde hair.

He chuckled at the thought of her indifference during their awkward encounter. But there was more to her beneath the chilly surface . . . he just knew.

Even if I never have a chance with her — I can still dream, can't I?

He gazed around the room, frustration fighting optimism.

Who am I kidding? She'd never be interested in me. "Dream on, fool," he mumbled, cooling a cup of tea with a lingering breath.

That night, as she slipped into bed, Sienna thought about all of the things she should have done on her day off — and facing another tomorrow.

The laundry still overflowed in a corner of the room. Random garments hung on a chair- back, a few things strewn on the floor. Washed dishes sat in the drainboard. Where had the day gone? She hadn't even played tennis as she sometimes did on her day off. Shopping must have taken longer than usual. Shopping. For a moment she thought of him, and the grapefruit he'd rescued which were sitting in a bin in the refrigerator, scrubbed and cold like her, with hair damp from the shower.

Mind, stop! Go to sleep, Sienna.

Rolling over, she punched her pillow into shape. Still, memories roamed as they did every single night. The guy at the plaza seemed kind — the complete opposite of Rob Lucas.

She wondered what had incapacitated him and how long he'd been disabled. Could he have missionary style sex? With the woman on top, of course. Could he have sex at all? Stupid thoughts. None of her business. She was too nosy. Anyhow, celibacy wasn't all that bad.

Then she imagined what her life would be like now if she'd met a guy like him instead of her ex. But it was neither here nor there because she was finished with men. All men. Cute men, nice men, sexy men. It didn't matter. She had been reduced to a shuddering mass of bloody flesh, left for dead on her own living room floor. Horror she tried to forget always blindsided her! *Shit! I refuse to give in. I won't be afraid. No more nightmares. No more Rob.*

She was finally in control. She had made a nice home for herself: pleasant friends, good job, money in the bank, hobbies. Well, maybe just tennis when time and energy permitted. Why the hell would she need a man? Even if he *was* nice, and hot, like the plaza guy.

Too bad . . . Erasing both men from conscious thought, she drifted off to sleep.

NIGHTMARES AND CAPE COD

Screeching, she flees the lower level leading to the deck where gusts of wind tug her hair at the root. Her feet barely touch the steps, the strength of her arms using the banister to double-time her legs. Fluttering locks snap like wings, whipping her face. Without breaking stride, she swipes strands from her eyes and dares a backward glance.

He's chasing her. Dragging a plaited rope behind him. No — he can't be . . . Rob is dead!

Her heart begins to pound.

In hot pursuit, the figure takes the stairs two at a time.

Another glance — he isn't far behind. A chill runs down her spine as she recognizes two distinguishing features: his eyes. His eyes are black rocks, not only lifeless, they're pure evil.

It is you. Her stomach tightens.

Oh, God . . .

She'll have time to double back, circle the deck, make it down the stairs to slam and lock the cabin door. Miscalculation — the length of his athletic legs will overtake hers in moments. She knows what he's about do to her. He's done it before. Her heart races.

The dream had been so vivid it could have been reality. When Sienna opened her eyes she was exhausted. Although she had drifted through unconsciousness for the past eight hours, she felt like she hadn't slept a wink. Her head was groggy, her mouth felt like cardboard, and her body ached. *Of course I'm tired,* she told herself. *I've been running all damn night. When are these dreams going to stop?*

Reaching down, she yanked covers off the floor and back onto the mattress where they belonged. From the look of the bed, it had been a wild night. Too bad she hadn't enjoyed it. She'd make the bed later. Right now she needed a cup of coffee. She sat up, wondering why she wasn't wearing her nightgown. Reaching down, she snatched it from the floor, slipped it on and dangled her legs over the side of the bed, taking deep breaths until her throbbing temples calmed. She felt dizzy. Low blood pressure, she was certain. But judging from her lively pulse, her blood pressure had to have skyrocketed during the night. She looked around the room. There were no shadows, no figures. There was no ocean, no yacht. And Rob was not beside her — or behind her, thank God. It was over. But her mind wouldn't rest. She had to do something to straighten out her life.

Morning glared through the Corolla's smudged windshield. Sienna realized she should have cleaned the glass before leaving her driveway. Maintaining an automobile was a task she had accepted a long time ago, but this morning she was late for work, so rather than paper towels and Windex, wipers and washer fluid would have to do.

She parked, grabbed her bag, and jogged through the doors of Manchester General. That special hush, found in early morning hospital corridors, still cloaked the first floor business offices, but the pungent aroma of coffee filled the air. The hard soles of her wedge shoes squeaked on the polished tiles.

"It's about time." The bellow shattered the silence of the office they shared.

"Sorry," out of breath, Sienna apologized. "It was a crazy morning." Settling behind her desk, she offered a sheepish grin. "I had to stop at a neighbor's house to see if she would take one of the guys."

"Still rescuing strays, huh?" The woman's voice softened. "You're something else, Sienna. You take better care of animals than you do of yourself."

"I'd take all of them if I could. Breaks my heart to see them sitting in cages, big sad eyes, little puffballs just waiting on the countdown. And they don't even realize their days are numbered."

"So are ours. That young guy they brought in yesterday died during the night."

"Oh, no. He was only twenty-five years old. Life is too cruel."

"Sometimes it is."

"Any calls? Emergencies? Anyone looking for me?"

"Nah, it's been quiet. And I've got your back. You know that."

"I know you do." Sienna smiled at the redhead seated across the room.

The script on her nameplate read Bonnie Murray. She hunched over her desk, rummaging through a sliding mound of pamphlets, and held up a glossy New England Tour Guide, waving it in the air, fanning her face. "How about the Cape this year? Vacation's around the corner, and Lord knows we both need it."

After a quick glance at the surf-covered guide, Sienna shook her head. "Bad memories. I went there with Rob — to rekindle, as he put it." She scowled. "Some rekindling. Dysfunctional bastard."

"Sorry I brought it up." Bonnie's voice was tight. "I didn't realize. . ."

"How would you?" Sienna scrutinized a computerized list of the prior night's emergency admissions, but took a moment to recall off-season Cape Cod, when motel rates were low. "Regardless. I doubt I'd go anyway. There's nothing to do this time of year," agitation revved her normal monotone, but her stare hung in the air, "other than bundle up, watch the ocean, gain weight on lobster dinners."

She had to shake off memories if she was going to survive. Shake off trauma, just as easily as she had shaken sand from their shoes after a run on the beach that ended in a raging argument.

That was ages ago — in her mind, anyway. "Yeah, I gained five pounds because it rained the entire time we were there. I thought you were going on a cruise where they have fresh fruit tables and diet platters?" She shot Bonnie a look of displeasure.

"I embrace my curves. So does Mickey." Bonnie chuckled. "You're gonna have to do better than that if you want to get a rise out of me."

Sienna remembered the tall flight of stairs leading to the motel room in Truro. If she let herself, she could easily relive the feeling of her hair coiling with dampness as it took flight in hammering bursts of salted wind.

The view from the second-floor picture window was of nothing but rolling ocean, with occasional seagulls in flight, like the ones she fed bread to each morning. Watching the furious waves made her seasick, but she loved it. She loved many things before . . .

"Fight or flight," her doctor had said. "If you don't want to take anti-anxiety medication, then learn how to relax. There's an RN who gives good meditation classes. Ideal for panic attacks. Here's the phone number."

The thought that she had almost agreed to marry Rob Lucas, before he tried to take her life, gave her chills — as well as recurring nightmares. Thank God Aunt Tessa was a good judge of character. Tessa never approved of Rob. Neither did her mother. Both women agreed he was a pressure cooker without a release valve.

Some incidents were too horrible to erase, memories striking without notice . . .

She doesn't need a Breathalyzer report to know that Rob is drunker than she has ever witnessed — or is it the drugs?

He must have lost his mind. As bad as things got, he never threatened to kill her before. Her heart thunders in her chest. She has to keep her wits about her if she's going to survive. She inhales cleansing breaths, deep and rhythmic like the counselor instructed, but her ears detect shallow gasps. Instinct takes over.

She knees him in the groin and runs down the short hallway. Now what? Not enough time to think!

"Bitch!" He corners her in the kitchen, within seconds reaching for her throat. She manages to dodge him, runs to the living room, snatching her portable phone from the counter. Rob is an athlete. He moves swiftly. She'll have to outsmart him.

She crouches beside the sofa, phone in hand, but doesn't have a chance to dial; her trembling fingers slip across the keypad, can't dial 9-1-1, and then she feels his breath, hot, sour, panting.

"Give me that fucking phone." He towers over her, taking a swipe at the air above her head, as usual, getting off as he watches fear consume her eyes. Droplets of frothy saliva pepper her face as he rants."Nobody's gonna come and save you."

He rips the phone from her hand and rifles it across the room like a football — but a football doesn't smash into a storm of plastic particles — and her living room floor isn't a football field. Her last defense is to try to calm him. How can she when she's falling apart? Still, she tries to strengthen her voice, "You don't want to do this. You'll be back in court, this time maybe prison."

He grabs her arms, wrenching her to her feet. "Nobody leaves me . . ."

Sienna blinked away memories and static luminance of her computer screen and closed her eyes. She massaged her temples, her fingers pressing firmly into her hairline. Her neck and shoulders were tight, but she refused to believe her doctor's diagnosis of tension headaches. She was over that, she told herself, she was strong. Now all she had to do was to kick the night terrors and she'd be just fine.

"I could use someone to talk to." Sienna sat with slumped shoulders, arms folded on her desk.

"Let me guess. Still no sleep." Bonnie spoke over her shoulder as she typed.

"A few hours, but restless."

"Gotta shut your mind off, sweetie."

"I can't. These dreams are driving me insane."

Bonnie swung around, watching Sienna's lips purse, then tighten. She raked her perm with long red fingernails, which signaled she was about to offer her undivided attention. "Well?"

"I think Rob is haunting me." Sienna shut her eyes, but the dream was unforgettable. Maybe sharing it would defuse it . . .

She dashes in another direction, to the yacht's bridge where perspiration seeps from her hairline, stinging her eyes. He's still behind her. Reaching out with muscular arms he grasps the trim of her flaring Sarong, but the slinky fabric trickles through his fingers like melted butter. She feels the tug and squeals, running faster, the pads of her feet thudding across the deck.

She risks another peek — he's hot on her heels, his face a mask of furious passion.

A scream catches in her throat. She knows the chase is about to end. She has to get away from him.

"Sounds very unpleasant. Maybe you should talk to someone."

"I am. I'm talking to you."

"I really wish I could help, but I don't know what to tell you."

"Just listen. I could feel wind blowing my hair. I could *smell* the air. I felt his hands, his fingers touching me. Ever have such realistic dreams?"

"Not often enough." The shameless look on Bonnie's face lightened the mood. Her eyes washed over Sienna who sat swiveling on her computer chair, her legs protectively crossed at the knee. "Go on."

"Thanks." The smile she feigned was sour. "Rob wasn't the only one in my dream last night. First I'm haunted. Then I'm having sex."

"In the middle of two men? Sounds good to me."

"If one wasn't trying to kill me, I guess it wouldn't be bad." Sienna's laugh was weak.

"Who was this lucky guy you were trying to seduce?" Bonnie's green eyes exploded with interest.

Sienna shrugged. "I don't know. Nothing makes sense anymore."

"Maybe your unconscious is trying to tell you something."

"What. I need to get laid?" Sienna rolled her eyes, then gathered her hair into a twisted knot on top of her head. She stretched tension from her shoulders, and after a thoughtful moment released a blonde rope that draped her chair back.

"Too many horror flicks, girlfriend. You ought to start watching porn before bed like Mickey and I do," said Bonnie, the tip of her tongue swiping her top lip.

"You know I detest horror movies." Sienna's eyes clouded. "This dream wasn't far from porn. He was hot. I was hot. It was so real I could almost reach out and touch him."

She pants to a halt, her heaving chest glistening.

"Tease." His growl is animalistic. "I've got you now." His ravenous eyes sweep her face, heating her ripening breasts. He peels down a strap of her bikini, angles his head, and swipes a startled nipple with his tongue, marking his territory.

"Like hell you do." She scrambles from his clutch.

Reaching out he fists her skirt — the zip of fabric tearing. Red chiffon curls like a bandage around his hand. Loosening his hold he shakes it free, letting the wind take her skirt up to fly like a billowing sail.

She heads for the stern, where he's a glimpse in the corner of her eye.

Small and light, she's fast. The only thing he can do is to hurtle forward, stretch out a tattooed arm to seize the clasp of her bikini top. Snap. It drops like an injured butterfly. She takes a few bouncing steps across the deck to where she pauses, turns with a devilish grin, then backs against the rail. Her pointed breasts heave sensual invitation as she struggles with her breath.

The look on his face — pure lust. His body is jacked, evenly tanned by a blistering sun. Smooth chest rippling into a taut waist and tight hips. A lock of wavy hair, darkened from a shower drapes a brow. She focuses on his lips — full, bowed, sexy and silent.

Bonnie's eyes narrowed. "So this was disturbing?"

Sienna's cheeks were flushed, her legs clenched. "The ocean was wild or the boat tipped. I don't know. But whatever it was — I lost my balance and fell overboard."

"Terrific, Sienna. You get this far into a sexy dream, but before you have a chance to screw a gorgeous guy you go and fall overboard. Leave it to you."

Leaning forward, Sienna gripped the armrests of her chair. "It freaked me out. I wasn't thinking about screwing. I woke up coughing."

"Your dreams would make great movies. You should sell them to Hollywood." She pushed away from her desk. "Listen gal. I know you've been through a terrible ordeal, but you need to climb back up on that horse again. It's time you stopped dreaming and started living."

"I don't want to hear about blind dates." Sienna waved her off.

"Whatever you say, Sienna." Bonnie snapped off her computer screen. "Coffee time?"

BREAK TIME AND MORE NIGHTMARES

Ready to head for the office door, Sienna stood and tugged at the back of her skirt, releasing the warmth that molded the fabric to her rounded buttocks. She didn't need a therapist. She already knew what was wrong.

"Quiet, Rob. I don't want the neighbors to hear."

"Fuck the neighbors," he snarls.

The living room picture window overlooks the courtyard of the New York apartment complex. Beyond the red brick building, a grass horseshoe separates the semicircle of parked cars from the roadway. Neighborhood kids pair off, playing on the concrete squares below. At the onset of the racket originating from the third floor apartment, the kids begin to buzz with interest, banning together like little thieves. A boy tags his friend's arm. "Come on, hurry up. That guy that keeps bothering her is back. They're fighting again," he whispers behind a hand stained with mud. "Don't want to miss any of it."

Rob tightens his hold and strides to the sofa table, dragging Sienna with him. Terror seeps through her limbs. With one hand he grips her neck while his other snatches an antique lamp. The pressure on her throat increases as his fingernails dig into her flesh. He holds the lamp inches above her head. When she screams, he snickers, then begins a tirade.

"There's nothing like gabbing all morning, then taking a break." The skin on the back of Bonnie's thighs squeaked as she slid from her chair. "Are you still with me?"

The Emergency Registration office they worked in was sandwiched between twenty other departments that spanned an entire wing of the hospital. Sounds of keyboards, telephones, and muffled voices wafted through flimsy walls partitioning the offices.

Bonnie rushed Sienna through the doorway, out into the corridor where their footsteps had no sound. "Come on. Let's grab that elevator first. The gals from the Business Office are heading this way." She elbowed Sienna. "If I have to ride with that bunch and listen to one more story about . . . Hey, you-know-who should be on rounds about now."

"Don't start that again," Sienna said as they stepped in and she pressed the lower level button. "Greg Trainer's the last thing I need."

Bonnie's overplucked brows flittered. "Why are you so dead set against going out with him?"

"Let's put it this way. Why would I want to?"

"Because your life is like a bland meal, Sienna. All the right ingredients. It just needs some spice."

Sienna's jaw slackened. Measured breaths extinguished the rise of anger. "See if I invite *you* to dinner again."

"I'm not trying to insult you, hun. You're a sweet, warm-hearted person, a good person. I hate to see your eyes filled with such pain."

"It's not pain. It's distaste for men like Trainer — and for some people who try to run my life when they don't know what the hell they're talking about."

"He's rich and good in bed. Need I say more?"

"How do *you* know Trainer's good in bed?" Sienna's brow shot up.

"Rumor." Bonnie tossed her hair, straightened her blouse. "And you could have confirmed it the night you were with him." Inside the cafeteria, her eyes moved from the pastry table to a rack of bagels and hard rolls.

"For God's sake, I had to pick up my car," Sienna clicked her tongue, "and he offered me a drink which I didn't even accept. Oh, how did I ever resist his charm? Gag." Her voice was as sour as her expression. "And who talked me into going to a medical conference with him in the first place?"

"That would be me." Selecting a plump Danish, Bonnie grinned.

Sienna held a bottled water. "I'll meet you back upstairs."

"Did I say something wrong?" Bonnie stumbled over her words while Sienna floated through the crowd and out of earshot.

The fury of his voice tears through her body with a jackhammer vibration. He drags her to the middle of the room where he spins her around as if in a hideous game of blind man's bluff — only Sienna isn't wearing a blindfold — and she knows he's not bluffing. She watches his face twist with hatred.

She knows there's no way out. The room begins to whirl. She focuses on his drooping eyelids, attempting to struggle free. I'm going to be sick . . . Don't panic!

Weakened by terror, tears flood her face. Can my heart pound this hard without bursting? I'm dying. Dear God, I'm dying. My chest pains. I can't breathe! I'll die before you kill me.

"I fucking hate you, Rob," trickles from her lips.

He stumbles, catches himself, latching on to her, hugging her like a grizzly.

Focus . . . Think straight! "Rob!"

"Shut up, bitch."

She's in his arms, he's crushing her. She's certain he's broken a rib when she feels the pain — hears a snap inside her chest.

"Stop it . . . You're choking me." She gasps for air, eyes darting around the room, climbing up and down the walls, to the doorway, open window, searching for the fastest way out.

Rob is savage, once handsome features distorted by a pint of

110 Vodka, and the cocaine he snorted on the way to the apartment — before breaking in to finish what he started months ago.

He stares with eyes so black and wet, they don't look human. His foul breath hits her face.

In a macabre moment, a thought flashes through her mind. A shark. I'm about to be ripped apart by a fucking shark.

"I told you she didn't mean anything to me," he screams. "But no — that didn't matter to you — you had to go and ruin everything — even after I warned you . . ."

Death seems seconds away, but Sienna isn't ready to die.

DOCTOR POLLOCK

"Tell Doctor Pollock I'm sorry. I overslept." Michael shifted the phone, masking a yawn as he slipped his Seiko onto his left wrist and pulled himself up to sit on crumpled sheets. His indigo pillows had been tossed to the floor sometime during the night, along with a lofty comforter half covering his chair. The only thing touching his bare chest was a matching percale sheet. A restless night had tousled his dark hair more sensually than a gust of wind ever could. He swiped mocha tufts from his eyes, squinting at the time on the titanium watch face. "Any chance of rescheduling for this afternoon, or possibly tomorrow?"

"Why don't you come right over, Mr. Chessler. Doctor feels these treatments are too important to miss, or postpone," Pollock's receptionist recited crisply. "Participating in physical rehabilitation is like performing in a fine symphony. Don't dare miss a single note for fear of throwing the entire movement off balance. Play a beautiful melody, Mr. Chessler, and your body will respond. But don't miss any notes."

Michael chuckled. "This is the first time I've been compared to fine music. About an hour then?"

"See you at twelve-thirty, Mr. Chessler."

Her voice was as cold as her disconnecting click, and the shower Michael took before leaving the cottage.

Doctor Pollock's office was located in a complex of suites adjacent to Manchester General Hospital, not more than a two-hour drive from Manhattan, where Michael had received his initial treatment.

He drove twice around the lot before finding a convenient parking space. He nosed his black Suburban between an elegant birch and a white Jetta. *Lucky I've become an expert at this,* he mused as he cut the engine and prepared to disembark. His arms, strengthened by heavy construction work, made getting around easier than he'd ever imagined — in his condition.

A far cry from the exotic sports car that had been on his *list of things to buy,* the Chevy Suburban was Michael's independence. He slipped the keys into his pocket, removed his polarized sunglasses, and mugged in the mirror. *Should've shaved.* He ran a hand from cheek to chin, then swept his breezy hair from his forehead. Long hair and five-o'clock shadow, a direct contrast from the pre-accident Michael who sported a military cut and smooth face. Although a man in uniform never failed to draw a crowd of fawning women, his wanton alternative attracted even more.

Michael had been young, straight out of high school and approaching eighteen. The learning experience the military offered would be a perfect opportunity both to give and receive. But he also knew there were other things he wanted to do with his life such as travel, especially to Germany and Greece, help run the construction company his grandfather had started, build his dream house. The rest of life would be left open to chance.

Although he hadn't minded the military and restrictions, Michael enjoyed total freedom. However, enjoyment and freedom were short-lived. Grunting, he hauled a lightweight Pollywog over his legs and onto the ground, deftly manipulating it into a readied position, then lifted himself out of the Suburban and into the seat that helped serve as his legs. This procedure, at first an emotionally painful hassle, was now routine.

Hospital visiting hours weren't to begin for another half hour, yet the shared parking lot was reaching full capacity. He headed for an entrance ramp, a necessity for visitors such as Michael.

Two young men skirted his chair, one on either side, walking briskly. Michael didn't notice their faces, but watched their pinstriped trouser legs flap with deliberate strides as he followed them through electronic glass doors, trying not to dwell on the rhythmic movements of superiority. *Easy to take things for granted, till you lose them.*

Pollock's office was posh and recently decorated in gradient shades of celery to forest green. Remnants of new paint and industrial carpet clung to the air. The length of the waiting room was paneled by tall panes of tinted glass, offering a spectacular view of the looping Connecticut River, and the sky dipping discreetly between distant peaks of the Green Mountains trudging through New England.

"Good afternoon, Mr. Chessler," said Grace Reed, aloof inside her polymer cubicle.

Grace could have been a typical grandmother, were she not so reserved. Had she been kinder, she would have been more like his.

Still, seeing her and the undulating mountains beyond the windows, reminded Michael of childhood summers in Vermont. As he waited he watched a smoky mist rise above the hospital's backdrop of evergreen peaks. When he was a little boy, the noble mountains carved a wall around his world. He thought life ended just beyond the last visible range. His grandmother passed away two years before Michael's injury. He thanked God she never saw him this way.

"Michael!" Pollock strode from his office into the empty waiting room. "You look great. How was L.A.?" If not for the white lab coat, Pollock could have passed for a Wall Street executive, tall and sharply dressed in double-pleated herringbone trousers.

The two men shook hands as would dear old friends. Pollock's firm grip then momentarily rested on Michael's shoulder.

"L.A. was terrific," Michael said with a grin. "Wild night life, beautiful girls. Whole lot of gambling and sex. I'm still recovering."

Pollock laughed heartily then cleared his smile. "I received the clinic reports last week. Encouraging."

"Funny. I haven't noticed any improvement, doc." Sarcasm had become part of Michael's new personality.

"Come on into my office, pal." Pollock led the way.

Grace forced a brief smile as they passed her cubicle, her eyes casing the movement of Pollock's door as it quietly closed. She then returned to her personal phone call.

Once inside the privacy of his office, Pollock removed his lab coat and positioned himself comfortably atop the corner of his desk. One leg dangled an onyx slip-on, while the other shoe was planted firmly on the gunmetal Berber rug. He smoothed the cropped sides of his chestnut hair, recovering from a hectic morning.

"I'm taking you away from lunch," Michael apologized as he sat almost leg to leg with his doctor, a vibrant middle-aged man who looked like he should have been on his way to lunch at a country club, then off to happy hour with a gathering of friends.

"No, it's fine. I'm clear for a while. I'm glad you made it in. We should talk." Pollock removed his wire-rimmed glasses and buffed his wispy brows. His steel gray eyes were determined.

The office windows were opened wide, and the third-floor wind billowed loosely woven draperies, spattering indiscriminant sunshine and the fragrance of just-mowed grass.

While he waited for Pollock to set forth the verdict that could affect the rest of his life, Michael focused on the ebbing whine of abrasive landscaping equipment.

"Michael. There's a surgery that might be effective." Pollock's words were careful. He flipped a pencil between his physician fingers, clicking lead point to eraser head on the top of his clean desk, preparing for an argument.

"I've already had one, Paul." Michael's jaw was set as he shifted his gaze from sunny refuge to Pollock's face.

Pollock's eyes hawked, then softened. He could have armed himself with statistics, but refrained. As past months indicated, Michael was unmistakably his own man. He would never base his decision on someone else's data. He'd do his own research, then weigh the results for as long as necessary.

"I know, Michael, and I know how you must feel. But I wasn't your doctor then. Things have progressed. New treatments and procedures. I'd like to try to correct what I feel could be your problem."

"What are the odds of it working? Can you make any guarantees?" Michael wished Pollock would say; *Of course, I'll make you whole again*, but he knew better. His hands, folded casually on the lap of his comfortable jeans, knotted into a tighter clasp.

"There aren't any guarantees, Michael. You know that. I realize you're discouraged, but you can't lose hope." Pollock loosened his cranberry tie to ease open the top button of his crisp, white dress shirt.

"Hell, I haven't lost hope. I've simply had eight months to adjust." Michael's uplifted arms gestured acceptance before his palms dropped heavily to his knees. "Getting accustomed to my sidekick here, too." He patted a wheel as if with affection.

Resentment settled on Michael's face. Nothing his doctor said would make a difference. When it came to surgery, he knew he was being evasive, and wondered if and when Pollock would give up on him. He wasn't ready to take the chance. Couldn't anyone understand?

"Michael. Why don't you head on down to therapy. See me when you're finished. There are a few things I'd like to go over, but I have some phone calls to make first." Pollock stood beside Michael, an outstretched arm motioning toward the door.

"Sure, Paul. Are you free for lunch?"

At first glance, Michael seemed to be joking, but when there was no follow-up wisecrack, it was obvious he was serious. His somber expression confirmed it.

He had never invited his doctor to lunch before. Pollock appeared puzzled. Did Michael need companionship or someone to vent to? Michael was not the kind of man to unload his problems on another, especially his doctor. Maybe at the moment, he merely needed diversion.

Pollock reached across his mahogany desk to check his calendar. "Lunch then." He nodded. "How's two sound? In the cafeteria."

"You've got yourself a date, doc."

LUNCH LINGERS

"**H**ow was lunch?" Bonnie's stare tracked Sienna across the room. The top drawer of the file cabinet she stood before was open, creasing her bosom as she leaned into it with her arms draped over the sides.

"Lunch was fantastic." Sienna's voice was flat. She squeezed her bourbon colored handbag into the bottom drawer of her desk. "The cafeteria was packed. They should have turned up the air conditioning because it was stuffy as hell, and to top it off, Greg cornered me and talked about breast augmentation the entire time I tried to eat my salad." Breathless, she reached up to loosen strands of clinging hair, then smoothed the sides of her skirt. "If we weren't at work, I'd have slammed him." She set her jaw.

"Breast augmentation? Was that supposed to be a subtle hint?"

"With him, who knows?"

"Well in my opinion, God gave you enough of everything stacked in all the right places. You don't need implants."

Sienna plopped onto her chair, pulling herself close to her desk. "Even if I did, I couldn't afford Trainer's fees." She rested her ankles against the casters on the pedestal. She chomped on gum, fighting off a roller coaster sensation that began to interfere with the Caesar dressing her stomach was struggling to digest. "Got any Tums?"

Bonnie went to her desk to pull a bottle from a drawer. "Here you go," she said, tossing it to Sienna, who looked like a wilting summer rose not quite ready to face fall. "Well, just look at it this way. I'm sure you'd get an employee discount." She chuckled. "And you'd certainly be in good hands." With swaying hips, she crossed the room.

"Yeah, right. That's a comfort." Sienna swiveled her chair to get a better view of Bonnie, who stood peering out the doorway.

"Who are you waiting for, Trainer?" Sienna chuckled. "Did you ever notice his eyes are like X-ray beams? They look right through your clothes."

"Stop it. You're giving me goose bumps."

"God, you're weird."

"Why, because I'm an easy turn-on?"

"Can't he get the meaning of platonic through his skull? I swear. He can be so nice sometimes. And then he ruins it by acting like a stuffy asshole." She shrugged, tossed her hands. "If he doesn't stop haunting me, I'm gonna stop talking to him all together. I try to be cordial, you know? We're at work. I can't be my bitchy self here. Especially if I want a promotion."

Bonnie shook her head. "You need to break out of that shell Rob stuffed you into. Start enjoying life again."

"I enjoy life." She shot Bonnie a sly look. "With my vibrator. That's all I need." She rifled through a stack of folders on her desk. Her bangle bracelets rang softly as she moved.

"I'm going down for a soda. Should I bring something back for you?" Bonnie grabbed a five from her wallet.

"Since my lunch was cut short," she smirked, " I'll forward the phones to Estelle and take a walk with you." Sienna was on her feet, wallet in hand, the first one heading toward the door.

Bonnie slung an arm across her shoulders. "Come on. I'll cheer you up. Maybe some dessert?"

"You had tuna again for lunch." Sienna laughed.

"I knew you were going to say that." Bonnie popped a mint into her mouth. "Now I'm thirsty as hell."

"You should drink water, not soda."

"You're hopeless. No soda. No sex. What next? No porn?" Bonnie laughed.

The two women hustled through the corridor. As they pushed

into the elevator, Sienna's lips pursed into a pout.

"You're going to get premature naso-labial folds if you keep making those faces," Bonnie said, "then you'll really need Trainer — and fillers."

Sienna frowned. "Trainer's not my problem."

"Lay it on me. I'm all ears."

They stood shoulder to shoulder, Sienna waiting for the doors to close, the elevator to hum, before moving close to Bonnie's ear. "Have you ever met a stranger and felt an immediate connection? An attraction for reasons you just couldn't put your finger on?"

"Chemistry?"

"Exactly."

MICHAEL'S CONDITION

"Here we go," Paul Pollock called out, balancing two lunch trays on his outstretched hands. By now he was tieless, his white shirt fully open at the neck. With movements resembling a waiter, he carefully set the trays onto a gray Formica table where Michael sat watching every movement he made.

Michael knew he was fortunate to have Pollock for a doctor, and felt he should have shown more appreciation. Not only was Pollock highly skilled, but he had a big heart, and was almost like a business associate rather than his physician. Manchester General was also a direct contrast from the clinical atmosphere of the New York hospital, where his pricey surgeon barely had time to speak to Michael before he was discharged in a wheelchair.

From his seat in the cafeteria, Michael had a clear view of the wide ceiling to floor windows that framed Manchester's scenic garden and outdoor lounge. Through the tinted glass he could also see the hospital's first-floor solarium, stretched out beyond a wall of rose azaleas.

The solarium's sliding doors opened onto lush grounds dressed with oaks and wrought-iron furnishings. Picnic tables and shade umbrellas encircled a patio of russet paving stones trimmed with zinnias and a sea of grass. *Like a country club, but how fallacious.*

Michael noted that almost everyone in the solarium was seated — either upon lounge chairs — or wheelchairs. *How confining,* he shrugged off the thought, not ever wanting to be part of that unfortunate scene, then noticed his reflection in the window. This was all wrong! He was Michael Chessler, a strong and independent thirty-year-old man. He no more belonged in a wheelchair than behind a desk in an office. He was an adventurer — an outdoorsman. He was in love with someone he might never be able to have. But for now, he chose to remain in his safe place, where there was no such thing as desire, or need, or unfounded hope, regardless of how hard Paul Pollock pushed him.

"I picked up two of everything I thought looked good." Pollock slid a tray in front of Michael. "Hope watery stroganoff and wild rice is a hit on your list of favorite entrees."

"Sure, Paul. It's fine. My gut is so used to my cooking, I can handle just about anything." Michael rolled the long sleeves of his plaid sport shirt to his elbows, and undid an extra button at his neck, then smoothed his hands down the soft front of the shirt so the tails rested flat on his thighs.

"How did the session go?" Pollock opened the subject after a taste of saucy beef. He tapped the corners of his mouth with a paper napkin.

"Like all the others." Michael nudged his food with a fork as if searching for a hidden prize, then picked up a dinner roll.

"Any improvement?"

"If there was, nobody told me. And I sure as hell don't notice anything different."

"L.A. was a hard run on you, wasn't it, Michael?" Pollock's face tightened.

Michael pushed his tray to the side and lifted a pint milk container. "Nah. Four weeks of indoor pools, lovely ladies in waiting, terrific meals."

"Don't consider it a loss, Michael. And don't let this get the better of you. You're a young enough guy who should be thinking about making plans for the future."

"I have plans. I have my investments to keep an eye on." Michael poured the last of the milk into a paper cup and swigged it like a shot of booze.

Whenever Michael spoke of his investments, a strong sensation of capability and self-worth replaced the paralyzing numbness that had become his legs.

"How are your investments, by the way?" Pollock sipped his coffee.

"Growing," Michael replied, triumphantly hammering a fist on the table as if to say: Hey, look at me, I succeeded at something.

"Good to hear it, Michael. See, things are looking up for you."

The two women stood before the cafeteria's self-service counter, waiting for an attendant to fill the ice dispenser. Bonnie held a wrapped corn muffin in one hand and a soda cup in the other. Sienna opted for an apple and a bottle of spring water.

Michael stretched his arms and stifled a yawn, half listening to words he'd heard before. As he looked across the cafeteria, he thought he recognized one of the women from behind. He tensed. *Could it be?* His eyes opened wide. Pollock didn't appear to take notice of the change and spoke almost non-stop.

The back of the woman's head was a mass of blonde curls. She wore a dusty-mauve top buttoning sexily up the back, and a dove gray pencil skirt that delightfully embraced her hips. And from Michael's view of the slender legs beneath the hemline, everything appeared enticingly shapely.

His interest ricocheted politely from Pollock's face to the woman's back as he waited, hoping for a closer look. It was not until she turned and glided through the checkout that he had a clear view. *It's her.* His pulse quickened in a sigh.

Pollock was explaining the latest therapy procedures, and future possibilities if Michael would agree to the surgery he vaguely detailed, but strongly advised. Michael couldn't concentrate as he watched her intently.

"How long for this round of sessions, Paul?" he asked abruptly, his eyes riveted upon her as she strolled in the direction of their table.

"Hard to say. We have to see how you respond. And there's still the spinal surgery to consider," Pollock continued to persuade, and added, "I'd like to conduct more tests."

"You know how I feel about that." Afraid she'd slip from sight, Michael didn't take his eyes off her as he spoke.

"We have new techniques. I've already explained this to you." Pollock wore a poker face. "Just because one failed doesn't mean another will."

"Or won't." Michael's voice was flat. "I'll ask again. Can you guarantee it will work?" He simply could not withstand another failure. And then there was she . . . Failure could kill every dream he'd ever had. Denial was a safer option.

"Once more, I'll explain." Pollock's voice rose. "Who can guarantee? We can only try and hope. You know how things are in medicine. We do the best we can. There are advances, breakthroughs. This one could be yours if you'll give it a chance."

Michael focused on Sienna, the way she walked, posture like a dancer, the way she held her head, how her lips moved when she spoke. That's right . . . nothing could ever be guaranteed.

A MERE GLIMPSE CAN HAVE IMPACT

On their way to the exit of the cafeteria, Sienna and Bonnie passed a safe distance from the small corner table occupied by Doctor Pollock and his patient.

"Hey," she whispered, jerking Bonnie's arm. "There's the plaza guy."

"What?"

"You know — the guy with the grapefruit. That's how much you pay attention to what I say." Viewing his profile, she could openly stare. His face appeared strained, not eager and gentle as the day they had met, but every bit as handsome.

"Where is he?" Bonnie asked, looking in all directions.

"Over there in the plaid shirt. With Dr. Pollock," she whispered. "Try to be low-key for once in your life, please."

"I see him now," said Bonnie as Sienna grabbed her hand, stopping her finger from pointing in his direction moments before he turned their way. "Oh, he's really cute. You never told me how hot he was. He was obviously trying to hit on you that day. Why don't you go over there and say hello?"

"Because I don't want to. Stop staring!"

"I'm not staring. How's he gonna see us in this crowd? " Bonnie sucked in a breath. "Oh, no. Now I see why you're not into him. He's in a wheelchair. You never mentioned that."

"I didn't find the need to. And what difference does it make?" Sienna glared before her voice softened. "I guess he's Pollock's patient. I wonder what's going on."

"One of the best spinal surgeons on this planet. He's such a doll, too."

"It's a shame. He seems like a nice guy." Sienna's pace slowed. "As far as me not being into him, who ever said there was anything romantic about him picking up my grapefruit? It was awkward, if anything."

Michael watched Sienna's graceful strides as she and the other woman began to move out of sight. Sienna's back was to him again. Then she was gone. Without realizing, he let out a groan.

"Lord have mercy . . ." he mumbled.

"What did you say?" Pollock's head snapped around.

"Nothing." Michael's face was as stiff as his voice.

The spell was broken. He redirected his attention to what Paul Pollock had been saying. Something about a chance?

"This chance . . . Just what it is — a chance — a long shot."

But maybe Pollock is right, Michael thought as another feeling surfaced . . . optimism. Maybe it would work. But if you don't get your hopes too high, you can't possibly be disappointed.

"Name one aspect of the gift of a healthy life that ever comes with an ironclad guarantee?" Pollock continued his pitch as he rearranged the remnants of lunch on his tray. "So there you have it, Michael. The ball is in your court."

Pollock had put enough pressure on the shoulders of the man who sat across the table, whose grinning mouth dropped into a frown, deep brown eyes shadowed with doubt.

"Let's hold this chance open for a while," Michael said as yet another sensation began to claw at him. Frustration . . . This latest nagging sensation equaled that of the overwhelming desire Michael had tried to overcome for months — the ceaseless yearning to get the hell out of the wheelchair and walk. Damn the sensations. When compared, they were one in the same. And this woman was the catalyst.

"We won't jump too fast," Michael heard himself saying. "There's time, Paul. Time to give it more thought." Near the edge of the cliff, would he feel himself fall?

"Ace in the hole, huh Michael?"

Pollock appeared to be catching on; his patient wasn't much of a gambler.

Michael nodded. "Let's call it my last hope."

Sienna fumbled around her desk."I have to bring these things up to Pediatrics. Be back in a few. Need anything?" She sipped the last of her water, capped the empty bottle, then stuffed it into her own personal recycling bin in the corner of the office.

"Nah. I'm fine." Bonnie loaded her computer software and an endless list of names, admission and discharge dates filled her monitor. "How does billing lose a patient? That's something I would love to know." She shook her head, stretched her back. "Now I have to search the past eight months of admissions." She frowned at Sienna, then turned her attention to the screen.

Walking out the door, Sienna cradled a stack of charts in her arms, strode down the hall and took the elevator to the third floor.

"Here you go, Marjorie," she told the charge nurse as she dumped the pile on her organized desk.

The woman smiled. "Thanks. Just what the doctor ordered"

"What's cookin'?"

"Coffee. Have time for a cup?"

Sienna laughed. "If I ingest any more caffeine I'll be bouncing off the walls — like the kids I'm hearing . . ." Shooting a questioning glance at Marjorie, she turned in the direction of laughter coming from the open doors of the playroom. "This place sounds more like toddler daycare than a hospital. What's going on?"

"They're being educated on what to do if their sailboats get caught in a storm." She rolled her eyes but wore a smile that filled her face. "Gives *me* a break."

Sienna's brows pulled together. She scrunched her mouth. "Huh?"

"Come on. I'll show you." Dressed in pastel scrubs, Marjorie glided around the desk, grabbed Sienna's arm and led her down the corridor, where they stood just beyond the open doors. "That's our friend, Michael."

In the center of the room sat Michael Chessler, a huge grin on his face as he addressed his young audience. On a desk beside him rested a scale model of a schooner. Next to it sat a sloop. Children in chairs, some with wheels, gathered close to Michael's wheelchair. They looked enthralled. Bombarded him with questions.

"What's the difference between a schooner and a sloop?" A boy, sitting in a smaller version of Michael's chair, asked. He wore navy blue sweats and sneakers, appearing as if he should be pumping a playground swing or screeching down a slide.

When Sienna recognized who she knew as the plaza guy her eyes widened, glazing when she watched the kids who seemed to adore him. And he was obviously having as much fun as they were.

He appeared comfortable with the hands sharing his armrests, small fingers pulling on his for attention.

"A sloop has a mast and two sails." He ran a hand across the model. "The mast is attached to the boom." He pointed to a polished dowel. "See how it's put together?"

The way he interacted with the children tugged Sienna's heart. There was something alluring about a man when he showed his softer side. His gentleness was arousing. *Stop it! He's talking to children. What's wrong with you? Rob. That's what wrong with me.*

"A schooner is bigger. It can have two or more masts, like this one." His hand slipped over the other model. "Like a pirate ship. Have all of you seen pirate ships in movies or pictures?" Michael glanced from face to face. "How about a dingy? Anyone know what a dingy is?"

"I never saw a pirate ship," said a young girl. She pouted.

Michael angled his head, mimicked her pout. "Then I'll bring you some pictures next time I come. How about that?" He scuffed the top of her head with his palm. "Now smile."

She brightened.

As he scanned the faces of the children, Michael's eyes caught the doorway and the women who silently watched. For a moment he appeared puzzled. When his expression registered recognition, he lifted a hand in Sienna's direction. From across the room, his eyes were powerful, then softened. Sienna could almost feel the emotion before he suddenly turned away.

"We're intruding." She nudged Marjorie's arm.

"Nah. Do you know Michael?"

"Not really." Sienna edged from the doorway. "Gotta run. Back to the grind."

Marjorie looked at Michael who kept glancing over. She shrugged, then smiled before walking back to her desk.

Michael sat at his kitchen table sipping cocoa. After returning from the hospital, he'd put in five productive hours at his drafting table, but decided to skip dinner; his appetite was not for food. The sensation he'd experienced while catching Sienna's stare still lingered. Motivated. Motivated him in a way he'd never expected. Things inside that had seemed lost, were beginning to return. *Why am I doing this to myself?*

His dreams had become disturbing. Not since the accident had he felt such lack of control. Those nightmares had lasted months. Learning to live in a wheelchair was not easy for a young and vibrant man. His loss of independence was brief, as Michael refused to rely on anyone.

With each passing day he regained strength, yet every effort he made to move his numb legs ended up with the same disappointment. Fighting depression, he refused to succumb to the unacceptable prognosis. He could not — would not believe he'd never walk again.

Before snapping off his bedside lamp, Michael checked his

alarm, then set the radio timer and in moments she was in his arms.

The tropical island is enchanting. Enjoying a fruity breeze, Michael sits on a sandy beach, watching lighthouse beams spin shimmering revolutions like a diamond Ferris wheel glittering through night.

Behind him rows of elegant orchids cling to a stone walk leading to an intimate white frame house. He's alone, enjoying slashes of moonlight pattern the waves as the aggressive Pacific hugs his bare legs, saturating the cuffs of his pants. He wiggles his toes in the foamy current, tucking them in and out of soggy patches of heavy sand that feels like wet cement. It's good — life is good — the ocean on his skin, the wet sand beneath his feet, thoughts of the woman who would soon arrive.

She approaches, starlight weaving champagne strands through her hair. Her sheer dress sways with the wind, revealing a luscious silhouette. She's breathtaking, warm, much warmer than any Pacific current, with lips moister than the tide. In fierce embrace their limbs intertwine. Michael senses they might not make it to the house.

OOPS WE MEET AGAIN

Clouds kept rolling in, along with rain. Dwelling on the summer months to come, Sienna strolled across the parking lot, the red hood of the Corolla in sight. Her studded peep-toes tapped on the walk, beating in time with wipers of passing autos, the blades swiping away remnants of a dwindling shower. The sky above the parking lot began to clear, but a haze disguised the range of mountains looming in the distance.

"Duh. What did you come here for in the first place?" Twirling a plastic bag of groceries: cat food and cereal, she spun around and headed for the plaza stationery store, which she preferred to call *the gift shop.*

She passed a huddle of high school girls gathered on the sidewalk, sipping sodas and giggling. She compared them to Mona who didn't look much different from the ponytailed teens. She certainly did not appear to be thirty-five. She didn't act it either. Dark gypsy eyes, lush red lips, not a line on her olive complexion. She could do so much better . . .

Mona's gift shop was a wall to wall assortment of pricey merchandise and every stationery item a soul could desire. Sienna enjoyed browsing the aisles of unusual wares. After admiring a display of ornamental cut glass, she stopped at the greeting card rack, picking up the first that caught her eye. A silk rose embossed the front of the perfume scented card. She checked the price on the back and reached into her wallet, pulling out six crisp singles.

Mona stood at the end of the aisle. Sienna shoved the money

into her hand. "There's no one at the register."

"Thanks." Mona snatched the bills and stuffed them into the pocket of her trousers. "So how's everything?" Without waiting for a reply, she craned her neck around a corner display. "Where's that counter girl I just hired?"

"Everything's fine with me, but you look stressed." Sienna glanced around the store.

"I'm fine. I love busy. And it's gonna get better yet." Mona puffed out a breath that ruffled her thick bangs.

"What do you mean? Are you expanding the store?" Sienna reached out to fluff Mona's hair back into place.

"No. I've got a bet going with Dyson that I can pull in more profit than he can by the end of this week." Her lips swelled into a sly smile. "The loser springs for a weekend in the Bahamas — for two — and the loser won't be me."

Sienna realized they were at it again, and Mona certainly wasn't trying to keep their affair a secret. She started to ask, "Why?" then clamped her mouth shut. *Who am I to ask questions? Or offer advice . . .*

"Listen, I'll see you later, Sienna. Time to patrol the aisles."

Mona was a self-sufficient businesswoman with an admirable life. Why was she fooling around with a married man? Sienna just didn't get it. Stepping from the store, about to stuff the *Happy Birthday Mother* card into her hobo, she heard him.

"No runaway grapefruit today?"

She turned in time to see him put his hands up like a shield.

Sighing, she shook her head. "You caught me in a foul mood the other day. I shouldn't have been so nasty."

"You weren't all that bad." He smiled. "Nice day, isn't it?" Motioning to the sky, he mocked.

"I know. It's been just miserable lately." Same as me, she thought, catching herself from blurting out the words. "I don't remember such an awful spring." Her frown deepened.

"I like those studs on your shoes. How do women walk in those things, anyway?" He angled his head, a silly look on his face making him even more approachable.

There was a moment of silence before she replied, "Well, you saw what happened to me the other day at Dyson's. I guess we like to live dangerously." A dimple dotted one cheek when her face scrunched with sarcasm. She shrugged.

"So what's on the agenda today?" he asked.

Ordinarily, Sienna would have nodded and said good-bye by now. But there was something about the way he looked at her that derailed her. His gaze was strong, but it wasn't hungry, like Rob's had been. She couldn't quite put her finger on it, only to conclude that it was different. He was different. But he was still a man.

"Just picking up a few things. So what are you up to today? Shopping? Working? Hanging around?" She eyed him with suspicion.

"I have some business to attend to, meet a few people, then I'm outta here." He studied the passing cars as he spoke, then faced her. "If we keep meeting this way, I guess I should introduce myself." He smiled and extended a hand. "I'm Michael Chessler."

"Sienna Alexander." She ran her palm lightly across his.

"Hey, I saw you the other day. With a red-haired woman." He began rolling slowly along the walkway.

"Oh, you did, huh?" Sienna followed at his side, a grin spreading across her face.

"Yeah, in the cafeteria at Manchester General."

"The redhead's Bonnie." She chuckled. "We work in E.R. Registration."

"You do?" He acted surprised. "Manchester General. I know that place pretty well." He gestured to his legs, but if he was self-consciousness, he didn't let on.

"Do you visit the hospital often?"

"Almost every day."

She shot him a curious look.

He smiled. "Physical therapy is demanding."

"Every day?"

"I visit with some of the kids in Pediatrics a few times a week. You know, talk about how to make the best of life in a wheelchair.

Stuff like that."

"A counselor?"

"Something like that."

She looked impressed. "I saw you in action."

"Did you . . ." He turned his head, gazed across the parking lot.

"It was Paul Pollock's idea," he clarified.

"But you're doing it."

"Of course."

"How wonderful. It must be nice. For you and the children."

"Yeah, it's fun. Rewarding and all. The kids are great, at times quite amusing." He laughed. "Some of the things that come out of their mouths. The questions they ask."

"I can only imagine."

"Do you live in Oak Haven?"

"Yes. Do you?"

"I do."

"Condo."

"Cottage."

The replies were simultaneous. They laughed.

"Do you have any pets?" she asked, turning serious.

"No."

"Would you like one?"

"I don't spend that much time at home, believe it or not."

"I didn't mean to imply . . ."

"I had a Golden Retriever when I was a kid."

"How about a cat . . . or another dog?"

"Do you own a pet shop or something?"

She giggled. "I help take care of abandoned pets at the shelter over on Croton. Try to find homes for every single one of them."

"Ah, nice. Maybe I'll wander down there sometime."

"That would be great." Her face relaxed.

"Day off today?" Michael picked up the pace.

"Yes. I work alternating shifts," Sienna explained. "I like having a day off during the week. Weekends are so crowded here. Tuesday's a better day to shop. I'm not one for crowds."

She wondered if her dress hung straight, or had the weather creased it? Then a breeze caught the polished cotton and plastered it against her thighs, outlining just about everything she owned. She wondered if he noticed. Why hadn't she worn makeup?

"I don't mind crowds. Kind of nice being around people," he said.

"There's enough activity at the hospital. I need down-time." She sounded exasperated as she faced him with a wide-eyed expression, her eyes burning into his.

He shifted from her stare that threatened his train of thought. "Speaking of activity." He pointed to the far end of the mile-long parking lot. "See how they're roping off that section?" When he raised a muscled arm, his shirt sleeve strained against his triceps, exposing part of a colorful tattoo.

"What are they doing, building another store?"

"They're getting ready for a carnival. Cotton candy, fried dough, fireworks . . . all that good stuff."

Thinking he looked like a little boy at the mention of fireworks, Sienna's face brightened with a smile broader than his. "Sounds like a fun way to kick off the summer, my favorite time of year." Her voice sounded whimsical, on the brink of laughter. So unlike her.

"I like warm weather too. I used to fish a lot in the summer."

"From a boat?"

"Yup, deep sea fishing is great. I love the ocean."

"So do I." She sucked in a breath. "Ever go to Cape Cod?"

For a moment he was silent. A woman like her could turn a guy's world upside down with something as simple as a sigh, when just looking at her made him tremble. "Used to go every year. How about Martha's Vineyard?"

"No." She sounded disappointed she'd never been there and he had. "Nantucket?"

"Yup." When he grinned his entire face lit up. "You have to see Martha's Vineyard. It's fantastic."

"I'd love to."

He was getting under her skin. To Sienna they were opposites.

He grinned a lot — she frowned a lot. But his behavior was appealing, contagious.

"I haven't been to a carnival since I was a kid. Game booths are my favorite. I used to be great at shooting hoops." She giggled like one of the teens outside Mona's store. "I have a good arm for throwing things," she said, looking deeply into the warmth of his eyes that seemed intense.

Michael ducked. "Remind me to stay out of your way when you're mad."

"Eh, I don't get mad." What a lie, she thought. "Will you be going to the carnival? I might try to go if I'm not working." She tilted her head, watching him with a questioning look that simmered in the air. Her face was close. Her lips moist and inviting.

"Not sure . . . I work every day. It was nice running into you. See you around." He paused for a moment before a glass storefront, avoiding her eyes. Then he was gone.

Her mouth dropped, but she managed a strong "good-bye" as he disappeared inside. She looked around for a minute, agitation rising. What was she doing here? He was gone. The bubble had burst. There was no need for her to be at this end of the plaza. Utterly out of place, she sprang from the curb and ran across the parking lot to the solace of her car.

Later that day the shock wore off and anger set in. *Who does he think he is, ditching me like that?* Her mind raced as she soaked in a bath sprinkled with scented salt. Did he think I thought he was hitting on me? Did he think *I* was hitting on *him*? Yeah, right. Little ol' me scare *him* away? Of course, he must be insecure. Insecure? He has no clue what insecure is! Or fear. Or what it feels like to be fucked over by someone you trusted . . . with your life!

Why do you always have to be a victim? Will you never learn? Do *not* trust the opposite sex! Who the hell needs them anyway? Go to hell, Michael Chessler.

When the anger subsided, she tried to concoct logical reasons for his curt departure. It had to be something she said. *I'd love to,*

ran circles inside her head. Holy shit. Did he think I was inviting myself to Martha's Vineyard? Yeah, right. Like I'd really want to be with someone like him.

"Break the cycle," the counselor had said.
"What cycle?" Temper flaring, she had asked.
"Negative dependency. Stand on your own two feet."
I have been! Hasn't anyone noticed?

Daylight overcomes darkness, and Sienna is no longer a timid creature, but rather a vixen, a libidinous siren, about to confront the man she yearns for.

With a mischievous smile she bolts to the bow, then draws a troubled breath. She wasn't expecting him. "Rob. You're dead." Her voice is hollow. Is his ghost about to make love to her? But she hates Rob!

Michael's steps are brisk, his arms powerful as he pushes Rob aside. "I've got you now," he tells her, sliding a tattooed arm around her waist.

Sienna is running. He's close behind. Is it Michael? She should stop and say hello. Make love to him. But she can't risk it. It could be Rob! Rob is always here. Haunting. Killing.

"Someone help me . . ."

Suddenly, Michael is at her side. He speaks with lash-swept eyes, broodingly dark and dangerous.

She reaches out, she touches him, pleasures at his arousal. He's hot. He's hard. She licks her lips. As she cocks her head, her pout slides into a grin. With an exaggerated sigh, she turns to the sea, arms braced on the rail. Bending forward at the waist guarantees the projection of her fully-rounded buttocks. She cranes her neck, closes her eyes, and lifts her face to the sky. The high wind cools, while the ocean boils at her feet.

With powerful arms he snatches her, locking their sweating bodies, his bold chest and muscled abdomen clasped to her spine. In one swift movement he spins her, pulls her close. Her breasts crush his bare chest.

"You drive me insane," he grunts, nuzzling her shoulders. He doesn't have to tell her — she feels it — inhales his anguished breath. He squeezes her supple buttocks as if they're mounds of sculptor's clay to be kneaded again and again. "Let me hear how much you want me."

Her arms coil around his neck, lips fusing as their bodies begin a grind, and after a baiting moment, she purrs, "More than ever."

LEONARDO GIBRALDI

The teen named Leo delivered Michael's grocery orders twice a week. His oyster gray hand-me-down Volvo wagon was certain to pull up in front of the stucco and stone cottage like clockwork, every Tuesday and Friday, by four in the afternoon.

"Here's my man, Leo." Michael greeted the delivery boy, who tapped twice on the kitchen door before entering the cottage.

Heaving a bulging carton onto the tabletop, Leo paused, slouching against the counter to face Michael, who was nursing a mug of tepid coffee. "Got anything cold to drink?"

"Sure. Grab a soda from the fridge. How are things?" Michael fished in a pocket for his wallet. "Grab a seat too."

"All good." Leo handed Michael a crinkled tally sheet.

"How's Linda? Or is it someone else this week?"

Leo shot him a shameless look. Along with grocery orders, he delivered an explicit week by week summary of the joys and perils of his active love life.

Michael refused to comment or offer advice, theorizing every man had to travel his own road, learning along the way when to cross over and when to hang around for a while and idle in one spot. Until Sienna, Michael had never found a reason to hang around and idle, but exchanged many stories with the boy about experiences he had encountered on the other side of the road.

"Heh." Leo smirked, rubbing the top of his tawny crew-cut with his palm. "Still Linda. Tomorrow's our third anniversary."

"Three whole months, huh?"

Michael enjoyed Leo's visits. The kid was a trip, always dressed in oversized T-shirts and baggy jeans, usually ragged. Sometimes he'd wear a casual button-down, but it would always be open, displaying a rock band logo or cartoon shirt.

"Yup. And we're celebrating. Tacos, a movie, a six of Coors at my place when my aunt and uncle are outta town." Leo swigged his soda from a pop-top can. From the corner of his eye he watched Michael intently.

Michael felt his stare, figuring the boy was waiting for a sign of his approval. "Yeah, I remember those days." He stifled a sigh. "Enjoy it now, kid. Doesn't last long, and then you're an old man like me with nothing to look back on but . . ." Michael stopped speaking when he saw the curious look cross Leo's face. "What are you looking at?" he asked with a shrug of his chin.

"What are you talking about old? My uncle's old. You're not old." Leo shoved the soda onto the counter and dug his hands into his pants pockets, striking an Abercrombie pose.

"I feel ancient today," Michael groaned and shook his head, a look on his face like the winner of a lost lotto ticket.

"Dude. You look a wreck. What's wrong with you?" Leo scrunched his thick eyebrows and pushed his broad top lip up to meet the carved tip of his nose. "Things not goin' good?"

"If you call ditching a gorgeous girl in the middle of a promising conversation good, then I guess my day was great." Michael's jaw dropped into a scowl.

"You didn't." Leo burst out laughing. He pulled out a chair from the table and plopped onto the seat, resting one lanky leg on the equally lanky thigh of his other.

"I sure did. I blew it." Michael palmed his forehead, then let his hand take the weight as he dropped his elbow onto the table. He closed his eyes tightly as if hiding behind his lids would stop the memory.

"Dude. Why'd you do that?" Leo's lively green eyes bulged beneath heavy lids trimmed by a row of thick, brown lashes. He switched leg positions and leaned forward as if to hear the shortcomings of someone other than himself.

"Cold feet, I guess."

"Why don't you write a poem and give it to her?"

Michael shot him a look. "Smart ass. I read it. I don't write it."

"I was joking, but maybe it wouldn't be a bad idea. I mean, if you can't man up and talk to her, then . . ."

"Quit while you're ahead, Leo."

"Sorry. You're a cool guy Michael. Not bad looking."

"Gee, thanks. You're pretty good-looking yourself."

"Well, you know what I mean. How's a guy gonna tell another guy he looks hot?"

"So I'm hot?" Michael's eyebrows shot up. His forehead furrowed.

"Linda thought so when we saw you at the mall a couple of weeks ago. And having money doesn't hurt either." Leo tossed a glance at Michael's drafting table. "So I heard you built the plaza. That true?"

"Yeah. I drew the plans right over there." Michael motioned to the alcove he called his home office.

"You own the whole thing?"

"Yup."

"What else do you do? Just work all the time?"

"Well . . ." Michael drew out the word. "I used to work construction if that's what you mean. I design commercial buildings and used to get in on some of the heavy work. I couldn't just sit at a desk all day." He was grim. "After the plaza was finished, I started a few other projects across town. But I'm not hands-on anymore — obviously."

"So that's your stuff goin' on over on Ridgewood? All those new buildings, you own 'em?"

"Till I sell or rent them."

"Was that a work accident?" Leo motioned to Michael's legs.

Michael shifted his eyes, staring at the forest outside the window, then refocused on the boy. "What do you do when you're not delivering groceries? And why don't you lace your sneakers? You're gonna trip yourself."

"Heh, haven't yet." Leo fumbled with a grimy shoelace and

grinned. "I'm in style." He took another slug of soda, then slapped a gangling hand over his mouth, suppressing the echo of a throaty belch. "Just school, you know. Stuff. So getting back to that chick, who is she?" He slammed the empty can on the table, indicating he was running the show.

"I doubt you know her." Michael rolled his neck and pulled at the collar of his shirt.

"How hot is she?"

"Very." Michael let out his breath in a low whistle. "I repeat — very."

"So why'd you ditch her then?"

"Scared I guess."

"Of what?"

"The unknown." Michael frowned.

That night, Michael had a nightmare. He relived the accident that had stolen his legs, as well as a big part of his life. The horrifying dream awakened him before it was over. In this dream the ambulance had not yet reached the hospital — but Michael already knew the outcome, for he had gone through it many nights in the past — and in reality.

He lay in bed recovering from the memory, trying to fall back to sleep. Impossible. This would be another restless night.

A bottle of pills rested in the top drawer of his nightstand, a prescription from Dr. Pollock. But Michael didn't believe in medication for the mind. He would face his demons head-on. Even if it meant he had to crash.

Then he thought of her, and how she made him feel alive again. She was what he needed, not a bottle of pills.

Why did he duck into Dyson's just when they were getting to know each other? What would Sienna think of him? He should have told her he hoped he'd run into her at the carnival. That could've worked without actually committing — just in case he was struck with another bout of cold feet.

Women wanted a strong man, physically and emotionally. He was tired of false bravado, tired of playing the upbeat hero. He drifted in and out of sleep, but didn't dream.

The next day brought sun and a brilliant idea. He'd thought about her half the night, their conversation, his insecurity. Maybe he'd give it another shot.

It was almost five when the Suburban wove through traffic, then eased onto a side street, taking Michael to the outskirts of the city. Uncertain of her hours, he drove at a moderate pace, thinking all the while. "What the hell will I say? Does that puppy come in any other color?" Would she even be there? He had a feeling she might work eight to four at the hospital. *She could very well be there.*

He knew the area he was heading into housed light industry, but he'd never been down this gravel road before. Behind him a warehouse, a water tower, not many trees. Less than fifty feet ahead a long building, squat and fenced. A signpost stood on an angle, embossed with peeling letters: Animal Shelter. *Almost like a refugee camp*, crossed his mind. The place was stained with weather and time, and looked imprisoned inside a chain link enclosure. An open gate softened the appearance.

Michael didn't immediately enter the yard. To gather himself, he spun the truck's wheels into a driveway where a building once stood, but all that remained were stone walls.

After circling a few times, the Suburban made a determined approach. Michael's breath quickened. Bingo. The red car was parked at the side of the building, pulled close to a brown metal door. A painted sign on the frame read: No Admittance. But taped to the door was a large handwritten note: Visitors please use the MAIN entrance in front. He wondered if she'd written it.

The precise location of her car left sneaking around the side of the building impossible. He'd have to face this like a man. Thinking of what Leo would say right now, he had to laugh. Then he sobered: He'd have to face her.

Cars of visitors, no doubt, were parked haphazardly on the

gritty front yard, not snuggled against the wall as the Corolla was. He warmed. Stopping before one of the few windows, he was able to get a good look inside: An office, surprisingly bare. A desk, scattered with papers. A double row of empty cages set against a far wall. Confining. Funds to run the facility had to be minimal. The place was in dire need of repair.

Jolting him from thought, figures moved inside, and then the front door was suddenly thrown open. Out popped a young guy holding a sleek black lab, looking comfortable in his arms, relieved. . . Alongside bounced a girl, smiling, patting the full grown animal who appeared groomed, cared for.

Standing at the doorway, waving and smiling: Sienna. Sienna dressed in jeans, sneakers, and navy blue smock. A headband covered the front of her head, a ponytail at the back.

What am I doing here? Michael wondered if she'd seen him. His heart drummed so hard he could count the beats in his ears. He heaved a sigh. The windows were tinted dark . . . and how would she know it was his truck?

As the Suburban rolled by he was tempted to lower the window, but without even noticing him, she pulled the door closed. He stole a thoughtful glance at the entrance to the shelter, then the truck picked up speed. Watching the building disappear from his mirror, his heart sank. "Fuck me," he said, swatting the dangling handicap tag. "This is too fucked up."

January Valentine

THE FAMED DOCTOR GREGORY TRAINER

The Chessler Medical Complex wrapped affluence halfway around one side and across the back of Manchester General Hospital. Greg Trainer leased a luxurious office and surgery suite that monopolized almost half of the fifth floor of one of the Chessler medical buildings.

Inside his office, Doctor Gregory Trainer's square jaw was set in a cordial position. He was about to begin a consultation with a prospective patient. The young woman had traveled a long distance from her southern hometown because of a word-of-mouth referral from a friend praising Trainer's expertise in the field of cosmetic surgery.

Perched upon a disposable pink table liner, she appeared notably frail. And with a ghostly wash from the overhead fluorescents, the young woman's porcelain features could have passed for the chiseled work of an exceptional sculptor.

As Trainer approached, her doe-eyes glistened with nervous anticipation. Her stare shifted from the embroidered insignia encircling the left breast of the doctor's white lab jacket to his female assistant, who remained mute and stationary, arms at her sides, leaning heavily against the edge of the desk Trainer seconds before had vacated. She was more of a room monitor than an actual assistant, with an olive complexion kinder than her swept-back ebony hair.

At the touch of Trainer's cold fingers upon her cotton dressing gown, the patient stiffened, and as Trainer opened the front closure she turned her head to the side, avoiding his eyes, focusing upon the mute assistant's flowered smock which brightened the neutral paint of the office walls.

A flush colored the young woman's cheeks, instantly shading her pallid porcelain scarlet. The palms of her hands were moist.

"Just relax now, Sara." Trainer's voice seemed to echo in the oversized room. "No need for stressing out. Just let me take a quick look." He assessed her small breasts. "Great potential," he whispered as if to himself. "Stand up please."

"I've been embarrassed since I was thirteen," Sara reluctantly confided as she grasped the hand helping her to her feet. "My girlfriends were all growing like mad, and I wasn't."

"I know what you're saying. Mother Nature can be awfully cruel at times." Trainer shared Sara's confidential tone. "And disagreeable hormones complicate matters. But we're going to correct that quite simply."

Trainer's empathy provided Sara with the courage to move. She shifted her dark eyes from the sympathetic assistant, staring at Trainer with a curious expression.

Trainer's hair was arrogantly styled, its impeccably layered sandy blonde shafts carefully blown away from his broad forehead and clipped sideburns. Identical silken strands formed his trimmed brows and the lashes softly framing his eyes. Sara locked on his eyes; their startling shade of forest green was powerful. There was an intensity boiling beneath the surface of the doctor's lubricated features. Sara looked impressed.

Trainer had to be at least twenty years older than his patient. In the past, girls such as Sara had regarded him as alluring. He'd overheard one whisper to a friend that he'd be unbearably handsome if the width of his long nose were just a fraction of an inch less defined. Trainer thought he saw a glint in Sara's eyes and frowned. He was a healthy looking man, standing tall, with a build honed by four-times-a-week workouts at the gym. Patients came on to him, but he remained aloof.

He dipped a hand into his jacket pocket and pulled out a tape measure, then proceeded to measure each breast from nipple to collar bone, calculating the distance from areola to crease. As an expert tailor about to design a double-breasted suit for royalty, his fingers moved deftly, cautiously.

"How big can you make me?" Sara asked unabashedly, now acting comfortable with her new best friend.

"Have you had a chance to hold the implants? Did my assistant help you slip them into your bra to gauge the size you'd like to be?"

She nodded. "Yes, we did that before you came in." Pausing, she gulped. "I'd like to be a full C. Would that be possible?"

"I'm confident I can give you at least two cup sizes," Trainer replied, smiling broadly. "You'll look wonderful."

"Okay, doctor." She let out a breath. "Whatever you think is best."

She began to pull the gown around her. Trainer halted her hasty motions, opening it wide.

"Fine, Sara. Perfect. All right now," he said with enthusiasm as he slipped the gown off her shoulders. "Ready for some snapshots?"

She appeared befuddled.

"Stand over there. We need before photographs, and in a few months we'll take the fantastic after shots." With outstretched arms Trainer motioned across the room as if he were a movie director and his patient his leading lady.

"Some of my photography." He smiled complacently as he pointed to a wall without windows.

With an expression of reverence, Sara faced the endless rows of eight-by-ten glossies decorating the honey wood paneling.

Trainer strode to the photographic equipment positioned beside the examining table. "Straighten up, Sara," he ordered. "Wrists locked at lumbar."

She continued to study the opposite wall.

"They're magnificent, aren't they?" Trainer boasted, snapping a waist-high frontal. "Now. Swing around to the side. Arms away from body. That'a girl."

Returning to her side, Trainer gently replaced the cotton gown to her shoulders. "Your next shots will transcend all. They will be exquisite enough to display in a gallery."

It was obvious that Sara admired Trainer, impressed by the mounted photos. One eight by ten glossy displayed a smiling Trainer dressed in full mountain climbing gear. Another was a panoramic of him skiing down a snow-packed slope sporting a daredevil grin. In a third he posed in defiance between a surfboard and an ocean of angry waves. And there were others. Each shared one thing in common; a radiant Trainer meeting the camera head-on with aristocratic dominance.

Doctor Greg Trainer loved sports, and ladies' breasts, deriving his greatest pleasure by transforming the latter into flawless assets, more impressive than Mother Nature's finest creations. After his patient departed, he left his office, a mask of satisfaction seizing his face.

Leapfrogging from one building to another, the Chessler complex was a maze of gleaming corridors. Taking the west elevator, Trainer exited at the hallway leading to the first floor business offices. His tasseled steps were brisk. Arms swinging at sides, he was on a mission.

DINNER TONIGHT?

Sienna was busy at work, typing up a furious storm when Trainer popped his head through the doorway. For a moment he simply admired the snapshot of a perfect secretary, chin up, hair clipped back, shoulders straight, breasts defying gravity in a purple v-neck curve clinging top.

"Hello, gorgeous," he sang out, a manicured hand resting lightly against the door frame.

At the sound of Trainer's voice, Sienna stiffened, while Bonnie simply stared.

"What are you doing here?" Sienna stopped typing to slide a chart across her desk. With the same brisk movement, her eyes darted from Trainer to Bonnie.

"Breaking for lunch. Have you eaten yet?" Trainer swooped through the doorway, heading straight to Sienna's desk, then gracefully leaned in toward her. The scent of musk filled the air.

"I'm not taking lunch today. I'm swamped." She barely raised her head.

His eyes drilled. "Oh, come on, Sienna. You have to eat." He grasped her chin with his thumb and index finger, leveling her face toward his.

She pushed his hand away, controlling the glare building in her eyes.

Bonnie was a peripheral flash as she rose and strode to the file cabinets, where she huddled behind Trainer. She proceeded to flag a series of hand motions at Sienna, like a cop directing traffic, mouthing, "Go to lunch with him."

Sienna appeared distracted — obviously not in the mood for Trainer — especially during working hours.

Trainer was determined. "Dinner tonight then?" He straightened his stance and adjusted his brown suede blazer, with long strokes of his fingers brushing imaginary lint from one boxed shoulder, halfway down the arm. "The River Lounge. How does that sound?"

Trainer was acting like they were an item. Why? Because of one pseudo-date that took place months ago?

"You really should go." Bonnie's voice rang like a dinner bell. "They have delicious food, Sienna, and there's a great band playing tonight. Mickey knows the drummer."

"See, even your co-worker knows what you'd be missing." Trainer pressed.

"I work till six . . ." Her voice was flat.

"Perfect. That will give me time to get the Porsche washed before I pick you up at, say, seven-thirty? Will that give you enough time to bathe and look even more dazzling than you do at this moment?" His voice was airy; he may have thought he was winning.

"I'll think about it," Sienna said with reluctance, her straight white teeth slightly visible through tightening lips. She lowered her eyes and fished through papers on her desk. *And why am I doing this again? Because I'm an idiot.*

Bonnie was the artist, and her Rockwell of the perfect couple was almost complete. Her lashes brushed a wink of approval in Sienna's direction.

"I guess I'll see you later." Was she actually agreeing? She shot Bonnie a scowl.

"Until tonight." Trainer sang from the doorway. As he left their office, his face looked like the sun breaking through an overcast sky.

Bonnie slid back onto her chair with a sigh, but did not start working. "Good for you. You deserve a night out. You'll have fun — I promise."

"How can *you* promise? You won't even be there." Sienna glared at her.

"Once you get out into that romantic night air, you'll feel like a different person. Just flow with it."

"Romantic night? I'm calling his cell to cancel."

"No you're not."

"I don't even like him. Why would I actually go out with him?"

"Because you need a change of scene. Because you'd have a better chance at a promotion if you'd go to conventions and other affairs with him. Rub elbows with the hot shots. Because he obviously likes you a lot and would be very good to you. He's bending over backwards for you, even though you treat him like crap." She shook her head and chuckled. "I've never seen anything like it."

"I'll get a promotion on my own."

"I'm sure you will. But maybe if you get some kind of social life, other than tennis and bingo, those stupid dreams will stop. Ever think of that?"

"I have a life. I volunteer at the animal shelter. It's fulfilling."

"They say you resolve problems in your dreams."

"Right now, my only problem is you."

"If you don't want sex, then why are you dreaming about it?"

"That's not fair. I can't control what I dream about. But I can control what I do when I'm awake. And I am NOT going out with Trainer. Or anyone else!"

"Would the *anyone else* by any chance be the plaza guy? It's got you bugged, doesn't it?"

"What are you talking about?"

"The blow-off. You're pissed."

Sienna grit her teeth. "I was doing fine on my own. Then he rolls into my life with those big brown eyes. He seemed so gentle. So nice. Not like . . ."

"What the hell? You can't be serious, Sienna. You wouldn't really go out with *him*." Bonnie's eyes bulged. "What could he . . . What could you . . . He's in a wheelchair for God's sake. What do you *see* in him?"

Sienna's nostrils flared. "For starters, he's not pushy like some people." Her stare could have lit a fire. "I don't have to have a relationship with him. I don't have to have sex with him. I don't have to put makeup on, or a damn dress and heels." Her voice rose. "I can be myself. Don't you get it? It would be fun to hang out with him. *As a friend.*"

"I *don't* get it." Bonnie threw her hands into the air. "Look at you, Sienna. You're about to fall apart. Forget the brush-off. Go out and have a blast."

Sienna smirked. "I will. I'm going to the shelter. At least there I get peace and loyalty." She plucked the receiver of her phone off its base, upsetting a ceramic cup crammed with markers and pencils. Plastic and wood cascaded over her desk like logs over a waterfall, rushing to the floor and scattering.

Bonnie was defiant. "You are not cancelling again." Reaching over she snatched the phone from Sienna's hand. "You're going this time. It's better than dog-sitting."

"Negative dependency?" Sienna whispered.

"What?"

"I thought I broke the cycle."

"I never figured you for dependent. Just the opposite. But your emotions are all over the map, Sienna. You fly around like a chicken without a head, doing things for everyone else. I worry you may be letting something good slip by, that's all. While you're deciding what to do with your life."

"Trainer is controlling."

"True."

"Michael is different."

"That he is."

"Don't be sarcastic. And I would call that breaking the cycle, wouldn't you?" A squiggly vein on Sienna's forehead bulged.

By then, her elbows rested on her desk and her head was in her hands, fingers nursing a budding migraine. "Give me two of your extra strength aspirins, will you please?"

Bonnie mumbled as she reached into her draw, then tossed the bottle of aspirin to Sienna. "Whatever." She shrugged, then turned her attention to work.

"Alright I'll go." Sienna snapped. "I feel like strangling you — and myself."

"Loneliness does weird things to people. You'll get old, cranky — dried up."

"I'm far from lonely. I have Frazzle and Dazzle. And I'm cranky already." Sienna's jaw clenched.

"True, but are you all dried up?"

"Who knows?" Sienna shrugged. "I haven't had the desire. . ."

As she recalled the dream, she tuned Bonnie out.

It was dusk. The air was damp. Her face was flushed and she was out of breath. His hands roamed feverishly, and in a moment her bikini bottom was tossed on the deck. Greedy fingers frisked her breasts, plucking her rigid nipples while his lips sucked ringlets of blood to each side of her neck.

She felt his bulge slip between the crease of her buttocks. A yearning nudge, then searing pressure. For a split-second, she thought he would strip and enter from behind.

"Leave me alone!" Sienna screamed.

"Sienna!" Bonnie sounded annoyed.

"What?"

"What planet are you on? Your extension is buzzing."

"Shit." Sienna lifted the receiver.

"I'll be right down." She reached for a clipboard.

"I know that look." Bonnie fixed on Sienna's frown. "Want me to go?"

"Nope. It's my turn. I'll be back soon, I hope."

Clipboard clutched to her chest, Sienna found the room the child had been taken to. It was her job to gather the insurance information for the emergency admission. *How cold. You're lying in a hospital bed and all we care about is how you're going to pay us . . .*

Entering a trauma room was like walking down a dark city street. You never knew what awaited behind the curtain of darkness. In this case, behind the curtain of fear and pain for the patient in the bed, worse yet, on the table.

"What do we have?" Sienna asked one of the nurses standing at the doorway. Before the woman spoke, Sienna's eyes washed over a figure so small it barely made a bump in the sheet.

"Seven year old girl. Auto accident. Possible concussion."

"Oh God." Sienna forced her eyes across the little girl's face; pale, closed eyelids encircled with a tinge of blue. "Will she be okay?"

"Should be. Her mom's in the next room. Must have been some impact. Her chest is badly bruised from the seatbelt. Possible internal injuries."

"Is family on the way? I should probably wait for someone. . . Not bother the poor woman. She's got enough to worry about."

"As far as I know, no one's been called. She's a single mom. Picked her child up from school to drop her off at daycare then go back to work. Never made it though."

Sienna's eyes burned. She knew any moment tears would begin a slow roll down her cheeks.

"Might as well get it over with." She sighed.

After another look at the child, she left the room to speak with her mother.

Technicians were just returning her from X-ray. The woman looked dazed.

"I'm Sienna," she touched her hand, "from E.R. Registration. How are you feeling?"

"Like I've been hit by a truck, which my daughter and I were." Tears gathered in her eyes.

"Are you in much pain?"

"They gave me something. I'll be fine. I'm more concerned about my daughter. They said she's going to be okay, but can I see her?"

"Of course. I just need to get some information," Sienna's voice sounded weak. She hated this part of her job. "I know this isn't the best time. And I'm sorry to be bothering you now . . ."

As if sensing Sienna's concern, the woman tried to smile. "It's okay. Shoot, and then shove me across the hall." She tried to laugh. "Or wherever Sandy is."

"Sandy. That's a nice name." Sienna gripped the woman's shoulder. "She looks like a Sandy. She's adorable." She smiled. "I just left her room. She's resting, and a nurse said she'll be fine. Try not to worry." She ran her hand gently down the woman's arm, stopping before her IV.

"You're compassionate," said the woman whose sleepy eyes clung to Sienna's. "You make me feel better. Do you have children?"

WHAT A COINCIDENCE

The restaurant of Trainer's choice was a dramatic reproduction of a Chattanooga riverboat, but this one was moored in a glistening New England bay. Tranquil Atlantic currents rolled into the Long Island Sound, forging a dramatic triangle around the stunning structure and rambling veranda. Its most desirable dining room perched on shoreline piers, straddling the ocean. The lavish room was paneled in rustic walnut, carpeted in crimson, and framed with windowed walls where gusts of salty air amplified the nautical scheme.

On his way from the shower Michael heard the phone ring. "Hey, Gus. Just getting ready now."

"You sound out of breath. Everything okay?"

"Give me a sec." Michael ran the towel he was holding across his wet hair. "I'm fine."

"Say again?"

Along with traffic in the background, static crackled through the line. "It won't take me long."

"Good. Pick you up in about twenty minutes, okay boss?"

"Who's coming?"

"About eight of us. Reservations at the River Station. Don't rush, Mike. We can wait."

"I'm starved. Haven't eaten all day." Beads of moisture clung to Michael's shoulders and upper chest. He slung the towel around his neck.

"I haven't eaten either. Had to stay at the site later than I expected."

"Problems?"

"Nah. Nothing to worry about. Electricians were late. I wanted to make sure everything went smoothly. I'll fill you in over dinner."

"Terrific. Don't pick me up, Gus. I'll meet you there."

"Gotcha, boss."

Michael returned the phone to his nightstand. Relieved to have a friend and foreman like Gus Argyros, the tension he'd felt all day faded. He whistled as he dressed, just like he used to, and then the thought struck; the last time he'd been at the River Station, he had walked in.

The crew arrived at the restaurant shortly after seven p.m. Ready to party, they were seated in the main dining room, at a round table opposite the entrance foyer.

"Who's gonna toast this celebration?" Gus spoke to the group. Each man wore a sport jacket, and button down shirt casually open at the neck. Involved in conversation, no one replied.

"Well, I guess it's me then." Gus chuckled and whacked the table edge with the palm of his hand.

Michael scanned the circle of rugged faces ranging in age from thirty to sixty, then smiled at Gus and shook his head. "Just like at work." He threw his hands into the air. "Always a damn racket, and you have to yell to be heard."

"Aye!" Gus raised his mug and his voice at the same time. "Listen up. A toast is in order. To Michael Chessler." He lifted a chilled mug of beer above his head. "To the completion of Chessler complex and condos — and for our jobs."

"Amen."

"To Mr. and Mrs. Chessler who gave him to us . . ." They tapped spoons against glasses. "And to Michael, the best boss a man could ever have."

"I'll drink to that." Rounded the table.

"Let's not forget William and Marianna Chessler." Following Gus's lead, once more they lifted sweating mugs of tap in salute.

"Amen. To Gram and Pops. May they rest in peace." Michael swigged his beer. "And to Mom and Dad who would be very happy to see the condo project completed, better than originally planned, and dedicated to Gram. She'd be thrilled if she were here."

"To the Chesslers." Gus toasted again. A boisterous cheer went up. The party had begun.

From her Chessler Cove condo, Sienna stepped into a brisk evening breeze. The sun hadn't set, and the sky was clear and vibrantly colored. To complete the tapestry of grace, she paused alongside a lamppost, looking like a stunning statue poised beside a Grecian column. She rolled her shoulders, shedding the day, and drew in a breath of lavender lilac blooming near the road.

She checked her wristwatch: seven forty-five. Greg Trainer was fashionably late. She soured. "I'll give you five more minutes, then I'm going back inside and cuddle with my cats. Well, maybe Dazzle. Frazzle seems to like the bay window better than my hip. Now I'm talking to myself . . ."

Before she checked her watch again, the metallic Porsche soared up Hilltop Road and jerked to a stop at the curb. Through the driver's window, she watched his face light as his eyes trickled over her stunning black sheath. Her red-soled stilettos brightened each step as she approached.

"Sorry I'm late," he drawled as he hopped out of the driver's seat, sprinted around the front of the idling car, and held open the passenger door.

He flaunted an Italian suit with striped tie and patent leather slip-ons. The look was classy except for what the wind had done to his usually perfect hair.

"No problem. I actually just walked out the door," she replied lightly with every intention of giving this night — and Greg

Trainer — a fair shake.

Trainer unavoidably gaped between Sienna's thighs as she slid onto the bucket seat, accidentally exposing her crotch covered with sexy black lace.

"Will you put the convertible top up?" she asked sweetly. "It took forever to do my hair."

Sienna's curls were piled into a crystal clip, with long tendrils grazing the nape of her neck, a few drizzling down the open back of her dress that dove and draped across her spine. She looked like a starlet about to step onto the red carpet.

"And it was worth every minute," Trainer cooed. "Let's forget dinner. You look good enough to eat."

Relaxing deeply into pewter leather, Sienna ignored Trainer's comments and focused on the scene beyond her window. The horizon was a remarkable creation of infinite brush strokes, streaking the sky above the broad stretch of curve-clinging coastline. She watched yachts glide with ease, some lingering, their lights launching daggers through dusk. The sight was captivating: passive bay, bowed sky filled with ripening stars, the moon pouring streams of molten silver onto the waves.

This could be a magnificent evening — *for someone in love* — flashed through Sienna's mind as the Porsche rolled to a stop before the paneled doors of the River Station.

A valet, fashioned as a sailor, took the keys, while the doorman escorted the eye-catching couple into the vestibule. In Trainer's name, an intimate table awaited them in the adjacent River Lounge. They'd be showered by lamplight and lulled by the tide; for Dr. Gregory Trainer, only the finest.

Drifting ahead of Trainer, Sienna stared above the bustling dining room, unaffected by the surrounding blur of faces as she paced the host. As she sailed by the table of eight jovial men, Sienna didn't notice Michael, or the surprise that wiped the smile from his face.

When Michael spotted her — with a man — he stopped talking and fell into astonishment that instantly morphed into envy. He couldn't believe his eyes, or the timing. *I know we keep running into each other, but why tonight, why like this?*

"What's the matter, boss?" Gus asked. "You look like you just saw a ghost."

"I just may have," Michael mumbled as he watched them from behind. The man strutted like a king on his way to his throne, while Sienna moved like a goddess, sleek and savvy, hips swaying as if she belonged on a Paris runway. "Nice dramatic entrance," Michael grunted, pressure pounding his temples.

"What's going on?" asked John, newest member of the crew, his face flushed with alcohol and the love of good times. "What am I missing here? We were just talking about our next project, weren't we?"

"Nothing," Michael snapped. "Nothing's going on. What were you saying, Dan?" He fought to manage hostility and regret.

"The land you were interested in, in the city, may be available soon. My uncle's a broker. I have him looking into it now," Dan said as he dug his fork into a tossed salad.

"Good," Michael nodded, "we could be breaking ground by. . ."

The entire table had watched them saunter by, but didn't make the connection between the couple and Michael's abrupt change of mood.

"Wow. Would you check out what just walked by," Jake blurted out. "What a knockout."

"Who — what — where?!" Chris turned so quickly in his seat, he jerked the mug of beer he'd been nursing, and it splashed across the arm of Jake's jacket.

"Asshole," Jake griped.

"Sorry, man. I just wanted to see what you were talking about." Chris swiped Jake's sleeve with his own linen napkin.

"That blonde over there. The babe walking into the lounge with that dude. Nice suit he's got on, but that hair's gotta go." As he laughed, Jake's barrel chest strained the buttons of his sport shirt.

"Easy for you to criticize another guy's hair," balding Chris shot back. "All you gotta do is pull yours back in a ponytail and you're good to go . . . Damn, she *is* hot."

"What's a guy gotta do to land a piece of ass like that?" Jake continued with a low wolf whistle as he threw his head to the side for a better view, flipping his elastic-bound wad of hair against his cheek. "I'd like to tap that," he drawled while motioning to the cocktail waitress. "Hey, doll, another round over here."

"I'll drink to that," Chris said, eyes still glued to the woman who was fading into the distance.

"Enough, you clowns." Gus glared, then looked at Michael, who appeared pensive, not finding their shenanigans the least bit amusing.

"The animals are out of their cages," Gus snorted.

"What a fucking fiasco," Michael grumbled under his breath, then cleared his throat and raised his voice. "So getting back to business. I'll have the blueprints ready for the new plaza suite by next week."

"It's going on acreage between Ridgewood and the 202 office complex, am I correct?" Gus asked, shifting in his seat as the waitress served him an oval dinner plate of lobster and baked potato flooded with butter.

"Yes," Michael replied tightly. For Michael, the evening had lost its charm, and with it went his self-worth.

"That'll be classy," Dan chimed in. "Plus bring a lot of business into the area. Hey, did I tell you the last Chessler Cove unit was rented today? Uncle George on the job."

"Full house. Another toast is in order." As Gus raised his mug, the last inch of beer sloshed against the sides.

If Michael angled his head in the right direction, he could just about make out their table through the twilight lounge. They sat opposite each other. Michael longed to hear the conversation, and winced when he saw the man reach across the table for her hand.

"I'm so happy you decided to come tonight." Trainer swooned. "Did I mention how dazzling you look? I love being with you." He paused for a sip of wine. "Did you see that table full of men ogling us as we walked in?"

"No, Greg, I didn't notice," Sienna replied dryly, snatching her hand from his grasp. He was already getting on her nerves. She tried to divert his attention from the obvious. "Look at the menu. What are you having? Everything looks so delicious."

Sienna and Trainer were seated at a linen topped table near the center of the room — not the intimate corner Trainer had requested. As they ordered, soft music strayed from the barroom, blending with the rhythm of cresting waves.

Sienna took her first long look at him since sitting down, then covered her mouth with her hand until she stopped grinning. "Fix your hair, Greg. It's sticking up from the convertible.

Feeling for loose strands, Trainer fingered the sides of his head then tapped his hair-sprayed crown. "That's the only downside to a Porsche convertible," he quipped, winking. "Better run to the men's room." He stepped to the back of her chair, kissed her cheek, and gave her shoulders a quick squeeze. "Be right back, dear."

Sienna clutched a long-stemmed wine glass half filled with Chablis. She sipped delicately and often as she waited for Trainer to return. With the help of the wine she convinced herself she had needed this evening after all. She refused to worry about masochistic tendencies or thoughts of the future. She was here. The time was now. And she was warmed by alcohol and the atmosphere, despite the narcissism of the man who stared longingly at her as he returned.

Watching what he presumed to be two lovers, Michael's heart ached.

Once more Trainer reached across the table, attempting to bring Sienna's palm to his lips, to nibble romantically one dainty finger at a time. Once more, she found a reason to pull away, knowing he was priming her for later — and something that was not going to happen.

"It's been a nice evening." She tactfully returned her hand to her glass.

"What do you mean *has been*?" He spoke huskily. "*Is* a wonderful evening. And will continue to be."

His gaze traveled from her crystal blue eyes to her dewy lips, then strayed lower to linger upon a gleaming locket that slipped between her cleavage. "Share a dessert?" He moistened his lips with the tip of his tongue.

"Sure," Sienna replied casually.

"How does chocolate mousse sound?"

"Fine."

Greg's demeanor struck a nerve. Bonnie had been right; the place was romantic. Could have been romantic; but sitting across from Trainer was not. Something inside her was triggered, an emotion long ago buried. She stiffened. No matter how independent she felt, acted, she could no longer run from it; something *was* missing from her life.

She couldn't wait for the evening to end.

"Here, dear," Trainer reached across the table, extending a long-handled spoon overflowing with mousse and fresh whipped cream, aiming it at her lips.

FIRST "REAL" CLOSE ENCOUNTER

During dinner, Michael stole glances at Sienna and her companion while only half listening to the voices streaming around him. Although the setting was intimate, and the man appeared indulging, Sienna seemed somewhat hesitant. Or was this just wishful thinking on his part? After all, she was there with him which meant there had to be something significant between them. From their attire it was not a business meeting as Michael had at first hoped. She was far too resplendent, with upswept hair, dangling earrings that caught a glitter of candlelight, and soft shoulders the man had possessively touched with his hands, his lips. *What else would he be touching tonight?*

"I reamed out Ryan Fredrick this afternoon," Trainer boasted as the waiter delivered the check.

"Whatever for? Ryan Frederick is almost as old as the hospital. Aside from the fact that he's the Administrator, and a very nice man."

"That nice man and his committee of aged hotshots are responsible for changes at Manchester. Changes that I, for one, don't agree with."

"Such as?"

"A certain clinic, for openers."

"I understand it's an explosive issue, but how will the new drug clinic affect you?"

"Indirectly." Trainer jerked his head. "I've visited the clinic's originating base unit in the city. Believe me, dear, they're producing nothing more than a hazardous collection of misfits. I don't agree with their methods of treatment. That's what I was trying to get across to Fredrick. But he continues to act like a fool."

"This tantrum wouldn't possibly have anything to do with the veto of the expansion of the cosmetic surgery department you thought you'd be heading, would it?"

"Let's drop it. This is not the time to discuss hospital politics."

"This isn't the time for a lot of things."

"Meaning?"

"Meaning I don't know what I'm doing here."

"What's wrong with you tonight? You're so—"

"Bitchy?" She glared. "Maybe it's the company I keep."

"You're going too far."

"Not far enough. I'm leaving."

"Sienna—" He reached for her hand.

"I need to be alone. I'll take a cab." Her face flamed.

Trainer's frown mirrored Sienna's as he threw three one hundred dollar bills on top of the check and pushed back his chair.

"I don't know how much harder I can try." He shook his head. "Have it your way."

Michael's eyes widened as he watched Trainer stomp off in the direction of the exit, while Sienna headed toward the bar.

What the hell?

While trying to keep an eye out for her, he sounded agitated as he announced to the table. "I guess we're ready to wrap things up?"

Gus had an odd look on his face. "Are you okay?"

"Couldn't be better." Before he moved from his place at the table, Michael slipped a credit card beneath Gus's hand. "Take care of this. I'll talk to you tomorrow."

"Is everything okay, Mike?"

"I'll let you know tomorrow," said Michael, fortified with resolve.

Michael made his way into the barroom, instantly spotting Sienna. She was seated at the far end of the bar. He watched her gulp the last of her wine, shove her glass to the bartender. She immediately attacked her refill. Michael shared the bartender's surprised expression. The woman appeared to be on a mission.

He moved to her side. For a moment he remained silent, hoping she would notice him. Wondering what he would do if she didn't. The drinks he'd had earlier, although not nearly enough to dull his senses, had relaxed him. He was about to do something he'd never dreamed he was capable of.

"Sienna, right?" His voice was strong, smooth.

Her head snapped around, her gaze leveling with his. Brows drawn together, her eyes narrowed. "Are you following me?"

Michael cringed. If her speech had not been slurred, he would have left her sitting there, digesting one of his rudest comments.

"I'm having dinner with friends. Actually," he cleared his throat, let out a breath, "I was about to leave and happened to notice you over here, by yourself, and thought you might need a friend — or a ride." He motioned to the table she and her companion had vacated, and the busboy who was in the process of clearing it.

"I'm sorry. I don't mean to be such a bitch." For a moment she stared. "I remember you. Hey, there's a room over there you can duck into." Her eyes looked as unsteady as her voice. "Men." She intentionally shuddered. "You're all the same."

The intensity of her stare was gripping. Although he knew he had it coming, she caught him by surprise. No woman had ever called him out before. But then, he'd never ditched one either. He felt the rise of a flush.

"Would you like a ride home?"

She looked at her glass, then back to him. "Maybe I do." With a seductive movement, she slid gracefully from the seat and stood before him, then wavered.

He was eye level with her slender waist, the front of her dress where a wrinkle beneath her tummy met the top of her thighs.

"I'd offer you my arm," he grinned, "why don't you lean on my chair . . ."

They looked straight ahead as they left the restaurant, Michael leading, Sienna resting a hand on the back of his chair. As the valet retrieved the Suburban, Michael rehashed the evening, his thoughts. He had earlier wondered what the starlit night had in store for Sienna and her companion. What had begun as one of the most disturbing evenings of his life, seemed to be progressing into one of the most exciting.

The night was warm and close, with dusty clouds overtaking the stars.

Seated in the Suburban, Michael turned to Sienna.

"Are you feeling alright?"

"Why wouldn't I be?"

"You're really something else," he mumbled as he drove out onto the highway. "I hope it's only the drinks."

Sienna rolled down the window, aimed her face into a stream of damp air. "It's going to storm."

"I know."

"I love the rain."

"These roads can be treacherous in bad weather." Michael carefully guided the SUV. "Exactly where are we going?"

"You mean, your place or mine?" She swung her head in his direction. The breeze had loosened her hair, and it framed her face, slipped over her shoulders. "I think I need a nightcap."

"I think you need to climb into bed."

Sienna sank into the seat, groaning. "I think you may be right. I couldn't fit in another thing. Thank you for the nice dinner. Now I really need to get home. I'm tired."

Michael stole a glance. For a sexy woman, the look on her face was funny. So was the nonsense coming through her lovely lips. He laughed.

"Give me your address."

"I told you I live in a condo."

"This isn't getting us anywhere." Michael pulled off the main road, stopping on a side street. There were no houses, just acres of forestland. Oaks. One of the reasons the town was called Oak Haven. He turned in his seat and faced her. "Can I have your wallet?"

"What, are you gonna rob me?"

He hadn't been expecting her to behave this way. She was actually delightful when intoxicated. And fortunate he had come along. He smiled and reached for her small purse.

Leaning close to the door, her thumb pressing against her lower lip, she twirled a lock of hair around her finger, watching him. Her eyes moved from his head to his shoulders to his chest. She watched his hands clutch her purse, intimately remove her wallet.

"Chessler Cove. I know that place," he said, tucked her license into its slot and replaced her wallet.

Before Michael knew what was happening, she was on top of him, pinning him to the seat with her body. Straddling him, her hips beginning to move. He sucked in a breath. He knew she was drunk, and he'd never take advantage of her, but that didn't stop his body from reacting.

Her arms went around his neck. Her lids covered half of her eyes; as she gazed into his, her lips parted.

All he could think was, *God help me.* How am I going to stop? I don't want to stop.

Her dress had slid up and was bunched around her waist. When he was finally able to move, his fingers clutched her soft skinned hips. Her panties felt almost nonexistent. Was she wearing any? His mind raced. His body stiffened. His hands gripped tighter.

When she sighed, her warm breath filled his ear. Her lips brushed his cheek, then came down on his, full force. He couldn't help but respond. Her tongue circled his lips then plunged. All the while, her body pumped against his.

"Baby," he moaned. "You don't know what you're doing to me." He pulled her into his chest, pressed her firmly into his lap. She moaned louder. Her hips moved faster. His hands roamed her back, stroking the soft skin bared by her thong.

"I need you," she whispered. "Make love to me."

She panted. He moaned. Then as suddenly as she had started it, he ended it.

"I can't," he said, peeling her arms from around his neck,

moving his face to the side. By the shoulders, he pushed her further away. "You have no idea how much this hurts." His breathing deepened.

"You don't find me attractive?"

"More than you can imagine."

"So why won't you?"

"Because you don't have a clue of what you're doing." His voice was firm. "And I'm not about to screw a woman who probably won't even remember me tomorrow."

The Suburban pulled close to the curb. Sienna had stared out the window the entire ride home. Neither she nor Michael had uttered a word. And now she was sobering.

"Looks like it's starting to rain." She tugged the door handle, but before stepping outside, turned to look deeply into his eyes. "Thank you," she said.

"Don't mention it," he replied. He watched her disappear into the condo, then drove away.

After unlocking her front door, Sienna stepped into the tiled foyer and dropped her keys onto a burl credenza. The moment Michael had appeared before her, thoughts of Trainer had vanished. But guilt began to surface. *What had she just done?*

Frazzle slept on the shelf of the bay window. Dazzle stretched and jumped from a chair. Like a puppy, she ran to Sienna, weaving in and out of her legs.

Sienna slipped out of her dress and let it drop to the floor, then kicked off her stilettos. In bare feet she padded across the tawny carpet in the direction of the staircase, then changed her mind and collapsed onto the sofa wearing only her black lace thong. She stretched and yawned, then curled into a protective ball. Beside her Dazzle purred. "You're such a sweet girl," Sienna said, stroking her soft white fur, whispering, "I love you, Dazzle."

Her head was beginning to hurt. She was restless; she knew

she'd be spending the rest of the night in the living room, and drew a peach colored afghan up to her shoulders.

Although a weight had been lifted, she wasn't at peace. How could she ever face Michael again? Well, she'd probably never run into him again anyway. She'd turn off her mind. She was good at doing that. Consciously anyway.

You should be rejoicing, Sienna. Obnoxious Greg Trainer is gone from your life — and so is the bastard, Rob Lucas . . . She dozed.

The pressure on her neck increases as his nails dig into her flesh. She tries to pry his fingers loose, but she's losing consciousness. He picks her up as if she's weightless. She's floating down the hall. The light from the bedroom beckons. "No!" she screams. "Not again!" He tosses her onto the bed. His chest is heaving as he pins her to the mattress. She freezes, stiffens beneath him. She'll die before she lets him touch her. Hands too big for even a dream wedge between her thighs. She fights him, but the muscles in her groin begin to stretch. Her legs are pried apart. She feels the pressure. Searing pain.

"Stop it!"

The words are magic. The horror of Rob's face is growing dimmer. His violence begins to fade away. Her hands fall limply to her sides, then everything goes black.

NOW SHE'S GOT HIM DREAMING TOO

Sienna awoke with a shudder, at the top of her lungs screaming, "Stop!" The assault had been too real. She felt him. His hands, his breath. His wet mouth on hers. Why was she tasting tobacco? Liquor? Her heart raced as her eyes searched the room. She reached for a tissue and wiped her mouth, inside and out, until it felt raw. Sliding a hand between her thighs, she touched herself. She was dry. Thank God it had only been a dream. She grit her teeth. She had never been violated *that* way. Why should she dream of such horror? Repressed trauma. Suppressed terror. One in the same to Sienna. The counselor had told her she'd face her share of darkness before things got better. How much darker could it get? She fought the rise of panic, blocking out the nightmare.

Phantom manifestation. Her unconscious brain was playing tricks with her again. Still playing tricks with her was more like it. Deep breath. Slow. Deep. Better. Clear your mind. That's right. He's gone. She would not let him back into her thoughts, and certainly wouldn't allow herself to feel remorse. She had tried to help him. Rob's actions were his problem. Not hers. Not anymore.

She felt the onset of a paralyzing hangover. Aspirin might help her head. Nothing other than sleep would help her stomach, or the room that still wanted to spin. Before she was able to drift off again, the phone rang. Swathed in the afghan, she tiptoed to the end table.

"Honey?"

"Greg?"

"It's me. I was a jerk. I misbehaved. I hope you're not still angry with me. I wanted to make sure you got home okay."

"I'm fine." Her voice was flat.

"With all of the activity tonight, I forgot to mention London." His voice was mellow. "I was going to wait until tomorrow to tell you about it. I hope I'm not disturbing you?" He didn't wait for a reply. "I want you to come to the seminar with me. A few days in London and then we're off to Ontario for this year's Cosmetic Surgery Convention. I'd like you to come to both. It's the first step toward that promotion you've been waiting for."

"I don't have money for a trip to London," she said tiredly, "and especially to spend on one of those high-priced hotels you doctors are used to staying in."

"Don't worry about money, Sienna. The hospital pays for everything, and of course, we'll have separate rooms."

"I'll think about it."

When she finally fell back to sleep, Sienna dreamed she was on a yacht, not on an airliner destined for London. And the man with her wasn't Dr. Gregory Trainer. He was someone gentle yet passionate, dark and lustful. Familiar but without defined features. She had a good idea of who he was.

He's an experienced male who knows how to satisfy a woman. In one swift movement he tears her from Rob's embrace, spins her around and pulls her close. Her breasts crush his bare chest. The bulge in his jeans pokes the softness just above her pubic bone. He begins a grind then lowers his pelvis, molding to her core. As his hips roll, his breath quickens.

"I'll have you before sunset," yanking her from the safety of Michael's arms, Rob rasps, raking his fingers up and down her back.

She pushes away, arches her spine, then offers a breast. Michael hungrily accepts, his mouth caressing the swollen nipple. Electricity ripples through her.

"Now, baby," Sienna murmurs huskily. Fire flashes deep in her tummy where a spot sweeter than her sigh begins to rage.

She knows exactly what to say in a tone that could drive a man to the edge. She can almost feel the ache in his groin as he moans, his hand moving to his fly. He drops his jeans to his hips, letting himself expand.

Her thighs clamp his hand like a vise. The groan escaping her throat is carnal — like his. She's beautiful, untamed, and finally in the arms of the man she longs for.

"The sun's setting. I thought you'd have me by now." In a whisper, peering over Michael's shoulder, she taunts Rob. Why is she doing this? She hates Rob Lucas. Rob Lucas is dead!

Michael's fingers respond by working faster. The clutch of her thighs draws out the singeing thrill of contracting muscle. Collapsing against him she gasps. "Baby, you're so good."

Digging her nails into his biceps, she wraps a smooth leg around his hip. But he obviously has something else in mind. A palm beneath each buttock, he hoists her up to balance on the rail. "Brace yourself," he says, his voice ragged with desire.

The metal is damp against her flesh. Pain. Painfully erotic.

Hands at her sides, she grips the steel tightly, her toes curling around a lower slat.

Michael's stare is dark, a predator to feast but first, to satisfy. He drops to his knees.

Sienna's legs strap his shoulders as his fingers hook her thighs. Trembling, she waits, bearing down as his tongue begins to swirl. He's the best thing she's ever had. Clawing at him, she's losing her mind.

Through a cloud, Rob watches with envy, his mouth twisted in a snarl.

Sienna gasps. Passion unlocks her grip on the rail. Before she falls, she rakes her fingers through Michael's hair, bringing his face so close that all he'll breathe, all he'll taste, all he will remember will be her.

Michael returned from the driving Sienna home, overwhelmed

by emotions too difficult to deal with. Even though he hadn't fully taken advantage of her, he felt ashamed. He shouldn't have let it go that far. Would she ever speak to him again? The feelings she stirred were almost unbearable. How could he fight them? She was tearing him apart. The crazy part about it was, she had no idea of what she was doing to him. *What a fool.*

He slept fitfully and kept waking, visions of Sienna weaving through his head. He wondered how serious her relationship was with the other man. How serious could it be if he'd left her? *He'd never leave her.*

Fighting despair, he reminded himself of all that was good in his life — then considered his limitations. Get real, he told himself; you're a guy in a wheelchair. What do you want from her?

They're nestled close together in a secluded booth. The hour is late. The restaurant has fallen into silence as everyone has departed for the night. The doors are locked, windows shaded. But they remain — not for dinner, not for love, but to fulfill a sexual need.

From beneath the suspended chandelier, her wild eyes flash like cobalt daggers, piercing his with intolerable temptation. The light illuminates her bare shoulders, tan and tempting. In one swift motion she unleashes her upswept hair, and with a shake of the head honey locks tumble down her back. She cups her breasts, forcing her cleavage over the top of her strapless dress. With a taunting grin she eyes his reaction, then slides her arms around his neck, pulling him to her. He resists. Eyes hungry for satisfaction, he'll watch her for a moment, tease her before joining in.

Shoving her roughly against the wall, he pins her arms above her head while his lips draw back in a vicious snarl, his throat emitting greedy sounds. His eyes flare with desire as he runs a hand over her dress, tasting every curve with searching fingers.

Since the waiter cleared the table, their eyes haven't moved from one another, but now he allows his to wander, follow the progress of his rough-hewn palms, down the side of her neck, across her chest, as he scrapes a torturous path on her skin. He feels her shiver beneath each stroke. With a groan she throws back her head and arches her spine, writhing upon the seat, urging the onset of decadence.

His breath comes fast as he watches the roll of her hips, her face overtaken by lust. He slips one of her hands beneath her dress, sliding it between her thighs, assisting her with a gratifying knead, then with a bow of his head mouths the trail of heat their fingers ignited. He raises his head, replaces her hand, and feels her quiver. "Don't . . . stop," she whispers.

He grips her shoulders tightly, then his hands join hers, releasing her stabbing ache soon to explode.

"Kiss me, bastard," her pouting lips snap. "More. I need more." She delivers a stinging slap across his cheek. Eagerly obliging, his mouth savagely clamps down on hers, his tongue wedged between her lips. Their mouths press fiercely as she rips the buttons from his shirt, sharp fingernails raking him from neck to waist before clutching the tenderness beneath his loose-fitting trousers. Her breath is hot on his face as she tugs him free of sharkskin fabric.

Admiring her at arm's length, he peels down the top of her dress. Sucks in a breath as he watches her breasts settle across her chest. He grows even harder.

Her breasts burst forth and heave, aching to be ravaged. Before he can move, she buries herself into his bare chest, shifting, grazing him with hardened nipples pleading for oral stimulation. The sight of her takes his breath away. He throbs.

"I want you so badly."

"Not yet." Her flicking tongue teases the outline of his mouth before tracing a tingling path across his chest, settling on his nipples.

From within his throat a painful groan rises as her grip tightens around him, vigorously buffing his erection. Torment. She's tormenting him.

He bites into the tendons of her neck, controlling the impulse to rip her apart, then lunges, catching one of her breasts in his mouth. As he chafes the swollen nipple with his teeth she squeals with bliss, her inside thighs once more moist and ravenous. His hand seizes her other breast, full and throbbing, its nipple bulging with jolts of electricity at the twist of his fingertips.

He stands, drops her onto the table. Tearing off what remains of her dress, he stretches her out on her back, sliding her to him while his full blown erection pulses at the table's edge.

Panting, she parts her legs. With one hand he clasps a breast, while his other slides beneath her hips, guiding her into position.

Her gasp turns ragged as he plunges inside, each thrust bringing them closer to orgasm.

Michael awoke with a start, his heart pounding, the dream still hideously graphic in his mind. He recognized the faces. The woman had been Sienna — her partner the man from the River Lounge.

"No . . ." he moaned. The dream was hideous. Reality was beautiful. He thought of how she had climbed onto his lap and kissed him. How good it had felt to hold her in his arms. Rolling onto his side he buried his face into his pillow. He was perspiring. He'd have to take a cold shower.

DERAILED ON SATURDAY

Pouring coffee, Michael gazed out the kitchen window. Surrounding the cottage, an evergreen fortress heavily cushioned with ash and oaks, broke into a marble sky. The forest was peace that normally transferred to Michael. But not today.

Cradling his cup in both palms, he stared into rising steam, waiting for a plume to disperse before taking a lingering sip of the dark roasted blend. For a moment he closed his eyes and listened. In its monumental stillness, morning was sweet. Spring birds found niches in sweeping boughs, their cadence rising above paths of ferns curling deep into the spectral woodlands.

Michael was exhausted. Regardless of how he tried, he could not shake the distressing remnants of last night's dream — or the reality of running into Sienna at the River Station while attempting to celebrate with his crew. Once more he closed his eyes, his memory filled with Sienna and her suitor. Sure, they had a tiff and he'd driven her home. She didn't belong to him. He felt more helpless than he'd ever felt in his life. Had he known they would be there, he would never have gone. But how could he have known? And wasn't it better to find out sooner than later? He'd already gone too far . . .

Although it was Saturday, and she would more than likely be at the plaza, he would remain at home, in his cottage office, attempting to concentrate on his work. His phone had been ringing off the hook with job offers. Business had never been so good. Work, he scoffed. He would more than likely use the day to lick his wounds, not as an animal dethroned by a clawed foe, but as a man whose dreams had been crushed by human hands.

He couldn't bear to see her today — or again for that matter. Disappointment was a fist inside his throat, and with each swallow the pain plunged deeper. Placing his empty cup into the sink, he let his mind re-focus on his opponent, acknowledging he had seen the man at the hospital — in the parking lot — springing out of his Porsche. The guy had a distinct advantage — his legs moved!

Michael thought of the Lexus LF-A Roadster he would love to order from the dealership, because he wanted it — then thought of the Chevy Suburban parked outside — because he needed it.

"Sienna!" Bonnie yelled from her red Durango, squeezing the SUV into a tight slot in the plaza lot. With her round face straining out the window, followed by an arm and wrist covered by bracelets, she waved frantically to capture Sienna's attention. "Yoo hoo. Sienna!"

"Hey, Bonnie." Sienna stood on the concrete aisle separating rows of parked vehicles, and returned the greeting — but not the enthusiasm.

"Where are you off to today?" Struggling to park straight while communicating through the window, Bonnie was breathless.

"I'm about to head for home," Sienna shouted above the roofs of cars between them.

"Wait for me. I just need to pick up a few things and then I'm off to see my psychic." Bonnie hopped out of the Durango, lugging an oversized tote. "Come with me." Megaphone voice, arms wide open, she beckoned.

"Oh, geeze." Sienna laughed as she re-locked the Corolla's door and strode in Bonnie's direction. When Bonnie behaved this way there was no escaping her. But, if there was one thing Sienna did not believe in, it was fortune tellers.

"I don't think so. I have a lot to do today." She frowned and shrugged.

"What do you have to do?" Bonnie scoffed and tweaked her arm. "Oh, come on, it'll be a blast. You ever been to a psychic?" Her eyes picked up the jade of her shirt and pleaded, corners crinkling into the tiny crow's feet she swore she didn't have.

Sienna shook her head.

"Then you *have* to come. It works you know. They can see things."

Sienna laughed, her gold hoop earrings quivering, catching the sun. "Sure. Right into your wallet." She arched a precisely penciled brow. Her eyelids were covered with rose shadow shades lighter than her glossy lips.

"No, really." Bonnie was adamant. She stood, hands on hips, her tote strap cutting into her fleshy shoulder. "That's how I met Mickey."

"Where, at a psychic fair?"

"No, silly. She told me I was going to run into my future husband at school. And she was right, because soon afterward I rammed into Mickey's car in the faculty parking lot." Her eyes slipped over Sienna. "You're nice and dressed up today. What's cooking?"

For a moment Sienna lowered her sweeping lashes, hiding a calculated glance across the plaza. "Just shopping."

Where is he? How embarrassing. Not only did I jump him. Now he's avoiding me.

Bonnie appeared annoyed. "So are you coming?"

Sienna sighed, "Okay. Why the heck not. You talked me into it."

She put Michael back into a guarded place, and fell into step beside chattering Bonnie.

"Great, c'mon. To the market we go, and pick up Mona on the way."

"Oh, Mona's coming too?"

"Yeah, Mona's been there before. She swears by this woman. She predicted Mona would be going on a romantic trip in the near future. Now Mona wants to know who she's going with and exactly where so she can shop for the right clothes."

Sienna shook her head and chuckled. "You two are nuts. You know that, don't you? Especially you."

"That's why you can never say no to me." Bonnie gloated with a grin.

The women were in and out of the market faster than the traffic pouring in and out of the plaza. Bonnie elbowed through Saturday shoppers, dragging Sienna behind her and through the door of the stationery store, where they found Mona standing at the register.

"Ready, gal?" Grocery bags in arms, Bonnie was the first to approach.

"I'm not going." Mona's voice was flat. Her thick bangs masked her brows but not the displeasure in her sultry eyes.

"Why not?" Sienna asked. Reaching up, she tightened the elastic band that bound her hair. As she tilted her head to adjust the waist of her shorts to meet the edge of her pink tank top, her ponytail slid over a bare shoulder, then spread luxuriously across one side of her perky bust.

"Aw, how come you're not coming, Mona? You were so into it yesterday." Bonnie turned down her bottom lip.

"I already know my future." A loose fitting navy smock covered half of Mona's tan trousers. She looked like a bored housewife about to bake cookies. "I found out this morning my only romantic trip is gonna be with Dyson." She twisted her mouth into a sour gape, creasing her rosy cheeks. "I won the bet hands down. I made more money than he did, so I'm going to the Bahamas with him instead of some handsome stranger. That's gotta be the romantic trip Persha predicted."

"How can you be so sure that's the same trip?" said Sienna, being polite. Did Mona really believe it had been foretold? Coincidence, she concluded, then thought of them together. The image of his clumsy hands groping Mona's curves painted a nauseating picture. *What was wrong with Mona? Was it money, or to fill a void?* Not long ago she could have related, but now, something had begun to fill the void Sienna felt inside.

"She told me before we even made the bet."

"Ooh." Sienna's brows arched.

Bonnie looked ecstatic, thrusting her words at Sienna. "See! I told you it works." She turned to face Mona. "Why are you disappointed? I thought you two had something going on?"

"His wife will never give him a divorce," Mona whispered beneath her hand. "Even though they're separated, she's still up his ass. She's such a bitch. I'm afraid he's stuck with her for life." She chewed her lip and sulked, then turned to check out a customer.

Sienna left her Corolla parked in the lot and rode with Bonnie. The trip was more than a half hour across town on a busy Saturday. After hustling through bumper-to-bumper traffic, the Durango pulled off the highway, driving carefully down side roads into a desolate area where it rolled to a halt on a dead end street.

"Here we are." Bonnie swung around and looked at Sienna, then grabbed her purse from the back seat. Before Sienna could move, Bonnie was out of the Durango and standing in the road waving her on.

"You sure? Looks deserted." Sienna slid off the high seat, stepping onto the crumbling pavement. "There aren't any other houses in sight." At the thought of entering the ominous looking house, apprehension rippled through her chest and settled in her stomach.

"Yeah, house on a haunted hill. I'm sure this is it. There's the welcome."

On a pole pitched into the ground, a white sign with bold red letters warned: *Curb Your Dog.*

PSYCHIC PERSHA

Bonnie grumbled as her sandal just missed a patch of dog-littered grass. There was no sidewalk, so they gingerly made their way up a treed incline, across what could have been a lush lawn had the parcel of drying land been cared for. Making their way along a pebbled footpath, shoulder-to-shoulder, they reached the two-story clapboard house sprouting from the hemlock dotted hill.

"Creepy," Sienna said, brushing against Bonnie.

"Has to be. Fits the mood, don't you think? I mean, suppose we were walking into a glass storefront. It wouldn't be authentic."

"You really think she's authentic? I'm starting to get butterflies." Arms folded across her chest, her expression guarded, Sienna took in every aspect of the aging structure.

The wooden shingles were painted pale yellow, with brown shutters flanking multiple sets of tall, narrow windows. The frames holding their dingy panes in place were chipped and splintered. On blustery days this house has to be awfully drafty, Sienna concluded, happy to be outside in sunshine. She imagined the crown molding topping two sets of first floor windows must have been lovely when the house was new, when they gleamed with fresh, white paint. She guessed those windows belonged to the parlor. The side windows climbed the wall straight up to the attic where an even narrower window met the pitched roof.

The entry doors were covered with brick red peeling paint, but the side lights were inlaid panels of gaily-stained glass fused together by strips of what appeared to be solid brass. Odd, Sienna noted, but at least the striking mosaic added ambiance.

Before Bonnie rang the bell she shook her sandals, one foot at a time, releasing a rain of grit. "Damn, I should have worn boots." They waited several minutes before the door creaked open.

A caramel faced woman, with softly gathered skin, met them at the door. She may have been attractive in younger years, when her complexion was firm enough to support the delicate area now sagging around her alert, amber eyes.

"Hello," she said in a raspy whisper pulled from a tired-sounding throat.

She wore a paisley scarf around her head, tied at an ear. Coarse black hair hidden from her shoulders ran halfway down her spine, partially concealing the back of the caftan that all but covered her bare feet. She wore no makeup.

"Hi there." Bonnie extended a hand. "I'm Bonnie Murray. I have an appointment with you?" It sounded as if she were asking. Was Bonnie perhaps intimidated? "This is my friend Sienna Alexander." Bonnie kicked out sharp grains of remaining grit from a sandal. Unsuccessful, she rested a hand on the house, bent at the waist, and fished a finger between sole and shoe until she found the annoying pebble. "Mona Vaughn couldn't come today, so Sienna's here in her place." Although Bonnie addressed the woman, she peered up at Sienna before she straightened her sandal and stood to face the psychic.

"Welcome to my residence." The woman was formal and spoke with a Bohemian accent. "Come in, please." With an outstretched arm she stepped aside to permit their entry. "My name is Persha." She moved with grace, like a figurine on the lid of a music box.

With a penetrating look, Persha's teal eyes scoured and held Sienna, making her uncomfortable, sorry she had accepted Bonnie's invitation.

There was something eerie about this place and its repulsive musty odor — about this woman who moved precisely, inspecting them carefully as she led them through the haggard vestibule, past an endless flight of stairs and down a narrow hallway. In silence they moved through a second peeling door frame. With sealed windows, the room they entered was even more dank and stuffy. Sienna sneezed from the dust that swirled in air they disturbed.

"One will wait here," Persha spoke deliberately, gesturing to a burgundy settee with a worn cover that no doubt sagged from the weight of many visitors, "while the other follows me to my reading room. Who shall be first?"

Bonnie and Sienna stood alert, regarding the woman's instructions as if they were children in school, indulging a teacher who commanded respect.

"I will." Bonnie jumped at the chance. "You mind if I go first, Sienna?"

Sienna shook her head. "No, go ahead." She considered foregoing her session. *A waste of time and money.* She would wait for Bonnie and they would leave. She slipped lightly onto the edge of the settee, legs nested, and checked for messages on her cell phone, waiting for what seemed an eternity; but in reality, only fifteen minutes had passed.

Bonnie emerged from the reading with a glow on her face, but her eyes were slits from the session in the darkened room. Her nose was swollen from airborne allergens and mold that even the scent of Febreze couldn't combat.

"Your turn." Pausing beneath the high doorframe, Persha pointed a pigmented hand at Sienna, waving her into the room.

"I don't think . . . I've decided not to—" Sienna slipped off the settee and moved toward the hallway.

Bonnie grabbed her arm and propelled her in the direction of the reading room, and said, "Your turn." Then under her breath mumbled, "You can't bug out now."

Sienna clenched her teeth and looked at her with narrowed eyes.

When she entered, Sienna stepped into a sinister chamber, or so she thought, and for a fleeting moment wondered if Persha had the ability to cast wicked spells befitting of the atmosphere. Dark satin draperies with time-stained linings covered the windows. Two armchairs were centered in spacious gloom. The only light was from a candle that rested on a drum table separating the chairs.

"Be seated," Persha said.

"I've never done this before. What happens now?" Sienna heard the echo of her voice. Her feet were crossed at the ankle, resting on marred hardwood that would have been spectacular if stripped and refinished.

"I do the work." Persha studied Sienna's frown. "You just sit. Try to clear your mind while the powers approach me. I can call them, but they do not always respond."

Powers? Does she mean spirits? Is this some kind of a joke?

"You do not believe in me. Before you leave, you will." With closed lids Persha nodded, then opened her eyes and stared deeply into Sienna's.

Sienna was mesmerized. Persha seemed to be reading her mind. She felt a chill, afraid to blink for fear a gruesome apparition would appear. A creature with black-rimmed eyes buried in a lipless face pressing close to hers, as close as the room began to feel.

"I've never been to a fortune teller before," said Sienna, as if entranced.

"I am not a fortune teller you find at fairgrounds. I am a psychic, as well as a medium."

"What's the difference?"

"A psychic reads your aura and can predict your future. If you have come to learn about relationships, your career, money, or perhaps love, I can do this for you. For your friend, I used Tarot Cards." Persha lifted a hand toward an ornamental box on the dusty table top. "But you are different. For you I am a medium. From the moment you entered my home I knew it would be this way. I felt distress in the aura surrounding you, but I also felt love."

"So I'm different?" *Distress? Love?* If she had a choice, Sienna would opt for the latter.

"Hush. We are not alone in this room." Persha closed her deep set eyes as if in meditation. "There is a presence trying to communicate with you. He is troubled. He grieves."

Sienna felt the rise of goose bumps. "What?" The word froze on her lips.

"From the energy surrounding us, I feel you were close at one time. He asks if you remember him — if you have felt him reach out for you." Persha's knowing eyes pierced Sienna's.

Skepticism turned to fear as Sienna watched the woman's chiseled features twitch, then tighten. "What do you mean? There's a ghost in here with us?"

Though the words sounded foolish, electricity filled the air with an unearthly presence.

"Not a ghost. A lingering spirit that cannot find rest. One that has the power to guide you. You must cooperate to learn the intention. Do you know a young man who not too long ago passed?"

"The only one I can possibly think of is . . . is." Sienna couldn't believe she was buying into this. "Rob?"

"Is this Rob?" Persha spoke in a stern voice.

The candle on the table flickered as if an invisible force nipped its brilliance, jarring Sienna. Persha did not move a muscle.

Sienna wanted to bolt from the room, but something compelled her to stay. Her stare darted from the candle to Persha, and the circular path of her neck as her head rolled in a hypnotic state. On the edge of her seat, she watched the woman's glazed eyes flash from side to side, synchronizing with shadows slithering across the walls.

"It is Rob. He knows your sadness and your pain. He cannot cross over. As in this life, there are rules in the afterlife. Before he can find peace, there is something you must know."

"What does he want?" Rob had always been the ghost of Sienna's tormented past, and the reason for her present troubled existence. Would he ever leave her alone?

"He is trapped because you are trapped. He needs you to move on with your life, to permit his soul to pass from this world to the next."

Sure, that's Rob. Always thinking of how things affect him.

"He tells me you are struggling with a decision. Choose the right one."

Move on with my life? Decision? Oh God, is he talking about Trainer?

"Tell me something specific!"

"Only you know. Only you can find answers."

Sienna's heart raced. She needed to know more.

"He is gone. I have no further information." Before she finished speaking, Persha was on her feet, walking to the door.

Sienna emerged from the reading room visibly shaken.

Before Bonnie and Sienna left the house, Persha draped an arm around Sienna's shoulders.

"You are special," the old woman whispered in her ear. She quickly closed the door behind her visitors.

From unsettling darkness, they stepped into sunshine. If Sienna ever needed loving arms around her, she needed them now.

"So how did you make out?" Bonnie asked excitedly as they headed for the Durango. "What did she say? Was it good? Are you gonna meet someone?" Bonnie's mouth dropped when she stared at Sienna's pale lips. "You look like you saw a ghost. What the hell happened in there?"

"She told me my dead ex-boyfriend wants me to move on."

"I agree with that," Bonnie said without blinking an eye.

WHO VANDALIZED THE SCHOOL?

"Look at those guns," Michael teased. "Phew . . . You been working out or what?" He watched a hydraulic piston help the screen door close softly behind Leo's straight back. Lean muscle strained the cotton of the boy's T-shirt.

"Eh. You know, here and there. I go to the gym sometimes, and lifting boxes at work and stuff helps," Leo replied as he plunked a heavy carton of groceries onto the kitchen countertop, then secured the tally sheet by sliding it halfway under the box. "And look who's talking. Look at *your* guns." His voice carried across the room to where Michael sat in the bay area of the kitchen.

"My guns, huh?" Michael grinned and clasped his bicep with a strong hand. "Hey, they're my arms and my legs. What can I say?" He reached for some twenties stacked neatly on the table.

"You should join the gym, Michael, come swimming with me. If you built that too it won't even cost you." For a kid his age, living almost on his own, Leo often wore a disarming look of innocence.

Michael chuckled. "Nope. Didn't build that one. The rec center's old, Leo. Older than I am." He extended a handful of cash. "Here you go. I got the total on the phone. Count it. Yours is in there too."

In several smooth strides Leo was at Michael's side. He folded the bills in half and crammed them into the pocket of his loose-fitting jeans. A crisp twenty would be his; he'd peel it off the stack before handing the rest over to the bookkeeper when he returned to the market.

"Thanks, Michael." Leo grinned over his shoulder as he turned to leave.

He had a hand on the screen door, then suddenly turned back. "So what do you do all the time stuck inside this place? You got a girlfriend yet? You ever go out?" He paused beside the refrigerator.

"No girlfriend. Not for a long time. But I go out often enough. I went to the River Station last night." Michael's sable brows knitted tighter than his lips.

"That's a cool place if you like seafood, which I don't. Who'd you go with?" Leo took a step toward the breakfast area, where Michael sat flipping carelessly through a car magazine.

"Guys from work." Michael's words were clipped. He stared at glossy pages of sports cars he really didn't see.

"Oh." Leo frowned. "Hey, you can always come out with me and my boys sometime. Did you hear the school was vandalized?"

"No. When?" Michael shoved the magazine aside and lifted his head.

"Last night, I guess. Janitor found it today. Broken windows. Spray paint all over the place. Desks and chairs thrown around. Somebody trashed the place."

"Anything of value taken?"

"Dunno."

"Did they catch whoever did it?"

"Nope — cops are clueless. Nobody saw anything, but rumor says it was druggies from that clinic that moved in across town."

"No kidding? That's messed up." Michael didn't like the idea of thugs moving into the area, near his building sites and condos, especially when he wasn't in a position to keep an eye on things.

"Anyway, how's that girl you ditched? Can I grab a can of soda?"

"Sure, grab me one too. C'mon and sit down. You look overheated." Leo's flushed cheeks darkened his hazel eyes to gunmetal, but they remained soft.

"Yeah, it's gettin' hot out there. So have you seen her again?" He dropped onto a chair and slid a can to Michael. After popping his soda open, he took a gulp.

"As a matter of fact, I saw her last night. Unfortunately, it wasn't planned."

"So did you talk to her this time, or did you run again?"

Michael frowned. "No, I couldn't talk to her. She was with someone."

"Ouch. That sucks. Must've been shitty."

"Sure was. I wished I was the one sitting with her instead of him." Michael tapped his soda can on the table, his glance shifting to gaze out the window.

"Sorry, man, must've been tough for you. Do you know him?" Leo fidgeted with his studded wrist cuff as he studied the strength of Michael's profile.

"Not personally." Michael returned his gaze to Leo, appreciative of the boy's concern.

"What's the guy look like?"

"Average, I guess. I only know him from the hospital. I think he's one of the doctors. He drives a Porsche." Michael tried to separate resentment from his words.

"Sweeet — The Porsche, I mean," Leo quickly corrected.

But Michael wasn't paying attention. His mind was on her, not Leo.

"I wanted to get closer to their table, hear what was going on," Michael was distant, almost as if Leo weren't there.

Michael had wanted to talk to Gus about the situation but felt awkward.

Having a man to man with Leo was easier. Leo was a kid with a lot going on in his life. He would forget their conversation the minute he left. Gus was a grown man with problems of his own, Michael seeming to be one of them lately.

"Why didn't you go over and say hello? So what if she was with some guy. You don't know what's up. Maybe they're just friends."

"Friends don't feed each other pudding." He shook his head and looked down at the floor, hands tightening on the arms of his chair. "I ended up driving her home though."

Leo's eyes bulged. "Now you tell me. So what happened?"

"It wasn't an ideal situation. Let's leave it at that."

"Well, did you ask her out?"

"No."

"What did you do, dump her out of the car and run?" Leo laughed.

Michael glared. "Drop the subject. I really don't want to talk about it."

"Sorry. Couldn't help it." Leo hunched forward. "I'm telling you. Just ask her to go on a date with you. Give it a try. If it doesn't work out, you can move on and stop wallowing." His gaze washed over Michael's face, settling on his broad neck, then fell to the collar of his olive T-shirt that was stretched out of shape, looking as worn as the man wearing it.

Michael let out a short laugh that sounded more like an exasperated breath. In momentary anger his nostrils flared, then he laughed and shook his head. "When did you get so wise?"

Since meeting her, Michael had no problem getting to sleep; Sienna was the sedative Pollack had ordered. And she was addictive. Staying asleep was the problem. The dreams always jolted him in the middle of the night, and then he would lie awake heavy as a boulder, falling helplessly into Sienna instead of sleep.

That night, as he wrestled with his bed sheets, he formulated a plan of action. He would be more aggressive, more inviting. He'd be the old Michael.

He's at the construction site. The night is cool. Sounds of the city tarnish moonlit silence. Michael cannot understand why he would be at the site at night, and why the spotlights usually washing the yard with security have suddenly gone out.

He's alone, the weight of a new project heavy on his shoulders. Seated on a concrete wall he unrolls the plans, comparing the integrity of the steel beams surrounding him to those on the blueprints he has created.

His palm grips a flashlight. When muffled voices interrupt, he shines a beam in their direction. The flash snaps a shot of two slouching men who creep from sight. He knows they are examining the heavy construction equipment.

The yard is full. His machines are worth a small fortune. Michael springs to his feet, picks up a metal rod and runs in their direction. By the time he reaches the two they are four, and the rod he's carrying is a .45 caliber handgun.

High on crack, they're easy targets. "We don't want any trouble, man." Michael hears one say.

His mind is as cluttered as the construction site. The next thing he knows, he's home, perched at the edge of his bed, bare feet firmly planted on the floor. He picks up the phone and calls her — he can't help himself. "I have to see you. Come over — now."

Michael's eyes snapped open, his body shuddering with desire.

THE BOOGEYMAN

Her queen bed felt too small for her aching body. Sienna stretched her legs, dangling one bare foot off the mattress, then tossed from side to side, trying to find a comfortable position.

She faced the window. The moonless night was a black wall. She fixated on the visit with the psychic, the flickering candle, the woman's face when she fell into a trance, the unwelcomed presence that made the air so heavy it was hard to breathe.

A light in the hallway trickled into her room, warming her back.

When she felt vulnerable, Sienna slept facing the door. She could then comfortably confirm no one — nothing lurked in the shadows, that she was alone in the condo. No flesh and blood creature or paranormal demon could attack from behind if she were facing the door.

But tonight Sienna needed to face the window. She sought signs of life beyond her solitary room. Wave upon wave of vehicle headlights grazed the window, assuring her she was not as alone in the world as she felt. Reaching out, she pulled her fluffy white cat closer.

Last time she checked the clock, the LCD read a blurry 12:10 a.m. Although she did not feel the need for sleep, Sienna shut her eyes to ease weariness, and to think.

Jolting lightning, followed by a series of thunderous claps corroborated the weatherman's prediction of rain, but not the furious eruption that sounded like Armageddon.

She felt Frazzle jump onto the bed, curl up at her feet. Soon, wind-driven rain clobbered the condo sending floodwaters rushing through gutters and downspouts. Sienna thought about closing the bottom inch of her bedroom window, but the sounds were mesmerizing. Rain could fill the room for all she cared. The storm was too beautiful to be silenced. Closing her eyes, her last thought was its fury, until she jerked awake, sensing something was wrong.

Sienna was not alone! Holding her breath, she reined the gallop of her heart to listen intently for the sound of footsteps. The air in the room was heavy, thickened by a presence. Someone or something hovered behind her in the dimly lit doorway. She felt it before she saw it. The fringe of hair on the back of her neck sprouted over goose bumps littering her skin. Alert mind, limbs numbed with familiar dread, she managed to roll onto an elbow and eye level with terror. Eyes darting around the room, her pulse raced. Then she saw him . . . saw it.

The figure loomed halfway between the doorway and her bed. There was no way out.

"What are you doing here? How did you get in?" Her throat clenched, cutting short her words, her breath.

"You left a window open. I always told you to lock the fucking windows — didn't I? That you never know what might crawl in."

"This is *my* bedroom. You don't belong here!"

Headlights brushed the granite figure. Lost in another dimension, for a moment its mournful eyes drifted beyond Sienna, until it sprang to life with twitching lips, a jugular hemorrhaging fury. And he was moving toward her.

Blood drained from her limbs, leaving them powerless as panic twisted her stomach into a knot. She knew what he was capable of — she had lived through it.

By the time she managed a scream, sunlight and fresh air filtered through the partially open window. She bolted out of bed, eyes searching the room. She watched the curtains stir and recalled his words.

Sienna slipped into a robe and hurried to the kitchen, hoping a cup of coffee would help clear her head.

Could Rob have somehow managed to find his way back to her through Persha? Had he really been there last night? Was he with her now? One thing she knew for certain, he hadn't tried to infiltrate her soul as he had attempted in New York, right after he almost killed her. He, his spirit, whatever it was, chilled Sienna to the bone. The night terrors, if that's what they were, were more than emotional; there was a physical connection — and it was mind shattering.

In her old apartment in New York, the thing had wanted to devour her, to hammer her with its will. With practice, Sienna had learned to deny it entry, for if she refused to quantify the presence by name, it was powerless. She was sure her unconscious had fended it off last night. Her mind recognized the presence as Rob — but she wouldn't call out his name — she wouldn't accept him for what he was. The ghost of her past.

Persha said Rob was sorry and wanted her to move on, yet he had found her again. Or was it all in her head?

Sienna overfilled her coffee cup and mopped the spill from the counter with a paper towel. She looked around the kitchen, dim in early morning, took one sip of coffee and poured the rest down the sink drain. She ran her palms up and down her arms and swallowed hard, then quickly left the room. From her bedroom closet she grabbed the first outfit her eyes settled upon. She couldn't dress fast enough.

The boogeyman had visited last night — in the form of Rob Lucas — time was in reverse, and the wounds she fought so hard to heal were fresh and raw. Would he haunt her forever?

LONDON REVEALED

The wail of an ambulance preceded the hum of electronic doors, cushioned steps and anxious voices. *Code Red* burst through the PA system, yet the speaker's voice was calm, as if paging for assistance in an understaffed department store.

"Somebody's in trouble," Bonnie said as her fingers beat her keyboard.

"Damn sirens give me the shivers. I hate them." Flipping through the folder topping the stack on her desk, Sienna extracted information and began to type methodically.

To Sienna, the siren was like a death rattle, a warning of imminent doom, and never failed to brace herself for the jangle of a gurney's wheels as uniformed attendants rushed someone to Emergency.

"Boy, we're morbid today, aren't we?" Bonnie continued to type.

Sienna knew she'd never share her co-worker's immunity to the hospital's sights and sounds. "That Persha woman gave me the creeps."

"Yeah, you never filled me in on the details."

"She educated me on the difference between a psychic and a medium."

"What do you mean? There's a difference? Did she use the Tarots on you?" Bonnie stopped typing and swiveled her chair in Sienna's direction.

"No. You got the psychic and the cards. I got the medium and the ghost." Sienna's mouth twisted, her face paled. "Psychics are more like fortunetellers, I guess. They foretell your future. Mediums talk to the dead who give advice it seems, or unload their problems on the living."

"Ca-reepy." Bonnie's forced shudder shook her cleavage. "Will you stop working and turn around please?" She yanked the chair, spinning the wheels so that Sienna faced her. "There, that's better. Now tell me more."

Freed from her desk, Sienna shook stiffness from her wrists then stretched her legs, crossing them at the ankle. Her feet were covered with white sport socks. Her pink Crocs rested neatly on the floor beside her. Today she needed to feel comfort; she wore a white cotton jumpsuit, with a looped belt clasped by a heart of brass, rather than her usual dress and heels.

"Oh, so you want to hear more? You want to hear all about communicating with spirits in the afterlife? Ugh, I'll take the cards."

"So, that's it?" Bonnie looked like she had been cheated out of dessert after paying for a five course meal.

"Well, you got good news, didn't you? You came out smiling like you just got laid or smoked pot with Mickey's hippy friends. I got nightmares that scared the hell out of me."

"You should be used to them by now."

"That's easy for you to say." Sienna's eyes tightened. "Maybe there's more to it."

"Come on. Share. You'll feel better."

"Sometimes I wonder if I'm just insane."

"Who isn't? But what's putting you over the edge?"

"Remember the night terrors I used to have?"

"The Incubus?"

"You call it Incubus. My doctor calls it stress. Whatever. It almost happened again last night. I'm getting sick of this. Why can't I live a normal life?"

"Because you don't want one."

"What's that supposed to mean?"

"You've got to climb out of the hole you're in."

"*How* is the question."

"For starters, try dating."

Sienna sighed. "Here we go again—"

"Don't look at me that way, Sienna. I'm not trying to upset you, but in your state of mind you're easy prey. And when you're vulnerable, it's easier to be reached by the other side. You don't want a demon on top of you, so you better be careful. Very difficult to get rid of dark entities." Bonnie quivered. "Exactly what happened last night?"

Bonnie sat with an elbow on the armrest of her chair, supporting her head with three fingers on the side of her cheek. Everything about her looked calm other than the yellow starburst growing around her shrinking pupil.

Sienna unsealed her lips, pale where her pink lip gloss had been chewed off. "Your psychoanalyst pose isn't going to get you anywhere. I've already told you everything, so you can turn around and go back to work." As she slid to her desk, she mumbled, "You and your psychic nonsense. Talk about being easy prey."

"Wait a minute," Bonnie huffed and set her jaw. "You can't dismiss everything Persha said. At least wait till I get my fortune. And by the way, my fortune is better than a bag of weed." Her gloat dispersed into fancy. "I just love telling everyone Persha said I'm coming into a bundle of cash in the near future. Can you believe it? I better tell Mickey to double the lotto tickets and be sure to sign them. He loses everything." She reached for the phone, but didn't dial.

"You still didn't answer my question. What all did the psychic tell you? You were so quiet on the ride home. I couldn't get much out of you, staring out the window like a zombie. It's bugging me. What exactly did Persha say about Rob? I want to hear every last detail."

Sienna wrapped her hair into a twist, securing it to the back of her head with a tortoise clip. "It's too freaky. You don't really believe her, do you?"

"Well, she kind of hit the nail on the head, didn't she? With the young guy dying and you moving on."

"Had to be coincidence. Those people have a way of reading your attitude, then they guess and hope they're right."

"If I don't collect my money, you can tell me Persha's a fraud. Until then, I'm a believer."

"There's something else. I wasn't going to mention it, but —"

"What? But what? Come on, now you have to tell me." Bonnie grabbed the back of Sienna's chair and wheeled it around so that they were again face to face. "Stop being evasive. I know when you're holding out on me. What's going on?"

Sienna tilted her head. Her parted lips flapped with a loud sigh. "Greg asked me to go to the London seminar with him."

"What?" Bonnie's eyes bulged. Her computer chair slammed into the side of Sienna's desk so that they sat nose to nose. "When was this? Friday night at the Station? Oh my God, I knew it. I knew he wasn't giving up." She scrubbed her hands so fast she generated heat, then palmed her cheeks. "I can't believe you were actually trying to hide this from me."

"Fat chance of that." Sienna used her foot to shove Bonnie and her chair a comfortable distance away. "London for a few days, and then to a medical convention in Ontario." She folded her arms across her chest, chomping harder on her bubble gum. "Don't get in a tizzy. It's a business trip, not a honeymoon. He claims it'll be good for my career."

"You accepted, right? London . . . You lucky little bitch."

"When you come into your fortune, per Persha, you can tour Europe."

"Good things come to those who wait." Bonnie tossed her head. A breath later, she said, "I can't believe you waited so long to tell me. I'm so excited for you!"

"Before you get your hopes up," Sienna's eyes closed with a long blink, "we had an awful evening at the River Lounge. Greg was Greg all night long. I couldn't stand being with him. I was so cold and distant, I couldn't stand myself. "It just proves you can't mix business with pleasure. I ended up—" She diverted her eyes. "I took a cab home."

Sienna fell into thought. "He sounded different on the phone, not his usual pompous . . ." Her brows shot up as the full magnitude of the situation hit her, and her eyes were saucers. "If Rob won't move on until I move on — does that mean I belong with Trainer? If that's my fate, I'd rather kill myself. And Ontario . . . My family's there, remember? I'm not sure I'm up to a visit right now." Her flush deepened with her frown. "And you know how my mother and Tessa feel about my judgment after what happened with Rob." She stared at her toes wiggling frantically inside her socks.

"That's ridiculous," Bonnie snapped. "You had no control over Rob's actions."

"I can't get that day out of my mind."

"This is what Persha — Rob — whoever it was, tried to tell you. Even if it was a freaky coincidence, you have to get past it and move on."

"She had no way of knowing what's going on in my life, now, or in the past."

"Right. Just what I've been saying. She SEES!" Bonnie's stomach growled.

"So, Rob's sorry for attacking me, almost killing me?"

"He was out of his mind. And it's in the past. It was horrible and you're still grieving. Get away from all this crap. You'll come back a different woman. Maybe even part of administration." Bonnie's brows twitched into crawling caterpillars. "Plus, Rob won't leave you until you're settled, *capice*?" She popped a piece of hard candy into her mouth.

"Did you know he tripped over me? I felt his boot hit my side just before I blacked out." Sienna's eyes clouded, but she refused to relive the terror.

Bonnie shook her head "I had no idea."

"Yeah. There must have been a reason I survived, though." Sienna sighed.

"Stop it. You're giving me chills." Bonnie shuddered. "And yes, you're here for a reason. To live your life! So go do it."

"I would like to see London. Maybe I will go. I'm sure there'll be free time to tour the city. There's nothing keeping me here.

Would you take care of the kitties for me? And make sure they don't get out! They won't know the neighborhood. They'll probably want to sleep with you."

"Terrific."

"Don't look at me like that. They're clean and cuddly."

"So is Mickey."

Sienna laughed, then sobered. "If I do decide to go, I'm flying home afterward. I'm not going to Ontario." She ran a soothing palm across her stomach.

"Don't worry about Ontario. It'll all work itself out."

"I hope you're right."

"Go to London. Pinch a Bobby's ass." Bonnie grinned. "I'm going to miss you." She threw her arms around Sienna. "Come on, kiddo. Let's go to lunch."

LOVE DREAMS

GUS ARGYROS

The air inside was stale. Nothing at all like the wind that churned construction dust into the afternoon sky. Blocks of wavering sunlight entered the trailer in bursts, consistent with sounds of droning machines and the boisterous men who ran them. Michael and Gus sat at a folding table, discussing the architectural plans Michael had drafted. The trailer served as their site office, where they now huddled. They were drank Pepsi from sweating bottles Gus brought in an insulated lunch cooler.

"Did you hear about the vandalism at Oak Haven High?" Michael pushed the plans aside, protecting long hours of meticulous work from moisture that dripped from the soda bottles.

"I did." Gus rolled his lunch wrap into a ball. "Unbelievable. A couple of houses were robbed and ransacked too — including the Mayor's mother's house. There's a reward out." Gus tossed the wrap into the cooler, closed the lid, and with his boot slid it from the walk space.

"I bet that would be worth every bit of fifty grand." Michael slid his half eaten peanut butter sandwich aside.

"Speaking about money. I was gonna talk to you about hiring somebody to watch the sites during the night. We've got a fortune in machinery and tools lying around. Not to mention all the material."

"I was thinking the same. Sorry I can't be more hands on." Michael frowned. "I hate watching from the sidelines."

"You're so much like your grandfather. He was more than an

architect and business owner."

"We could use him now."

"This has got to be hell for you, Mike. I can't imagine how hard it must be." Gus slugged down the last of his Pepsi and tossed the bottle into a bucket on the floor beneath a window. As well as catching recycling, the bucket captured rainwater during heavy downpours. "Living alone out there in the woods can't be easy either. I know what your social life was like before the accident. I remember the mornings you dragged your ass in here hung over." Gus smiled.

Michael shook his head. "I don't need to hear this. Thinking about it's bad enough."

"I'm not gonna dredge up the past, but I wish you had more of a life other than drawing plans and worrying about job sites." Gus looked out the window as he spoke . "You'd be so damned disheveled on Monday mornings." Turning back to Michael, he combed a worn hand through his mop of coarse hair. "Now look at you. Neat, clean and fashionable. You need to get out more."

"Now you're sounding like my father probably would have."

"If he were here, I'm sure your dad would have told you you've got to be with a woman again. You're too young to be missing out on life. Take it from me — time's a-wastin' — and there's no going back."

Michael studied Gus, then grinned, yanking a sketch pad from the saddlebag strapped to his chair. "On the bright side, we've got more projects."

"Whatcha got there?" Gus slid a thick forearm across the tabletop, sweeping a space clear, then held out a hand.

"I want to donate some time to the animal shelter on Croton Street."

"Okay." Gus cocked his head. "What are we talking here?"

"What that place really needs is to be demolished and rebuilt from scratch, but for now, I want to give it a facelift. Inside and out. Maybe you'll go down there? Take a look around. Kind of figure things out and then go full steam."

"Of course."

"Better figure on a parking lot too." Michael pushed the sketch pad closer to Gus, lips moving faster than his hands. "And I told you about the kids at the hospital, right?"

"Yup. And I think it's a great thing you're doing." Gus lifted the glossy cover, smoothing out a folded page. "Looks like you've been busy designing. What's it, a club?"

"A rec center for handicapped kids. What you're looking at is a rough design — but it'll give you an idea . . ."

"Basketball court. Cafeteria. Look at the size of that game room. And pool? This is really something, Mike. But it's gonna run you some big bucks, son."

"Money's the one thing I don't have to worry about."

Gus nodded, skepticism giving way to a smile. "You gonna use the court?"

"Hell, yeah." Michael beamed as he folded the pad and stuffed it back into his bag, then stared at Gus. "So you think I should date?"

"Why not?"

"One thing at a time?" Michael appeared overwhelmed. "Where am I supposed to meet someone? Internet dating sites?"

"Come on, Mike. You know I didn't mean anything like that." Gus sighed. "Where did you used to meet girls?"

"In bars." Michael's laugh was stiffer than the look on his face. "Unfortunately, I no longer inhabit bars."

"There are other ways to meet women. Community events. . ." Gus stammered.

"You can stop right there. I'm not going to church functions or town hall picnics if that's what you have in mind." Michael stared out the window, at the beginnings of a courtyard office buildings would soon surround.

"No. No," Gus's lips were tight, "I meant you should get yourself out, rub elbows in public places, that's all, where single women hang out. Don't stay cooped up in that cottage all the time. Your life is either the cottage or a trailer. It's not healthy for a young guy."

Michael knew damn well who he wanted to spend time with,

but cringed at the thought of approaching Sienna and asking for a date. How awkward would that be? Sexy Sienna whose beautiful long legs could transform an ordinary sidewalk into a private dance floor, out with a guy in a wheelchair? It was absurd. The thought made him want to run. But of course, he couldn't. He was trapped. He loved watching her movements; he loved watching her, period.

The image of her with another man twisted Michael's face into a scowl. Suppose he was never anything more than a guy in the background watching life pass by?

"You know, Michael. Tina has a friend who has a daughter about your age."

"Oh yeah? What are you thinking, blind date?"

"She just moved back from someplace down south and has no friends here." Gus cocked his head.

"Divorced?"

"From what I understand, never married."

"Smart girl. What would she want with me? Unless she's worse off . . ."

"She's shy. Needs somebody to make the first move. Tina and I could have you both over for dinner. You know. Friendship only."

"There *is* someone," Michael interrupted.

Gus's jaw dropped. "Who is she? Do I know her?"

"I don't think so." Visualizing Sienna prolonged the smile spreading across Michael's face.

"Wow. I haven't seen color like that since Alaska and the Northern Lights. Tell me about this girl who's bringing back old Michael."

Michael exhaled. "I ran into her a few times at the plaza. She seems like a loner — you know, kinda single looking. On the other hand — that night at the River Station when Jake and Chris were talking about a blonde . . ."

"Friday with the guys?" Gus's brows gathered. "Oh, was that *her* our idiots were hawking?"

Michael nodded. "Oh yeah. That was her, and she was with someone. A date I guess. She doesn't have that *settled* look, and from the way he was hanging all over her in the lounge — in love or not — couples don't usually act that way." Michael forced himself to consider the worst case scenario. "None that I know of anyway, although I'm not an expert on relationships."

Gus laughed. "Oh really? Well you haven't seen me and Tina on a night out." The weathered skin beside his eyes crinkled as he winked. "I should be so lucky."

"I ended up driving her home." Michael grinned.

"That's why you split in such a hurry. You dog." Gus laughed hard. "So'd you ask her out?"

"We didn't do much talking."

Gus shook his head, beamed. "Sonofabitch. You got laid."

"Not quite." Michael's face cleared. "Must be amazing to have someone like her to come home. I can't stop thinking about her. Someone like her should have her nose in the air, but she seems so down to earth approachable."

"So approach her."

"She can be kinda snippy, but funny as hell. She makes me feel good, makes me forget. But I just can't bring myself to do anything but look at her, and that hurts like hell." Michael's glow faded.

"We're gonna work on this one."

That night, Michael painted Sienna's face in his mind as he drifted off to sleep.

Her eyes, radiant blue, shine with emotion as they sit, side by side on a sofa. The only sound in the air is the quickening of his breath as he moves closer, positioning her on his lap. He feels the pressure of her body melt into his. She fits snugly into the curve of his arm, and as she rests her head on his shoulder, he brushes aside stray curls that fall across her face. Her eyes never leave his as her lips part in waiting. Her beautiful lips — soft and inviting — plush like Cupid's pillow — sweetened by the piece of chocolate he places on her tongue.

"Now that I finally have you in my arms, I'll never let you go," he whispers. His breath catches in his throat as she kisses

him, moaning, "Make love to me, Michael," and leads him through the doorway.

"Come on," she whispers, pressing him down onto the bed. She's gentle yet demanding, and he's falling . . .

Without a sound, he allows her to remove his clothing and position him on the bed. The sheets are crisp, cool on his warm skin. From the open window comes a touch of a breeze, or is it her sweet breath falling lightly upon him? He's tense, but as she kneels beside him, gently stroking his hair and face, he relaxes. With one hand she raises his arms above his head, while with the other she unties her bathrobe, stripping the soft belt from its loops and binds his wrists to the headboard. For a second he thinks he should stop this . . . maybe he doesn't want this — gently push her away — out of his sight — as he has pushed her many times from his thoughts. But this time is different . . . she's gentle yet demanding — and he is falling . . .

"Just relax," she murmurs, husky, determined. She has a calming effect upon him. And as she holds a blindfold to his face her eyes twinkle, a devilish grin spreading on her lips. "May I?" she purrs.

Closing his eyes, he consents, he waits.

As darkness falls upon him, his senses enliven. She's beside him. He hears the rhythm of her breath quicken, draws in a honeysuckle fragrance as her hair brushes his face. He slips into passion as the softness of satin engulfs him. This could feel so good . . . If only I could let myself go . . . it could be so good.

She kisses him, then her mouth moves to his neck, his chest. Every care fades as he anticipates her next move. He begins to feel better than he's ever felt in his life. He's letting go . . . He's feeling . . . He's free . . .

Blindfolded, hands cuffed, he drifts in another dimension. One where her knees are wedged between his legs, spreading apart his thighs. She runs a finger around his lips, sticks it inside his mouth, drags it around his tongue and when it's good and wet, her mouth starts to work again, licking, nibbling. She sucks harder, then her finger eases inside.

About to explode, Michael sprang awake with a gasp. He lifted the sheet and looked down at himself. "Holy shit," he mumbled. "What the hell is this woman doing to me?"

SOMETIMES SHOWERHEADS MUST SUFFICE

Cradled in persuasive arms, Sienna floated on satin sheets. A stranger kissed her long and deeply, his tongue a gentle wave that swept her parted lips. Strong hands gripped her intimately, more with caution than demand. Whispers, breathless promises glazed her neck. As his mouth sipped the softness of her shoulders, her gown slid to her waist. While fingers brushed lightly, each breath was an ardent message. His hand caressed her stomach, then a thigh, and then the phone in her bedroom rang.

Only seconds before their lips had fused. As Sienna awoke, her moist mouth pressed not on a lover's lips, but on a droplet of drool clinging to her forearm. "Shit," she moaned, the spell broken as she opened her eyes and adjusted to reality.

Although his features were elusive, the man in her dream had a familiar smile. Her dreams were insistent. Sienna failed to understand why her focus seemed to be upon someone she barely knew. By the fifth ring she reached for the phone.

"Good morning, princess. Did I wake you?" Greg Trainer's greeting poured into her ear.

"I must have slept through my alarm." Caught up in dream, her voice wandered.

"Have you had breakfast?"

She took a moment to process. *What the fuck?*

"What is it?" Her voice cracking, her response could not have been more harsh.

"I thought it would be nice to meet for coffee before work."

"Why?" She rolled onto an elbow, blinking at the clock.

"I wanted to reiterate — London would be very . . ."

"Why do you keep nagging me?" She had been drowsing on an elbow, but with annoyance twisted, sat up, plumped a pillow and fell into it. "Why are you so worried about my career?"

"Because I care about you. I think I'm falling . . ."

Avoiding his next words, she cut him off. "I'm just getting out of bed." The soles of her feet grazed the oriental carpet covering the floor. "I'm going to be late if I don't get up and shower right now." She stood and crossed the room, reaching into a dresser drawer for her bra and panties while balancing the phone on her shoulder.

"Sure, honey. I'll see you around noon. Drive safely."

Sure? Honey? Was this the same Greg Trainer she had known for the past year? She whisked a bath towel from the linen closet.

In the shower, Sienna lathered with scented wash. Thoughts revolved like a flaming baton in the grasp of a handler who defied the fire she was playing with. The dream had been invigorating. She still felt as if she had actually been with the bewitching man who left her aching for his touch. She longed to slip back into the realm of desire, to finish the unfinished. A magnet could not have had a greater draw than her desire for this man, even if she were tumbling through fantasy. When she felt this way, why was it *his* face that controlled her mind? *Oh God. Now I have to dream about him too?* What was it about Michael Chessler that let him breeze into her life like the Atlantic, stealing her breath, making her wary.

What would it be like if he could stand, stand beside her in the shower, their wet bodies sliding together? Her legs would surely buckle. She imagined her hardened nipples pressed to his chest. Her arms would grip the width of his powerful shoulders as she worked her tongue between his lips. He would moan when she backed him against the wall beneath the shower's stimulating flow, and she would wrap her legs around his hips. As she sank against the tiled wall, his hands would hold her firmly, kneading her flesh with each powerful thrust.

She switched her hand-held showerhead to vibrating pulse mode and twisted the lever so the faucet shot out a titillating massage. A sigh, originating from deep within, ambled from the drape of her lips.

PHYSICAL THERAPY CAN'T HEAL AN EGO

In the bright room, he didn't stand a chance of drifting into slumber as a CD player circulated soothing music throughout the physical therapy office. Michael's vision clouded as he stared up at square ceiling tiles, with long fluorescents embedded between every fifth row.

His therapist manipulated his legs in marching maneuvers, lifting his knees from table to chest, bending them in a simulated walk.

"Your hamstrings are in good shape."

Michael lay on a padded workout table, his stare shifting to an air exchange vent mounted in a corner. "Too bad they don't feel as good as they look." *Droll* was becoming his attitude of choice.

"These exercises will keep your muscles supple and strong."

"So I can start jogging the minute I'm back on my feet?" Michael's laugh was strained.

"Hey, you never know. Technology advances every day. You could be our miracle patient. Hang in there," was a mechanical response most therapists used.

"I'm not a quitter — just being realistic while I hang." Michael hated the pep talks. Despised relying on others to move for him, artificially pumping up his morale, along with his legs. His mind was independent. His circumstances were not.

"Let's roll you over, get the old back, loosen up those knots. Geeze, your back is tense, Michael, but your glutes look fine."

"That's a first. I've never had a guy tell me I had a fine ass."

The therapist guffawed, then focused on pressure points in his upper back and neck. "Christ, you're a mass of hard muscle," he said, leaning firmly against him as he massaged. Air, forced from Michael's lungs, sounded guttural.

"You're knocking the wind out of me, but it feels great," Michael said after exhaling. "Do you make house calls?" His voice wavered under the pressure of his therapist's punches.

He snickered. "If you were a hot blonde, I'd consider it."

"You married, Dave?"

"Fifteen years."

Michael grunted. "Ouch. You're hitting something there, buddy."

"Yeah, serious knots. And if I don't break them up, you're only going to feel worse. I'm trying to get under your muscle."

"I've heard of getting under a guy's skin," Michael coughed, "but never under his muscle."

Dave chuckled. "Each therapist has his own method, depending upon what he's working on and trying to achieve. I could rub gently and relieve the top layer, but that wouldn't do much for the pain that's underneath the muscles pressing on nerves."

Following a quick tap on the door, Dr. Pollock poked his head into the room. "I want to talk to you when you're finished, Michael."

"Should only be another ten minutes or so, and he's all yours, doctor."

"I'll wait for you in the cafeteria, Michael." The tone of Pollock's voice was in professional mode.

"You got yourself another dinner date, doc. And please, don't order for me again. I hate cafeteria stroganoff." From the surprised look on Pollock's face, Michael felt his sense of humor may have caught the doctor off guard. *Joking makes it easier . . . doesn't he know that by now?*

"Is it okay if I choose a table, or should I leave that up to you too?" Pollock stared at him. "What's wrong, don't you like hospital food?" Then his face broke into a smile.

"It's the greatest thing next to my gourmet cooking." Michael shifted the position of his head to launch a smirk. "Hold a table and have a hot waitress on hand. Dave's limbering me up. I'm in the mood for some wrestling."

Shaking his head, Pollock withdrew from the room with a lingering grin.

JUST A MOMENT AT THE OFFICE

"**I**'m getting sick of being cooped up in this tight office, especially when it's beautiful outside. And I'm too exhausted to concentrate on work thanks to these damn dreams." Sienna paced a circle around her desk, then walked back to face the window. The lawn was thick and trees were sprouting pink and white buds. "Crap. Everything's getting to me, and it's not even that time of the month." She turned to make certain Bonnie noticed her exasperation.

"Someone's cranky today." Bonnie nodded her head like it was hinged. "You need a vacation, girlfriend."

"That too, but I need to start getting a good night's rest." She sauntered to her desk, sat, pulled in her chair and, in the same movement, pushed it back out. "I can't work today," she said emphatically. "I feel like throwing a tantrum. Maybe they'll send me home. I'm so wound up. Ugh, I hate my life."

"You're still drowning at night?" Bonnie shot her a sarcastic grin.

Sienna mugged back. "No. These are pleasant dreams. Too pleasant if you know what I mean. Disturbing when you're a woman alone." She huffed as she leaned to rummage in a bottom drawer. When she bent, her hair almost reached the floor, tickling her face. Annoyed, she swept satin locks up into a ponytail bound with a pink elastic band. "Damn, this drawer's a mess. I really should organize this freaking desk." She dragged her purse loose from a tangle of headset cords, rubber bands, booklets and note pads, then kicked the drawer closed.

"So what's the latest in your saga? You haven't been explicit lately." Bonnie squinted at her.

"You sure?" Sienna had challenge written across her face. "It's pretty graphic."

Bonnie's mouth stretched. She stared. "Don't stop now."

"It was so dark, I couldn't see his face."

"What else is new?"

"Do you want to hear this or not?"

"I'm all ears."

"He was running his hands all over my body. Holy fuck, it felt so good. I think we were shipwrecked, or something like that. You know how scrambled dreams can be. One minute you're here. The next you're there. I remember saying, *all I want is a bed.* And the next thing I knew, he spun me around, bent me over the side rail, and I could actually feel him pounding away."

"Oh — my — God." Was all Bonnie could say.

"I woke up with rectal pressure." Sienna watched her reaction.

"Ewww." The tendons in her neck strained when Bonnie clenched her teeth.

"I ran to the bathroom. I had to make sure."

"Maybe it was the Chinese food?"

"You're disgusting."

"I'm disgusting? Look at the floor under your desk. You've got a bigger collection of crumbs than I do."

"Do you think I'm gaining weight? Shit. It's all this stress."

Sienna looked seriously close to tears. "I'm joking," Bonnie soothed.

"I need to vent. I need a punching bag."

"Don't look at me."

"I hate being alone when I feel like this." She resumed her prowl.

"Stop pacing. You're making me nervous. What's the matter with you?"

If she mentioned her make out session with Michael, Bonnie would be all over her. She wasn't up for that.

Should she mention she was feeling the urge to give a relationship another shot, but was not quite sure of how to go about it? How could she feel comfortable with someone else when she wasn't comfortable with herself? Frozen was safe. Dreams were delightful. Desires could be kept under control. So what if her dreams were like Internet romance? Sexy. Satisfying. Harmless, if you never acted on impulse.

When Sienna didn't reply, Bonnie stopped typing. "You're not alone, you have me. And there's always Greg to slap around. I'm sure he'd let you. He might even like it."

"Everything with you revolves around sex." Sienna shook her head, then plopped onto her chair.

Bonnie finished the file she was working on and put her computer to sleep. "I'm starved." She pulled a box of diet cookies from her tote and began to munch, then offered some to Sienna.

"How did I ever get mixed up with him, anyway?"

"Take a look in the mirror."

"Oh, please." Sienna rolled her eyes and grabbed a cookie. "I should shop for clothes, I guess, if I'm really going." She crunched on half a Toll House. "I've got to get the fuck away from here. Clear my head."

Bonnie's jaw dropped. "You just said fuck." She let out a laugh. "This doesn't sound like you at all."

"It doesn't? Who am I, anyway?"

"If you don't know . . ." On the verge of a wisecrack, her tone changed. "It just sounded funny coming out of your mouth. You've been acting weird lately. Is there something I don't know about?"

"Nope." As she chewed, Sienna tested her memory. "You know, with all of those stupid dreams of mine, Trainer's never been in one." Her stare fell across empty air.

"He doesn't bring out the woman in you?" Bonnie chuckled.

"Oh God. As if." Sienna seemed to be thinking out loud. "We can never be more than friends. Haven't I made that perfectly clear?"

"Let him get his rocks off, while you enjoy the ride." Bonnie stuffed the last cookie into her mouth, then tossed the empty box into the trash can beside her desk. Crumbs flittered through the air. With a swipe of her hand she brushed her skirt clean, indifferent to littering the rug. "I love shopping. Let's go tonight, right after work. Mickey volunteered to be a school guard a couple of nights a week. I'm free as a bird," she said, still munching.

"Isn't he teaching science anymore?" Sienna dusted her palms free of crumbs, took a tissue from her desk and dabbed at the corners of her mouth.

"Yeah, but the school budget can't afford to hire extra watchmen. And after that break-in, some of the faculty decided to keep an eye on things. So they're taking turns. Plus he gets stuff done while he's there, so he doesn't have to bring his work home — well, not the paperwork." Bonnie rolled her eyes. "I don't like the idea of him staying so late, but this is one thing I can't talk him out of, no matter what I say. He's being stubborn. And I don't feel like being alone tonight. Now I sound like you." Bonnie's loud burst of laughter didn't impact Sienna.

"Interesting." Only half listening, Sienna walked to the window again, wishing it were open wide. She needed fresh air to clear her cluttered mind.

"I know how you feel."

"What do you mean?"

"Feeling lonely and can't do anything about it because some men are pigheaded."

Sienna frowned. "Yeah, it stinks, doesn't it? Speaking of pigheaded, I told Greg I'd let him know today. Suggestions?"

"Yes. Go."

"Why did I even ask?"

"Are you meeting him for lunch?"

Sienna scrunched her face, looking more sour than the milk in the morning coffee she'd forgotten to finish. "Maybe later."

"When later?" There was a mischievous twinkle in Bonnie's eyes.

"I'm not sure. Why? What do you have up your sleeve?"

"Nothing." She huffed. "Geeze, I was just asking."

SPUR OF THE MOMENT DECISIONS

"**H**ere you go, Michael," Pollock's voice rang out as he gingerly lowered a tray of sandwiches and drinks.

They sat near the elevator. Michael made sure of that.

"How's the construction business?" Pollock asked casually, settling himself at the table. Before biting into a tuna wrap, he made sure his beet colored silk tie was tucked securely beneath his leather belt.

"It's good, Paul. How's your surgery schedule?" Michael pulled his burger off the tray, lifted the bun and doused the grilled meat with ketchup.

"Are you asking that because you're comparing our careers? Or do you want to schedule an appointment?"

"Maybe. What did you want to talk to me about?"

Surgery? Maybe? The surprised look on Pollock's face remained. "I wanted to talk to you about construction, actually, but we can start with my schedule first." He took a sip of bottled water.

"No, that's okay. You first."

"My nephew is moving into the area. He's looking for a medical office across town. Nothing large. He's just starting out. Those are your offices on 202, aren't they?"

"Just about finished and almost fully rented," Michael replied, washing down his lunch with ice cold cola. "I'll call Dan. He handles the rentals. I'm sure we can find something for your nephew. A small unit, right?"

"Yes, he and another young fellow are opening an office together, pediatricians. These days it's easier for a group. They may be expanding."

"We'll take care of him, Paul."

"I know you will, Michael." Pollock nodded, then polished off half of his spring water in one long swallow. "So about the surgery, what did you have in mind?"

"Sienna, can you get my phone please? I'm in the middle of a mess here." Bonnie sat on the floor, rummaging through a pile of folded computer printouts. "Damn, so many patients, they can't even keep this stuff on data drives anymore?" Her stomach grumbled like a clogged sink trying to drain. "Everything's archived on old fashioned paper. Who was on the phone, Sienna?"

"Medical records. They said they don't have your information. What are you looking for? And what are you doing on the floor?"

"Oh, nothing special. Just organizing."

"Looks more like you're destroying the office. Get off the floor before someone sees you." Sienna's voice trailed off to a mumble. "Too late."

"Good afternoon, ladies." Greg's prattle filled the room. He remained in the doorway, hiding a bouquet of flowers behind his back. "Are you ready, Sienna?"

From the euphoric look on his face, she visualized him bouncing up and down with joy on a pogo stick, and hid a chuckle behind her hand.

When his eyes shifted to Bonnie, Trainer scowled. "What are you doing on the floor? Are you staging a sit-in?" He roared at his joke. "What are you protesting?"

"I'm doing Yoga while I work. You should try it Dr. Trainer. It's very relaxing."

"I'm afraid Yoga wouldn't be appropriate in my attire," Trainer pursed his lips, then turned to Sienna, who sat at her desk biting back laughter. "Are you ready, dear?"

"Um — I guess so. Bonnie, would you like to join us?" With hands folded in her lap, Sienna was a portrait of innocence, but for a cagey grin.

Bonnie's quizzical look developed into a frown.

At the mere mention of sharing Sienna, Trainer's face strained.

Bonnie shot Sienna an arched eyebrow as if to say, you're using me to worm out of this, aren't you? "No thanks. You two run along and have fun. I'm buried in Yoga down here." She tugged at her skirt, attempting to cover her bare thighs as she perched over the papers like a nesting eagle.

"These are for you." Trainer placed a stunning arrangement of red tulips and blue irises into Sienna's hands. "A dozen hugs, and a dozen kisses, just for you."

She brought them to her nose, inhaling their fresh scent, then looked at him with an odd expression. "Thank you, Greg. These are absolutely gorgeous. How thoughtful . . . Bonnie, will you find a vase and put these in water?"

Trainer rested his hand lightly on her arm as they strolled to the elevator. "Hungry?" His breath grazed her cheek. Coffee and mints.

"Not very."

"Busy day?"

"No."

"Everything alright with you?"

"Yes."

"Not very talkative, I see." The elevator door closed behind them. His brow automatically furrowed, a frequent occurrence when with Sienna. "So?" He moved closer, practically pinning her against the elevator wall.

"So what?" She side-stepped him.

"Are you coming? It's the perfect time of year."

The prospect of her first trip to London was exciting, yet Sienna would rather be going for reasons other than a seminar, and with someone other than Trainer, who was becoming unnerving with this pleasant, almost humble attitude. And bringing her flowers? What next?

She thought of Rob, and how he had hidden himself until she had fallen for him. And now she was torn apart, living in a world of dreams, some of which she wished *were* reality. Would she ever forgive herself for being such a fool? For letting Rob control her to the point of losing her identity? She would have to step outside herself to recover the person she had once been — happy, confident, idealistic — rational.

And then there was Michael. She thought of the day she had watched him with the kids. After explaining the different parts of a ship, he described exactly what it felt like to be out on the ocean when it was calm. How scary it could be if you were caught in a storm. The children had looked mesmerized as they listened to his stories. Small jaws dropping, they stared — bursting with questions. What else had Michael been saying to them? She hadn't been able to hear it all. Something about playing basketball? What was he up to? They seemed to love him. It melted her heart. He was everything she'd ever wanted in a man. But he had rejected her. Twice. *Is it me, or is it him?* She couldn't face another failure.

She began to panic . . . Then made a spur of the moment decision.

"What should I bring? I'm going clothes shopping after work. Formal? Casual? What's the usual attire for a seminar?"

Trainer folded his arms around Sienna's waist. "I'm thrilled you're coming with me. It will be a wonderful getaway. When we're not working, I'll show you the sights. Bring both, causal and formal. We'll be enjoying lots of fine dining."

The elevator door opened wide into the cafeteria. As they exited, Trainer rested an arm around Sienna's shoulders, as if to keep her from straying.

From his table, Michael had a perfect view. "Bingo," he mumbled. "There they are again." Focusing on how Trainer's arm slung around her like a cape, he grit his teeth.

"Who?" Pollock asked.

"Just a friend. What were you saying about surgery?" Eyes fixed on Sienna, Michael said something he knew would make his doctor happy. "I'm seriously considering it. From the way I've been feeling lately, surgery might be the best option, and sooner rather than later."

Pollock beamed. "When you get home, call Grace. Tell her to schedule an appointment as soon as possible. We'll go over everything in my office. I'll explain the procedure. We'll have to schedule a work-up first. If all goes well, I can have you in surgery by the end of the month."

"The end of the month is Memorial Day, Paul."

"Let's shoot for June . . ."

"I think it's time I moved on her." Michael watched Sienna and Trainer cross the cafeteria and disappear into the crowd.

A puzzled look crossed Pollock's face. "Her?"

"This." Michael's face heated. "I think I should have this surgery. I'll call Grace. Guess it can't hurt to get the tests out of the way."

Pollock reached to pat Michael's arm. "Good call," he said with one of the broadest smiles Michael had ever seen.

One step closer. Deep breath. For a moment, Michael closed his eyes, then slowly opened them as he exhaled.

THE OTHER WOMAN

It was five o'clock. A long line of cars waited for a green light to turn into the mall. "We'll start at one end and work our way to the other," Bonnie said. "This is so exciting. Then we'll have dinner."

"I don't have a lot of money to spend on clothing," said Sienna as they inched their way into the underground garage.

"Don't worry about it. End of the season and pre-season sales. I'm a smart shopper, believe me. I look good, right? Like I spend hundreds of bucks on outfits. Well I don't." Bonnie whipped her head to the side and grinned as Sienna squeezed the Corolla into a space and cut the engine.

Sienna took a moment to assess her best friend, from her flaming shoulder-length hair to her tan two piece suit and mango blouse, lingering on her eager expression. She smiled. "You sure do." She felt a sudden urge to hug Bonnie, but reached for the door handle.

"Let's get going. We've got a big night ahead of us." Her stomach churned. "I can't believe I'm really going through with this."

"That makes two of us," Bonnie said as she hoisted herself out of the small car.

Sienna headed toward the plate glass entrance to Macy's. When she saw the window display of evening wear, she stopped short and gasped, then whirled. "Would you look at those gorgeous dresses?"

Despite rush hour traffic, the spacious stores appeared deserted.

Bonnie dragged Sienna through aisles of fashions with clip-on sale tags, pausing before racks with signs boasting 50% off bargains. "This is fantastic. We've got the place to ourselves."

"It's dead in here, eerie," Sienna remarked. "Reminds me of the shopping mall scene in *Night of the Comet*." They approached an elevator that would take them to the fashion loft. "All we need are guns."

"Yeah and rock music. We can start dancing in the aisles." Bonnie laughed. "I loved that movie — how the comet turned everyone into red dust, or zombies. Oldies are so much better than new releases. Don't you agree, Sienna?"

"It was a good flick, but I'm not much for horror anymore. I've had enough in real life. Hey, look at this." She held up a citrus pink strapless gown with a sweeping hemline.

"That's your color. Is it your size?" For a closer inspection, Bonnie grabbed the dress. "You'll knock out some eyeballs in this. It's beautiful, try it on." She shoved the dress into Sienna's arms, turned her back and trotted off, calling over her shoulder, "You stay here in petites, I'll be over in plus sizes. Meet you back here in a few. I feel like Chinese, how about you?" Her tomato red hair faded from sight.

Dusk faded to night while they spent more than three extravagant hours in the mall.

Bonnie, still overheated and flushed, yawned as they approached the hospital parking lot.

"This was a great night, Sienna. I bet you can't wait to get home and try everything on."

"I can't wait to get home and fall into bed."

"Yeah, me too. But I wish Mickey weren't doing this damn night watch. I won't sleep until he's home."

"Call me if you get lonely," Sienna called out, watching Bonnie climb into the Durango.

She powered down two bottles of spring water as she headed for home, the car windows open to air out the lingering odor of takeout Bonnie carried home for her husband.

"That's what I forgot," she said as if Bonnie still sat beside her. "Damn it. There's nothing home to feed the guys." She sighed. "No biggie. I'll wash by the market."

She turned up the radio, sang along, then laughed at the cracking sound of her voice, comparing herself to the female who screamed her lungs out. She cringed. "Guess it's good I'm focusing on an administrative career. I'd never make it as a singer." She chuckled.

The streetlights lining the road beamed, and the moon with its halo lounged high. Sienna checked the clock on the dash. "Duh. One minute past nine. Shit. They're closed."

About to drive straight by the plaza, she jerked the wheel and the Corolla sailed into the parking lot. Sienna cruised by storefronts, hoping against hope for a sign of life. A place where she could grab a few cans of cat food. "Shit. Do they have to roll up the sidewalks exactly at nine? Perish forbid they stayed an extra five minutes — for idiots like me. She enjoyed talking to herself. She could then say whatever came to mind without having to square off with someone who just didn't understand her dry sense of humor. Sarcasm. Or was it downright misery that made her a first class bitch these days?

"Ah ha!" She spotted the glowing windows of the Plaza Restaurant just up ahead. Not many cars were parked out front. "Please be open."

She zipped into a space, cut the engine, at the speed of light disembarked and as she jogged toward the door, the car locks chirped. Through the glass entrance, she saw a cluster of waitresses and a hostess. Music from outdoor speakers greeted before she even entered.

"Hello," said a girl whose voice was on autopilot. She was dressed all in black, as were the other staffers.

Why was everyone who worked in these types of restaurants young? Were they the only ones willing to work nights? Lug food around to strangers? Clean off tables. Slave away for peanuts? *Ha. I should talk.*

"Table for one?" the girl asked, her eyes washing over Sienna who appeared disheveled and exhausted after working all day and following Bonnie around the mall.

"Actually. I'd like to buy a few cans of tuna?" Sienna's eyes pleaded.

The girl looked puzzled.

"For my cats." She explained. "The market's closed."

"Oh." The girl then smiled. "One kitty bag coming right up."

Sienna sighed relief. "Thank you. My cats will love you for this."

Lights as low as the mood music, the restaurant was a perfect hideaway for lovers. Along with soft voices, delicious aromas filled the air. Why hadn't she ever tried this place? Why would she? She scowled.

While she waited for the hostess to return, her gaze traipsed across the paneled walls, crept over knotty pine tables, faces. Faces? What the hell? She sucked in a breath. No way. You've got to be kidding me. She tried not to stare, but unless her eyes were deceiving her, remaining inconspicuous would prove impossible.

At a table tucked against the wall alongside the bar, two couples seemed to be enjoying the evening. Backs to the door, a man appeared to nurse a draft, a henna haired woman sipped from a straw. And across from the two, beneath the strongest spray of overhead lighting, sat Michael and a young woman.

Sienna felt her stomach fall. What she stared at seemed to be an entirely different Michael from the one who'd stolen her heart at work. The guy who made such a hit with sick and disabled kids, seemed to be doing quite well for himself with women, namely the brunette who sat practically on his lap. Was she leaning on him or was he leaning on her? And oh boy, was she acting coy or what? Lowered lids? Come on, lady. Her hands were probably all over him — under the table.

Sienna couldn't figure out what they were doing. One more step . . . No, they'll see you! A tug of war raged in the lobby where she was glued to her vantage point in a corner. Faces inches apart, he seemed unable to tear his eyes away from the girl's. Was he kissing her? His arm was slung around the back of her chair.

First his hands were fingering her silky long hair, tucking it behind an ear, then a hand rested on her bare shoulder. What was he doing pulling on the strap of her tank top? Trying to undress her? The restaurant's dim but, hello people — we happen to be out in public here, are we not? He appeared so damn attentive, she envied and hated the girl, simultaneously. What a head of hair . . . If she turned around, I'd probably see a unibrow. Sienna wanted to chuckle, but the sight wasn't laughable.

The lineup of empty glasses on the table said they must have been here for a while. They all looked pretty sloshed. Drinking their dinner no doubt. Did he have a thing for drunken women? Would he push this one away? As he'd done to her? That had been a first for Sienna. Her face flamed. She had never been 'thrown out of bed' before.

She strained to see the woman's entire face. Her profile alone was striking. And she was built like a weight lifter. Firm and full figured and shapely as hell. Sienna looked down at the width of her hips, or lack of, then checked her bust line. Hmm. Her boobs didn't protrude nearly as far. Sonofabitch. *Fatal attraction . . . I can't believe he's turning me into a freaking stalker!* Why was she evaluating her anyway? Screw him. She turned her head, but gaping was irresistible.

The hostess returned with a bag. "Here go you."

Overly enthusiastic, Sienna reached for her wallet."Thank goodness." *Thank goodness I can get the hell out of here.*

"It's on the house. I have little ones home too." She smiled.

"You're sweet. Thank you so much."

Sienna stole a last glance at their table, where the two woman stood, headed toward the ladies room. Michael and the other man were huddled in serious conversation. She was dying to know what they were talking about.

Had it not been an automatic door, it would have slammed shut after Sienna stomped out.

Men. They're all the same. Why did she think he'd be any different?

The overstuffed Corolla soared through the night, miraculously catching every green light. Sienna felt like Santa in his sleigh as she pulled down the driveway and parked. Heaving a sigh, she looked into the back seat, grabbed her keys and began gathering. It took three trips to unload, scurrying beneath lamplight, up and down concrete porch steps, lugging garment bags, shopping bags, and a five piece set of floral luggage she had found on clearance. "You'd think I was going for three weeks instead of three days," she grumbled, rubbing a hand along her new paisley satchel as she dropped to the floor along with her packages. "Wait till the credit card statement comes." She grimaced. But who knew how many trips she'd be taking in the future? The luggage might come in handy. *Screw the bills. Screw Rob. Screw Michael. Screw Trainer. Great. I'll be spending the next three days with him. Shit. How do I get into these messes?*

Lying on the living room carpet, she stared at the array of lights recessed into the cathedral ceiling. Dimmed by a wall switch, the lights twinkled like early stars in a summer sky. She had better bolster her morale, and fast, or she'd end up in the kitchen with a half gallon of moose tracks and a spoon. Like she was their mountain, Frazzle and Dazzle climbed over her, purring.

After catching her breath and tiring of the view, she stood, eyed the mess of packages strewn around her, and collapsed onto the sofa, car keys still in hand. "I'll feed you in a minute guys. Mommy's tired." For a moment she closed her eyes, reliving the sight at the restaurant. Well, she was going to London — with a man. Was it a wave of satisfaction she felt?

Maybe things that feel the best aren't always the best for you, she told herself as that one afternoon with Michael flashed through her mind, bright and lively as the lights. She let her heavy lids slip down, remembering how he looked the first day they met, the softness of his eyes, his heart-melting smile. Then she thought of how he'd ditched her. Which she'd probably never recover from. She'd never forget how his lap felt, either. *Stop it!* She looked around the room, at her beautiful new clothing, thinking of what she'd be doing while wearing the sexy dresses, wishing she were going with . . . *Snap out of it. You've got a lot to do . . .*

She dropped her keys into her tote, where her fingers found a fortune cookie buried there by Bonnie as they departed the Chinese restaurant. She went to the kitchen, took a bottle of green tea from the refrigerator, sat on a stool at the center island, and tore the wrapper open. She wasn't interested in the cookie she snapped in half, dropping crumbling pieces onto a napkin, but pulled out the paper tab and quickly read: *A lifetime friend shall soon be made.*

HEADING TO LONDON

Bradley International Airport surged with tides of travelers when Sienna and Greg arrived in a white limo. They bypassed waiting lines . . . Trainer had thought of everything. The Gulfstream he chartered was a winged brute, waking from slumber as it idled smoothly on the runway. Their luggage had already been stowed. Boarding the jet, Trainer concentrated on the seat of Sienna's linen trousers as she mounted the folding stairs ahead of him.

"This is incredible," she said as she sank into an overstuffed brown recliner that cradled her body much like her memory foam mattress. "Feel this leather, Greg, it's so soft." She was on her way to London! She felt adventurous. Oak Haven, Manchester General, even Bonnie Murray, were non-existent.

"Just like you." Trainer gently stroked the side of her cheek with the back of his hand before easing into the seat across the aisle. "We're so far apart." He stretched an arm, theatrically reaching through the space between them. Cheek on headrest, he watched her with a lazy stare. He appeared to relax and enjoy what he had obviously been working so hard to acquire.

Sienna's eyes rolled like a camcorder, filming every square inch of the Gulfstream. Every pore in her body absorbed luxury. She couldn't hide her admiration of what Trainer — and the jet — had to offer, and gasped. She fought the urge, but succumbed to the trappings of high society, until she was grounded by memories — and thoughts of what she might be leaving behind.

From the look on Trainer's face, he was enjoying the innocent side of Sienna, her inexperience and lack of exposure to the *finer things in life*, which he was about to help her explore. She was like a little kid in a toy store, eyes wide with awe. He seemed to adore her naïveté. She knew he wanted to show her the world, and possibly much more . . .

Two pilots boarded, and soon a speech that sounded prerecorded was broadcast through the PA. "The weather's clear. Might feel some mild turbulence over the Atlantic, but nothing of concern. This is a perfect day for flying. Good forecast. Should be a smooth flight. We'll be right up front if you need anything. Fasten your seatbelts, we're on our way to London. Should be there in about six hours, give or take."

The powerful aircraft plowed through morning in an aggressive climb.

Sienna's stomach tightened as the plane heaved into the sky and angled. Although the jet had eight seats in its roomy fuselage, she brushed off a sense of agoraphobia and a bout of vertigo. Squinting, she glanced at Trainer, who said, "Don't worry, dear, she'll smooth out as soon as we're above the clouds. I do this all the time. It's fine."

"I'm used to commercial airliners." She cradled her stomach, reverting back to the ordinary Sienna Alexander, not the world traveler she'd been pretending to be.

"You won't get this on commercial." Trainer snapped his fingers and a male attendant immediately appeared with a bottle of *Dom Perignon Rose* planted in a stainless steel bucket of glittering ice. He set two crystal wine glasses onto a blonde wood table in front of Sienna's seat before retreating to the back of the plane.

"It's a bit early for champagne, isn't it?" She looked surprised, then her lips spread with delight. She hadn't enjoyed champagne since a sorority sister's lavish spring wedding, when birds sang love songs and skies showered happiness, and worry was something for others to contend with.

"There's no such thing as time in flight. Wet your lips, darling, sip it slowly, it's so delicious." Trainer lifted his glass in a toast.

"To us, Sienna, and to London."

She sipped champagne while gazing through the portal window, relaxing as the pungent alcohol migrated to her limbs, and the jet dissolved in buttermilk haze as it swept a blue sky, thundering dense tracks of exhaust in its wake.

She glanced at Trainer, who sat in repose, listening to a concerto on his iPod, full blast. From across the aisle, she heard melodious piano keys reach a dramatic peak.

The attendant returned to pour more champagne. He pushed a button, then twisted a dial near Sienna's seat and a flirtatious rhapsody by Kenny G's sax filled the air, and Sienna, with sensuality.

"Do you like this music?" the charming attendant asked.

"It's nice." Sienna nodded, and sucked in her breath when he leaned in close. She assumed he was in his twenties and was striking, with sooty eyes that gave her a feeling of turbulence when he stared into hers as he refilled her glass.

Once again, he retreated to the curtained catering area at the back of the plane. Impulse turned Sienna's head to watch him from behind. A masculine bottom filled the seat of a pair of relaxed black trousers he wore better than a centerfold, accentuating the lean muscle of his long legs. The sleek black ponytail that rested on the collar of his white shirt was the icing on the cake. European? she wondered. From the accent, Spanish, of course. She could see women flocking around him in a bar, and wondered how he behaved when "off duty". His appearance brought to mind another scrumptious man, the one who had ditched her in front of an Oak Haven hardware store.

The plane pitched with another burst of vitality. Her arms felt heavy. Time was slowing; she felt dreamy . . .

They're on a flight to Ontario. Sienna is fearful of what awaits them, but with him at her side, things will be so much easier. She can lean on him, gather his strength as her own. The airport is dark. Mist fills midnight. His arms fold around her. Her hands slide from his shoulders to his neck, to his thick, dark hair.

It's raining. Dampness twists his hair into waves.

The ocean is raging. She's in his arms, his words silenced by tidal thunder — her words mere thoughts — raw thoughts. She grips him fiercely. His lips search gently, then crush hers in a fit of passion.

She blinks raindrops from her eyes. The hospital looms in the distance. Together they stroll down the polished corridor to a room lighted only by machines supporting withering life. Her beaded gown is heavy, making it difficult to move. In slow motion, she drifts down the aisle to where he's standing. Her veil is raised, pressed neatly into place at the back of her head. He's so handsome. He's smiling. He's standing. She's in heaven. It has to be a dream . . .

The Gulfstream glided gracefully onto a Gatwick runway. Field attendants approached with a motor driven luggage cart.

"Wake up, Sienna, we're here." Trainer was on his feet, smoothing wrinkles from his trousers, plucking his shirt sleeves, adjusting his onyx cufflinks.

Sienna shook free of unconsciousness. "I'm coming. Give me a minute to collect myself. It was a long flight." She felt drunk. Lifting her head, she arched her neck, rolling it in a deep muscle stretch. Her wristwatch confirmed the elapse of eight hours, but she felt like the jet had just taken to the air.

"You slept almost the entire way. I didn't have the heart to wake you. You looked so peaceful. Making funny sounds too. Were you dreaming?" Trainer was at the door preparing to disembark, yet his probing stare reached her, along with his voice. "Smiles and moans. I hope it was about me." He stifled a yawn, but not his interrogating cocked brow. "This is always such a tiring flight, but we'll perk up on the ride to the hotel. It's quite luxurious. I've stayed there before."

"I know, Greg. You've already told me." Feeling the after-effects of champagne and dream, Sienna held onto the seatback for balance as she stood, then joined him at the portal. "All I want to do is shower and sleep." Her voice echoed in her ears.

"Come on, lean on me."

"I'll be fine." She lifted her face and fell into step beside him.

The air smelled fresh from a recent rain. There was no moon, no stars, only runway lights glaring in every direction. She squinted, then held up a hand, shielding her light sensitive eyes.

Big Ben struck midnight miles beyond reach of the terminal floodlights. Sienna imagined the sweeping hands of the famous tower clock shrouded in mist, the same as the runway the jet had landed on. She inhaled deeply, feeling awake and wonderful. *This is London. I'm really in London.* Her stomach filled with butterflies and her feet moved faster.

Commercial flights emptied travelers and cargo, but the Gulfstream taxied straight into a hangar packed with private jets and charters.

A man dressed as a chauffeur held a sign that read, TRAINER, printed in bold letters.

"That's for us," Trainer said, whisking Sienna, who was walking ahead of him and in another direction, by the arm.

She didn't mind being ushered from the terminal and tucked into the back seat, and barely noticed the firmness of Trainer's grip as he took command. She was too entranced with everything around her to acknowledge Trainer as the reason she was here.

The limo was black and sleek, stocked with more alcoholic beverages and scrumptious hors d'oeuvres of no interest to Sienna, although Trainer indulged on delicate pastries filled with blended cheese and berries.

Much like the jet in the sky, the limo took to the road as if suspended from clouds, overpowering spiraling intersections. Through crowded lanes they dodged traffic on looping roadways until they sped onto a highway. The ride was a tangle of further disorientation for Sienna, unaccustomed to driving on the left side of the road.

"With all these taxis and congestion, it's as bad as New York City." She watched structured outlines and vehicles flash by faster than her mind could register.

As she looked to the right, Trainer's profile merged with

skeleton trees riding level with the road. When she looked to the left, the impressive horizon of one of the most alluring cities in the world stretched as far as she could see. Outside her window, for miles around, there was nothing but London, drawing her through a dazzling maze of brilliance.

"This is London, darling. We're in the pulse of the world. Piccadilly Circus, historic museums, theatres." Trainer handed Sienna a colorful travel brochure.

"It's incredible, I want to see everything. I hope we have time between sessions. Where's the hotel?"

"At the West End of London. Tomorrow we'll see Buckingham Palace, Trafalgar Square, oh we're going to have a time of it. But you're right about this bloody traffic." Trainer was already taking on a British air.

"Tomorrow? What about the seminar?" Suspicion took hold of her face.

"Don't worry. We'll squeeze everything in."

She seemed satisfied with his answer. "I don't think I could drive here. I'd be on the wrong side of the road all the time. How does anyone get used it?"

"I've driven here. A bit of concentration is all you need. You could do it, dear. Maybe we'll rent a car."

"I'd rather ride the trolleys and the underground. Seems safer to me." She sipped an iced Perrier poured into a fluted glass. "It looks a lot like Times Square, but what fantastic architecture."

As they reached the city, Sienna was ready to fall in love — with the enchantment of London, not Trainer. She snuggled close to the door of the limousine, leaning against the padded interior as she marveled at the surroundings.

Trainer slid closer and took her hand. "If this trip works out, I'd like to take you to Paris. Can you free your calendar for a few days next month? Traveling by Lear is a dream, don't you agree? The world is at our fingertips, Sienna. All we need to do is enjoy the journey."

She recoiled. "Will Paris be for business too?" Her eyes narrowed.

REALLY? ONLY ONE ROOM?

The luxurious hotel stretched its pride more than two city blocks. Nine stately floors of Old World charm awaited them in shadows of torchlight, adorned by awnings of emerald green. Hotel banners flapped a welcome in the wind. Mounted at the highest architectural precipice, a British flag marked its territory.

Gazing from the window of the limousine, Sienna said, "Oh my God," and sucked in a long breath. "Would you look at this hotel —"

As the vehicle came to a stop, uniformed doormen stood ready to assist, properly attired with unemotional eyes.

"Smashing reconstruction. Fantastic, isn't it? We can dine on the terrace tonight if you like. Midnight snack perhaps? I'm sure the staff will accommodate us." He flashed his brilliantly crafted set of white porcelain veneers.

"I'm tired, Greg. Right now I want nothing more than a long hot bath and nice soft bed."

"We have to make the most of every moment we share here, Sienna. We only have three days." Was there a wistful tone in Trainer's normally authoritative voice?

"I know, but I don't want to walk around in a daze. I want to enjoy every minute and be able to remember absolutely everything when we're back home." Home. Twinges of loneliness crept in. *Stop it. You're going to enjoy this trip with an open mind and heart. There's no such place as Connecticut . . .* She looked at the sky, squelched the ache, shifted her gaze toward the doorman and walked into the hotel with a set jaw, her head held high. After tipping the driver and attendants, Trainer sauntered in and went straight to the registration desk.

The lobby was a behemoth three stories high, marble floors at one's feet, a celestial ceiling above — an abridged version of the intricately gilded dome of Grand Central Station. Only this ceiling held crystal chandeliers, dangling nearly to the floor.

With every step, Sienna compared this wonderland to her own reality. Vases of flowers scattered the lobby, with a five foot jardinière stationed before the glossy ebony desk where hotel attendants waited to serve. The buttery brass holder overflowed with long-stemmed calla lilies.

An alabaster bust of Roman Emperor Augustus postured on a fluted pedestal, gracing an intimate alcove alongside an impressive scarlet carpeted staircase leading to an arched loft where other statues lined a wall.

Sienna compared the lobby to one of New York's historic Hudson Valley mansions she had toured, only this structure was a hundred times larger than the mansion, and that had been long ago. She had run into Rob there, shortly before hell consumed her life.

As Trainer walked back from the registration desk, he looked uncomfortable. "I hope you won't be too upset." He smiled apologetically. "They screwed up our reservations."

"What do you mean? We have to find another hotel? At this hour?" She appeared on the verge of tears.

"They have us down for only one room. And with all of the conventions, they have nothing at all free."

"I should have know." Her lips tightened.

Trainer smiled, whispered in her ear with moist lips. "How about a midnight swim? The water in the pool is sapphire blue, extremely romantic, just like your eyes. Would that take the edge off?" He grinned and tilted his head. "Our room does have a large whirlpool, which might be even better."

"Don't even go there." Her eyes searched the lobby. "This is a business trip. Where is everyone else?"

His face shaded. "Scattered around. We'll all meet tomorrow." He patted her shoulder. "Don't worry about anything. Just have a wonderful time, which is what I intend to do, starting right now. I'm on overdrive from the flight. I think I'll mull around the barroom if it's okay with you." Before stepping into the elevator, he casually added, "Maybe we'll trot over to Spain. You know, continental beaches encourage nude bathing. That's what I love about Europe: natural beauty, pure bliss."

Sienna's stomach sank as she watched the doors snap shut; she felt confined and ill at ease. But there was something about Trainer she couldn't quite put her finger on. He talked the talk, but when it came right down to it, would he? When he mentioned nude bathing, she hadn't seen lust on his face, just his driven passion for life. Maybe his arrogance was as unintentional as her envy of the way he seemed to view and handle the world.

The suite seemed endless. Where sliding glass doors led to a terra cotta deck from the bedroom in her condo, patio doors spanned half the length of the Great Room, with leaded panes of glass encased in cleaved hardwood, opening onto a private veranda of concrete, iron scrollwork and granite.

The furnishings in the Great Room were of mahogany and cherry woods, decorated with striped damask fabrics in rich gold and shades of blue. Suddenly excited, Sienna ran her hands over everything. *I can handle Trainer. This is going to be fun.*

Four carpeted steps brought Sienna to level two, where two king-sized beds garnished with white brocaded spreads were set in the center of the master bedroom suite. She wished the beds were positioned further apart, with a dresser stretched out between them. But at least she'd have her own bed to sleep in, even if not the separate room she had been promised.

She explored the massive rooms that were divided by plaster archways painted in peach, much like the Oak Haven plaza outdoor arches, she thought. Come to think of it, the plaza had been built in a stunning design, not at all like an average shopping mall. Someone with a flair for elegance and beauty must have put a lot of heart, and a lot of cash into it.

She kicked off her sandals and sank into a plush, royal carpet with ivory scrolls carved into it; luxury for bare feet. After wandering, she padded back into the Great Room to see if Trainer had departed. She found him sorting through his wallet, and handing a few bills to a bellman who then stuffed twenty pounds into the slash pocket of his cardinal red and gold striped jacket. The bellman wheeled the luggage cart into the spacious foyer, where Trainer stepped aside and once more dipped deep into his wallet. "Here you go, mate, and keep us in mind. I'm certain we'll be needing things." He spoke in a hushed tone as he handed the man an additional gratuity, the equivalent of fifty US dollars.

"Very well, sir, and thank you, Doctor Trainer." He took a quick glance at Sienna. "If there's anything you and the Mrs. need. . ."

Trainer stood, one hand in the pocket of his jacket, smiling briefly. "We'll be sure to call you," his eyes dropped from the man's smiling lips to his nameplate, "Charles."

The bellman nodded, slipped out and silently closed the door. His crepe-soled oxfords chirped as he hurried down the polished corridor, and as he stepped into the elevator, he took the money out of his pocket and counted it.

"We should be well taken care of — Mrs." Trainer winked at Sienna, moving to take her in his arms.

She sidestepped him. "Oh, I'm sure we will be." Sienna knew Trainer had everything under control. Everything but her.

"I'm going to change for the evening." He strode to the center of the room before he turned and looked into her eyes. "Are you sure you don't mind being alone for a while?"

"Mind? How could I mind? I'm still drooling over this suite. There's a lot to keep me occupied. Believe me, I'll be fine." She rounded her shoulders, clasped her arms around her upper body, and shuddered.

"Are you cold? Do I have to be concerned about you? Are you feeling ill?"

"I'm just excited. Don't worry about me." She rolled her eyes with delight. "I'll be making plans for tomorrow while you're gone. If you don't see me in bed when you get back, check the tub." She chuckled, then her face went blank as she realized she had inadvertently sent him an invitation.

Trainer lifted a brow, shot her one of his adoring looks, then turned to his luggage stacked in the foyer. "If you want me, I'll be rummaging through my bags."

"I'll be upstairs in the bedroom." *Not another invitation.* I have to stop sending him signals, she cautioned herself. *There's no way he's getting me into bed with him.*

Sienna loved exploring. From the bedroom, she climbed three marble steps leading to a spacious loft and bath suite on the third level. *Let's see. A steam shower or a slow soak in the sunken tub?* "Ooops, forgot my clothes," she whispered, giggling, heading to the Great Room where Trainer was in the process of changing into white slacks and black silk pullover, topped off with a blazer that was a muted blend of charcoal and white wool, and mohair.

"This place is amazing," she practically sang as she danced down the stairs. "I could really get used to this." While tiptoeing across the carpet, she turned a quick pirouette before coming to a breathless halt. "You've already unpacked?"

"No, just pulled out a few things. I won't be long, dear." Trainer adjusted his jacket and brushed his palms down the sleeves. "How do I look?"

"You look great. I'll see you in the morning." Without a smile, Sienna blew him a kiss, although they stood only inches apart.

He planted a peck on her cheek and on the way out the door whispered, "Do wait up for me." His sandalwood scent floated with him to the door.

"I'm sure I'll be fast asleep by the time you get back."

She was relieved she didn't have to contend with him tonight. And conferences should take up a good part of tomorrow. She needed her own downtime. She would relax in a warm lavender soak, maybe use the powerful tub jets, slip into her silky violet nightgown, then slide into bed. She would be fast asleep before he returned.

THE CHAIR HITS ANOTHER BUMP

Sienna was about to light up his life. She would appear soon, and he would be there to greet her with a smile and lively conversation. After his talk with Gus, Michael's confidence was rehabilitated, even if his legs were not. Today would be the day. He would ask her if she'd be coming to the carnival. They would let things unfold from there. He had it all planned.

It was a mild afternoon, and the plaza was busier than usual. As he waited outside Dyson's, he stared at wave upon wave of shuffling feet, lifting his eyes to scan faces of women who passed. Broad shouldered bodies, some pausing before store windows, blocked his view of the parking lot. He craned his neck from side to side, peering through the tangle of arms and legs. Would her small red car drive down the entrance ramp? The chair didn't move from the spot he had chosen. He knew he blocked the walk. *Who cares? I own the place* . . . He detested sympathetic smiles, and the occasional look of annoyance if someone had to step around his chair. Then he saw her, and his heart began to thud. She was walking toward him, and her hair was a mass of blonde curls, springing off her shoulders.

He sucked in a breath, deciding how he'd stop her from walking right by if she didn't notice him. How could she not notice him? Would he call out her name? He might ask her to join him for a cup of coffee on the restaurant's breezy terrace, or perhaps an intimate dinner. No, too soon for dinner. Coffee would be a good start — away from the plaza — someplace like the River Lounge, offering privacy where two people could leisurely get to know one another. Just to speak with her again would satisfy the ache inside his chest that was his heart.

The blonde woman neared. She looked rather tall. For a better look, he moved to the center of the walk, his heart beginning to race. She stopped, hesitated, walked the other way. Should he follow her? She wasn't making it easy . . . Suddenly she turned, heading straight for him. He swallowed hard. Then her face came into focus. Michael's heart sank. Wearing sneakers and trousers, she slowly passed him, tugging along a toddler. He checked his watch. He would wait all day if he had to.

Three p.m. and Sienna was nowhere in sight. *She's not coming* . . . Michael heaved a heavy sigh, angry with himself for not having been more aggressive when he had the chance — the day he ducked into Dyson's. If things did not work out as he hoped, he would never forgive himself.

When a man paused and lowered his face, asking if he needed help, Michael's stomach dropped, snapping him out of fantasy. His face felt hot. Then Leo crept up from behind. "Hey, Michael." He tapped his shoulders, then skirted the chair to face him.

If his legs moved, Michael would have jumped up and grabbed him by the collar. "Nice way to give someone a heart attack."

"Sorry. Couldn't resist." Leo's eyes were filled with youth and mischief. "What's up?"

"Nothing. Still delivering?"

"Nope. Done for the day." Leo took a deep breath and smiled. "Great afternoon, huh? Why are you sitting in the middle of the sidewalk?"

"I had some things to do. I was just getting ready to head for the hills. Cook an early dinner, maybe watch a movie." Michael stared past him, out into the parking lot.

"Earth to Michael."

"Huh?"

"No wisecracks today? What's the matter?"

"I can't take center stage all the time. What are you up to?"

"I'm going over to the field. Wanna come?"

"What's doing there?"

"Soccer. Wanna watch?"

"You playing?"

"No, just gonna watch a practice."

"Sure, why not." *Soccer. Will it take my mind off her? Doubtful...* Destination: Oak Haven High.

Leo parked the Volvo in the area assigned to students with permits.

"Still looks like a used car lot," Michael said and chuckled, remembering his bright green GTI. The age-old oak that could shade a row of ten cars still stood. "I used to have my own spot."

"How'd you manage that?" Leo, who stood beside the car, ran a hand over his head, then opened the tailgate to haul out the wheelchair that was folded in the back.

Michael pushed the car door open and swung around in the seat so his legs dangled over the pavement. "I made sure everyone knew which spot was mine." He laughed when Leo's eyes bulged.

"Don't tell me you were a bully."

"Actually, I got here early every day."

"Why the heck would anyone come to school early? What, did you need to study?"

"I ran laps."

"You ran track before class started?" Leo's jaw dropped.

"Yep. So did my father."

Growing up the son of an army colonel brought responsibilities, offered privileges, although Michael preferred to earn them on his own. Even as a child he knew right from wrong, when to lead and when to follow. The night he was born his grandmother held him in her arms, looked into his alert eyes, and claimed he was an old soul in a new body. Her loving smile said Michael would be the kind of person who would put the welfare of others first.

Leo helped him with his chair and led the way. Boys wearing baggy knee-length shorts and Wife Beaters gathered in groups on the sidewalk. Some had tattoos on every imaginable body part. They talked and joked, sparred and rough-housed, showing off for girls who strutted by in hip hugging short-shorts, push-up bras and tank tops.

Through wide open doors, along with a wash of sun, spring flowed into the gym. The oak floor was heavily scuffed, black scratched foul and point lines more worn, needing paint. The place had aged, so had he. Michael felt old, and although school had been a big part of his life, he was as out of place in the gym as he would have been in the middle of a crowded dance floor — as long as he was sitting in a wheelchair.

Twelve years was a long leap into yesterday. He eyed the orange rim of a basketball hoop, and a row of bleachers. He noticed that juice replaced soda in the dispensing machine.

"This is my old stomping ground. I remember it well." To Michael, returning to the school was like the ghost of a movie watched long ago, one rarely given much thought but available for instant recovery and capable of rousing deep-seeded emotions.

"I can't wait to graduate." Leo shoved his hands deep into the pockets of his athletic shorts and squared his shoulders.

"Things here that bad?"

"Like being locked up in jail." Leo leveled his furry brows.

"I imagine changes had to be made, Leo. The world's a lot different now than when I was here. More things to worry about. The school's got to protect the kids."

"Yeah. Protect themselves from lawsuits you mean."

"Maybe."

"You're pretty serious today."

"Ever hear of jitters?"

"What?"

"The smell of this place brings back memories."

"Oh. Like you could smoke in school, right? We can't." Leo lumbered at Michael's side.

"You shouldn't be smoking. It's bad for you."

"How about weed?"

"I don't know. I guess you shouldn't smoke anything."

"Did you smoke?"

"Sometimes."

"Anything stronger than weed?"

Michael laughed. "What are you doing, a documentary?"

"Just wondering if you had fun before . . ."

"I did."

"You miss it a lot, huh?"

I miss her more, Michael wanted to say but replied, "Sure I do. Big lifestyle change, you know? Well you wouldn't know. Hope you never do. And since when do you ride a motorcycle?"

Leo's voice jumped an octave."How'd you know?"

"I saw you on the bike, flying through the dust you were kicking up. Those things are dangerous, even off- road."

Leo made a face. "It's only a dirt bike, plus I aced my driver's test and it's registered for road."

"I understand, but accidents happen, usually when and where you least expect them."

Leo became defensive. "I could handle a Harley, ya know."

"Ahem." Michael remembered how invincible had felt.

"When did you see me?"

"The other night when I drove by our Lakewood housing site, private property, which I'm sure you know."

Leo cleared his throat. "Looks like it's coming along great, Michael. That'll bring in some major cash."

Michael's eyes narrowed. "You can butter me up all you want, but the bottom line is, stay out of there." He grinned. "Come here so I can smack you." For his own good, the kid needed to be kept in line.

Leo faked a move. "You da man."

WET WITH MORE THAN SUDS

They exited the gym through the back doors, and headed toward the field where a soccer match was underway. Leo plopped onto a ground-level bench beside Michael, who was immediately engrossed.

"I thought it was just practice? This looks like a kick-ass game to me." Michael, crunched at the waist, hands folded in his lap, had to yell so Leo could hear through the cheering.

"Wild aren't they? That's Hager." Leo pointed to a perspiring boy with a red and white headband stretched around his curly mop of hair. "He's the best. Look — look at how he steals the ball. Ha. The other team doesn't know what they're up against." Leo's eyes were glued to the field, even while conversing.

Michael watched the teens play, hustling with sweat-soaked shorts and T's, slamming the soccer ball with determination as if defeat would end their perfect worlds. They were kids; he tried not to envy their blissful ignorance. "Why aren't you playing?" Michael asked Leo.

"Basketball's my game," was Leo's distracted response.

"Sure, with those long legs of yours you're probably good."

"I'm the best. Speaking of best. Check her out up there." For a moment, Leo ignored the game and motioned toward a well-endowed, cinnamon haired girl perched in the bleachers across the way. She wore a choking maize tube top trussing her breasts, and shorts so brief her panties showed from the side of her crossed leg.

Michael wasn't impressed. "No more Linda?"

"Nah — we had a fight. She doesn't like me taking off weekends on the bike."

"Why don't you take her with you?"

"Her parents are strict. They'd never let her out with me for a weekend." Leo threw out a grin, swinging his stare back and forth from the soccer match to Michael. "So she gave me an ultimatum. Her or the bike."

"And you chose the bike, of course."

"Sure. We have fun. Campfires, rowdy chicks like Spice up there. She came with one of the guys last week. They're only friends," he added quickly, "she was checking me out the whole trip."

"I can see why," Michael teased, although the kid's biceps and triceps were admirable despite his lean frame.

"Check out the jugs and ass. Damn. Some eye-candy, huh?"

"You're getting out of control, Leo." Michael concealed his amusement. "I always figured you as a one-woman kinda guy."

Leo laughed. "That'll be the day. How about you? You had your share of ass, didn't you?" Leo's expression changed as if he regretted the remark."Don't mean to make you feel bad or anything, Michael. I just meant . . ."

"Don't worry about it. My day'll come again." Michael smiled and slapped Leo's leg.

"You're thinkin' about her, ain'tcha," Leo blurted.

"All the time," Michael said in a low voice, showing no emotion.

"Where is she today? It's Saturday. I figured you'd be waitin' for her at the plaza like you always do."

"I don't *wait* for her. We just seem to run into each other now and then. If she's there when I'm there, fine. If not, whatever."

Leo grinned; having caught someone else in the act for a change seemed to make his day. "Yeah. I know why you hang around there all the time. You're waitin' for her to come along and the chance to ask her out. Right?" He gloated.

Michael smirked. "I do happen to own the place, Leo." His

forehead creased with more lines than he'd had the prior year. "But I did want to talk to her — today actually." He surprised himself by admitting this to Leo, but why not? Things were coming to a head. "I was going to ask her if she'd be at the carnival next week." He lowered his gaze, locking in an awkward stare that fell to the grass at their feet. "Are you going?"

"Yeah, I'll be around. Not sure who with, but I'll catch you there. And you better be with her." Leo cocked his head, then gave a knowing nod of approval. Struggling for the right words, he scuffed his sneakers back and forth into grass and dirt. "Wonder why she didn't come today? How do you plan on asking her when the carnival's next week and she's not around? Can you call her?"

"Never." Michael's voice was harsh. "Besides, I don't know her phone number."

But I do know where she works . . . A design began to take shape in his mind, but this one was not a construction project.

"Eh, she's probably doing woman stuff today, like laundry or something." With his sneakers, Leo scraped a hollow into the dirt as he tried to sound consoling.

"Maybe." Michael wondered where she was, wishing she would magically appear, although something inside said she was far away.

She runs along the beach, skipping in and out of surf that slaps at her ankles. Like a gilded kite caught in an upward spiral, her hair flows with the breeze.

She knows he's been sitting there since sunrise sprinkled the shoreline with diamond light. She makes certain she's standing erect, arching her spine provocatively so he will witness every inch of bounding cleavage.

From his perch on a bluff, he can't help but notice. He's entranced.

Beneath the morning sky, her bronze skin glints with moisture. She's perfection; firm breasts stuffed into a skimpy bikini bra, tied with a string between her shoulder blades. Her slim waist bows gracefully into rounded hips connected to the shapeliest legs he's ever seen.

She's irresistible. In moments he's standing at her side. "Morning."

"Hello," she replies, her heaving chest calming.

"I'm Michael. And you are?"

"Sienna."

"Hello, Sienna. You're beautiful."

Beneath her tan excitement heats her body faster than rays of blistering sun. As they speak, his gypsy eyes steal a breath from her throat.

"Can I walk with you?"

"I'd like that."

Slipping an arm around her waist, he leads her to the shallows. The ocean is cold, but his presence is warming. Within moments she's wrapped in his embrace. His arms are strong, careful hands roaming to the small of her back, fingers dipping beneath the hip-tie of her bikini. Waist-deep water fails to cool his heat.

As the ocean tugs, he pulls her closer. Her mouth traces the length of his neck with appetizing kisses. Lost in the moment, she doesn't feel his hands untie her top, or see it drift with the tide, but feels her nipples harden in the chilling water as they slide across his chest.

His warm breath is a moan in her ear.

Don't lose it now, she thinks as she feels him pulse. Inside me — grow inside me.

His muscles ripple as he lifts her, first cradling then extending her before him. While her body rocks with ecstasy, she feels each beat of her heart.

He knows exactly what to say — he must have read her mind. "I'm here for you," he whispers. "I'll never let you go."

Sienna awoke in the bath, wet with more than lavender suds. Nearly insane with desire, she slipped her hand beneath the churning water. "Where are you?" she groaned, then her imagination went wilder than her fingers.

TOO MUCH TO DRINK

The hotel lounge overlooked the lobby. On the mezzanine level, Trainer sat at the mahogany bar trimmed with rails of polished brass. A row of glowing lanterns mirrored its length before advancing into the lavish nightclub. The barroom lanterns were placed so high they illuminated the vaulted ceiling more than the ground level surroundings. After two Martinis he switched to straight vermouth. Sipping the smooth liquor well after two in the morning, his thoughts bounced from Sienna to the convention he would be attending in three days. His presentation was slick and polished, saved on the hard drive of his laptop and stowed safely in his room. He had prepared a photo slideshow of his finest, most current achievements. He was certain he would receive the recognition he deserved.

Trainer wished Sienna would be accompanying him to Ontario. Dressed as counseled, she would turn heads, draw attention to him. And he was perfectly willing to share the limelight, if only she would fall in love with him.

Riding the elevator to the penthouse, he found their suite dimmed and silent. He quickly discarded his clothing on the carpet of the Great Room, then stumbled up the steps, passing the bedroom on his way to the bath. The robust steam shower, combined with gin and vermouth, invigorated his ego as well as libido.

Sienna slept partially on her side, hair a halo on a white satin pillowcase, angelic expression on her face. Standing over her,

Trainer detected a lavender scent. As he leaned closer, he inhaled the fragrance of delectable honey shampoo. He was drawn to her like a wolf to the wild.

"She's a vision," he murmured, his body still damp from the shower. The Turkish towel he had fastened around his waist dropped to the floor. He wouldn't disturb her, just slip soundlessly between the sheets to cuddle. He luxuriated in her softness, curling his body around hers. Her essence fired his senses. He rolled her onto her back, and smiled as a moan escaped her parted lips. *She wants me . . .* Pressing his heat against the side of her leg, he began to writhe rhythmically.

In a sensuous storm brewing between dream and reality, Sienna drifted upon waves of unconscious desire; but in reality, it was Trainer's lips covering hers, not her dream lover's. She responded by sleepily draping her arms around his upper back, pulling his face closer, returning his kiss with passion. Arching her back, she clung to him. As his hands traced her curves, a grunt caught in his throat, his heat tapping with the beat of his heart. Before she realized what was happening, the covers had been tossed to the floor along with her nightgown, and she lay deliciously naked in the glow of lamplight. Trainer, ready to mount her, nudged her thighs apart. She felt him, rigid and fumbling, but as her hips began to rock, something flashed across her mind and she sprang awake.

"Greg! What the *hell* are you doing?"

"What the hell do you think?" he panted. "Making love to you."

"You're more like *attacking* me! Get the hell off me." She squirmed beneath his weight.

"Nature is like a freight train thundering on rail. You can't stop it dead in its tracks," he slurred, his breath heavy upon her face.

She smelled the all too familiar aroma of liquor. "Stop it!" With more strength than she knew she possessed, she shifted her body, raised a knee, and shoved him to the other side of the bed. "I told you I didn't want this. This trip was supposed to be for business. You're drunk. Do you even know what you're doing?" Sickening memories of Rob tumbled through her mind. "This was a big mistake. I'm out of here!" She reached to the floor, grabbed the sheet, and wrapped herself like a mummy before jumping off the bed.

"I'm sorry, Sienna." Trainer was sobering. "You looked so beautiful and tranquil. I got carried away. Please don't be angry. Please don't leave." He gripped the pain in his crotch.

He would have to make it up to her tomorrow if he wanted to win her over. He hopped into his own bed and within moments was snoring.

"There goes *my* night's sleep," she muttered as she stumbled over a tangle of bed covers on her way to the Great Room. The plush sofa looked comfortable and inviting, but sleep was impossible. Hugging a blanket, she curled into a ball. Trainer had almost been inside of her! "Oh my God," she whispered into the cushion tucked beneath her chin, "I should have known better than to come here with him. It's my own fault. I'm partly responsible for this." Her stomach quivered, guilt creeping like a flush to her face. She was about to vow to be wiser, then realized she had a bad habit of breaking such vows. What was wrong with her?

As she waited for sleep, she tried to focus on something other than Trainer. Other than Rob. One thing was certain, she would never be a victim again. She'd proved that tonight.

"It's not our bedroom — it's my bedroom. We broke up months ago, or are you too drunk to remember?" Although she attempts to appear dominant, Sienna knows she sounds desperate. She wants to stare him down, conquer the demon of her nightmares, to face him with the heart full of hatred and pain his presence ignites, but her expression is far from threatening.

She watches his lips twitch, his jugular pulse with anger. Her strength begins to crumble, along with her legs. She can't believe he's back.

"Oh, God, Rob. I don't want to fight anymore. I just want you out of my life." It's almost impossible to match his stare as she bravely challenges him, repeating words she's said hundreds of times. "It's over."

"It's over when I say it is." Rage flushes his weathered Irish face, a stark contrast against the white creases hugging his boiling green eyes.

"I have an order of protection. If you don't leave, I'm calling the police."

He lunges for her. "I don't like threats. You want a threat? I'm gonna fucking kill you."

Sienna had grown accustomed to hit and run nightmares that struck and faded during the wee hours of the morning, disturbing what should have been restful sleep. Refusing medication, she had learned the natural way to avoid a panic attack. She sat up straight on the couch, hugging the blanket to her chest, and deeply inhaled calming breaths to slow the beat of her heart. After she stopped trembling, she snuggled against the sofa's padded back as if it were a warm body.

BARING IT IN LONDON

She awoke at sunrise, the outrage of the prior night momentarily shelved by the splendor of London. A world of historic architecture and cultural wealth awaited her. Shielding her eyes from daylight, she peered through the terrace doors. In the distance, a statue of Eros saluted the city with his bow. An aging double-decker chugged along the busy road, passing modest vehicles parked at the curb. She thought of her Connecticut condo parking lot, fraught with SUVs and dog-walkers.

Making her way to the bedroom, she tread softly. She snatched her robe from the chair, then spotted the tour booklet on the nightstand. Tiptoeing around the bed, she picked it up, leafing through the colorful pages, wondering how much of the city they would actually have time to see. Caught by the view outside, she crept from window to window, gasping at the beauty. Beyond the towers with spiked peaks and pitching rooftops, she could almost detect the layout of Piccadilly Circus with its neon signs. "So this is the renowned Piccadilly," she whispered with a smile of admiration, as if curtsying to the Queen herself.

From his bed Trainer yawned, stretched and grinned as he lifted his tousled head. "Good morning, dear. Did you sleep well?" His voice was groggy. "Do we have an analgesic handy? I feel like I've been kicked in the head by a mule."

Apparently, he recalled nothing of last night's fiasco — and she was more than happy to forget the incident. She was a big girl. She could handle herself. After all, she had been through worse. Knowing Trainer had been thoroughly intoxicated made it easier to excuse him.

If he tried anything else, she'd set him straight in a way he would never forget, and by the time they returned home he'd be tamed, as far as she was concerned.

"I slept fine." Eager to attend her first seminar, she shot him a look resembling a smile. If she wanted to become part of management, she would have to remain civil. She handed him two Ibuprofen and a glass of water.

"What's on the agenda for today?" she asked as she walked toward the upholstered bench that held her luggage. "What time does it start?"

"We'll be sightseeing first." He shot her a wary look. "Dress comfortably."

He slid from bed, wrapping the satin sheet around himself. His morning heat bulged beneath the slinky fabric. He headed straight to the bathroom, appearing befuddled as he limped.

Sienna opened her suitcase to an array of colorful fashions. "The seminar *is* starting today, right? she asked, holding up plum satin-stretch capris and matching bolero jacket, she called to him, "How's this for sightseeing?"

"Smashing," he shouted through the half-open bathroom door where he stood shaving. He poked his head around the doorway, a cheek lathered with foam. "Those pants will deliciously outline your hips, thighs and calves. What about a top?" With Trainer, everything had to fit into an aesthetically pleasing puzzle of flesh or fabric.

"A mauve tank top?" She sounded tired.

"Perfect, dear."

"Jet lag?" he said, continuing their room-to-room conversation. "Would you like to breakfast in our suite this morning? I'll call room service if you like."

"No," she replied, the bottom half of her body already clothed beneath her nightgown. "I'd rather eat in a nice restaurant."

In a rush to finish dressing before he returned to the room, she pulled the gown over her head. In shimmering low-rise capris and slip-on heels she stood topless, then bent at the waist to rummage through her luggage for the lacy tank top that would be an ideal match.

"Stop right there." Bare-chested, Trainer stood on the last marble step, a towel wrapped around his waist.

She hadn't heard him enter the room, and froze, folding her arms over her chest as she whipped around. "What's wrong?"

"Nothing is wrong. You're breathtaking is what's right."

She felt a flush and stiffened, hugging herself tighter. "Get out of here. I'm getting dressed."

"Lower your arms, darling. Let me see you in daylight. Don't feel shy."

A slice of morning flowing from the window dripped glitter in her hair, painting a diagonal stripe from shoulder to hip. Half of a creamy breast peeked from beneath an arm. Her throat was as tight as her reacting nipples.

This wasn't a hospital atmosphere where he could be his usual aggressive self — no clattering gurneys, no intrusive voices. They had never before been this intimate, never alone in a hotel room, no less a foreign country. She could startle like a delicate fawn in a forest. He would have to approach with caution.

In a moment, he was at her side. "You *are* perfection. Do you know that?" he said, gently tugging her wrists.

She had no idea why she released her hands, exposing her breasts, or why she let her arms drop protectively against the sides of her body.

Perhaps it was because she felt like she was dreaming, or had forgotten how it felt to be desired. Was it her ego?

"Damn it. You promised you wouldn't do this. We're here on business." Did he hear her gulp, or notice the goose bumps on her flesh as she stood before him, latex clinging to her hips, and nothing but cool London air covering her chest.

"We *are* here for business," he insisted, studying her. "I'm not touching you, I'm admiring you."

He rested his hands on her shoulders, urging her toward an alcove where she faced a mirrored wall. He unzipped her capris, then tugged them to her ankles.

"Look at yourself. You're beautiful. Chiseled features. Sculpted body. Beautiful women are my specialty, as you know. Do you see this?" he gestured to the obvious bump beneath his towel. "You've done this to me. I haven't felt this way in years, not since she . . ."

Was she feeling the rise of desire prompted by dreams? she asked herself. Because it certainly wasn't a result of Trainer's soft hands and eyes.

Her breasts were firm, the mid section of her body lean. Her slim waist curved gracefully into hourglass hips. What Rob had almost destroyed was struggling to resurface.

Trainer's stare drifted to the patch of blonde hair beneath her tummy, that grew into a perfect triangle. His face was unreadable when he said, "There's a spa downstairs. You should consider a Brazilian wax, dear."

She frowned, jerked up her capris and stomped to the bed.

He looked confused. "You should be proud of your natural body. Don't hide it."

"I *am* proud of my body. I'm just not used to walking around naked in front of men." She was furious with Trainer, and herself.

"I'm not just *any* man, Sienna."

"I know who are you."

"What are you — thirty?" He appeared immune to her sarcasm.

"It's none of your business," she snapped.

"No stretch marks, no sag. You've obviously taken care of yourself, never been stretched by pregnancy."

Speechless, she winced as he thoughtlessly continued his assessment of her body. She was stunned, confused that his advances were more clinical than sexual. If not for sex, what were his motives?

"With a glance, I can tell if a woman has been enhanced. I can expertly decipher nature from surgery, and when I cannot, then it must be the work of the gods, or an excellent surgeon — one in the same." He cocked his head and swung his palms into the air, strutting around the room, inspecting, then dropping his expensive clothing until he found the right outfit.

SO THAT'S WHAT MAKES HIM TICK

"**I**'m ready," Sienna's lips were tight. She attempted to behave as if Trainer had not just acted stranger than anyone she had ever met. She hoped deep breaths would settle her nerves, stave off the urge to gather her things and take the next flight home. *Bizarre,* was the only way to describe the experience.

She was angry with him, angry with Rob. She was also upset with Michael for hurting her in a way he more than likely didn't realize or intend. *Men!* Why did she let herself be put in these situations?

It had taken a lot to push her into this trip, including Bonnie's nagging, and she was not about to have it end without completing her mission. One way or another, she was going to rub elbows with the brass, get that promotion. "Most of the sights I'd like to see *before the seminar* are within walking distance of the hotel. These sandals should hold up nicely." She kept her voice steady, although there was a lump in her chest.

"You look stunning." Trainer checked his watch. "I also think we'll be having brunch instead of breakfast. Where did the morning go?"

"Brunch sounds good. Where?"

"Considering the time, right here at the hotel is fine with me. Is it good for you?"

"I guess so. Half the day's already gone."

"I have to confess. The seminar begins on Monday."

She glared at him. "Are you serious?"

"Don't be angry, dear. I wanted to surprise you. Show you the city . . ."

The day was perfect for terrace dining. They sat beneath an awning, at a white clothed bistro table that held a bouquet of red roses secured in an ebony vase. A spray of sunshine streamed across her face, painting her porcelain.

Trainer's eyes were shaded by dark lenses, protecting his sensitive irises. When he lifted his sunglasses to read the travel brochure, his eyes brightened in color, matching his open-neck emerald shirt.

She had to admit he looked handsome . . . in a worldly way, not rugged . . . sun-bleached shag usually sprayed into place, now casually framing his face.

"What would you like to see first?" he asked, sipping a cranberry juice cocktail the waiter set before him.

"The Thames, I guess. I saw it in the brochure this morning, and the Eye looks interesting." She sounded deflated.

"I assumed that," he said with a wink, "so I purchased these." He fanned the air with two tickets for The London Eye. "Private capsule, Lenore."

Wait a minute . . . Had he called her Lenore? *Who the hell is Lenore?* Sienna stared at him, wide-eyed. "Greg . . ." she was cautious, as if he might at any moment explode. "What did you mean this morning at the hotel about not feeling the same since — she? Who is *she?* Why did you just call me Lenore?"

His expression fell from pre-programmed machine into a mask of human frailty.

"You look pale. Are you alright?"

Rays of sun dipping beneath the canopy accentuated fine lines around his eyes and mouth. Sienna wondered what caused the melancholy that suddenly overtook the cool and confident doctor.

"It's been so long. I'd rather not discuss it now." His face looked strained, a frown tightening more effectively than Botox.

"It's *me* you're talking to. If I can stand naked before you, you can certainly confide in me. What could be so terrible to change your mood so drastically?" The tables had turned. Sienna now perched on the peak of the pyramid, speaking to Trainer as if he were an adolescent who was not leaving the table until he presented a plausible explanation.

Sighing, he looked out over the city, then faced her. "If you must know, I was referring to my wife."

"You never mentioned you were married. Are you divorced?" Great, stuck in London with a married man who tried to attack me. Lied to me. What next?

"No, she passed away over twenty years ago."

"I'm sorry." Watching Trainer crumble was startling.

"I've never told anyone at the hospital about this." He rolled his glass between the palms of his hands as he stared into the distance. "I was a doctor, unable to help my own wife. She was so young . . ."

"It must have been terrible for you." She reached across the table for his hand, placing it between hers. "What happened?"

"You know the saying: wrong place, wrong time?"

Sienna nodded, trying not to appear stunned, but could not hide confusion.

"A sick bastard, filled with hatred," his face was lined, "ended more than one dancer's life."

"Dear, Lord." She was witnessing a defeated man baring his soul.

"Ruled as arson, but I call it cold-blooded murder. She was barely alive when the ambulance brought her in. We did all we could." He lowered his head.

The pain on his face was contagious. Sienna was close to tears.

"She was horribly disfigured by the explosion. Had she lived, I would have made her whole again, as perfect and as beautiful as the day we met."

"And in all this time you've never moved on." She considered her own tragic history, how difficult it was to find closure."You must have loved her so much." She shrugged off bitterness; love wasn't the reason she had not moved on.

"Lenore was my world. We grew into adulthood together, certain we'd grow old together. I met her while I was in medical school." He twisted a ring on his right hand, staring at the ruby set in gold. "We met in San Francisco, the summer she was the lead in her company. I was on a short break. She was a vibrant young woman." His eyes clouded with a determined look, chilling Sienna when he stared deeply into hers and said, "Some individuals do not handle loss well. Some find a way to win, at any cost."

Was he trying to tell her something? She broke from his stare.

"Lenore was everything to me. Life without her was never the same — until I met you."

Until he met me? His confession shocked Sienna, as did his sudden transformation.

"I'm sorry this happened to you. I know what it's like to lose someone."

Reaching across the table, he took her hand. "I'll not lose again. Let's not let this ruin our time here." A wild look in his eyes, he disregarded her words of comfort and without warning, reverted to Greg Trainer extraordinaire. "Back to the Thames. An evening cruise, see the lights of the city. London nights are magnificent. But today we ride the Observation Wheel. It's breathtaking. You can view the entire city from the elevation, even the Queen's backyard garden." He smiled. "I hope you brought your camera."

She tilted her head and studied him. He seemed capable of turning his emotions on and off like one of his pulse lights.

This is insane. What was I thinking?

"And I brought along these." Reaching into his blazer pocket, he dangled a pair of folding binoculars. "We'll see everything, darling, together."

"We won't be needing them." She stared him down.

"What are you talking about, Sienna?"

"I'm moving to another hotel. Attending the seminar on Monday. And then I'm going home."

BFF BONNIE

$\mathbf{M}$ichael awoke to an early morning thunderstorm. Along with a flash of lightning, a cawing crow sailed past his open bedroom window, followed by the furious flutter of sparrow wings. As quickly as they arrived, the birds absconded to the shelter of foliage behind the cottage like feathered jets disappearing into cloud-driven skies.

The wind was strong. Rain pelted the roof . . . tranquilizing. He'd stay in bed a while longer, snuggled beneath the covers, thinking.

It was Tuesday. He would grab a cup of coffee and hang out beneath Dyson's awning, have a gabfest with friends. She would usually arrive around noon. He would greet her with a smile, ask how she was doing on this gloomy day, draw out the conversation so he could learn more about her. Sienna was a mystery he would never be able to solve, not without her cooperation. He had no idea whether or not she'd participate, but it was a gamble he had to take.

By the time one p.m. rolled around, Michael had consumed three cups of coffee and a turkey club from the deli. She's not coming, he thought. Another letdown.

He hadn't seen her in days. He wondered where she was and what she was doing. He wanted to be with her, wanted to talk to her, not tomorrow or the next day — now. Do I even remember how to flirt with a woman? The thought was humiliating. He was being foolish. She barely noticed him.

His pre-testing appointment was scheduled for two o'clock. If he were going to be on time, he would have to leave the plaza immediately. He had to tear himself away, wondering if her schedule had changed, if she would show a bit later than usual.

On the drive to Manchester General, he wondered why he had agreed to the MRI and other scans, as he had not given Dr. Pollock a definitive answer. Surgery was not something he wanted to think about today. He'd much rather think about her, which was what he did the entire time he lay inside the capsule, tuning out the loud buzz and clang of the ticking machine that usually gave him a headache.

"Okay, Mr. Chessler," the technician said. "All finished." She helped him off the table and into his chair. "Dr. Pollock should have the results soon."

"Thanks, Deborah. Should I call Grace to set up an appointment?"

"You could, or they'll phone you when the results are in."

"Right. Well, have a nice afternoon." He checked his watch. Two hours had flown by, "Or what's left of it." A smile slid across his face. "End of the day for you?"

"I should be so lucky," Deborah said. She pulled the door open and with a shoulder, held it for him. "I'm on until eight."

Michael figured he would be back in about a week. No doubt Pollock would say his vertebrae looked the same. Why should these tests matter? Why did he bother to have them? Nothing had changed since his last workup and experimental therapy in L.A. Now Pollock wanted to do his own evaluation, and even though Michael was uncertain of how he would proceed, he would humor him, but spare the hope.

He left the ground floor lab, heading for the exit ramp. Why not? he told himself. Maybe she worked today and that was why she didn't show up at the plaza. Maybe he could catch a glimpse of her sitting at her desk. She wouldn't notice him as he quietly slipped by. He needed a fix. Just laying eyes upon her would be enough. He would be too tongue-tied to speak, even if she raised her head and smiled. Although she had no way of knowing what went on inside his mind, his thoughts and dreams of her were vivid enough to make him anxious in her presence. Imagine if she knew? What would she think of him?

The craving was too powerful. He couldn't leave the hospital just yet, not until he stopped by E.R. Registration, not until he saw her. Decision made, he turned in the direction of Sienna's office. What reason could he give for being there? *Oh, hi — I've just had an x-ray of my broken back and figured I'd drop by to say* hey? That would entice any woman, wouldn't it? It was four o'clock. She would more than likely be gone by now or possibly ready to leave. He wouldn't want to disturb her, or worse yet, run into her while wandering the hospital corridors. Not cool. He was just about to swing around and head back toward the exit when he heard her.

"Hey there." It was a woman's cheerful voice, high-pitched but pleasant. "Anything I can do to help, like direct you or something?"

Bonnie could be so helpful — at the wrong times.

Who is she? Michael wondered as he turned. "Hello," he said. "No thanks. I'm just heading out."

Then it hit him. She had been with Sienna that day in the cafeteria.

"The elevator's the other way." She pointed down the winding corridor. "You're headed for the business offices." Her smile was never-ending. "Hey, have I seen you around here? I never forget a handsome face." She fell into step beside him.

"Um — I'm always around here. Maybe the cafeteria?" Michael remembered her balancing a cup of coffee and a Danish as she and Sienna passed him and Pollock. His heart skipped a beat.

"Oh sure, that day with Sienna. Now I remember." Did she just put her foot in her mouth? How would Sienna feel about her talking to this guy, who, from what Sienna had told her about their grapefruit incident, was obviously smitten or on the verge?

"Sienna?" He feigned surprise, as if to communicate, *who is she?*

"Oh, I thought you two knew each other. I just took it for granted because she told me . . ."

She had told her about him? His interest in this talkative redhead spiked.

"She told you? What did she tell you?" He couldn't help but grin as he felt an instant boost of camaraderie, then felt guilty for using this woman to get to Sienna.

"Oh nothing really, just that you helped her out when she dropped her groceries. It was nice of you."

"By the way, I'm Michael Chessler."

"Bonnie Murray, Sienna's best friend. Well, we work together in E.R. Registration, but we are definitely, BFF's." She flashed her toothy grin.

"So do you see her often?"

"Not often enough." He couldn't believe he was tipping his hand, and decided he might as well go all out. "Where is she? Have you seen her today?"

"They're in London at that conven …"She sucked in a breath.

"London?" They? The smile on his face sank, along with his heart.

He watched her eyes soften. She apparently felt bad for breaking the news to him. Then her jaw set and he sensed she was trying to convince herself she'd done the right thing. He agreed.

"She'll be back in a few days. I'm sure you'll run into her." She acted giddy, like someone concealing discomfort. "Maybe you shouldn't mention London if you see her, okay?" When they reached the elevator, she lunged for the call button.

"Don't worry, I won't." He looked past her, avoiding the unremarkable faces of other riders.

They rode in silence. Michael left the hospital wondering why he hadn't flat out asked if she was in a serious relationship. Obviously, he didn't want to know the answer.

THE FLIGHT HOME AND BONNIE

Declining the generous offer to use the Gulfstream, Sienna booked a seat on a commercial flight back to the USA. Trainer would take advantage of its availability and jet to Ontario, privately.

They said a cordial good-bye at British Airways terminal.

"I'll miss you," he whispered, giving her a bear hug and peck on the cheek.

"I'll see you at the hospital." With tilted head she stared into his eyes. "Friends. You know that's all we'll ever be . . ."

"See you in a few days." He patted her arm. "Have a good flight."

She watched him sprint off with his briefcase in his arms, his laptop pressed against his heart. She had to admit, regardless of what he had done, she felt a pang of sorrow.

On the flight home, she analyzed the past three days: London, Trainer, the success of the seminar she'd attended alone, then thought of what awaited her at home. Overwhelmed, she shut off her mind by discreetly watching a middle-aged couple who sat across the aisle. The woman's hand rested on the man's hand, which rested on the arm of his seat. Her head was turned in his direction, while his ears were covered by a headset.

Finishing a glass of ginger ale, Sienna pressed into the seat and closed her eyes, not wanting ever to be the woman who loved a man who enjoyed music more than her company.

The flight home was entirely different from the flight to

London; the 757 was crowded and noisy. There was no hot-looking personal attendant serving champagne, no Trainer to exhibit romantic gestures, no soothing sax of Kenny G. The commercial airliner did, however, offer a movie and microwave meal, along with disturbing bouts of turbulence.

During her stay in London, she had not had much time to think of Connecticut, the hospital, her condo, but she had thought of Michael. She wondered why he kept popping into her mind. He had a way of making her feel whole, maybe that was it — or maybe it was the way she felt when she looked into those deep brown eyes faceted with gold, reminding her of gemstones. As she drifted to sleep, she wondered if they'd meet again.

Sienna arrived at JFK at six a.m., and boarded a commuter flight to Bradley where she was met by a cranky Bonnie who had to drop her off at home and get to work on time.

"Oh, I missed you," Bonnie said as she ran toward Sienna, the moment her feet hit the tarmac. She tackled her.

"I missed you too. You didn't have to meet me, Bonnie. I could have taken a taxi home." Sienna yawned; already feeling the effect of jet lag, her eyelids drooped.

"No buddy of mine is met at an airport by a cab. Besides, the Durango wouldn't hear of it." Bonnie chuckled as they walked to the baggage area.

"You don't know how much I appreciate it. I brought you a surprise."

"Ooh, what is it?"

"You'll see later. I'm not sure which bag I packed it in." Bonnie's perfume reminded Sienna of the office. Her stomach clenched.

"No wonder. How much stuff did you bring? Holy crap, look at all these bags."

Bonnie grabbed the heaviest pieces of luggage and hauled them off, Sienna beside her with an overnighter, vanity case, and garment bag.

"So how was your flight? How was London? How was Trainer?" Bonnie bubbled with questions, surprisingly alert and energetic for pre-dawn.

"Flying home wasn't as bad as I thought it would be. London was wonderful, more fantastic than I could ever have imagined. And Greg was — we didn't spend much time together. I saw so many places in three days, though. I was flabbergasted. London is absolutely fascinating," she breathlessly described, flashbacks of the trip revving her footsteps. "Getaways are great, but so is coming home."

"How was the seminar?"

Sienna's eyes shifted. "Trainer kinda went his way, and I went mine. The stuffed shirts stick together, you know? But all and all it went fine. Anyway . . . I can't wait to take a shower in my own bathroom and fall into my own bed."

"I'm happy things went well. I know this is gonna pay off." Bonnie gave her an exhilarated nudge. "You look beat. Didn't you sleep on the plane?"

"A bit, but . . ."

"Let me guess. You had a dream. Even in another country, Sienna?" Bonnie clicked her tongue. "What's up with you and this crap? Leading a double life I don't know about?"

Sienna laughed. "You know I tell you everything."

The airport felt far too big in early morning repose: no check-in lines, gates pulled down over shop entrances. No bustling travelers rushing about, just a trickle of frequent flyers pulling bags, some with totes slung over shoulders. Still, staff seemed to be gearing up for the usual onslaught of commuters, striding to their stations with coffee cups in hand.

On their way to the parking lot, Sienna and Bonnie stepped around puddles of the prior night's rain. The sky tried to kindle with sun. Patches of ground fog parted for them, dissipating as they passed.

"It's going to be hot today," Sienna said, "could this be summer? London was cooler, damper." She yawned again. "I'm exhausted. I'm gonna rest my eyes for a few . . ."

"Forget the weather — and no! You cannot nap, unless you plan on talking in your sleep," Bonnie said as Sienna slid into the Durango's soft bucket seat.

"And speaking of telling me everything," Bonnie rambled, thumping her way to the back of the Durango where her voice echoed from inside the cargo area as she stowed the luggage.

Sienna heard the tailgate slam shut, and Bonnie climbed into the driver's seat, still chattering, "I saw a friend of yours the other day."

"Who?" Sienna snapped the buckle of her seatbelt shut.

"Oh, that Michael Chessler guy. He was at the hospital again." Bonnie said nonchalantly, turning onto the highway.

Sienna's head snapped to face Bonnie's profile, which at the moment looked stiff and uneasy. "Michael Chessler?"

"Yeah, the guy you told me about from the plaza, remember?"

"Of course I remember."

"I could've sworn he was on his way to our office when I caught him in the corridor."

"What do you mean, *caught* him in the corridor?" Shocked awake, Sienna's tone sharpened. "What's this all about, Bonnie? What did you say to him? Look at me."

"I can't look at you. I'm driving."

"Damn it, Bonnie." Sienna sucked in a breath and stared.

"I just — I mean he was — I asked him if I could —"

"What are you stammering about? What did you do? Did you tell him anything I said about him?"

"Well, no. Not really."

"What do you mean, not really?"

"Just that you were in London, but I didn't tell him who you were with. He's too sweet to play games with, Sienna."

"Who's playing games? I met him a few times, casually, that's it!"

"He likes you."

"He apparently likes stocky brunettes too."

"What are you talking about?" Bonnie's head spun.

"I ran into him after our shopping trip. At the Plaza Restaurant." She made a sour face. "He appeared to be on a double date."

"Did you go over and talk to him?"

"What are you crazy?" Sienna shook her head.

"So how do you know it was a date? Always get your evidence when it's available."

"Whatever. Like I said, we've only run into each other a few times. Finish telling me about the hospital."

"Well first of all, I know he must have been on his way to our office when I saw him kind of wandering around the hall, so I asked him if he needed help."

"And?"

"We got to talking — sort of — and your name came up and his face immediately lit up. He has the greatest eyes. I thought brown and gold meant hazel, like Mickey's. But his have green specks in them too. Now I personally know what you meant by magnetism."

The thought of staring into Michael's eyes sent chills through Sienna. His easy grin, inviting arms, were enough to melt her heart. Not to mention, his warm lap.

"Maybe we were wrong about Persha," Bonnie said, lips tightening. "I mean Rob talking through Persha. Oh my God, imagine if she meant you're supposed to be with Michael Chessler?" Hands tightening on the steering wheel, Bonnie shook her head.

"Why are you telling me this? You're upsetting me." Sienna faced the window without paying much attention to passing vehicles, or the sun beginning to rise over a post and rail pasture of golden mares with pure white manes.

"Let's not jump to conclusions." Bonnie's voice calmed. "He's in a wheelchair, remember?"

"So what! Tell me again, what did he say about me?" Sienna turned to face Bonnie who seemed happy she had the road to concentrate on, along with her story.

"It wasn't *what* he said, it was how he looked when I mentioned your name."

"Like?" Sienna tried to form a mental image.

"I don't know. Like a kid waiting for Christmas. Something like that. He beamed when I said it was nice of him to help you out. Oh, I don't know, Sienna. Why don't you just find out for yourself? Talk to him. See how you feel. There's something about him. He's teddy bear adorable."

"I know that, Bonnie. I'm not blind or emotionless."

"Maybe he doesn't believe you'd really go for a guy like him."

"What do you mean?"

"You know . . . In his situation, wheelchair and all . . ."

"God. I'm sick of hearing you say that. When I look at him, I don't see the chair . . ."

"Why aren't we talking about the trip?" Bonnie's eyes narrowed. "I have a feeling you're avoiding . . . Did you have sex with Trainer? Did he propose or something and you're keeping it a secret?"

"Are you kidding me?" Sienna said, too tired to do anything but roll her eyes. "Not that he didn't try very hard. And I emphasize hard."

"Wow. How's he look naked?"

"Did I ever ask you how Mickey looks naked?"

Bonnie laughed. "Okay — you've got me there. So what about the sex? Why didn't you?"

"Are you serious? Plus he was smashed out of his mind. He spent half the night at the bar."

"So, what happened? Don't leave me hanging."

The Durango sped along the dawning highway, the wipers intermittently swiping condensation from the windshield. Each time their breath clouded the interior windows, Bonnie snapped on the defroster.

"Not sure I should spread gossip about a doctor's privates."

"Come on, you little bitch. You said you'd tell me everything, so give. How did Trainer come on to you? Oh, this is so romantic."

"No it isn't. He gave me a full body exam, without his hands. And it was clinical."

"What do you mean full body exam? And he didn't touch you?

You're different, Sienna. Trainer brought you out of your shell over there. You had sex with him, didn't you."

"Okay, he had sex with me."

"I knew it. I told you you were horny —"

"With his eyes. I didn't participate."

"He had sex with you with his eyes? Okay. I give up. What, did you both come while you just stared at each other? I have to try that with Mickey." Bonnie guffawed, struggling to maneuver through rush hour traffic. "Next time he wants to get laid I'll tell him we'll take off our clothes and just stand there staring at each other, that we're having sex." She laughed so hard she coughed.

Sienna turned serious. "What did Michael say when you told him I was in London?"

"Nothing, he looked upset and left."

A PROMISING BEGINNING — FINALLY

After a shower, Sienna crawled into bed, curling up peacefully between percale sheets. Too warm for even a lightweight blanket, she tossed the covers aside, stretched out on her back in a T- shirt and panties, and let herself sink into memory foam. For once she didn't toss and turn; thoughts of the conversation during the ride home from the airport, and Bonnie's description of Michael's reaction to her absence, were sedating.

With most residents at work, the condo was quiet. The whir of lawn sprinklers beyond the bedroom window was a perfect backdrop for slumber. Morning collided with noon, sunlight bursting into the room, rousting Sienna from a deep sleep.

The dreamless sleep had been refreshing, but she took a second shower anyway. Wrapped in a towel, she wiped steam from the mirror and stared at her spotless complexion, rosy and moist. While brushing her teeth, her stomach growled with hunger. Emerging from the bathroom, she patted her gurgling midsection, thinking about breakfast . . . then realized she should be considering lunch — or dinner, had she still been on London time. She sighed.

The kitchen cabinets were empty. Knowing she would be away, Sienna hadn't shopped before the trip. There was nothing in the refrigerator either. She thought of the plaza — and of him. Since their first meeting, the plaza would always be special, as if it were "their place." Silly . . .

Sliding into a pair of denim shorts, pink T-shirt and flip flops, she left with her damp hair picked straight to her shoulders and beginning to curl as it dried in the heat of the day.

Sienna parked near Dyson's. She might as well drop off her London garb before grocery shopping. When she opened the car door, she spotted a bronze dress tossed across the back seat. Struck with nostalgia, she wondered how Trainer was doing at the convention. Had he given his presentation? Would he call her later? She placed the satin dress carefully on top of the mound of clothing to be cleaned. Dyson would surely have something to say, or think, when he ticketed her provocative garments.

Arms loaded with folded fabrics, she left the Corolla with a chirp of her key fob, and hurried across the parking lot. As she stepped onto the curb, her bronze dress slipped from the rest, gliding gracefully toward the ground like a slinky kite in a breeze. *Oh no, here we go again . . .* Bent at the knee, clutching the other garments closely to her chest, she tried to catch the dress before it dropped to the sidewalk.

On his way through the arcade separating Dyson's and the coffee shop, Michael saw the scene unfold. He remembered their first meeting, almost at that very spot, and here she was, struggling once again. He shook his head, but didn't grin. She sure was a klutz. He considered rushing over to help her, then remembered London.

From the corner of her eye, she noticed him. Her mind raced through a list of interesting things to begin conversation. As Bonnie had said, "Take a chance."

"Hey there." His voice was cool. "How's it going?"

He passed with a nod, disappearing into the UPS store two doors away. Her stomach dropped, along with her jaw. Was he blowing her off again? She hunkered down and began picking up her things. Muttering to herself, even more items fell from her grip.

Within moments he emerged from the store, a teen at his side, mouth and hands moving faster than the wheels of Michael's chair. Michael stared straight ahead, avoiding Sienna who strained to hear their conversation.

"Talk to her," Leo said. "You may never get this chance again, especially if there's another guy after her. Hey, all's fair . . ."

"Look, Leo. I know you mean well, but it just wouldn't work."

Michael felt more inadequate at that moment than the first time he left the hospital in a wheelchair. Just the sight of her would have weakened his legs, had he been able to stand. Seeing her struggling with her garments, he relented and headed toward her.

"Need a hand?" he asked, unable to smile.

"Sure." Her reply was soft. Sunshine on her shoulders, she tilted her head upward, squinting. Fortunately the glare obscured her view; she wouldn't have to look him square in the face, gaze into those dreamy eyes. Her stomach tightened, she hoped the tension she felt didn't blow her cool. What cool?

"Hey. Let me give you guys a hand." Leo began picking up the clothing.

Sienna remained crouched above the sidewalk, the striking flex of her muscles enhanced by the sun. She'd remain in that position, regaining composure, until she absolutely had to move.

"Thank you," she said, then faced Michael.

She flipped strands of hair into place with a toss of her head, avoiding his eyes. "How are you?"

"I'm good," he said, grasping the bronze dress he had snatched from the walk. "This is pretty. I like the color. It matches you . . ."

"It matches me?"

He shifted his gaze. "You know, your tan, your coloring."

"I think I overloaded myself, yet again."

She watched his hands clutch the dress and tingled as if he were touching her, holding her almost as tightly as he now gripped the satin fabric.

"I see that. Guess you took on more than you could handle." His voice was as tight as the swallow rippling his throat. "Day off today? Cleaning out closets?" His expression was difficult to read.

"Just running a few errands." She was level with his eyes. Her knees ached as she perched above the walk.

When the dress passed from his hands to hers, a familiar fragrance filled the air. For a moment their fingers touched, their eyes met and held. His were smoky. Hers felt the fire.

He was losing concentration. Did she sense it?

Leo's attention fixed momentarily on a brunette touring the lot in a shiny black BMW. When the car disappeared from sight his interest settled on the definition of Sienna's legs. Perfect opportunity . . .

"By the way, I'm Leo." He stuck out a hand, first wiping the palm on the pocket of his khaki shorts. "Any friend of Michael's is a friend of mine."

"Nice to meet you. I'm Sienna."

"Do you work out?"

"What?"

"Your biceps and quads are well-toned. Nice form."

Tension broken, Sienna laughed. As she stood, her knees creaked.

Shaking his head, Michael whispered, "Here it comes."

"Tight calves too. Turn around, let me see your hamstrings."

"Leo!" Michael shot him a look. "I think the lady needs to drop off her dry cleaning."

"It's okay," she said, a surprised look coiling into a smile. "Thank you for the compliments, Leo. I try to work out regularly, but unfortunately, not as often as I should. I was in pretty good shape while I was taking self defense classes. But that was a while ago."

Michael ran a hand across his chin.

"You know how to fight?" Leo's bright green eyes widened. "Very cool." He shifted his gaze to Michael who was motionless; his face growing rosier each time Leo opened his mouth.

"Sort of, well I only took a few classes. Barely enough to. . ."

"Sweet. Show me some moves."

Clowning with men wasn't like her, but she shocked herself by striking a menacing pose while balancing her dry cleaning on a hip.

Leo jumped back, mimicking her.

"Not exactly Karate, but intimidating?" She scrunched her nose. Some of her hair spilled over a shoulder, the rest tucked back, glistening in the sun.

"Yeah." Leo drew out the word, running a hand over his crew cut, doing a side-step.

"I hope so." She grinned. "I'd really hate to face a mugger and have him laugh at me. Although maybe that would work in my favor." Her eyes shifted to Michael.

He watched her thrash the air with a few playful Karate chops. *She has it all. What am I doing here?*

"Remind me not to mess with you," he said, his smile so stiff it could have been a grimace.

"Hey, Sienna. Why don't you come to the gym with me and Michael? We were just getting ready to go."

Michael didn't look happy with Leo. "Oh, sure, Fitness and Fury, right, I almost forgot. Thanks for reminding me, but I didn't bring my gym clothes with me."

"That's okay," said Leo. "You guys can treadmill, um, or eat lunch, I mean while I lift, or do whatever you want." His words gave way to the kind of smile he flashed when talking about a hot girl. The kid seemed to enjoy playing matchmaker.

Michael cocked his head and shrugged, studied Sienna.

Her brow arched. She tilted her head, looking at him as if to ask, do you want company?

"Would you like to join us?" His voice sounded higher than usual. His heart rate increased again. He took a breath. *Damn, this is becoming annoying.* He'd have to learn to control himself if he were going to be spending time with her. His heart beat even faster . . .

Without hesitating, she said, "I'd like that. I really would. Let me drop these things off. I'll be right out. Wait for me." Without batting a lash she flashed a cute, wide-eyed pout.

"You know it," Leo said.

"We'll wait." Michael smiled. "Take your time." He let out a deep breath as she rushed into Dyson's. "She's really something, isn't she?"

"F'n ay." Leo whistled, dancing around the wheelchair like a boxer. "Was that so hard?"

"For once I appreciate your audacity, and your big mouth. You can stop punching me now." Michael smoothed his hair into place and straightened the collar of his sport shirt. "I'm surprised she said yes. Do I look okay?"

"Yeah, you look real cute. Why are you surprised she'd like you? You're cool. I told you that already, but listen, follow my lead, you gotta learn how to handle these things. She's into you, dude, I can tell. Just stay cool."

"She's into me, huh?" Michael's pulse began to race faster than his thoughts. "Yeah, but I told you she just got back from London with," he couldn't say the name, "or did you forget? Maybe this isn't the greatest idea. Take it easy, okay?"

"I know what you're thinking. Don't worry about the other guy. I saw her face when she looked at you. She wouldn't smile like that if she was into him. Trust me, I know all the signals. Plus she wouldn't be coming with us. You think she's coming for me?" Leo slammed his chest once with a palm and stared at Michael, a goofy look on his face.

"I would hope not. Hey, I caught those gestures you were making." Michael chuckled, shaking his head. "I hope *she* didn't notice."

"So I have ticks." Leo laughed so hard he began to cough, then hiccupped loudly.

Sienna returned, smiling. No one would guess her stomach was filled with butterflies.

"All set?" said Michael.

"Yup. I'm ready, and hungry. I haven't eaten since last night." She watched his lips shrink, fading from pink to white.

"So I guess I'll follow you with my car?"

"Why don't you come with us. My ride's behind the plaza. I work here, have you seen me around?" Leo was like a sheepherder, corralling his flock.

"I think so," she said.

NATURE TAKING ITS COURSE

The Volvo departed Oak Haven Plaza, Leo and Michael in the front, Sienna in the back. Leo played the radio low so they could talk as he drove the short distance to Fitness and Fury. She shoved Leo's backpack aside and relaxed against the door, seated directly behind him.

While the vehicle moved with a steady line of traffic, she analyzed them, not more than three feet away, their heads like bobble-head dolls moving with bumps in the road. She could watch Michael freely, stare at every visible part of his features as he moved and occasionally turned to glance at her with a quick smile. She drank in every angle. His profile was stunning: smooth skin, sprinkling of beard from sideburn to chin, arched brow and densely lashed lid. She had never noticed the slight bump on the bridge of his nose, imparting a ruggedness. Rugged in bed. . . The thought was enough to make her body tingle. She had wanted to study him other times and now that she had the opportunity, found looking wasn't enough.

As Leo shifted gears, she watched his shoulders and arms stretch. A typical teen he was lanky, unlike Michael, whose neck was thick and enticed, shoulders broad, filling the width of his shirt, and her head with ideas. His right forearm, sinewy beneath a rolled up sleeve, rested on the curved door panel, window half open, his fingers tapping now and then. How would that muscular arm feel around her?

She listened to the hum of tires drowning their voices, then the side of Leo's face turned slightly toward her.

"Is the wind bothering you? I can close my window if you like."

"I'm fine. I'm enjoying being chauffeured."

She should be riding up front, crossed Michael's mind, but he'd never be able to sink easily into the back seat, no less be hauled out by Leo, especially with her eyes upon him.

She saw three-quarters of Michael's face when he swung his head, chin pressed to shoulder.

"How are you doing back there?" he said in a gentle voice.

Ears flooded with wind, humming tires, and loud diesel engine, she strained to hear, reading his lips, and his face, which looked apologetic.

He smiled, his voice deepening. "This isn't the best place for conversation."

Sienna rode with a hand holding back one side of her hair, strands occasionally flicking across her face, tickling her nose. Smiling, she shrugged, and again stared at the back of Michael's head when he turned, his windblown hair so inviting.

Once inside Fitness and Fury, Leo strode straight to free weights and acquaintances in various workout stages. Michael and Sienna settled at a corner table in the adjoining café. Through the club's court glass wall, they could watch Leo and the others pumping iron, glistening with perspiration.

Charcoal liner and black mascara warmed Sienna's eyes, but sitting across from Michael set the blue on fire.

Michael wouldn't have to close his eyes to imagine her. She was real, she was close, she was stunning. Glistening locks of hair framing her oval face covered her shoulders; her sun-toasted features looked porcelain, painting her angelic.

Sienna stole glances as she slung her shoulder bag over the back of a chair. Had they been together in moonlight, she might have thrown herself into his arms. She controlled her face, her body, her emotions, but her eyes gave her away as she leaned back with a frozen stare.

Fearing awkward silence could risk everything, she took a breath and blurted the first thing to come to mind, "He's cute." While her mind raced, she busied her hands by rolling the edge of a napkin in her fingers, peering into the gym through the rippled court glass. She leaned forward to get a better view, hands now clutched in her lap, neck craned, midriff pressed against the edge of the table; the picture of perfect posture. With each graceful movement, her fruity fragrance made its way to Michael, already entranced by the unexpected pleasure of sitting across from the woman of his dreams.

As Sienna focused on Leo, Michael concentrated on her: her creamy neck contoured by taut tendons, long and inviting; her tank top, snagged by one shoulder, unveiled a hint of cleavage, leaving the magnitude of her breasts to be imagined. A faint outline of a lacy bra beneath the knit fabric did nothing to conceal her femininity.

Michael couldn't have cared less about Leo, who was laid out on a bench, knees rounded, sneakers flat to the floor, struggling with a barbell. Or the two jacked-up spotters who guarded either side of his young friend, exhorting and coaching. Snagged. . . Sienna caught him staring, and they both blushed. She looked away.

Michael was sure his desire was evident. If he didn't clear his expression quickly, she'd return her focus and be shocked by his gaping face strained with desire.

Michael picked up a menu, flipping plastic pages. "Good thing they don't serve alcohol here."

Her jaw dropped. "I have to apologize for that night. I'm mortified."

"I wasn't sure you'd remember." His grin endured.

"Haven't forgotten yet." She tried to laugh.

The look on her face told him to change the subject. "Leo's taken with you."

"Teenage crush?"

"Just a guy thing, I guess."

She laughed.

"You're athletic?"

"I play tennis now and then, if you want to call that athletic."

"Ah." He smiled.

"Did you used to? I'm sorry . . ."

"Don't worry about it. I've been asked worse." His brows tightened.

"People can be cruel, I guess, which is why I love animals."

"You've got a point there." He looked across the café, then refocused on her. "I played a lot of sports in high school and in college. I used to ski, hike, bowl on a league." He smiled. "You name it, I probably tried it. So, what else do you like to do besides playing tennis and soliciting homes for strays?"

She looked thoughtful. "Dance."

He sobered, then asked, "What are your pets like? You must have a houseful, huh?"

"Just two cats. Frazzle and Dazzle," her eyes darted to the wall clock, "who I should be picking up shortly. They've been staying with a friend."

"Frazzle and Dazzle." He laughed. "How did you come up with those names?"

"I brought Dazzle home as a kitten. She's a white ball of fur, beautiful long-haired, soft and sweet. She loves to cuddle. She dazzled me." With an innocent face, she shrugged.

He watched her intently, his smile growing broader as she spoke. "And Frazzle?"

"There was the cutest little guy at the shelter, who I brought home as a surprise for a neighbor. I had been rushing around that day. My hair was wild, my face all red. I guess I looked like a train wreck. When I rang the doorbell, Mary took one look at me, and said, 'Sienna, what have you been doing? You look absolutely frazzled.' When I held out the orange kitten, and told her he was hers, her mouth almost dropped. She loved him, but her husband's allergic to cats. So, I took him home, and called him Frazzle."

"That's adorable. Your cats sound like something else."

"They're something else alright, especially Frazzle. He's a sleek and aloof calico climber. And Dazzle is a clinger. She loves to hang all over me, licking, purring. Their dispositions are entirely opposite."

"Ah, that's a cute story. I bet they're good company."

"The best. So when are you coming down to get yours?" She raised a brow and smiled.

He laughed. "Leo comes around a lot. He's like a pet."

"He seems like a great companion, too. And he can take care of himself." She chuckled.

"I leave food and soda out for him." Still laughing, he added, "Yeah, he's a good kid. When he delivers my groceries we have some very interesting, not to mention amusing conversations." He rolled his eyes.

Leaning back, Sienna gave his face her full attention. "It's really nice that you're so close, Michael."

It was the first time she had called him by name. He liked the way she said it, soft and provocative. It had never sounded so appealing, so personal.

"What would you like to eat?" he asked, avoiding those sapphire eyes that could easily derail his concentration.

"Hmm," she mouthed with lovely pink lips, studying the menu. "When you're hungry, everything looks so good."

"I know what you mean." Instead of reading the menu he took in as much of her as possible, this time ready to shift his eyes the moment she lifted hers.

"I'm tired of turkey clubs. They have delicious pastrami."

"Hmm, pastrami." For a moment she was thoughtful. "How about a Rueben? I'll have mine without meat." She grinned, her eyes sweeping his face, which had suddenly tightened.

"With fries and dill pickles? Can't beat that. So how was London?" How could he not ask the question that had been haunting him for days?

Her eyes widened, then narrowed. That explained the tight look on his face. Why was she feeling guilty? She had done nothing wrong by going to London with Trainer. They were, after all, on a business trip. She wasn't committed to anyone. Or was she? She looked across the table at him, her jaw clenching. She chose to pretend she didn't know that Bonnie had told him about the trip. Her face calmed, but her fingers, fidgeting with a napkin, were as edgy as her voice.

"It was nice. How'd you know I went to London?" She angled her head. What would he think of her if he knew that less than a week ago she had stood naked before the eyes of another man? Would he look at her the same way he was looking at her now?

"Your red-haired friend."

"Oh, you mean Bonnie? Where'd you see her?"

"At the hospital, briefly. I had an appointment for some tests."

"Paul Pollock is your doctor?"

"Yes." At the mention of his doctor's name, he angled his head. His wide eyes narrowed.

"He's one of the best in his field." Don't probe . . .

"Yup. Manchester is the place to meet the best doctors, that's for sure."

Was he making a dig or just digging for information? Her eyes became like a cat's.

"In Registration we deal mainly with patients, not doctors. So what kind of work do *you* do?" Keep the focus on him . . .

"Construction. Well, I used to work heavy construction, but now I just run the company. Actually, we built the hospital's pavilion which I designed." He paused to gulp some ice water from a glass the waitress set on the table.

"I had no idea." Her brows shot up then settled.

"I'm an architect by trade, but I liked getting down and dirty with the crew."

Down and dirty; the words sent a shiver down her spine. He had quite a way of expressing himself. It cleared the air. She smiled. His voice was rich and deep, his words well-enunciated. He was much like the professionals she dealt with at the hospital on a daily basis, but not at all aloof.

"Must be nice not being cooped up in an office all day, especially in the summer." She pictured her cramped cubicle with one window almost always closed, then imagined him at work, sweaty and sexy, tousled hair, pecs straining against a form-fitting

T. Witnessing such a scene would tantalize any female.

Sienna found herself wondering about Michael's past romances. The woman she had seen him with in the restaurant. Before today he had been a fascinating mystery, now he was a fascinating puzzle that had to be solved.

"That it is. We built the Chessler Suite at Manchester General and the condos on Hilltop."

"I live in the Hilltop condos," she blurted, then grinned, "which you already know." Her eyes widened, "they're magnificent, Michael. You designed those too?"

There it was again, his name, smooth as silk slipping through her beautiful lips. His stomach went roller-coasting. He was letting his guard down, unsure if that was a good thing. Would it matter? There was no turning back now.

"Yup, and the Oak Haven Plaza."

The last thing he wanted was to brag, but words simply flowed. He controlled the tone of his voice, the rhythm of his breath, even the beat of his heart. Things seemed to be coming together better than a well-designed blueprint; the framework was bolted in place, and the structure felt strong.

"That too? Wow, you've been busy. And all of this must have happened almost at once, because all of the buildings are relatively new." She was thinking aloud. "You must do nothing but work."

The moment the words left her lips, she feared they sounded critical. But the pleasant look on his face remained. Still, she was thankful for the waitress for giving her a moment's reprieve by taking their order.

Watching his behavior, how his lips moved, his hands, brought matters to a head. And now that she seemed to be on a roll, she couldn't help herself.

"How's your girlfriend?" she asked, her face filled with innocence as she played with her fork.

He looked confused.

"The dark haired woman you were with at the restaurant the other night."

His face went blank.

Her heart skipped. Was she crazy asking an almost-stranger about his personal life? If she could have strangled herself, she would have. His silence was almost as bad as the picture of the two of them still rolling across her mind.

"Ohh. You mean . . ." His face broke into a smile. "The other night at the Plaza Restaurant." he laughed.

"Why are you laughing?" Indignation masked embarrassment.

"Because you're cute." He reached for her hand. "That was an acquaintance of a friend."

"I'm sorry." Her face flushed. "You don't have to explain. I shouldn't have brought it up."

"I'm glad you did." He grinned. "It gives me a chance to share an awkward experience."

"Gee. I thought only I had those." She twisted her mouth to the side and rolled her eyes.

"I was railroaded by a good friend who sprung her on me at the last minute."

Unconsciously lifting a brow, she didn't appear convinced. "Just so you know, I wasn't spying." There it was again, the attitude, and she couldn't blame alcohol for acting bitchy. "I needed dinner for my cats." Her voice was flat.

He lowered his head and slapped a palm against his forehead. "Now I get it. You thought we were?" He laughed loud enough to draw stares. "You must have caught the tale end of me trying to untangle her earring from her hair and her shirt. Don't ask me how she did it, but somehow everything got stuck together and she didn't want it to rip her shirt, or her hair." He shook his head, threw his hands up. "Gospel truth."

Sienna smiled, let out a sigh. "A tale like that has to be true. Like your eyes. They show emotion."

Her assessment surprised him. He looked uneasy.

Get off the damn subject, Sienna. "You must love your work. I guess it's rewarding, huh?"

She seemed to be full of surprises. The look on his face calculating, he raised a brow as if trying to understand the sputtering woman who sat across from him.

"I mean, you provide so much. I can't tell you how many times I've silently thanked the ingenious individual who planned the condos." She nodded, beaming. "Closet space galore, a roomy linen closet in the bathroom, tons of kitchen cabinets and a center island. Even a pantry. I must sound like a realtor." She stopped for a breath, and a sip of ice water. "I understand Chessler is a family name?"

Michael appeared amused, his eyes roaming her face before replying. "I appreciate your compliments, and I'm happy you like your condo. I grew up listening to my grandmother moan about closet space." He chuckled, then shrugged. "We named the condos and professional complex in honor of my grandmother Chessler. Actually, I inherited the business from my father, who inherited it from my grandfather when it was a small company. Although my dad didn't spend much time in the construction business."

"So you're the reason it's grown into what it is today. That's amazing."

No, you're amazing . . . His delight was so deep that his face was stiff and sore from smiling. She was driving him wild, without even realizing.

"When you say we, do you mean you work with your dad?" Sienna shifted her chair, making room for the waitress who placed tall glasses of iced tea onto Corona Extra coasters she set before them.

"No, I was referring to my foreman, Gus. He gets most of the credit." Michael lifted his glass and sipped. "My dad was retired Army, but still flying as an instructor. He flew for business and pleasure, so he hired Gus to help my grandfather handle the business while he was away, which was most of the time. Gus is like family."

"So your dad wasn't actually involved in full time construction? And he's now retired from the service?" Her expression was one of admiration, and she wondered if Michael looked like his father. From the sound of it, he had inherited his father's multi-dimensional ambition.

"He wasn't hands-on, but he kept an eye on the business when he could. He passed away a few years ago." Michael lowered his eyes, fumbling with his straw wrapper.

"Mine died too." Sienna frowned. "We lost him when I was little. I don't remember much about him, only stories and photos . . ."

"I'm sorry," he said, his eyes reaching out to hers. "We lost my mom at the same time." Michael's face held less expression than his voice.

"No, no, no." Sienna shook her head, a hand to her chest. "I'm really sorry, Michael. An accident?"

"They were flying to the Carolinas. My dad's Cessna had a mechanical malfunction a half hour into the flight. He tried his best for an emergency landing, but the plane went into a nosedive not too far from a field that could have been a runway."

"That's absolutely horrible. What a tragedy." She reached for his hand, noticing a tattoo peeking from beneath his shirt sleeve.

Her fingers charged his skin with electricity. The tips of his fingers returned the thrill. If they never met again he would at least know what touching her felt like.

As he repositioned his arm, Sienna saw more of the vibrant ink. Her fingers crept up his forearm, gently lifting his sleeve, exposing the entire tattoo. She cautiously ran a finger around but never touched it, as if the artwork were too sensitive to be handled. "Wow." Her voice was as soft as her touch.

His fingers left hers to lift the sleeve, unveiling the head and wingspan of an eagle whose talons gripped a heart from which droplets of blood fell. "With my dad being a pilot, of course I got my license too, and the eagle after my first solo flight."

"How sentimental and beautiful. I really like it." She reached for his hand. "You were with them when it happened?"

He lowered his head, obviously still plagued by pain. "I wasn't with them. This . . ." His hand brushed his thighs. "This isn't from the plane crash. After my parents passed, I had the heart added beneath the eagle." His eyes clouded. "Had I been with them . . . That's something that will always bother me. But I doubt there was anything I could have done to save them. My dad was a highly experienced pilot. If anyone could have pulled out of it, it would have been him. The heart is for my parents, and in my mind symbolic I guess. You know, the eagle catching them before they hit the ground."

A lump rose in Sienna's throat, and she fought tears. She wanted to rush around the table, take him in her arms. A teardrop slipped through her lashes and dotted her cheek like a tiny diamond.

"It's okay." Michael's voice was soft, his fingers once more sliding across her hand. "I didn't want to upset you. Don't look so sad." He smiled.

Where a spark had ignited, a full-blown fire was growing beyond control. In the gym, Leo stood statue-still, watching their faces inches apart, their arms reaching across the table, fingers locked.

AN INVITATION TO THE DRIVE IN

Placing lunch before them, the waitress broke the spell. "Here you go. Two grilled Reubens, one no pastrami."

Toasted Rye bread, sauerkraut, melted cheese, and pastrami flavored the air. Russian dressing dripped from the sides, seeping onto the pickles. Overstuffed paper cups of coleslaw sat beside golden fries, juice trickling.

"Can I get you folks anything else?" she asked. "Refills?" She motioned to the drinks.

Rosy-cheeked, Sienna quickly dropped her hands to her lap, but her eyes held onto Michael.

"Not for me. I'm fine, thank you." She drew her plate closer. "This looks so good."

Recovering from one of the most blissful moments of his life, Michael stared. *What had just happened?*

"How about you? Anything else?" said the waitress.

"No thanks."

"Mustard's over there." She pointed an acrylic nail shining with red polish and something greasy, perhaps mayonnaise, then disappeared through the kitchen doorway.

"Uh — So, where were we again?" Michael asked, his cheeks warming.

Sienna covered her face with her napkin, a snorting sigh sounding so strange they both laughed, looking like bright-eyed kids sharing a secret.

"I have no idea," she said, giggling, spreading the napkin on her lap.

"I think I was about to ask about your family?" Michael inspected his sandwich and lifted half to his mouth.

"My family." Sienna sighed. "Well, my mom's up in Ontario, which is where I'm originally from."

"Really? How did you come to migrate to this neck of the woods?"

"Also a long story, but in short, after my dad died, my Aunt Tessa came to visit and ended up staying permanently, which was wonderful for Mom."

"And you?"

"My mom and I get along fine. Aunt Tessa on the other hand. . ."

She looked adorable when she wrinkled her nose, and ate her sandwich with a fork.

"She's kind of overbearing, but means well. Growing up I had an average life, I guess." She shrugged. "I absolutely hated elementary school, but I loved high school and college."

"Homecoming queen and the frills?" Michael grinned, wiping dressing from his lips.

"Nothing that exciting, but life was pretty good. After college though, things changed." Thinking of Rob, her grin faded.

"You don't have to explain. Change of subject."

"It's okay. There are things that happened, but in the past. I'm dealing . . ." Sienna sipped iced tea through a red straw. "I met Bonnie in Ontario," she said before biting down on a pickle she had speared with her fork.

"She's from Ontario too?"

"No, she was on her honeymoon." Needing her hands to tell the story, Sienna pushed her plate aside. "I was working at the hotel where they were staying. Someone had mixed up their reservation, gave them a regular double, not the bridal suite Bonnie had booked. When she checked in and found out, she was like a Brooklyn wildcat."

Michael laughed. "I can imagine. She seems to have an effect on people."

"You should try working with her. It's an experience."

"I bet. She kind of gave me that impression."

"So anyway, because I was a business major, it was my job to keep things running smoothly. So I switched their reservation to the penthouse, at no additional charge — and I got fired. Guess I went overboard. I also accidentally double-booked and lost a ten suite wedding party in the process." Arching a brow, she shrugged, then took a big bite of her sandwich. "This is so good."

"Oh no, you didn't."

"Ah-ha." She nodded, swallowed, sipped more tea, then tapped her lips with a napkin. "I did, and Bonnie felt so bad about it. She has such a big heart. She told me about her job at the hospital and that they were expanding and could probably use help in her department. So here I am, still waiting for my promotion to management."

"That's quite a story." Finished, Michael pushed his plate aside.

He watched every expression alter her face as she spoke, wondering if she could ever feel about him as he felt about her. He also wondered how he would handle being without her once they parted, when he returned to the cottage, alone.

"What kind of movies do you like?"

"Hmm. I have a long list of what I *don't* like . . ." She grinned.

"Go for it."

"Well. I don't like war or gangster movies. I can't sit through James Bond flicks. And I hate horror."

"That can be limiting. So what *do* you like?"

She was thoughtful and sighed. "Romcoms, I guess."

"Romance and comedy. Sounds appropriate." He chuckled. "There's a good flick playing at the Ridgefield." He paused for her reaction.

"The drive in?"

"Yup. It's a comedy. Not sure if it's romantic."

Her lips pursed, her eyes smiled.

"And it's supposed to be a nice evening." He cocked his head and grinned.

"Is that an invitation?"

"Would you like to go to the movies with me tonight?"

"I'd love to."

Sienna wasn't surprised at how relaxed, content she felt. Her first glance into his beautiful eyes had hinted it would be this way. And now they were having such a wonderful time; why had she been doubtful? He was fun to be with, easy to talk to. She couldn't remember being this comfortable with any man before, or feeling as elated in a simple atmosphere such as a café. She didn't need London to experience excitement. She was thankful she had decided to shop today — and happy Michael had been there.

Finished with lunch, her hands rested on the tabletop, artfully folding her flattened straw wrapper into bird wings.

Michael fought the urge to confess his feelings, to reach across the table and take her hands in his. Now what? Would she want a guy in a wheelchair? Was he was deceiving himself? Maybe she just felt sorry for him.

Leo popped his head around the doorway. Not a sight Michael was ready for.

"Hey, guys. How was lunch?"

"Delicious," Sienna said. "You look thirsty. Sit down, have some iced tea. The waitress brought refills and I haven't touched mine." She slid the fresh glass toward him.

"Be happy to." He ignored the look of annoyance on Michael's face.

"So I benched two hundred today. You believe it?"

Sienna smiled. "That's terrific!"

Although Michael seemed miffed by the intrusion, he had to give the kid a pass. If not for Leo, they would not be sitting here, together at last.

"That's just great, Leo."

Sienna slid her chair aside so Leo could take the seat beside hers.

"You don't want the other half of your sandwich?" he asked Michael.

"No. Why, do you want it?"

"Sure do. Gotta feed the bulk."

226

Michael pushed the plate across the table, grinning, shaking his head as Leo attacked the rye bread, plucking out pieces of pastrami, dangling them into his mouth.

"So, Michael," Leo asked as he munched. "Where'd you learn how to design all those awesome buildings?"

"Yale."

"You went to Yale? Wow, that's awesome. I'm thinking about colleges now. I'd never get into Yale though. Plus I want to get out of Connecticut for a while."

"Have you applied to any schools yet?" Sienna asked.

"I'm checking out a few next week. Partying schools . . ."

"Do your partying after school, Leo. Take it from me. Don't waste your uncle's money."

"You partied in college."

"I worked my ass off in college."

"Come on, admit it. You partied and look where you are now."

"I partied *after* college," Michael corrected. "I traveled Europe for a while. That's when the party started. You'd love Amsterdam."

"So you were a wild child, huh?" said Sienna, curiosity growing. Her head was tilted, resting on her folded hands, hair spilling over her shoulders. Her earrings caught the overhead light and sparkled, but not half as much as her eyes.

"No. Just a flower child." He laughed.

Her jaw dropped.

"I'm teasing. I wanted to see another side of life before I settled down."

"Were you ever married?"

"Nope. Not even close."

She seemed relieved. *Not even close* must have meant he had never been deeply in love. She didn't understand why the thought of his past relationships troubled her. Maybe she didn't like the idea of him gazing into another girl's eyes as he was hers, turning her on.

She'd keep her past to herself, at least for now. What would he think if he knew she had almost been pushed into marriage to a monster? Would he still look at her this way? When would she confess her dreadful secrets? Certainly not now, not when he was beginning to — beginning to adore her — or so his eyes hinted. And she was weakening by the minute. He was her beloved Atlantic, and she was wary.

"Speaking of partying, you going to the carnival, Sienna?" Leo asked.

"I haven't given it much thought, but I saw the tents are up. When does it start?"

"This weekend," Michael said. "You should come."

Of course she would be there. She wouldn't miss it for the world.

"Hmm, seems like it would be fun, especially with both of you there." Although, she meant, it would be fun being with Michael. "Sure, I'll come. Maybe I'll bring Bonnie."

"Great, so we've got a date." Leo stood and lifted a jangle of keys out of his pocket. "Listen, I have to get back to clean up the storeroom at the grocery. We better get going."

"A date it is." Michael winked. "Pick you up tonight around seven?" If Sienna had been leaning against him, she'd have felt the drum of his heart.

Leo did a double take, then his jaw dropped.

Sienna had just stepped from the door when the Suburban pulled up to the condo, right on time. As she neared, Michael reached over, pushed open the passenger door.

"Hi." With a soft breath, she slid onto the seat.

"How's it going?" His eyes glided over her.

"Good. You were right about the weather. It's beautiful out."

"It's good you brought a sweater. It may cool off."

She looked at him and smiled. *I doubt it.* Wearing a pale blue shirt, its long sleeves rolled to the elbow, and jeans that were a perfect fit, he looked delicious. He smelled it too. Once the door closed, the inside of the truck filled with a blend of spicy cologne, and fruity perfume, even though his window was wide open.

"You look nice," she said. "We match." She tugged at her tank top and smiled although he was looking straight ahead, driving.

"You look very pretty." He stole a quick glance. "Your hair is up." He smiled, turned his head back to the road. "I like it. You look so young."

"Is that a good thing?"

"It most certainly is."

"Do I usually look old?"

He laughed. "Not at all. I just meant — with a ponytail, you look like a little girl."

She relaxed into the seat. There was something about being near him, alone with him, that triggered the sensation. And her eyes were obviously displaying her emotion. As he drove, now and then he'd turn toward her, even if they didn't happen to be talking.

The outdoor theater didn't appear too crowded. When they entered the parking lot, Michael chose a row near the back.

"Can you see okay from here?"

"It's fine."

"I don't like to park up front. With the height of the Suburban, I don't like blocking anyone's view."

"That's very thoughtful." She smiled. "People with big heads and hairdos should be that kind *inside* movie theaters."

He laughed.

"There's a cooler in the back with bottled water, soda, juice." He turned and motioned to the blue Igloo that sat at the center of the back seat. "There's a bag back there too. In case you get hungry. I brought cookies, chips, even some candy. I wasn't sure what you'd like."

"You think of everything."

"Well. Since a trip to the concession stand would be kind of difficult . . ." He looked out his side window. The sun had set but the night was clear and bright with stars.

When the opening credits rolled across the huge screen, he looked at her and said, "I hope you like the movie."

"I'm sure I will."

During the following hour they laughed and joked, sometimes about the movie, other times about things more personal. Like Bonnie. Or Leo. Their childhoods, old friends. They seemed to be opening up to one another. She waited, and his hand finally made it over the console and onto hers. She gripped it and smiled. "This is so nice. I'm happy you asked me to come."

"I'm glad you're enjoying yourself."

His laughter indicated he was having an amazing time as well.

Halfway through the movie, Michael turned to her and said, "If you work tomorrow, we don't have to stay for the second show." His eyes remained on her face.

She remembered how she had attacked him and felt a wave of uneasiness, but couldn't break from his stare. And when his hand rested on her shoulder, she sucked in a gulp of air.

His fingers traced the slope of her neck, then slipped beneath the strap of her tank top, smoothing the fabric, caressing her skin. If she didn't hold her breath, he'd know it was growing louder.

His arm draped her seatback, then slid around both of her shoulders. She was certain he had no idea of how his touch was turning her on.

For a moment they sat in silence. Then without notice, he pulled her toward him. Lips parted, she faced him. The look in his eyes sent a chill down her spine. With his fingertips, he gently stroked the side of her face, twirled the tendrils of hair, then rounded her ear, swept over the hollow, down her neck, her arm. His gaze never once left hers.

Swiveling in the seat, she brought up her knees, scooted over the console so she could face him. She worked a hip and a buttock onto his lap, wedging herself between the steering wheel and his chest. Instinctively, he slid his seat all the way back.

Twisting sideways she shifted, unfolded, easing her entire ass into his lap. With one hand she gripped his firm upper arm, while the fingers of her other hand toyed with his hair, the side of his face, traced his lips.

He took a loud breath then his mouth closed over hers, gentle at first. But when her breasts pressed into his chest, his kiss deepened. She drew in his tongue, encircling it with hers. Her lips never moved so precisely, without even trying; they were a perfect fit for his. Their mouths crushed so fierce their teeth clashed, and she almost swallowed his tongue as she moaned.

Her arms locked around his neck. Without straddling him, once more she had him pinned.

His hands roamed her back, while hers brushed through his hair, followed the strong lines of his neck, rested on his broad shoulders, squeezing, caressing.

A hand ran down the outside of her thigh; the lightest touch of fingers trailed up the inside. She hoped her panties would hold the moisture, and her cotton shorts would conceal what they didn't. Her body reacted by writhing, arching. Squirming in his arms, legs parting, she offered him easy access.

Moaning, he cradled her like a baby, his touch more demanding, reaching, exploring. He caressed the side of her breast, cupped it entirely, with a firm grip rounded both, then he stopped, swung his head to the side.

"Maybe we should slow down. I don't want to push you into anything you might be sorry for in the morning," he said huskily.

"Believe me," barely able to speak, she whispered against his cheek, nibbled his ear. "You're not." She ran a hand across his chest, pulled his face back to hers. Eyes wide open, hips grinding, she brought her lips to his.

THE ANNUAL CARNIVAL

The carnival was a kaleidoscope of colors, garish lights decorating the wide entrance gates. Streamers hung and fluttered like luminous kites in bondage about to be swept up and away by the wind. With each gust, the vibrant triangles beat the lofty air like flocks of heavy winged creatures flying south for the winter. But it was summer in Oak Haven, and the carnival had become an annual event.

The evening was clear, a balmy breeze wafting generously off the glistening Connecticut River. The moon was full, the sky a sleek sheet of satin. Flood lamps illuminated the rides and thrilling attractions.

The parking area full, vehicles overflowed into the plaza store lots. A mob of adults and children merged with dusk, waiting to enter into the land of enchantment.

Michael and Leo were already at the carnival when the Durango pulled off the highway, parking on the grass at the shoulder of the road.

"This place is a madhouse," Michael said to Leo, their eyes scanning a hundred dissolving faces.

Michael searched for Sienna, while Leo hawked his latest love interest, a voluptuous brunette wearing Daisy Dukes and a halter top.

"Tonight's the night," Bonnie whispered, rolling out of the Durango. "I can feel it in my bones."

She shook her perm with her fingertips, then repositioned the waistline of her walking shorts so her tunic overhung in perfect alignment with her hips.

"What's happening tonight?" Sienna asked, amused. Bonnie would be livelier than the carnival, this she could already detect. But Sienna had more on her mind tonight than the carnival.

"Where's Mickey?" Bonnie continued in a hushed voice.

They paused in an area the floodlights couldn't reach. Eerie shadows fell around them.

"He's locking the car," Sienna mimicked Bonnie's whisper. "What's gonna happen?"

"I think we're gonna hit the jackpot. I brought three hundred dollars with me."

"What? Are you crazy? That's close to a week's salary."

"Shush. I don't want Mickey to know. He'd kill me. Besides, I want to surprise him. I'm investing in jackpot tickets tonight. I'm thinking this is what Persha might've meant. This could be the fortune she was talking about."

"Well, I hope you share the wealth." Sienna humored her, and then thought of Persha and Rob, Trainer and Michael. If Bonnie really hit the jackpot, would Sienna's happiness follow? Would it be Trainer, or would it be a man she had technically only been on one date with, and was already falling for. Could this be possible? Silly… She was being superstitious. But the night promised its own kind of magic, and Sienna was feeling as giddy as a high school girl sneaking out on a hot date.

"Come on, girls," Mickey shouted, already ten paces ahead of them. "I want to get in line for the funhouse."

"Not me." Bonnie's voice sang out. "I want some fried dough first, then the funhouse. Wait up."

They hiked half the length of a football field, toward the carnival entrance. The grass was moist with dew and summer rain. It brought pungency into the night to blend with the aroma of Philly cheese-steaks, popcorn and other appetizing foods.

"I love this time of year." Sienna inhaled deeply. The thought of seeing Michael was thrilling. "How do I look?"

Rock music blasted from speakers as they neared the

ticket booth.

"Let me see you in the light." Bonnie grabbed Sienna's arms for a better view. "I didn't get a good look at you when we picked you up. Let me see."

Sienna noticed Bonnie's face glowing in moonlight. "You outlined your red lipstick with that brown liner again, didn't you? Your lips look huge, like butterfly wings. Didn't you learn anything at that make-up show we went to?" She laughed as she turned to face the gate, and a shoulder to shoulder wall of people.

"I know. They're great, aren't they? I want to look festive. Come back here, let me see what you're wearing." She pulled Sienna beneath the spray of a spotlight. "Okay, let's see. Phew, wait until he gets a load of you in that dress. I love you in red. Wow! I wish I could wear something like that. Oh, and look at that French manicure. You're really decked out." When Bonnie winked, her lashes brushed the top of her cheek like a child's baby doll.

Sienna's strapless dress clung to her breasts, soft fabric glued to her hips. The hem was knee-high on one side where a slit revealed a lovely leg. The other side flowed like a scarf to mid-calf.

"Those splashy roses look terrific against that ivory background."

"I know. I love the roses. This dress cost a fortune. I got it in New York." She held up a foot, "New ballerina flats. I figured we'd be doing a lot of walking."

"I guess, unless Mickey wants to ride around the funhouse all night, or park his butt at one of those rifle stands. You know how much he likes target practice and running around in the woods with his pals."

"Yeah, you said he's a pretty good shot with a paintball gun." They laughed.

"Look, he's already inside. Mickey!" Bonnie called, flailing her arms.

They slowly moved through the gate, merging with the herd. Rambunctious children ran with cotton-candy-hands, balloons floated in the air, lovers cuddled on the Ferris wheel, amid floodlights and music and carnival barkers beckoning to their booths.

"Hey, there's Mona," said Sienna.

"Where?" Bonnie squinted.

"Over there, in the white shorts. Standing by the frozen custard stand."

"Let's go." Where there was a chance for gossip, Bonnie could be found. She grabbed Sienna's hand.

"Oh wait. Forget it, she's with Dyson." Sienna saw that they stood close together, and Mona seemed to be wildly gesticulating with her hands. "They look like they could be arguing." Her mood began to bottom out. "I wonder where his wife is tonight? She's usually around, harassing him."

"Hopefully she's out doing her own thing." Bonnie shook her head. "Let's follow them. I could get into their business, and some custard too." She chuckled and dropped Sienna's hand as she began to stalk the couple.

INTO THE SHADOWS

"**H**ey. You made it." Michael's voice was bolder than usual.

Sienna stopped abruptly and spun around. "Michael . . . I'm shocked you found us in this crowd." Her face lit up.

"I'd find you in the middle of a million faces." His eyes raked over her.

She was stunning. Perfect hair, smooth arms and legs, one of the sexiest dresses he'd ever seen. But the woman beneath it all made it happen, flooded his mind, made his body tingle, his stomach lurch with expectation. "Let's move to where we can hear each other."

Butterflies filling her stomach, she followed him into the shadows beside a concession stand, where a row of crimson-leaved maples offered privacy. "This is a relief. I couldn't hear myself think in that bedlam."

"I remember you saying you're not one for crowds." He sounded short of air.

"Where's Leo? Isn't he with you?" She caught the vibes he was sending.

Sienna wanted no interruptions, not from Leo, or Bonnie, or the crowd. Her focus was on Michael. He was the reason she had come, why she had spent hours selecting the perfect attire.

"Where's Leo?" Michael grinned and motioned across the parking lot to a savage-looking ride, where wire cages held passengers in place as it spun and moved skyward, eliciting screams. "He found himself a cute little playmate. They're on that thing together. It's like a milkshake machine." He shook his head, then shrugged. "Leave it to kids. They'll try anything."

"Ooh," Sienna gasped, "not for me. My stomach couldn't take it."

Michael's eyes traced her movements. "You look very nice. I like that dress, but I can see you didn't plan on getting on any rides," he said with a look of male appreciation.

"Only you," she said, turning serious, staring him down.

She thought he flinched. If he did, he covered it with a chuckle.

Darkness loosened restraints, digging up feelings that had been buried for too long. Moonlight drenched her hair, splashing champagne into platinum. Feline in the night, her translucent eyes intensified, gleaming like sapphire gems.

Michael appeared to be catching the heat. She was coming on hard and fast as the beat of his heart. Almost as fast as the night he would never forget. *Keep it light. A gambler never shows his hand.* And vying for the affection of such a woman was an incredible gamble. He was relieved they hadn't fucked in the truck, although they'd come close to it. He didn't want to take the risk of screwing things up.

"I'm content just watching them." Her voice was soft, her smile spreading slowly. "And you." She seemed to enjoy taunting him.

Just looking at him was growing impossible. She wanted to wrap her arms around his neck, feel his lips on hers, touch him again. Was she coming undone? She'd had a taste of romance at the restaurant, where they briefly held hands. That was in a moment of compassion. What had been developing recently was passion. Like in the Suburban, when she'd almost screamed when he gently set her aside. He controlled himself well. That had to stop. The thought of sharing a bed with him left her trembling. It has to happen tonight . . .

What they had assumed was a safe zone, actually attracted some stragglers and odd stares. She angered at their expressions, then suddenly experienced a conflict of emotions. Was she being shallow?

"I don't plan on staying in this chair," Michael said, his eyes deep as his voice.

She flushed. It was as if he had read her thoughts.

"It wouldn't matter . . ." Her breath came fast. Was the look on his face doubt, or lust?

"Where's your friend? Or did you come alone?"

"She's over there with her husband." She pointed to where Bonnie cheered for Mickey as he attempted to toss softballs into miniature basketball hoops.

"Do you see them?"

Michael peered through the crowed. "Can't say that I do."

She closed the space between them, pointing out they were safe from intrusion.

Her arm brushed his; they were almost cheek to cheek. She rested her arm on the back of his chair, her skin grazing his neck, then let it fall deliberately across his shoulders. He sucked in a breath. Her breast pressed his shoulder, warm. A chill ran the length of his spine. His impulse was to pull her onto his lap, wrap her in his arms. Her hair draped his shoulder, vanilla scented, overpowering. Her sweet perfume, growing stronger with passion, was intoxicating.

"Now I see them." His words sounded thick.

Sienna faced him, eyes heavy-lidded, her lips irresistible.

She felt delirious. Her gaze dropped to his neck, his chest, his arms, his hands that were helplessly splayed on his thighs. His hands her body longed for. Her limbs began to tingle. She pressed closer. His freshly shampooed hair smelled of citrus, the fragrance of his cologne was of spice, a delectable combination. "Michael," she whispered, her breath reaching his ear.

The way she spoke his name was pure magic, fueling the storm. "Come here." His voice strained as he cupped her cheek with his palm and drew her face to his lips.

His legs were numb, but every other part of his body was in perfect working order. His need was growing; a rise of long overdue passion erupted.

"You're beautiful," he murmured.

Without a word, she guided him deeper into the shadows, halting before the wood line, a barrier between fragileness and the road. Immersed in darkness, she could still see an outline of her hands on the back of his chair, but not much else. His face, streaked by starlight, radiated surprise, expectation. She raised her skirt, lifted her knees, first one then the other, finding a way to slip between his thighs and armrests of the chair. Perched above his lap she melted against him. Her lips slid off his long enough to whisper, "I can't get the other night off my mind."

"I know what you mean." He pushed her lips back onto his.

Her hips moved as fast as her hands that massaged his shoulders, his chest, then dropped lower.

"What are you trying to do, kill me?" he groaned, breaking their kiss for a breath.

Her lips were all over his face, his neck. Then her breasts crashed into his face. Allotting time for each, in a slow shimmy she grazed them, one at a time, across his mouth.

He tilted his head for air. "You wouldn't get off so easy if we were in my truck." His breath heated her breasts. He snaked a hand between their bodies, running it back and forth over her chest, clutching, lingering on her nipples, then mouthed them through the thin fabric of her dress.

She tugged down one side of the elastic bodice, offering. "You're gonna make me come." Gripping his head, she rubbed her face into his hair as he tortured the nipple.

His hands slid over her hips; one made its way to her crotch. He pressed, then massaged. "I'd make you come so damn hard you'd beg me to stop." By then he was panting, aching.

"How would you do that?" Her chest heaved.

"I'd throw you onto my bed. Rip off your panties. Spread your legs wide."

Shifting, she kneeled in as close as her legs would permit. "Let's go to your place." Her words barely made it through her lips.

"Baby," he blew the words into her ear, "you're so wet. You're driving me nuts." His fingers slid beneath her panties. The longest slipped inside while his thumb circled then strummed her throbbing clitoris. "I want to sink into you. Right here."

She moaned. "What are you waiting for?" A hand flew to his fly, while the other tightened around his neck. "Baby, I want you to know . . ." she started to whisper.

A small spotlight wove between the trees. Sienna ducked to escape the beam.

"Hey you two. Here you are," said Leo, coming out of nowhere, his hand locked around the arm of the brunette. His other hand held the lighted screen of his cell phone, which he was waving about.

"Put that damn thing away," Michael growled.

Sienna sprang up, wavered, adjusted her dress, then shook out her hair.

Michael looked disoriented. Folding his hands across his lap, he stifled a moan. *She wants me to know? To know what? Damn, Leo.*

"Yup. Here we are. Great timing, Leo."

"I've been looking all over for you. What's up? This is Gina." Leo swung the girl in front of him as if displaying a trophy, and slid his arm around her tiny waist.

It took excruciating moments for Sienna's legs to strengthen, for her heart to resume normal pace, the butterflies in her stomach to settle.

"Hey, Gina. Hope this guy's showing you a good time." Michael smiled, then shifted his eyes to Sienna, pleased she seemed to be struggling with a similar aftermath.

Gina's mouth curled briefly. Her reply was a nod and giggling, "We're having a blast."

"Gina, this is Sienna, Michael's girl — er, Michael's friend I mean." His arm, nestling beneath Gina's chin, wrapped around her shoulders, backing her against him. His chin rested on the top of her head.

"Hello, Gina." Sienna tried to sound engaged, but concentration was difficult.

"Hi, Sienna." Gina clutched Leo's arm as if she were suspended from a chinning bar. "I like your dress."

Gina seemed reserved, although her attire was the same as every other teenage girl in Oak Haven.

Sienna's eyes skimmed the shapely girl, whose long wavy hair was layered and thick. Her full-lipped greeting was virtuous. She reminded Sienna of the way she looked the night she met Rob; the main difference was the hair color — and Leo held a can of soda, not a bottle of beer.

"Thank you," she said, focusing on the apparent sweet and innocent teen relationship. *Enjoy it, Gina . . .*

SHOWDOWN AT OAK HAVEN CARNIVAL

A sudden commotion interrupted their conversation. Loud voices overwhelmed laughter and music as anger belted through the air.

"What the hell's going on?" Michael strained to see, frustrated by being stuck in the chair. Would he ever get used to his limitations?

Leo replied, "I don't know, but I'm gonna find out. Who's down for it?"

Sienna and Gina followed as Michael and Leo pushed through the wall of people gathering around two women and a man wrestling beneath spotlights, the center of the carnival their ring. The man's arms separated the women who struggled to get at each other. The man appeared dismayed, intimidated by the throng of thrill-seekers, and the females who seemed ready to kill each other. He looked helpless.

Sienna spotted Bonnie jostling to the front of the crowd, dragging Mickey behind her. Bonnie wore a red Ten Gallon cowboy hat with a huge brim that flapped as she walked, fanning the top half of her face. Surreal, flashed through Sienna's mind . . . Violent behavior and Bonnie crashing through the crowd in an outlandish hat, all transpiring within the confines of intended amusement. Within moments they stood in a tight circle.

"Any idea of what's going on?" Sienna said, then added, "Where'd you get the hat?"

"I won it." Mickey looked proud. "Doesn't it look great on her?"

"Cool hat," said Leo. "We gotta get you one of those, Gina. Wear it on the bike." He winked.

"I thought someone had a heart attack or something," Bonnie burst out, panting, "until I saw them fighting."

"Who are they?" said Sienna.

"It's Mona and Dyson."

Sienna sucked in a breath. "What are they fighting about? Why are they even here together? Shit, say no more. . . his wife. . ." She covered her mouth with a palm.

Bonnie balanced on her toes, neck pivoting as she tried to get a better view. "Holy shit, you're right. It *is* his wife. She must have caught them together."

"I wondered how long they'd be able to hide the affair, especially since Mona's been shooting off her mouth. Well, the secret's out now."

"It's a cat-fight. Cool." Leo beamed.

Bonnie reeled to face him. "Who are you?"

"He's with us," said Michael, tossing Leo a warning glance.

"Oh." Bonnie looked from Sienna to Michael, eyes widening at the apparent intimacy brewing between them. She shot her a look that seemed to say; So you're really going through with this?

Sienna returned a cold stare. "I think you know Michael."

"Yeah, we met. Hi, there. This is my husband, Mickey." She jerked him to her side.

Michael held out a hand. "Good to meet you. Would have been nicer under peaceful circumstances instead of in the middle of a rumble." Unlike the women, he appeared unaffected by the chaos.

Mickey gripped Michael's hand. "Nice to meet you. I know what you mean. Those two look like they're ready to square off, and the poor guy in the middle is the battered referee."

Leo turned to Michael. "We're gonna get going. Catch you guys later." He and Gina disappeared into the shadows of the parking lot.

"Enough intros — getting back to this." Bonnie motioned to what was becoming an outright brawl. "Look, Sienna. Dyson's wife is a loon. She's about to knock him over. Poor Mona. If that woman ever gets her hands on her . . ."

"What can we do?" Sienna's eyes ricocheted from Bonnie to Mona, who seemed dangerously close to a black eye or a broken nose.

Mona and the wife screeched. Dyson wavered, losing his footing as his wife stretched her arms through his hold, throwing punches in Mona's direction. One hit Dyson's shoulder, almost knocking him over.

"Enough of this," said Michael. "Someone should call security before they kill each other."

"Yeah, poor Dyson," Mickey agreed. "Imagine being caught in the middle of that?"

"It's his own damn fault. Don't ever get any ideas, Mickey. You've never experienced my full wrath." Bonnie squeezed his arm.

"Maybe it's good things have finally come to a head . . ."

"Why don't you go in there and break it up with a few Karate chops." Michael broke the tension.

"Oh sure. I'll take care of business and be right back," Sienna snapped.

Michael's eyes widened. "Sorry. Bad joke, I guess."

Despite the situation, Mickey chuckled. Bonnie punched his arm. "Why's she taking it out on Mona?" she said, "when she should be kicking Dyson's ass. He's been cheating on her for years."

"I know he has," Sienna's lips were drawn. "But the irony is, she's been carrying on behind his back longer than he's been fooling around on her."

"Why don't they just call it quits?" Mickey's head swung from Sienna to Bonnie.

"He probably stands to lose too much money," Michael commented. "And she might not come out with a big enough settlement." He shrugged. "Who knows why people do the things they do . . ."

"I don't even think they live in the same house anymore," Sienna mumbled. "I hate fighting." Her pink lipstick had been kissed off, and despite her tan she looked pale beneath the lights."Let's get Mona out of there."

"I'm with you." Bonnie pulled her by the arm.

The men exchanged concern, and watched the two women march off. Michael was the first to let out a noisy breath. "I hope they know what they're getting themselves into. Maybe we should go over there."

By the time Sienna and Bonnie reached Mona, the fight was ending, a security guard escorting Dyson's wife to her Cadillac CTS, with Dyson, head down, lagging behind. Mona stood sobbing.

"Come here, hunny." Bonnie took her by the shoulders. "Don't you cry. It's not your fault. He's a conniving bastard. You need to find somebody nice and settle down. There's this new guy who just started working at the hospital . . ."

"Don't even . . . I'm done with men."

"I'm sorry, Mona. Hang with us, we'll cheer you up." Sienna put her arms around them both.

"Okay," Calming, Mona almost agreed, then said, "Thanks anyway, but I'm going home. I've had enough for one night. Wait till I see Persha tomorrow . . ."

"You have an appointment?" Bonnie dabbed Mona's face with a tissue.

"Well, no, but this is an emergency."

"Oh God, you two. Come on, Mona, we'll walk you to your car." Sienna took her arm.

"No, I'll be fine."

"Call me," Bonnie said as Mona edged away. "I want to know everything Persha says."

"I'll bring a tape recorder," Mona tossed over her shoulder.

Bonnie turned to Sienna, lips clenched. "Was she laughing when she said that, Sienna?"

"I'm sure she was. Where are Michael and Mickey?" Sienna stared through the blur of faces behind her, squinting to see through the glare of lights.

"Sienna? What are you doing in the middle of this?" Trainer

put his hand on her shoulder, swinging her around. He whispered in her ear. "This is an awkward involvement for you. You didn't tell me you were coming here." When his eyes swept over her dress he looked even more surprised. "We could have come together." He squeezed her shoulders, dropping a kiss on her cheek.

She forced a smile. "Greg — you're back." *Michael . . . Where was he?* Her stomach sank. *This could be more awkward than you think, Greg . . .*

Eyes shifting from Trainer to Bonnie, then returning, she said, "How was Ontario?" Voice wavering, she took a step back.

"Ontario was a smash. My stellar presentation decimated the others. They held onto my slideshow, possibly to implement a few of my groundbreaking techniques in a forthcoming seminar."

"Oh shit," Bonnie mumbled, her eyes catching Mickey's rust colored shirt and the light glinting off the wheels of Michael's chair.

From a distance Michael watched, eyes drifting from Sienna to Trainer. Talking was one thing, but when he touched her, adrenaline surged. His face colored, then contorted.

"So, Michael. What do you do?" Mickey stepped in front of him, blocking his view.

"I own this plaza, and others."

"Nice. So you know most everyone around here."

"I don't know *him*." Michael craned his neck, motioning to Trainer.

"Unfortunately, I do. He's a dick."

Mickey towered over Michael, but was slight of build. His plaid flannel shirt hung open, a tan T–shirt beneath it tucked into loose-fitting cargo pants. His salt and pepper hair looked windblown.

Michael stared at Mickey's black and white Converse that had obviously seen better days. "What do you do, Mickey?"

"I'm a teacher. Want to get a drink or something to eat while we wait for the girls?"

"No thanks, I'm good. Where do you teach? Oak Haven High?"

"Yeah, for a few months now. I transferred from Hartford."

"Leo's a senior at Oak Haven. Do you know him?"

"He looks familiar, but I really only know the kids in my own classes. I teach eleventh grade science. Summer classes too."

Staring into the distance, Michael couldn't have looked less interested in Mickey, or anyone else.

"We should head back to the guys," Bonnie said, tactfully drawing Sienna away from Trainer, who appeared more willful than usual.

Sienna was dying to grab Trainer's crotch, squeeze, and say, "Get the point creep? Fuck off." But with Michael just feet away, there was no way she could confront, no less ditch, the overzealous doctor. A scene would, no doubt, bring to light things she'd never want Michael to know.

Trainer looked dazed, then agitated. "What guys?"

Bonnie answered. "Mickey and a friend."

He ignored Bonnie. "Did you drive yourself here? Why don't I take you home? Maybe we'll stop for a nightcap."

White lipped, head spinning, Sienna spoke through a clenched jaw. "How many times do we have to go through this, Greg?" She forced her voice to calm. "You and me are never gonna happen."

As she took another step back, her heel caught a rut and she lost her balance. Trainer caught her in his arms. She pushed him away, but not before Michael watched the rescue unfold.

The excitement and beauty of the night had worn off. Sienna looked fatigued, her shoulders slumping.

Bonnie watched the determination on Trainer's face intensify, gasping when his arm clasped around Sienna's waist.

"As I told you in London, I'm not one to give up."

Michael had a clear view of Trainer's hold on her. "Just like in Manchester's cafeteria," he mumbled. Blood slammed his temples. He wasn't helpless — he was furious.

"Let's go over there, see what that clown's up to." His voice didn't sound like his own.

"Sure. We should be heading out of here anyway. They're starting to shut the place down," Mickey waited for Michael to make the first move, then strode alongside the chair.

When they joined the others, Mickey immediately moved to Bonnie's side. Michael didn't enter the circle they formed.

"Honey," Bonnie said, squeezing Mickey's hand, gesturing to Sienna with a "What do we do now?" expression. Her mascara was smudged, lipstick caked the corners of her mouth, and the cowboy hat sat lopsided on her head.

Mickey plucked off the hat, brushed a hand over her hair, and kissed her forehead. "They have to work it out themselves," he said, close to her ear.

"There you two are," Sienna said with a bright voice, edging away from Trainer. Her tone was exaggerated, as was her demeanor as she moved closer to Michael and folded her arms across her chest.

"Mona was so upset. We were trying to calm her." Her eyes were watery, imploring.

Poised in awkward silence, her mind raced: Greg, please don't bring up the hotel room in London. Her heart began to pound. She tried to hide a relentless shiver.

Mickey and Bonnie exchanged easy to read glances.

Trainer looked strained as he gauged the situation, glancing from Sienna to Michael, obviously puzzled, yet maintaining a confident air.

His gaze settled on Michael. "Aren't you one of Dr. Pollock's patients?" He drew a sharp breath. "Haven't I seen you around the hospital? Is that how you know Sienna? I'm Dr. Gregory Trainer, by the way."

Michael's eyes were so cold they looked black. "Paul's actually a good friend of mine, and Sienna visits my plaza all the time. She's also a good friend."

Trainer took a step toward Sienna, who stood frozen between them.

"I didn't realize this is where you shop for odds and ends, darling." He motioned toward the rows of shadowed storefronts on the opposite side of the parking lot.

Bonnie's jaw dropped. Mickey seemed to be grinding his teeth.

Darling? Did Michael really hear that? *Is she playing me?* He glared at Sienna, who would have looked exactly like a ghost had she been wearing white.

She dropped her arms to her sides, hands curled into fists, like a bad child awaiting punishment. Biting back tears, she stole a glance at Michael. He looked different— his soft shell hard. Would things ever be the same? Everything she'd worried about seemed to be happening. Oh God . . .

Michael sat, a stubborn look gripping his face.

Sienna knew he was waiting for a sign, something to tell him he hadn't been wrong about her, that he hadn't been a fool. She thought her eyes had sent him the message. Why was he looking at her that way?

Her legs felt weak. She watched Trainer with dread. If he were to disclose anything that had happened between them, she would be mortified, and it would be over with Michael before it had a chance to begin. She needed to control the situation, but how?

Trainer scrutinized Sienna and Michael. Their discomfort was obvious, although Michael appeared perplexed, rather than someone caught in the act.

Trainer wasn't about to surrender. "You have a nice little plaza here."

"Thanks, Dr. Trainer. And I understand you lease one of my office suites," Michael taunted.

Trainer flushed. "What do you mean?"

"The Chessler complex — it's mine. I own the construction company that built it. I hold the lease on your office." Adept at concealing pain, Michael's voice was steady.

"Oh . . . Functional building. You must have an insightful designer."

"Why, thank you, doctor. I designed it myself."

For a moment, Michael's eyes sought Sienna's, wishing hers would fall softly on his face, prove he wasn't mistaken, and that everything would be okay. But she stood stiff as a figurine — a beautiful figurine about to be shattered.

He swung his stare back to Trainer. "I'm an architect, as well as the owner of most of the new buildings you'll be seeing around here."

"Go Michael," Mickey said under his breath.

Trainer had no comeback. His jaw stiffened, his face looked arrogant, he stood his ground. He shifted from one foot to the other, then stilled, legs apart, arms locked behind his back in defiance.

The ringtone of Sienna's cell phone interrupted the standoff, the male posturing.

"Who'd be calling me this late?" She flipped the phone open. "Aunt Tessa? What's wrong? Oh God, no. Is she conscious? I'll be there as soon as I can."

She turned to Bonnie. "It's my mother. She's had an accident. I have to get to Canada."

Bonnie gasped. "Is she okay? Can we do anything?"

"I don't know." Tears brimmed, then rolled freely down Sienna's cheeks, her chin, streaming to her neck.

"Sienna . . ." Michael said, then stopped and stared as his rival sprang into action.

Ripping his cell from the pocket of his linen blazer, Trainer's fingers pounded the dial pad.

"Steven, I need the Gulfstream — now. No, this cannot wait until morning. Make sure she's stocked and ready for takeoff. We'll be at Bradley in twenty minutes."

"I can't believe this guy," said Mickey in a low voice. "He's like mister wonderful."

Bonnie nudged him, her face a combination of sullenness and shock.

Mouth open, Sienna turned to face Michael, but he was already moving away, disappearing into darkness. She called out to him, but Trainer's heavy arm around her shoulders smothered her words as he whisked her to the exit.

"Keep me posted," Bonnie shouted. "Call my cell . . ."

Sienna didn't reply.

"You feel cold, dear. I have an extra jacket in the Porsche."
. . . were the last words Michael heard as they faded from sight.

By the time Michael reached the exit, Bonnie and Mickey were there waiting for him.

"I hope her mother's accident isn't serious. Will he be going with her?"

"I don't know, Michael." Bonnie said, watching his jaw clench, the heartbroken look on his face. "He's just a relentless pain in the ass."

Mickey slid an arm around Bonnie. "You're shivering. I'm gonna get you home, then I have to get over to the school."

"No. Not tonight."

"I have to, honey. It's my turn."

"This has been one hell of a night." Bonnie's words were muffled as she pressed her face into Mickey's shoulder.

"Michael, do you need a ride? We can drop you home," Mickey offered, his voice tired.

"No thanks. I've got it covered."

FACING A BAD SITUATION

The cottage was dark. Not a ray of moonlight slipped through the forested backdrop. In his haste to get to the carnival — and Sienna — Michael had forgotten to turn the driveway lights on manually. He made a mental note to fix the timer. He pulled the Suburban around the circular drive, stopping at the front of the cottage where a pole lamp had a sensor. He would make his way around the side to enter through the kitchen, where a ramp had been built for him.

Inside, he thought of pouring a glass of scotch, although he knew it would only make things worse. Alcohol made him mellow; he needed to harden to face this challenge.

He fought back tears and pounded his unresponsive legs with his fists. He felt so stupid. How could he have allowed himself to believe he was worthy of a woman like Sienna? Even a dolt like Trainer was better for her than he was.

In bed he tossed and turned, longing for sleep so he wouldn't have to think. Images of Trainer and Sienna flashed relentlessly through his brain. After a while he moved to his recliner and turned on the television. He needed a diversion.

The TV screen flickered. Michael half-watched a drama unfold. He couldn't concentrate. He closed his eyes, listening to the dialogue, but within a few moments snapped off the TV and threw the remote across the room. Then he began to drift . . .

He's finally alone with her. He's waited so long for this moment.
"Let's move into the shadows where no one can see us."
Maybe she knows what he has in mind. At last . . .
She follows. "That's better," she says. "I like the darkness.
It's gentle."
His eyes move slowly over her. "You look nice. I like that dress."
You're turning me on, Sienna . . .
She leans close, breath touching his face. Her hair drapes his
shoulder, vanilla. Her arm grazing his neck, a jolt of electricity.
His immediate instinct is to pull her onto his lap.
"Baby," the rasp in his throat deepens to a painful moan as
her hips shift, swelling him even more. It feels so damn good, his
mouth goes dry. Swallowing hard, he'll soon confess his love. He
hasn't said that to a woman in such a long time, and never with
such sincerity. He wonders if the words will find their way to his
lips without sounding hollow. But she's different from other
women.
She shivers as his fingers skim her neck, rest on her breasts.
His arousal growing, again she shifts. He's never ejaculated in
his trousers and isn't about to start now, although restraint is
torture.
"I want you," she murmurs.
The sound of her voice trips his heart. He slips a hand beneath
her skirt, fingers gliding up her thigh. Her panties are damp. He
finds the throb that confirms her need, the moisture clinging to
his skin.
"Michael," she pants. "I can't wait any longer."
"Come closer." His voice strains with passion as he crushes
her against him so tightly air escapes her lungs, then a groan.

Michael bolted awake. Eyes adjusting, he squinted, blinking
to focus through shadows. He felt her presence, but immediately
realized she wasn't beside him.

His gaze fell to the bed; it was crumpled, uninviting. He looked
around his bedroom; it was dark and lonely. He would throw on

sweats and sit outside for a while. Perhaps fresh air and the fragrance of pine would relax him so he could sleep. He needed her as much as he needed sleep. No more dreams of her. He wouldn't permit it. He would force himself to think of work, he would always have his work.

AUNT TESSA — MOTHER — ONTARIO

The flight to Ontario stretched into dreadful hours, the darkest of her life — almost. Although there was no turbulence, she felt sick. She sat alone in an aircraft that seated eight. The overhead lights were low, eerie. She longed to sleep as she had on the flight to London, but rest was impossible. Thoughts of Michael collided with worry about her mother. Sienna was torn in two.

A driver met her as she disembarked. Once more, Trainer had thought of everything. Inside the cab she dialed Aunt Tessa's cell, but instead of a cantankerous "Hello", a pre-recorded computer message followed four urgent rings.

Sienna feared what she might find when she arrived. Sienna didn't know if their connection had been terminated because of lost signal, hospital interference, or if Aunt Tessa had been too choked with grief to speak.

As the cab sped through night, panic gripped Sienna. Would her mother be alive when she arrived? She had no idea of what had happened. Why did Tessa hang up without explaining?

She should have visited more often. She should never have relocated to New York. After what happened with Rob, she should have gone home. She vividly recalled the last time she saw her mother, standing on the front porch waving good bye, watching intently as Sienna drove away. Her mother's smile had been filled with tenderness, but her expression had been strained. Sienna could still feel their last hug, how comforting her mother's soft body felt in her arms, the coarseness of her hair pressing against her cheek, the perfume that had sweetened the fibers of Sienna's sweater until dry cleaning removed it. She was sorry she had dry cleaned it. Her mother's scent may have been with her forever.

Gripped by waves of nausea, Sienna began to shake. Her head pounded and her body ached. She reached into her bag for aspirin. Sighing raggedly, she pressed firmly into the back seat of the taxi. When she closed her eyes, she imagined her mother in the Intensive Care Unit, connected to machines, wires from head to toe. Grotesque. She shivered, but even ICU would be better than a casket.

Intermittently, Michael's face ricocheted with beauty across her mind, a carbon copy of his provocative essence earlier that evening in the shadows of the carnival, when she finally found her way to him. They had been so close until Trainer arrived. The look on Michael's face was like a sword thrust through her chest. His eyes had begged for an explanation, and she had stood there, dumbstruck.

His face had asked every question his heart, his lips didn't have the courage to.

Instead of freezing, she should have rushed to his side. She wanted him with her now, holding her in his arms, whispering that everything would be all right.

One move had made a mess of her life. Things began to fall apart the day she met Rob Lucas. She hadn't known him long enough, or well enough to fall in love, and her mother had warned her. Mothers have that innate intuition. But who ever listens? Why hadn't she listened?

During the fifteen minute cab ride from the airport to the hospital, she had time to relive the last day in the apartment, the day Rob broke her heart for the last time. And now, while struggling to recover, she had broken someone else's — a beautiful, innocent man unaware of her past.

Maybe she was meant to be alone. Maybe she should stay in Canada, never return to Connecticut. Would she ever see Michael again? Could she ever not?

She didn't even have his phone number. Sienna's mind moved faster than her feet as she rushed through the hospital doors.

256

HIGH SCHOOL GUARD DUTY

The Durango pulled up in front of the brick-faced colonial. Bonnie hadn't uttered a word on the drive home from the carnival. So unlike her.

Instead of hopping out, chattering as usual, she hunkered in the bucket seat, staring glumly out the window.

Concern gripped Mickey's face. "We're home, Red." He acted cheerful as he opened the car door, planting a peck on her cheek.

She swung around to face him, feet landing on the running board. "This has been one of the worst nights. I can't stop thinking about Sienna and her mother."

"Try her cell," he said, grasping her elbow, urging her out of the vehicle.

"I did. She must be in the air by now so it's probably turned off."

"Let's go inside. We'll have a cup of tea before I leave."

"I really wish you weren't going tonight. I have the creeps. Besides thinking about Sienna up there in Ontario, now I have to worry about you."

"Nothing's going to happen to me." He placed a reassuring arm around her, guiding her up the walk to the side door of their home. "There haven't been any problems at school since that one case of vandalism. I'll just grade a few papers and be back in a couple of hours. Now let's go inside."

"How awful it must be for Sienna," Bonnie moaned with every animated motion her face, arms and hands could conjure.

Mickey snapped on the kitchen light and stepped aside, letting her enter first.

She dropped her leopard tote onto a center island stool, then slipped off her sweater, hanging it on the stool-back. She fluffed her hair free of dampness. "I know how I'd feel if it were my mother." She went to the sink and leaned against the cold cabinet, filling a kettle with water.

"Be logical, honey. If it were that bad, you would have already heard from Sienna. You're the first one she'd call. They're probably having a reunion by now, while you're tearing your hair out."

"I hope you're right," she paused and added, "I wish you had a gun to take with you."

Mickey jerked in her direction, a stunned look on his face. "Come on, silly head, I'll be fine. I wouldn't shoot anyone anyway." He tweaked her chin on his way to the cupboard. "Stop worrying."

Bonnie shrugged, dangling four teabags under his nose on her way to the table.

"I know, but still. You're in that empty building, all alone. Anything could happen. They never caught those creeps."

She poured boiling water into a teapot and steeped the bags, then opened the pink bakery box of raisin bran muffins resting on the counter.

They sat at the breakfast nook, drinking raspberry pomegranate tea out of red ceramic mugs, munching flakey muffin tops they pulled off moist bottoms.

"I better get going, honey," Mickey said as he placed his empty mug into the kitchen sink. He leaned over and kissed the top of her head. "Stay out of trouble."

"And you be careful, you hear?" Bonnie raised her face, waiting for a full kiss on the lips. "Don't be so cavalier, Mr. Smarty Pants. I love you."

"I love you too," he said on his way out the door. "I'm taking my car."

"Make sure your cell phone is turned on," she screamed out the window as he slid behind the wheel of his charcoal BMW.

LEO AND HIS HONDA

After the carnival shut down for the evening, Leo took Gina straight home. It was one a.m. He wouldn't meet the guys tonight; he would drive straight home. He wasn't tired, but his mood was melancholy. The evening had been fun. Still, he felt empty inside, unfulfilled. He parked the Volvo at the curb, but instead of entering the white frame house, he went to the wooden shed huddled beside a detached two-car garage. He would check his bike. He knew the Honda would be sitting in silence where he had left it with mud-caked tires, scratches scoring the metal. The bike had seen better days, but to him it was like a priceless toy he'd yearned for but never had as a kid.

The Honda was perfect for when Leo needed to cut loose. Gingerly, he wheeled the bike from the garage, balancing its weight with the strength of his arms, resting it on the kickstand, and quietly closed the shed door. It felt good to straddle the seat, even though it was worn. The bike was powerful and could still run with the best of them. He coasted down the driveway, tires crackling on gravel, knees bent, his boots resting on foot pegs. He wouldn't ignite the bike's fury until he reached the road.

Leo did not want to disturb the folks he lived with, whom he referred to as aunt and uncle, the caring couple who had taken him in after his parents deserted him when he was ten. He would never use drugs as they did. He'd have a beer or two, but never hardcore stuff. He'd also never father a child while a teen.

Leo thought of Gina. He really liked her. She was different from others, and he respected her. She was the kind of girl a guy could think about settling down with. Even at his age, the thought of permanency was appealing. He had been alone most of his life. It would be nice to share experiences with someone faithful.

They hadn't been intimate yet; he hadn't even tried, which was a first for him. After being with Gina, recalling her long legs in scant shorts, he was wired. He had to release the smoldering tension. The best place to accomplish this would be at one of Michael's deserted construction sites. There he could race the bike to his heart's content without the risk of being seen by police.

Visualizing Gina's indulgent smile, still feeling the brush of their lips in their goodnight kiss, he realized he had coasted further down the road than he'd intended. Reaching the brush-rimmed corner, he pop-started the engine. The bike was loud. He would wake the neighbors if he dawdled, so he launched the machine as quietly as possible then shifted gears, lighting up the tires when the road became isolated.

He sped past fenced-in farmland, then turned a corner, flying freely down the highway, effortlessly crisscrossing lanes in the absence of traffic.

The night was cool, the sky overcast. The only glow on the road was the glare of the Honda's headlight.

He was loaded with pent-up emotion. What would he do with his life? How far could this thing with Gina go? Was it just a fling? They would both be heading off to college soon. What then? Would he become the hot-shot attorney he'd secretly dreamed of being?

Veering onto a side road the bike skidded, wheels almost parallel with the ground. Leo felt the thrill of power. Winding the engine for takeoff, he blasted toward a familiar shortcut known only to cyclists and hikers. Inside the forested tunnel, a biker's wonderland awaited, reasonably safe during the day, perilous at night. Fallen logs and boulders were invisible to the naked eye, but Leo, a free-spirited eighteen-year-old, did not give it a second thought; he knew this route like the back of his hand.

The Honda sped across soggy trails, tires bouncing as it tore through puddles of stagnant rainwater, splashing mud against the legs of his jeans. The engine groaned, changing pitches at the command of his grip.

He rode like a demon, following a trail along a shallow ravine formed by the river's runoff. Leo had the instincts of a motorcycle racer, avoiding deadly ditches and grooves. He was aware that the tangle of gullies and projecting limbs could trip a wheel, hurl a rider headlong into the barrier of trees. An acquaintance had died in these woods in a head-on collision with a massive oak that had broken his neck.

As he rode, Leo's thoughts weren't on danger, they were on Gina. He relaxed into the seat, his mind uncluttered, his head protected by a shiny black full face helmet decorated with seething silver flames.

The Honda thundered down the abandoned trail, roaring engine a threatening warning to anything in its way, a fleet creature in pursuit of game.

This was what he lived for, he told himself — freedom. But now Gina had come into his life. Now things might change.

With each tightening grip of the accelerator, the bike exploded through the blackness that would soon release into an abrupt clearing, the Lakewood construction site. Michael owned the land in and around the site, including the forestland Leo had just blown through.

The main sign, *Chessler Construction*, was cast in the shadows at the rear, but others were floodlit and staked out the territory.

January Valentine

MOTHER IN THE HOSPITAL

Sienna was disheveled, both inside and out. She had on the same strapless dress she had worn at the carnival — the one that had driven Michael finally to act on his emotions.

Recent tears and stale mascara drew spirals down her cheeks. Her lips were white, her mouth dry with bitterness. Emotions brittle, Sienna was about to crack.

Trainer's jacket covered what the dress didn't. She was ashamed of the sensations Michael aroused. There she was, ready to hump a guy's brains out at the same time her mother was taken to the hospital.

Ducking into a restroom, she splashed cold water on her cheeks, rejuvenating her face, then ran down the corridor in the direction of ICU.

Sienna knew Mount Sinai and the busy roads leading to it. It reminded her of the hospital in New York where she had been taken after Rob had left her for dead. With each step, she recalled the horror of the night the ambulance rushed her to the trauma unit. Sienna prayed she would never face anything like that again, but here she was, approaching the nurse's station.

"My mother was brought in earlier tonight," she panted, leaning against the counter. "Margaret Alexander. Where is she?" Her voice sputtered, her eyes watering, pleading.

The nurse was sympathetic, her scrubs cheerful, her expression bland. She had seen worse, Sienna knew. Sienna's misery was routine to the middle-aged woman, whose dark ponytail wound into a knot at the nape of her neck.

Tessa must have heard the familiar voice in the corridor, because she peered out the door, staring in the direction of the woman who was slumped against the nurse's station. "Sienna?"

"Aunt Tessa," Sienna called out to the aging woman rushing toward her in tan blouse, navy slacks and white tennis shoes.

"Sienna — I'm so sorry." Aunt Tessa had been crying. Her pewter eyes were puffy, her rounded nose swollen beyond its normal smooth shape. Her shoulders hunched wearily as if she had just stepped out of her own grave. The burgundy windbreaker she wore hung open, crumpled, like Sienna's life.

Sienna stared at her, wild-eyed. "What? No — please don't tell me my mother's…" Her hands clasped in prayer beneath her chin.

Before Tessa could reply, Sienna dashed toward the doorway from which her aunt had emerged.

Tessa caught Sienna by her wrists and breathlessly explained, "She's okay." She patted her tangled hair in a futile attempt to calm her. "Don't go in there looking like that. You'll frighten her," she warned sharply, "She's been worried sick about you. Pull yourself together. Your mother's going to be fine."

Tessa's words brought Sienna to an abrupt halt. On the verge of emotional collapse, her mind ran rampant, requiring information faster than her aunt provided. Unable to absorb the good news, Sienna stood speechless as a fashion designer's mannequin, with a complexion just as flawless, replaying Tessa's words.

Tessa hung her head. "I'm sorry I phoned you like that and panicked you. Afterwards, I worried about you rushing up here because of how foolishly I acted. If anything happened to you, I don't know what I would have done."

Tessa, whose tears had already been cried, threw an arm around Sienna and gave her shoulder a feeble squeeze.

Finally able to heave her own sigh of relief, Sienna let her guard down and sobbed, leaning against Tessa for support.

"I'm okay now, Aunt Tessa," she said. "It was such a shock

hearing your voice like that. I couldn't take another . . ."

Tessa's face was worn with subtle lines. She pulled a ball of soft white tissues from her purse and dabbed at Sienna's face.

"I know." Tessa patted Sienna's shoulder, a rare act of compassion on her part. "That's enough. Come on now. Come see your mom. She's been waiting for you."

Entering the room, "Mom," Sienna cried, throwing herself across the bed while her mother's arms reached out. "I thought the worst things on the plane ride up here. I didn't know what I'd find. Thank God you're okay. You *are* okay, right?" Her glistening eyes narrowed. "What happened?"

"I'm just clumsy." Her mother's laugh was cut short by a bruised rib.

Margaret Alexander wore a coral smock sprinkled with tiny white stars, the shoulders too large for her small frame. Her auburn hair had been brushed severely from her youthful face and spread across a flattened pillow that pressed against the semi-reclined bed. She appeared worn but not broken by the fall, or by her difficult life.

"She was carrying laundry down to the basement," Tessa huffed, "and the next thing I knew, I heard a scream and a thud and found her layin' at the bottom of the stairs, splayed out like a bug splattered on a windshield."

Tessa stood at the foot of the bed, arms folded like a sentinel, mumbling, "Clumsy. Like mother, like daughter, in more ways than one."

Sienna brought her hands to her face. "What are your injuries? Did they take x-rays, cat scans?" she rambled with a pale doe-stare. "We're going to do whatever's necessary. I'll bring you to the States, there are fantastic doctors at Manchester."

Margaret tucked a lock of Sienna's hair behind her ear. "I had the works. I'll be fine, honey. I'm just sore and twisted an ankle, that's all. They only want me to stay here overnight for observation."

Sienna ran her soft palm across her mother's forehead and down the side of her cool cheek. It felt clammy. Margaret's face was ghastly pale, her lips chalky white against her ginger skin color. A purple half-moon impressed the delicate skin beneath each of her striking turquoise eyes.

"You look so tired, Mom," Sienna said, distressed.

"So do you, and with good reason," Margaret replied. "I'm sorry for adding to your problems."

Sienna had inherited her mother's fine features. People who didn't know better thought they shared the same cosmetic surgeon. "Please don't apologize, Mom. Just take care of yourself. I'm fine now that I'm with you."

"Look at you," Margaret touched Sienna's cheek. "Whose jacket is that? It's falling off you. You look like the little girl who used to play dress up, but without my makeup." She smiled. "Your face is shiny. You've been crying your eyes out."

"I'm fine," Sienna insisted, holding back tears.

She ran her hands over her face and through her hair, then wrapped Trainer's jacket around herself. Her mother's analysis of her appearance made her feel like that little girl, and abruptly rolled back the years. She snuggled closer to her mother, careful not to press against her ribs.

"I love you so much, honey," Margaret said, hugging Sienna for a moment, then holding her at arm's length. "Look at you, you're a beautiful wreck."

Sienna chuckled. "Thanks. You're beautiful too, and I guess we're both wrecks. I love you too," she whispered. "I'm so happy you're okay and we're together. I can't tell you how much I've missed you."

"I've missed you too, honey." Margaret turned to her sister. "Tessa. Take her home and tuck her into bed. She looks worse than we do."

"No. Now that I'm here, I don't want to leave you. I'll sleep on the chair." She sat at the edge of the bed, squeezing her mother's hand so tightly her fingertips turned red.

Tessa snorted. "Like hell you will. Come on. Let your mom get some rest."

"You can stay, but just for a little while. These aren't supposed to be visiting hours, and the nurses here are worse than Tess." She winked, watching for her reaction with heavy lids, then stifled a yawn. "When I get home, you can fill me in on all that's been going on with you. We don't get to see enough of you, young lady. I want to know everything you've been up to."

With Sienna holding her hand, her mother's eyes closed.

FACING AUNT TESSA — BITTER MEMORIES

During the ride home, Sienna watched Tessa from the corner of her eye. Noticing the toll time and life had taken upon her aunt, her stomach sank. Sienna remembered Tessa to be flamboyantly attractive and neat as a pin. But now her sixties hairdo, still honey blonde, was flattened to the back of her head, a result of her bed pillow, Sienna assumed. She wanted to reach across the seat and fluff it into place, but would never do such a thing. Tessa wouldn't let anyone but a beautician touch her hair.

"How have you been, Aunt Tessa?"

"Busy with antiques, buying and selling."

"How's the shop?"

"Busy."

That was Tessa, straight and to the point, a perfect businesswoman.

"But you're feeling well? Not overworking, I hope."

"The shop's bustling so I can't complain. The money's good, I have my health, and now that your mother hasn't gone and crippled herself, I feel even better."

Crippled. Sienna hated the word. Although she would not admit it, the word now represented a big part of her life, her emotions, and the man she was forced to leave behind with a frown on his face.

When Tessa pulled the car into the driveway, Sienna noticed the Tudor still stood in glamour amidst a flush of streetlights, and almost every light inside the house was turned on. The place was on fire with one hundred watt glare. Anyone could look right inside, Sienna thought, annoyed. At least it was neat and beautifully decorated. She shrugged and smiled. Aunt Tessa and Mother were quite the self-sufficient pair.

The lawn was abundantly green, impeccably mowed into thick cornrows. Mother's flowers were in radiant bloom. Bucketed Hibiscus flanked the portico while rosebuds followed the path of a whitewashed trellis, climbing toward the pitch of the roof outside the kitchen window. Lilacs hedged the window's other side. Mother loved to meet the perfume of roses and lilacs head-on when she opened her kitchen window, especially during breezy morning breakfasts.

Once inside, Sienna paused in the center of the living room, her eyes drinking in every facet of the home in which she had been raised. She had forgotten how high the ceilings were, and how white the plaster walls appeared against the glistening crystal candelabras distinguishing nine-foot doorways. The patterned draperies had been replaced. Now solid burgundy damask gathered in neat pleats beside lofty windows, admitting a sparkling array of starlight into the spacious living room.

Lightheaded, Sienna inhaled a series of lumbering breaths and bolstered her faltering limbs.

"Are you okay?" Tessa asked, lines in her forehead drawn tighter.

"I'll be fine. It's just going to take me a while. This has been one of the worst days . . . nights of my life." With a sigh, her breathing began to ease. "I forgot how lovely it is up here. The house looks wonderful."

Tessa scowled. "You should have stayed here with us, instead of running off to New York."

"I'm a lot wiser now." Sienna attempted a smile. "And I moved to New York for a better job if you recall."

"You should have stayed."

"I had to get away. I couldn't bear all the fighting with Rob. I had to make a clean break. Do you understand what I'm saying?"

"Perhaps," Tessa replied wistfully, recalling how quickly she departed the south after her husband left her. "And he still went running after you. We could have protected you if you'd stayed here."

"Nothing would have stopped that maniac. He was hell-bent on destruction."

"Of both of you." Tessa's words were icy. "I'll put on a kettle for tea, take the chill off the night. Maybe we'll be able to squeeze in some sleep before picking your mom up tomorrow." She looked at the clock. It was four am. "I should rather say today." She paused at the doorway to add, "Thank God he's out of your life," then left the room.

Sienna was antsy; she'd never sleep, and if she did she was sure it would be interrupted by a nightmare.

While Tessa was in the kitchen, Sienna studied the living room, padding softly on the carpet in bare feet. The fireplace captured her attention. She affectionately ran her hand the length of the mantel. She had spent many a night curled up on a Persian rug, reading novels and magazines before a spitting fire. She missed those days.

The mantel was lined with family photos. Sienna smiled at her image in stages of growth. As her fingers lovingly stroked a portrait of her parents on their wedding day, she fought a lump in her throat. She noticed a creased photo of herself in cap and gown tucked behind the rest. When she unfolded the hidden half, there stood Rob beside her. Her stomach clenched. She remembered her urge to tear it to shreds before heading off to New York, and wondered why she hadn't. Suddenly, the room threatened to spin. At the sound of Tessa's footsteps falling lightly on the hardwood hallway, she shoved the photo behind the others. Later she would shred it.

Taking a last glance at the mantel, she admired framed memories of Tessa and Margaret in their youth, along with adoring grandparents and distant relatives she couldn't seem to place.

What a lifetime of memories this mantel holds, she thought, then smiled, wondering how long it took her mother and Tessa to dust the photos and all of the shelved and tabled knick knacks.

Everything inside the room was spotless. Her condo came to mind, bare and easy to keep clean. If not for her cats, it would have been unbearably lonely.

Sienna rubbed her hands up and down her arms, stroking the crinkled arms of Trainer's leather bomber. Realizing she now felt warm, she slipped the jacket off, shook it, and placed it neatly across the arm of a chair.

By the time Tessa entered the room, carting a teakwood tray supporting two cups and Victorian rose teapot, Sienna was perched at the edge of the walnut-trimmed sofa.

"I might stay this time. I've made a mess of things in Connecticut." Pained, she pictured Michael. He had looked so puzzled, so angry, so sad. Would it be better if she . . .

"Here we are," Tessa announced. After lowering the tray to the sofa table, she directed a sharp look into Sienna's red-rimmed eyes, then scrutinized her bare shoulders and upper chest exposed by the dress. "Here." She plucked a lacy crocheted throw from a nearby chair and tossed it across Sienna. "Cover yourself, you'll catch cold."

OUT OF THE BLACK

Dressed in midnight blue sweats Michael went outside, hoping the night air would clear his head. He would study the stars like he did as a kid, through hands curled up like a telescope, but tonight the sky was black. A solid layer of clouds masked the stars, and the sliver of moon would soon fall into dawn. Storms were near; the air smelled like rain. The weather channel didn't have to alert him, the trees did, as bending branches hissed.

Michael wondered how Sienna was, if she had reached her mother safely. He hoped everything in Ontario was had turned out well. Although he was devastated by the carnival bedlam, he still cared enough to worry about her. He now knew nothing could ever come of their relationship. What relationship? There had never been anything between them; it had been all inside his head. How stupid could he have been?

The Suburban was parked in front of the cottage. Michael sat in the darkened driveway, not far from the garage, cloistered by evergreens. Although the forest was alive, he'd never felt so alone. He listened to sounds he had never concentrated on before: the creaking of limbs, murmurs of branch rubbing against branch in blustering breeze, leaves crackling like eerie footsteps. But the cadence of the forest was not human, its calming effect minimal. Anticipating the storm, he would remain outside, melt into darkness as he fell with the rain.

He thought about where he was now, and where he was heading — nowhere.

He made his decision. After the current projects were completed, he would move to the beach. The ocean was calming. He needed that atmosphere now. He had never lived at the beach. It would be something new. Changes were on the horizon. Maybe he would move soon. Why wait for skyscrapers or a surgery that would probably fail anyway? At this point, Michael didn't care much about anything.

At the edge of the forest, Leo throttled the engine then stalled the bike in a skid along mossy ground. There, the Honda stood in a tilt, with Leo relying on his left leg for balance as he scanned the area to confirm he was alone. He re-started the engine, revved and jumped a low barricade.

Inside the yard, once again he lit up the tires, grinding gravel into earth leveled by bulldozers. Leo knew Michael's heavy machinery was locked inside a chain link fence far from where he frolicked recklessly. He could enjoy himself without concern.

Construction at this particular site was just beginning; there weren't many valuables lying around to worry about — or so he thought.

"Wheeeww," Leo shouted, lifting the front tire of his bike in a brazen wheelie. He felt a rush as he easily overcame gravity and charged the clearing like a bull attracted to crimson.

Another orgasmic release: "Yeeaaahhhh." Leo was carefree, ravaging the perimeter of the yard. His tires cut an obstacle course as he wove through piles of cement blocks, jumping over lengths of discarded pipes and planks littering anthills of sand and gravel. In the distance, floodlights illuminated the construction trailer where Michael met with his men every day.

The Honda throttled down as thoughts of Gina escalated. "I wonder if she's still awake?" Taunted by her image, he deliberated.

He wanted to hear the sound of her voice. At rest in the shadows near the trailer, the bike produced a mellow idle. "I'm gonna call her," he said aloud. "What the hell do I have to lose?"

Her cell phone was probably in bed with her, where he would love to be at this moment. Maybe he could sneak in, climb into her darkened bedroom window concealed by the leaves of overhanging branches. Who would know?

Their kiss goodnight had been brief, but her lips held promise. He had wanted to plunge his tongue into her mouth, but the porch light suddenly came on. Even though they were in the privacy of the Volvo, he had been uncomfortable, certain her parents were watching from a window. Besides, the Volvo had bucket seats. What was he supposed to do — pull her over the console and onto his lap? Of course. But did he? No. At the thought of her full lips, her inviting arms gripping his neck, so close that her hazel eyes bore into his as she strained toward him, Leo became aroused. Had she wanted more? Did he disappoint her by sending her into the house with a mere brush of sealed lips?

He shoved a hand into the side pocket of his jeans. No phone. He reached into another pocket. No phone? What the hell?

"Shit," he muttered, remembering he had taken the cell from the Volvo's console and stuck it in his pocket.

The phone had cost him a month's salary. He needed to find it, but it could be lying anywhere between the highway and the site. He would never find it if it had dropped onto the darkened pathway. He began his search in the yard behind the trailer, making his way toward the clearing bordering the thickest part of the forest. That's where he had pulled his most daring wheelies.

He rolled the bike behind the construction trailer where the light was stronger. He pulled off his helmet and cut the engine. The only sounds in the night were annoying crickets, reminding him his phone could be lying in a patch of tall grass where he'd probably never find it. Now, on foot, crouched low to the ground, he continued to search, wishing he had a flashlight.

Thinking he heard voices, he paused abruptly, perched on a knee, a boot ground into solid earth. Nah, it's those damn crickets. A moment later he heard them again, this time more audible. *Who the hell would be here at night other than a biker like me?*

But he didn't hear any bikes, only muffled voices. He crept to the trailer's edge, then ducked behind coils of wire. Peering into the darkness, he strained to see. The voices grew louder, along with an occasional ragged cough, or was that a laugh? His adrenaline surged. A flashlight scanned the area, not far from where he listened intently. Three derelicts came into focus, possibly the ones who had been vandalizing homes and shops in town, maybe the school. Now they were about to hit Michael's site? *I don't think so . . .*

The flashlight's beam shuddered then fell on a van, its back doors wide open. The men were picking up scrap metal, loose tools, anything that wasn't nailed down. Leo knew there was valuable equipment in the yard. He wanted to stop the thieves, but doubted he could handle the situation alone. He also remembered he had no cell phone. The bike . . . Leo crawled back to the Honda, hopped onto the seat and started the engine, ready to rev and raise dust. He would try to scare them off. That was the best he could do for Michael. As he took off, his helmet lay discarded on the ground in the same place he had dropped it. Beside it was his black cell phone, pressed into the sand by the weight of a boot, or perhaps a tire?

The bike roared. Leo was so close, his headlight glared against the side of the van. It was murky green, with a rusting roof rack and twisted left front fender. He got a good look at the men, stringy haired vagrants wearing dark baggy pants and long-sleeved shirts. They saw his headlight, froze momentarily, then scattered. One, well over six feet tall, disappeared behind the van. Leo couldn't make out their features, but would bet they were the vandals the police were looking for.

With the skill of a champion racer, Leo darted around them like a cowboy ready to lasso. The bike churned dirt and gravel, hurling it into the air, the Honda rearing like a bucking horse. The men shouted, one above the rest, cursing loudly. Leo encircled them with a wall of choking dust. He heard them coughing, and shortened his own breaths to avoid inhaling dirt.

"You little shit," the loud voice yelled, throwing a wrench that hit Leo in the shoulder, almost knocking him off the bike.

Head down, hunched over, a death-grip on the handlebars, Leo shouted back, "Fuck you, assholes. You'll be in jail in about five minutes. I called the cops."

Although the exchange had been sudden and swift, the timing seemed off to Leo, who saw himself as if through a spectator's eyes, careening in slow motion. He experienced his first bout of de-realization and had to concentrate to remain alert.

Whatever tools they had been holding immediately dropped to the ground as the three men ran to the van, the tall one leaping head-first into the open cargo area. The engine sputtered, then roared, and the van bounced across the yard heading straight for Leo. "Get the bastard and then get us the hell outta here," the one in the back yelled to the driver.

"Fuckers," Leo yelled, almost dumping the bike as he sent up such a thick wall of dust it blinded the driver. They had no choice but to flee, with the van's back doors slamming open and shut.

Leo watched their taillights disappear onto the highway. With no cell to call Michael or the police, he would head to Michael's cottage, fill him in on what had occurred and from there they would call the police. He repeated the van's license plate number over and over in his head and gunned the bike. He'd take a shortcut that should deliver him in less than ten minutes. He headed toward the denser edge of forestland, the area that bordered the back of Michael's cottage. He felt drunk, without the enjoyment of drinking a beer.

Michael heard it before he saw it, a powerful roar accompanied by a vague sound like cracking saplings. At first he believed it to be thunder, yet the air overhead was undisturbed. Although strikes of lightning brightened the sky far across I-95, the storm was too distant to create such commotion in the backyard. He stared in the direction from which the sound originated. As it grew closer he realized it wasn't weather related; it was something else, an anomaly thundering through the trees. The sound morphed into a distinctive whine, and it was affixed to a glaring light surging almost out of control. *What the hell?*

Michael then realized it had to be a Quad, perhaps a motorcycle. But who could it be at this hour, racing through the woods like a lunatic? That was dangerous, potentially lethal. *Leo?* Michael barely had a moment to think, let alone react before the glaring beam hurtled through the barrier of evergreens. The bike headed straight for him. *What the fuck?* was his last thought as he felt himself being plowed, lifted and hurled by a tsunami. Then the rain-filled sky hanging low overhead began to spin.

In his haste, Leo didn't spot Michael until the last possible moment. He braked fiercely, then felt a thud, and watched in horror as Michael's body landed on the pebbled driveway. Without even turning off the engine, Leo dumped the bike and ran to him. "Michael!" he screamed. "Michael, are you okay?" His heart pounded.

Leo threw himself onto the ground and hovered over Michael, a frightful sight sprawled out upon his back. He panicked when he saw Michael's limbs bent in awkward positions. One arm was tucked beneath his thigh, the other splayed out, fingers curled, beckoning. Leo was afraid to move him. The glare of the bike's headlight was macabre, shimmering against the side of Michael's face, which was smeared with blood. Leo checked his neck for a pulse; it was slow, rhythmic, while his own was racing.

"I'll be right back," Leo panted into Michael's ear, then scrambled into the house to phone for help. He returned within moments and kneeled beside him.

All the while Leo watched the rise and fall of Michael's chest. "You're gonna be fine. I promise."

"Oh, man," Michael managed to groan. "I told you . . . be careful with that damn bike."

Tears gathered at Leo's lashes. His voice was charged with emotion. "I'm so sorry. Hang in there, the ambulance is on the way. They're calling Dr. Pollock. He'll meet us at the hospital. Everything's gonna be fine."

THE BREAK IN

The school was a fifteen minute drive from home, during which time Mickey received three text messages from Bonnie, the last advising if he called her and didn't get an answer, she'd be in the tub.

Mickey pulled the BMW into the faculty parking lot. Although it was void of vehicles, the lot was lined with bright flood lamps amplifying the heavy downpour that erupted shortly after he arrived.

When Mickey leaned over the driver's seat to find an umbrella, he noticed that the paintball gun he'd used the past weekend was still lying on the floor in the back of the car.

"Hmm," he mumbled, picturing Bonnie's face. After a moment's deliberation, he decided, "Why not?"

He snatched his umbrella from the back seat, grabbed the gun and threw it into his satchel. Exiting the car, he fished in his pocket for the key that would let him into the school. With long strides he dodged widening puddles. There would be nothing worse to top off this night than to sit on a wooden chair with damp clothing and soggy tennis shoes.

As he paused at the door, a police car cruised into the lot and shined a spotlight on him.

"What's your business here," an officer called out.

"I teach here," Mickey replied. "My turn for guard duty. With the vandalism, we can't be too careful."

"Can I see some ID?"

"Of course." Mickey stepped back into the rain, reaching into his satchel, his fingertips brushing the barrel of the paintball gun. Thank goodness it was hidden deep inside the satchel. How would he explain that one away? He suppressed a laugh and handed the officer his license and school identification.

The officer examined the plastic cards, comparing the photos to Mickey's face. "Okay, Mr. Murray. Not a great night to be out. Have a good one." He returned the ID's and tipped his cap. "How long do you plan on staying?"

"A few hours," Mickey replied, wiping rain from the side of his face. "It's good to see you patrolling the area. I hope you catch those punks before they do any more damage. They're scaring the hell out of my wife. And a lot of other people," he admitted with a nod of his head.

The patrol car left as swiftly as it had arrived, tires spitting water as it crossed the lot. Mickey watched the taillights recede then went inside, trying the door handle to make sure it had locked behind him.

The sight of the authorities was comforting; Bonnie had spooked him, gotten under his skin, as usual. He laughed off the jitters as he walked through the faintly lit building, heading down the hallway leading to the Science Lab. He passed the English Office and Teacher's Lounge, pausing at the Computer Lab to make sure that room in particular was secured, as it held the most valuable equipment.

Mickey entered his room, flipped on the light switch and dropped his weathered satchel onto his desk. Reaching inside, he removed a few pens and markers,. For a moment he held the paintball gun in the palm of his hand, noting it appeared an authentic .45 caliber weapon. He dropped it into the top desk drawer. He'd have to text Bonnie before starting anything. She'd be in the tub relaxing, but worrying. The phone face read, "Message Failed."

"Must be the storm," he muttered. "I'll call her later."

Lightning flashed, illuminating the room more effectively than the fluorescents, which now began to flicker. The wind drove pelting rain against the windows. "This is going to be a short night," he said to himself, thinking of his warm bed and wife.

About to dive into his work, Mickey opened a side drawer and pulled out a stack of exam papers. A sharp clap of thunder, followed by strobe-like lightning, circled the room. The cracking sound he heard was so emphatic, Mickey thought something struck the roof, a power line or a split tree limb perhaps. Before he reached the window to see what was happening, the lights flickered then the school and grounds went black.

"Great," he grumbled, feeling his way back to his desk to rummage through draws for a flashlight. The desk held no flashlight, but streaks of lightning bleached the room.

NEED DRUGS . . . NOW

The van barreled down the highway then swung off onto a dirt side road, jerking to a stop.

"Close the freakin' doors," the driver yelled at the guy in the cargo area.

After doing so, the tall man climbed into the back seat, his pants wet from wind-driven rain. Two were in front, smoking pot. Their clothes were covered with dust and dirt from their earlier encounter with Leo's Honda. The interior was thick with the smell of burnt grass.

"Gimme a hit," the tall man demanded, snatching the joint and inhaling deeply.

The smoke coursed past his stubble beard up across his mustache, curling sideways into the nostrils of his hawk nose as he sucked in two hard drags.

"Gimme that back," snapped the man in the passenger seat. "It's all we got."

The tall guy flopped back against the seat. "We don't got much stuff in the back. Tonight was a waste of time thanks to that fuckin' shit on the bike. I'd like to wring his neck."

"We gotta do something," said the driver. "We've got no cash. And now that we're out of that shithole rehab, we got no place to crash 'cept this van, and it's startin' to smell like B.O. We gotta make another hit. That's all there is to it. This weather's perfect. I gotta take a piss first."

Stopping at the side of the road, he opened the door into driving rain and without exiting the van, unzipped his fly, leaned out and voided into a puddle, laughing as his urine splashed and mixed with mud.

In the darkness of the school lot, the three didn't see Mickey's BMW parked a few yards away.

As the storm raged, Mickey didn't hear the crunch of the crowbar against metal, or the snap of the door lock. He didn't hear the squishing noises of their wet rubber soles on the slick tiled floor, either. All he heard was thunder, the furious rain as it pelted the windows.

Preparing to leave his classroom, Mickey inched toward the open door, feeling his way out. Beads of perspiration gathered around his hairline, and not because it was hot inside the building. He should have listened to Bonnie and stayed at home. *Where's the janitor when you need him? It would be great to hear the generator start.* He had one foot out the door when he heard a gruff voice not far down the hall. Was it the janitor? No, there was more than one voice. He stopped dead in his tracks and stiffened, then quickly backed into the room, tripping over a chair that slid across the floor, slamming into his desk. *Shit.* He froze, hoping the storm had covered the sound.

The thieves made their way down the hallway, flashing lights upon every door, peering inside each room. At the brink of withdrawal, they were agitated, angry. They needed drugs, and sooner would be better than later before they crashed and became really lethal.

The one with the crowbar began to smash the glass paneled upper portions of the oak doors of each lab and classroom.

Again and again Mickey heard the shatter of glass. "Shit, for sure that's no janitor."

Clutching his cell phone, he punched in 9-1-1. "Still no signal."

His only hope was to escape undetected and drive to the police station. But how would he get out of the building? The only available exit was in the path of the thugs, who were on their way toward him. From the sound of it, there were a few of them — and no doubt, they wouldn't hesitate to bash his head in. He'd be helpless against them.

They were closer now. Mickey winced as he heard the glass in the Teacher's Lounge, three doors away, shatter and crash to the floor. What could he do to protect himself?

Then it occurred to him. The paintball gun he had dropped into the desk drawer. He quickly grabbed it. It looked authentic enough to hold them off, hopefully get him out of there alive.

They were just outside the door as he stood, gun in hand ready for — for what, he didn't know. He ducked behind his desk as flashlights shined across the room. Had they seen him? His heart pounded as he heard footsteps enter. His gut contracted at the sound of shattered glass nearby, followed by the thud of heavy boots kicking down a door.

"Jackpot," a voice called from the corridor. "Get your asses in here. Look at all these computers."

Footsteps receded; Mickey released his breath. His mind raced.

He knew they had found the computer room, loaded with thousands of dollars worth of equipment. How would it look if the school were ransacked and robbed while he was on the premises? He took a deep breath.

"Be careful," one thief snapped. "Don't break anything. This shit's worth big dough."

Gun in hand, Mickey crept into the hallway. The thieves were loud and careless. They'd never hear him; they were too excited by their potential haul. All Mickey had to do was to slip around the doorway and ambush them.

He stood just beyond the splintered door, listening to their obnoxious banter. He didn't understand how anyone could be so vile and destructive. His fear subsided as anger emerged.

He burst into the room waving the paintball pistol as if it were a heavy gauge handgun, adopting the pose he'd seen so many TV cops use.

"School Security!" He shouted from the doorway. "Don't move."

For a moment the three froze in confusion. "What the fuck?" the driver snarled, shining the light directly into Mickey's face.

Mickey raised an arm, then shifted his stance to avoid the light.

"You're no security guard." The driver advanced, crowbar in his hand. Seemingly stunned, the other two held back.

Remembering his paintball survival skills, Mickey acted with a clear mind. "Stop or I'll shoot," he said in the most menacing tone he could muster.

The driver ignored him.

Lightning burst through the room, turning shadows into flesh and blood figures.

Mickey aimed for his midsection and without further warning, pulled the trigger three times. The gun had a strong blowback action. It functioned like the real thing. The impact sent the man reeling back into a table where his foot caught the leg. Body twisting, he fell heavily to the floor, his head striking the corner of the desk on the way down. He sprawled on his back, groaning, red paint spreading across his chest, stains highlighted by the glow of his own flashlight as it spun to a stop at his side. Blood dripped from his forehead, coating his eyelids.

Motionless, the other two stared.

The one on the floor must have thought he had been shot, and writhed in pain, hands hugging his stomach as he moaned.

Mickey had to act fast before they realized his gun wasn't real, and the guy on the floor was coated with paint, not blood.

"Face down you two. On the floor." Mickey never would have dreamed he'd be so cool in such a situation.

He hit redial on his cell phone, praying the call would go through.

Still, there was no service, but he spoke into the dead phone anyway, reporting the incident, stalling for time.

"Just stay where you are. The police are on the way."

Mickey knew he couldn't hold them off much longer. The guy on the floor would soon realize he hadn't really been shot. Then what? They'd beat him to death. Think, he urged himself, as every muscle in his body vibrated.

THE HERO AND THE HOSPITAL

The patrol car looped around the city. It had been well over an hour since their tour of the school grounds.

"Drive by the high school again," the rookie officer who had confronted Mickey said to his partner. "I want to see if that teacher's still there."

"You're edgy tonight. What is it, the storm?"

"No, just call it a hunch."

They drove back to the school, expecting to see only Mickey's BMW at the end of their spotlight beam. Through the rain the spotlight illuminated the parking lot, and the van, where it was pulled close to the side door, its back open.

"Call for backup," said the driver, bolting from the car, hand on his revolver.

Soon, another squad car arrived, carrying two more uniformed men.

Mickey, still standing in the computer lab doorway, held the three junkies at bay. Sweat dripped from his hairline into his eyes, stinging them. His hands were clammy, and the gun no longer fit his palm the way it had earlier.

The men began talking amongst themselves.

"Shut up," Mickey shouted, trying to sound menacing.

And then he heard the footsteps coming down the hall. He saw flashlights cut through the dark. Guns drawn, the officers approached with caution.

Not a moment too soon . . . Mickey heaved a sigh. *Thank you,*

Lord. "In here," he called.

One came up behind him. He felt the barrel of a gun press against his back.

"Drop it," an officer ordered.

"It's me," Mickey stammered. *How could they think . . .?* "I met you outside. You saw my ID. It's a paintball pistol." The gun fell from his hand, making a tinny sound when the aluminum barrel hit the floor.

"Turn around — slow," he said.

"They broke in during the storm. This's my class," said Mickey. "Can I sit down before I faint?"

"Nice goin' teach," said the rookie.

All three were cuffed and led from the building.

One officer remained behind with Mickey.

"Are you okay? I can't believe you did this with a paintball pistol."

"Neither can I."

"If these are the guys we've been looking for, you've done the whole town quite a service, and you've hit a personal jackpot."

Puzzled, Mickey looked up at the officer. "What do you mean?"

"Seventy-five grand, reward presented by the mayor himself."

As he followed the police to the station, Mickey yielded for an ambulance that sped by in the direction of Manchester General Hospital. He assumed it was a storm related accident, and didn't give it another thought.

Leo rode in the ambulance with Michael. An attendant monitored Michael's vitals.

"He's not dying, is he?" Leo questioned in a hushed voice.

Michael was pale and moaning, his eyelids fluttering, as if blinking away raindrops still dotting his face.

"I don't think so," the attendant replied without looking, pumping a blood pressure cuff. "Tell me again what happened?" He raised one of Michael's lids, flashing a penlight across his pupil.

Dr. Pollock met them at the hospital. He assessed Michael, and asked Leo to repeat once again exactly what had occurred. "He's conscious, but I'm ordering a brain CT," Pollock said to the nurse. "No visible trauma other than a scrape on his forehead."

"Well, that's good," Michael grunted, suddenly alert. "Because I feel like I got hit with a brick. And you better check my back, doc."

"I *am* checking your back, Michael," Pollock replied, a curious look overtaking his face.

"Feels like the shrubs I landed on tore a hole in me."

"Oh . . ." Pollock smiled, obviously relieved Michael wasn't suffering memory lapse. "Sure, Michael. We'll take a look at your back now."

"Michael," Leo wailed from the doorway. "You're okay."

"Just great, as you can see. What the hell happened?"

"I'm sorry. I didn't see you sitting out there. What were you doing sitting in the dark, anyway?"

"None of your business." Michael's tone was flat. "Now give me a damn ride home, will you?"

"Not before we run some tests," Pollock cut in.

Sighing, Michael rolled his head to the side. "More tests . . . great. You may as well leave, Leo. I have a feeling it's gonna be a long night."

The defeat in Michael's voice, along with the urgency of the doctor's, stopped any possible optimism from inching across Leo's face. "Michael . . ." he sputtered, hopping aside as the bed was shoved through the doorway. For a split-second, he glimpsed Michael's grim lips, pale as the linen sheets, then focused on the attendants' blue scrubs and receding footsteps as they disappeared down the corridor, pushing his friend into what seemed like another dimension.

There were no voices to relate to, but the hospital breathed echoes: whining electronics, doors snapping shut. Leo retreated into the room, now stalled in silence — and in time. In the distance a phone rang, a keyboard may have clicked. He checked his wristwatch continuously, comparing his time to the wall clock.

Sitting in a stiff chair beside the one that held Michael's clothing, Leo sank back, resting his head against the wall. As he shifted positions, his foot hit something pliable. Someone had kicked Michael's running shoes under the chair. Leo let out a groan, wiped the corner of his eye with the sleeve of his sweatshirt, then noticed the tissues on a shelf. He grabbed for the box. The time in his head dragged more than the hands of the clock. At the jangle of wheels that grated on the floor tiles, and voices sounding muffled, Leo's eyes snapped open and he jumped to his feet.

"I thought I told you to go home." Michael said, facing him with a grin of relief.

"How did it go? What did they say? Can we leave now?"

"Well — I still can't seem to move my legs, so I'm not sure." Leo stared at him, appearing dumbfounded. "But . . . What? . . ."

Michael's grin spread. "Relax. It's nothing life-threatening, but Paul has to sign me out. Give me my clothes, will you?"

"Michael . . ." Flipping through a chart, Dr. Pollock entered the room, reading and speaking as he walked. "The scans were negative for serious injury. Other than a few bruises, you seem to be okay. But . . ."

"But what?" Michael said, reaching a hand out to Leo, who held his clothes but halted when the doctor shot him a look.

"While I have you here," Pollock said. "The MRI . . ."

"Not now, Paul. I just want to go home. I'm beat."

"Something's changed. The fall jarred the alignment of your spine. If we're ever going to do anything, now's the time."

Michael evaluated the expression on Pollock's face. For a moment, he looked more like an anxious relative than a doctor.

"You're in great shape. Testing has all been completed. I'd like to keep you here, and within a day or two . . ."

January Valentine

LUNCH AT THE OVERLOOK

"**W**ere you able to sleep at all?" Tessa asked as she approached the sofa carrying a mug of black tea and a blueberry muffin on a small, round breakfast tray lined with a frilly bakery doily. She had showered but still wore a white bathrobe and scuffs. Her hair was swept into a loose French braid, emphasizing her attractive face which had a fresh, scrubbed look.

Sienna was curled up on a blush-toned traditional settee, snuggled beneath the rose colored afghan Tessa had tossed to her. The windows were open. A faint breeze rhythmically ruffled the ivory lace curtains, chilling the room.

At the sound of Tessa's voice, Sienna stirred, squinting through eyelids swollen by exhaustion and emotion.

"Hi," she replied groggily. "I slept on and off. Did you?"

"Somewhat. Why don't you stay here while I go and collect your mother?" Tessa offered. "You look terrible. Try to get some more rest so you don't give her a heart attack when she gets home. Use one of the beds upstairs." She frowned.

"No, I want to go with you, Aunt Tessa. But I didn't bring anything with me. I can fit into Mom's things. I'd like to get out of these clothes and take a quick shower. Give me ten minutes and I'll be ready."

"Eat your breakfast first, so you don't fall over. I'll dress and be waiting for you in the kitchen." Her voice was clear and cool. Leaving the room, she mumbled, "Thank goodness she wants to get rid of that awful dress."

In the upstairs bathroom, Sienna peeled off her clothing and luxuriated beneath the strength of a steamy shower. She shampooed her hair and cleansed her skin thoroughly, as if to wash away sin.

She found tan linen slacks and a floral pullover folded neatly on her mother's bed. Tucked beneath them was a bra and a new pair of white cotton briefs. She towel dried her hair, combed it with a pick and quickly dressed. She slipped on her shoes and met Tessa in the kitchen within her ten minute ETA.

On her way out to the car, Sienna noticed something hanging from the side of the trash can that was partially concealed by the three car garage. Tessa had stuffed her dress in with the morning trash. She shrugged. That's where it belonged. It was connected with a horrible experience. She'd never have worn it again anyway.

When they arrived at the hospital, Margaret was ready to leave, dressed in a heather shift and ivory shawl Tessa had thoughtfully brought the prior evening, along with clean underwear. A nurse wheeled Margaret to the hospital's discharge exit, where Tessa helped her settle into the front seat of their pristine sedan.

"Maggie," Tessa addressed her younger and only sister, "if you feel strong enough, would you like a decent brunch before I take you home?"

"That would be lovely." Margaret turned to Sienna, who rode silently in the back seat watching the coiling Muskoka River still gushing spring runoff toward the falls. "We can stop at Holly's Overlook, eat outdoors. It's a magnificent morning. Would you like that, Sienna?"

Margaret's voice was agile. "I'm happy to be alive and walking."

"Lunch would be nice, if you're up to it," said Sienna, although her stomach was still tied in knots. The last thing she wanted was food.

"It's wonderful to relax and enjoy this unexpected visit with you."

"I'm not sure how long I'll be staying, Mom. But before I leave I want to visit the —"

"Thank the good Lord this is developing into a pleasant reunion," Tessa interjected, hijacking the conversation. "Holly puts out quite a spread. A lot has changed since you were last here, Sienna. They have outdoor dining now, with a spectacular view of the river and some good looking waiters." She half turned in the driver's seat, tossing a hardy wink at Sienna, who barely noticed.

"Tessa," Margaret reprimanded, "you're driving past the entrance."

"For Pete sake, that damn highway department keeps moving things around — like road signs! Every damn time I drive into town, something's in a different place."

"Are you alright, Tess?" Margaret's voice wavered.

"I'm fine."

"Did you take your blood pressure medication this morning?"

"Don't worry about me, Margaret," Tessa snapped. "I know where I'm going. It's the damn city council that can't make up their minds about what they want to do next. My brain is working fine, thank you very much."

From the back seat, Sienna patted her mother's shoulder reassuring; they were together, and nothing would spoil the day, not even Tessa's bitter outlook.

"Here we are," Tessa announced as they pulled into Holly's gravel parking lot. "Do you remember this place, Sienna?"

"It's changed."

"We all change. Now come on you two." Tessa was out of the car, hurrying toward the entrance. "I'm so hungry I could eat a pig."

Margaret and Sienna exchanged glances and locked arms, following Tessa through the lounge, to the outdoor dining area dotted with white canopies and umbrellas.

They sat at an oval table beside poplars, shielded from the sun by elegant willows. The grounds were trimmed by blackberry bushes, magnolia, and tulip trees. In the distance, the Muskoka churned into rapids before reaching the next town.

"Isn't this beautiful?" Margaret said. "Look, we can see the river. I love it here, and we have a good table." She rubbed her palms together. "It's good to be out of that awful place." She peered over the menu at Sienna, who remained pale and emotionless.

"How is your job at the hospital?"

"It's a job." Sienna shrugged. "But at least I'm with Bonnie. She's someone to be around when your problems get the best of you." She lifted her face to the sun, for a moment closing her eyes, then focused on her mother's face. Noting her concern, she squeezed her hand, her expression saying: there's nothing you can do to help me, Mom. Only time can.

"Oh, I remember the story of *that* one," Tessa sassed. "Wasn't she kind of chatty with puffy red lips? That Bonnie was a surly one."

Margaret and Sienna exchanged glances. "The pot calling the kettle black," Margaret mouthed, nudging Sienna under the table.

"We almost ruined her honeymoon, Aunt Tessa."

Tessa huffed and slapped her menu onto the table. "I'll have the tuna melt," she announced to the waiter. "And an ice cold lemonade. And don't forget the ice this time."

"I'm sorry I rousted you from bed last night, Sienna. It must have been a terrible flight up here." Margaret was apologetic.

"Stressful," Sienna corrected. Emotion ricocheted from mother to daughter and back. "It wasn't your fault, Mom. Besides, I wasn't sleeping." Now was as good a time as any to mention other things . . . "I wasn't sleeping," Sienna repeated in a stronger voice to pave the way. "I was at a carnival, in the middle of a — let's just call it a situation." She sipped peach iced tea through a pink straw. "Aunt Tessa's phone call actually rescued me."

Bug-eyed, Tessa recoiled, then her lips slipped into a smug smile. "Well child, just what did I rescue you from?"

"You both know about Greg Trainer, right?"

Tessa quickly said. "Of course we know about the eligible doctor."

Margaret watched Sienna, with an anxious look on her face.

"We smoothed things out a bit in London."

"What was ever wrong?" said Margaret. "I kind of hoped you two might . . ."

"London? You never told us," a hand to her mouth, Tessa gasped, then frowned. "I remember my trip there. Of course it was years ago, and so many things have improved."

"Things got rocky, Mom." Sienna paused and turned to Tessa. "Greg and I took a long weekend, business mixed with leisure. It was nice, but . . ." She fell silent, her expression turning sour. "I'd never be able to give him what he wants. And he's not what I'm looking for. Not that I'm even looking . . ."

"It takes time to return to your old self, dear," said Tessa. "It took me years to get over the death of my husband, even though I only had him for a short time."

Margaret and Sienna rolled their eyes. "When are you going to come to terms with the fact that your ex-husband is alive, healthy, and wealthy? Tessa, you can't keep going around telling everyone you're a spinster or a widow because you're still mad at the man for divorcing you." Margaret shook her head. "For a cougar, no less."

Tessa returned a bitter glance, about to object, but tightened her jaw instead.

Margaret turned back to her daughter. "So what's been going on with you at the hospital? Besides Bonnie, do you have any other friends? Do you go out much?"

Her mother had that look again. The one that said she couldn't bear the thought of her lovely daughter spending lonely nights at home, when she should be experiencing love, and more.

"As a matter of fact, there *is* someone," she faltered, "I'm kind of interested in."

Sienna's face went from bland to radiant.

"Amazing," said Margaret, grinning. "Am I witnessing a sparkle of life here?" Sliding her glass of lemonade to the side, she leaned across the table, reaching for Sienna's hand. "Tell me, tell me. Who is he?" Her cheeks began to flush. "When can we meet him?"

"Is he a physician?" Tessa chirped in, her eyes narrowing.

Sienna was not sure how to proceed.

MY MICKEY

When Mickey returned home from the police station, Bonnie was asleep, breathing heavily through parted lips. He wouldn't dare wake her. Jarring Bonnie from dead slumber was like wrestling with an angry bear.

He tiptoed around as he undressed and got ready to shower. For a moment, he watched his wife. She wore a fluffy rose colored blind over her eyes as she snuggled on her side, facing the night stand. The radio was on but turned down low, to the rock station she liked so much. If she were awake, she'd be dancing, especially after he told her the news.

After a shower, he dropped his bath towel onto the rug and slid naked into bed. As he stretched out on his back and closed his eyes, he replayed the night. Exhausted, he simply conked out, spread-eagle, beside his wife.

Mickey awoke with a start, the past night's events fresh in his mind. He hadn't dreamt but rather experienced several hours of dead sleep.

"Red," Mickey whispered, gently nudging Bonnie's shoulder. She didn't budge.

The alarm was set for seven. It was only six-thirty. He tried again, a bit louder. "Honey. Bonnie."

"What?" she grumbled, yanking off her blinder, squinting as her eyes adjusted to daylight.

A huge smile spread across Mickey's face. He was unshaven and stubbly, and puffy around the eyes.

Bonnie tossed her blinder onto the nightstand and pulled herself up to slouch against the headboard. She yawned, then spoke with a morning rasp.

"What the hell happened to you? You look like crap. The last time I tried your cell it was two a.m. and the damn service was still out. Where the hell were you? I was worried sick." Her cheeks went from pink to red. "I'm exhausted, and I have to be at work in an hour. Start explaining."

He put his hand over her mouth. "Shush. Take the day off. We're celebrating."

She glared at him and pulled away. "Celebrating what? I can't take the day off. Sienna's out, or don't you remember what happened at the carnival." She sat up straight, concern sweeping across her face. "Oh my God. I still haven't heard from her. I wonder how her mother is."

"Calm down, honey. No news is good news." Mickey tugged her closer. "Now listen. I have something to tell you."

"Terrific, what's this, confession time? More bad news? Flimsy excuses? Where were you all night?"

"This might not be the right time." He frowned. "I'm going to make some coffee. Want some breakfast?"

"Breakfast? What were you going to tell me? What is it? Tell me." She grabbed his shoulders and shook him until the sheets slid off the bed.

A teasing grin spread across his face. "If you give me a chance, I'd like to tell you that — We're Rich!" Mickey leaned back to get the full effect as soon as Bonnie digested his words.

"Rich? What do you mean? Lotto? Did you hit lotto?" Her eyes bulged. "I knew it. I knew buying all those tickets would pay off. Damn, Persha was right. I have to visit her more often." Leaping off the bed, she wrenched her hands.

"Not lotto." Mickey swaggered across the room, opened the blinds, and faced her. "Your husband is a hero. We're getting a seventy-five thousand dollar reward."

"Hero? Reward? Tell me everything. I'm so excited." She snuggled against him. "I'm sorry if I was cranky. You know how

I am early in the morning. Now tell me everything!"

Her mouth hung open as he relayed the details, and when he reached the part where he single-handedly captured the junkies, she used her dramatic arm to brow pose, then screamed loud enough to wake the neighbors and pounced onto the bed, dragging Mickey with her.

"We're rich!"

After she finished jumping up and down on the bed, she threw her arms around him.

"My Mickey's a hero!"

It took half an hour for Bonnie to regain composure.

"I'll be late, but I still have to go to work," she whined. "You stay right here and get some rest. I'll see if I can get out of work early and we'll start our celebration as soon as I get home." She picked the sheets up off the floor and threw them onto the bed.

Mickey rolled into a comfortable position, gathering the bedding up to his neck. He still couldn't believe what had happened.

"I love you, babe," Bonnie called out as she left the house.

By then, Mickey was dreaming of where they'd vacation this summer. Forget Maine. He was thinking more like Europe, maybe the Caribbean.

HE'S IN ROOM 624A

Sienna showered and collapsed into bed. After two days with Aunt Tessa it felt good to be back in the solace of her condo, although she already missed the comfort of her mom. Had it been just the two of them, she would have stayed longer, but Tessa wore on her nerves.

At the airport they had exchanged tearful goodbyes. Even Tessa's eyes glowed with emotion, but the rest of her face remained sour.

"Michael sounds like a wonderful man," Margaret had whispered into Sienna's ear as she hugged her. "Bring him up to see us. I'd love to meet him."

Sienna grimaced. "If he ever speaks to me again after what happened."

"He'd be crazy not to," said Margaret. "He'll never find anyone better than you."

"Oh, stop it," Tessa scoffed. "Your mother was in the hospital for Chrissake. What would he expect you to do? Ignore her? You're overreacting."

"I don't mean my trip up here. I'm talking about the tension between him and Greg."

Sienna had been secretive about what had transpired at the carnival, not offering too much information about Michael.

The phone rang, interrupting her thoughts. It was two in the afternoon. She was disoriented, half of her mind still in Ontario. Was Tessa calling? Her stomach dipped.

"Hello?"

"Sienna? Is that you?"

"It's me."

Bonnie sputtered. "You don't sound like yourself. What happened up there? Is your mom okay? I kept calling but you didn't answer your cell."

"She's fine. She fell but wasn't seriously injured. I'm sorry I didn't call you. Everything happened so fast I didn't get a chance to do much more than . . ." Think about the past and deal with Tessa the entire time, Sienna thought, but didn't mention. Nor did she tell Bonnie about her soul-cleansing visit to the rural cemetery, where she stared at Rob's headstone for half an hour, praying for his eternal rest, promising to leave his memory behind once and for all.

"Why didn't you stay longer? I could've handled things here."

"She has Tessa to take care of her." Remembering her aunt's grunts and grim expressions, Sienna's voice strained. "I had to get out of there."

"Oh, hunny. I'm sorry. I wish I was there to give you a big hug. Are you sure you're okay? Maybe you shouldn't be alone. I can send Mickey over."

This wasn't the time for Bonnie to tell Sienna that Persha's prediction had materialized, at least for her.

"That's nice of you, but I'm just going to relax. It's been a long three days. Thanks for taking the guys for me. Were they good?"

"Yup. Mickey's getting attached to them." Bonnie chuckled.

"I can remedy that. We have a couple of new litters . . ."

"That's okay. I'll pass. You can pick up your kitties later, tomorrow, whenever."

"I miss them. I'll get over there soon." For a moment, Sienna paused. "Bonnie. What happened after I left the carnival? What did Michael say?"

"Michael's here." Bonnie blurted, then slapped a hand over her mouth.

"He's in our office?" Had he come looking for her? Her

stomach tightened.

"He was admitted to Manchester General the night of the carnival."

"What? What happened to him?"

"Don't panic. He's okay."

"What's wrong with him?"

"You sound terrible. Maybe I shouldn't have said anything on the phone. Look, it's a long story, but to make it short, Michael had a minor accident and was taken in by ambulance. He ended up having the surgery."

Sienna sprang to her feet and felt the blood rush to her head. She leaned against the dresser. "Surgery? What kind of surgery?"

"You know, the one Pollock's been bugging him about."

"How do you know Pollock's been bugging him to have surgery?"

"I poked into his records, okay? There, I confess."

Sienna remembered her on the floor of their office, computer printouts spread out all around her. No wonder Bonnie had been so anxious to send her out to lunch.

"How did the surgery go? Is he awake?" Sienna imagined Michael attached to tubes and wires.

"He's out of Recovery so he must be doing alright. Why don't you come over and see for yourself? He's in room 624 A, in the post surgical unit."

IRONING OUT THE WRINKLES

Sienna parked the Corolla in a shaded area of the staff lot. Arching elms with graceful boughs minimized a relentless shower of afternoon heat, but deep purple sunglass lenses failed to stop the glare. Using her hand as a visor, she headed for the entrance, up a curb, down a curb, snaking around sun-broiled bumpers and fenders.

On her way through the doors, she glimpsed her smoked-glass reflection. Desperate to see Michael, she had thrown on a pink halter top and shorts and burst out the door, her ponytail swinging like a pendulum. What would she find? Why did she doubt Bonnie's assurance? She knew exactly why; tragedy seemed a permanent part of her life. She prayed Michael would be awake and well, wise-cracking and grinning.

Her pink flip-flops squeaked as she traversed the gleaming tiles. She dashed off the elevator at the sixth floor, where high fluorescents turned the broad corridors into a dizzying tunnel-like maze. Passing door after open door, her urgent strides lengthened, breaking into a jog as she neared his room.

The door was ajar. A piece of paper was taped to the outside, with the name Michael Chessler penned by one of the nurses. Sienna came to an abrupt halt, holding her breath. For a moment, all she could do was stare. The sight of Michael's name on a hospital door was chilling; a representation that someone she knew, someone she cared about, was being held captive inside that room.

The halls reeked of lingering lunch. A resolute hum of familiar machines further thickened the stifling atmosphere. Sienna's breath, at first heavy with haste, flowed evenly as she entered. The room was chaste, dimmed by tan window blinds, slats partly closed. Two burgundy arm chairs squared off in a corner. Her eyes swept across an enamel closet and a small bathroom baring stark white porcelain. A bedside table served as a mantle, holding colorful greeting cards lying on their sides like dying birds, wings stiff in the air.

She'd always wanted him in bed, but never like this. He rested near the window, his head slightly elevated on a flat pillow. Her eyes settled first upon his pale face, then darted over his blanketed body. Recalling their last encounter, her heart ached. He had been lively and talkative, his fingers sawing his five o'clock shadow as he joked about a beard. Today he was clean shaven, expressionless, his lips like chalk. His sooty lashes curled toward the ceiling, and his dark hair was in disarray. He seemed a mere shell of the man who'd been overheated with lust just a few days ago. Michael's body was motionless, a figure draped in white, solemn, as he had been when she walked away with Trainer.

Sienna tiptoed to the bed. Leaning over him, she checked his breathing, which was rhythmic, calm, gentle puffs of slumber reaching her face. She took his hand. It felt cold. The moons of his nails were tinged purple. She brought his hand to her lips, then tucked it beneath the blanket. He appeared peaceful. Was he dreaming? Was she on his mind? Would he even care after what she had done? Would he be feeling his legs when he awoke? To Sienna, it wouldn't matter if he never walked again. She'd care for him, be there for him always. But she knew Michael wanted his legs back, more than anything.

A nurse, dressed in cranberry scrubs and polished white clogs, quietly entered the room. "Hi, sweetie," she whispered, halting at the foot of the bed. With a swipe of her slender fingers, she tacked loosened strands of golden brown hair back into a French braid that hung between her shoulder blades.

"Hello." Sienna replied, unable to return her smile.

"How is he?"

"I don't know. He hasn't moved a muscle since I got here."

"I'll just be a minute." She checked the monitors and IV that stood between the bed and window, then swung a stethoscope from around her neck to listen to his chest. "Sounds good. Pulse is strong, breathing is normal."

"When do you think he'll wake up?"

"Probably not for a while. He's got a lot of sedation in his system. He was awake earlier though, and his vitals are good. He's been through a lot the past few days. Try not to worry. He's a strong young man. He'll be fine."

Sienna managed a brief smile as the nurse patted her arm and then left the room.

The wall clock read five p.m. Visiting hours wouldn't end until eight. She went to the window and peered through the blinds. An immaculate raspberry sky formed a stunning backdrop for the mighty oaks that dominated the landscape. She hoped the idyllic view, so like a painting of a skilled artist, was a good omen.

She moved to a chair and watched Michael, focusing on his face while her mind jumped from one thing to another. She relived their first encounter. He had been so chivalrous. She smiled as she recalled how he had rushed to her aid — his grin — the compassionate look in his eyes — his gentle stare.

The clock read seven p.m. She stood and stretched, then once more, tiptoed to the bed.

"Still asleep," she whispered as if to tell him something he didn't know. She bent and kissed his forehead, then rested her cheek on the place her lips had just touched. His skin was cool and dry. "I'm so sorry."

She studied his face for the millionth time. Long hours of surgery had not diminished his handsomeness. Sienna couldn't quell the urge to lean over him, to care for him as if he belonged to her. She moved in closer, gazing at his lips, parted and sumptuous. She might never have the opportunity to do this again.

With one hand securing her ponytail, she carefully lowered her face, easing ever so slowly toward him. His breath was close now, a sweet stir in the air, his lips defenseless. His gown smelled of hospital and antiseptic, but she didn't care. She pressed her lips to the stillness of his. They were soft. She let her mouth slip to the side of his face, planting a chain of kisses on his smooth skin, his pulsing neck. She braced herself with one hand on the side of the bed, imagining what might happen should she lose her balance.

The thought snapped her back to reality. She felt warm and carefully lifted her body. Unleashing her ponytail, she shook her hair free, smoothing straying locks from her face. She'd leave now, before it was too late, before she fell so completely in love with him, life without him would be impossible. But had that not already happened?

Taking her purse from the chair, she slung the pink braided strap over her shoulder. "I'll be back tomorrow," she whispered, turning toward the door.

"Hey, don't run away so fast, sweetheart."

At the sound of his groggy voice her stomach lurched. Her legs felt weak. Doe-eyed, she whirled, her hair whipping the air. Mouth open, she stared at him.

"Sienna," he rasped, unfolding an arm from beneath the blanket.

Was that a grin? Had he forgotten what had occurred at the carnival?

"Come here," he whispered, his voice persuasive as it had been that night.

The words sent a chill down her spine. Move, she urged herself. Move!

"You're awake?" she said, vocal chords unlocking.

"No, I'm talking in my sleep," he groaned. "How long have I been out?"

"Almost all day."

"Come here. I won't bite."

She was rigid. Had he been awake the entire time she was kissing him?

"How are you feeling?" She inched closer to the bed.

302

"Give me your hand and I'll let you know." He reached out for her.

She dropped her purse onto the chair and slipped her hand into his.

"Closer, so I can see you better."

"Have the drugs worn off? Are you in pain?"

His eyes were sleepy. "Don't look so worried. I'm not in pain." A grin spread across only half of his mouth. "And I know exactly what I'm doing . . . I feel great, but my throat's dry. Can you get me some water?"

She snatched a cup from the tray on the nightstand, and poured ice water from the pitcher. "Here you go," she said, directing the straw to his lips while helping him lift his head.

He sighed. "That's better. Thanks."

Her heart melted. She squeezed his hand and the butterflies returned. "I'm so happy to see you." She smiled, then frowned. "You've been through so much. Was it awful?"

"Not so bad. How'd you know I was here?"

"Bonnie told me."

"Oh yeah, the nutty redhead. Boy she's loud. I was going to surprise you, walk into your office like what's his face does. Take you to lunch, but not here in the hospital."

She quickly changed the subject. "When will you know if it worked?"

"It works, believe me." He managed a weak laugh.

She giggled. "I meant the surgery."

"I know. Just testing." He tugged her arm.

"Ouch."

"Sorry, just wanted to make sure you're really here."

She ran her fingers softly across his cheek.

"Are you ready?"

"Ready for what?" She drew her brows together.

"Hold on, I'm going to try something. Hold my hand."

"What?" She'd never seen his face so strained, or noticed the tiny lines etched around his eyes.

He took a deep breath and gripped her hand, squeezing until

her fingers hurt. She winced. He stared at the ceiling. She sensed he was afraid. Afraid of what? What was wrong? She placed a hand on his shoulder. He was trembling, expelling short breaths in succession, as if he were doing sets in a weight room. His eyes glazed. He grit his teeth, continuing to squeeze her hand. She gripped his shoulder tightly. Finally he let out a breath.

"What's wrong, Michael? You're scaring me. Should I call a nurse?"

He nodded toward his feet. "Look." The blanket fluttered as he wiggled his toes.

Sienna brought a hand to her face. "Oh my God! You moved."

A smile broke his tension, but Sienna noticed beads of sweat forming at his hairline, while tears gathered at his lashes. She couldn't hold back. After months of wishing, praying that Michael would walk again, it seemed a dream come true. She began to sob.

"Sienna." Michael pulled her toward him. "Don't cry, honey. Don't cry." He stroked her hair and pressed her face to his.

"Kiss me again," he whispered.

"What?"

"Kiss me like you did before."

"You were awake the entire time?" she said against his cheek, then raised her eyes to his.

"I thought I was dreaming. So glad I wasn't. Were you thinking about taking liberties with me?" His laugh was soft.

Her cheeks turned crimson.

"The truth revealed," he teased.

She held him close. "It feels so right."

"Because it *is* right. I knew it all along." He lifted her chin and looked deep into her eyes, then pulled her down beside him.

She was cautious at first, fearful he might break if she unleashed the full force of her emotions. His initial response was tender, but only for a moment. His tongue traced a burning outline around her soft lips, tasting, searching, until his mouth engulfed hers. Then the tip of his tongue slipped between her lips, teasing. Her gentle nibble told him she wanted more. She moaned with pleasure. He moaned for more. She ran her fingers through his hair. He stroked her cheek, his hand drifting to her shoulder, dropping to her hip, pulling her as close as he could. "After the way things were left off, I wasn't sure we'd be doing this again." he whispered, his lips sliding to her cheek, her ear, her neck.

Her throat was tight with emotion. "We have to remember where we are."

She sat up, composing herself at the edge of the bed. She brushed her hair from her face and straightened her top. "I should probably go, and let you get some rest."

He ran a hand up her back. He nudged her shoulder. "Turn around, you." Her lips were red and swollen.

"I was just fixing my . . ."

"I'm a little warm myself." He let out a long breath. "Disappointed you yet again. Well, at least the bed is here." He took her hand, nibbled each finger as he spoke. "Dumb luck. We've got a lot in common. We belong together."

"I think our luck is changing."

"For the better I hope. I should have asked sooner. How is your mother?"

"She had a bad fall, but she'll be fine. She's in good hands." Sienna grinned mischievously and said, "My mother and aunt want to meet you."

"They do, huh? And what exactly do they know about me?"

"That you're wonderful." She brushed loose strands of hair from his forehead. "It's eight. Visiting hours are over. I have to leave." She pouted.

"You're not sneaking away so fast."

Footsteps and voices gathered in the hallway.

"Great timing," Michael said with a sigh. "There's always something to interrupt."

"I don't want to leave you."

"I don't want you to. Sneak under the covers. You're small. Maybe they won't notice you. Hey, maybe you can pose as my therapist."

"Too late. I've already met your nurse."

"Good vitals, huh?"

"You're terrible, you know that? You were awake the entire time. I'm mortified." She snuggled her face into his shoulder.

"In all fairness, I was really drugged the entire time, and you're adorable when you're mortified. You're adorable any time, actually. Although the first time we met, you were a little snob." He gripped her chin, pulling her close for a kiss then eased back. "Speaking of snobs, what's happening with your doctor friend?" Michael frowned. "What's he going to say when he finds out about us?"

"There's never been anything between Greg and me, although it wasn't easy convincing him." She rolled her eyes before her gaze softened. "He doesn't matter to me. Not like you do."

"If he gives you any trouble," he winked, "give me a week on my feet and I'll take care of him."

"That won't be necessary."

When she flexed an arm, he laughed. Pulled her in for another kiss.

The nurse popped her head through the doorway.

"How are you feeling, Mr. Chessler?"

"Just fine. When's check-out time? My bags are packed."

She laughed. "Not for a while. But by the look of you, who knows. You're making one of the fastest recoveries I've ever seen." She winked at Sienna. "Visiting hours are over. Sorry."

"I better get going. You need your rest." Sienna brushed his lips with hers. His were also plump with passion.

"Okay, but only for tonight." Michael cradled her, as if she were something too precious to release. "Can't wait to get out of this place and start living my life. We have a lot of catching up to do."

"Soon," she said, then kissed his cheek. "I'll be back tomorrow."

Michael relaxed into the bed. "I'll be right here," he mouthed a kiss, "waiting for you."

When Sienna left the hospital, her feet barely touched the ground. A full moon on the rise bleached the night. Everything looked beautiful, as beautiful as she felt. The sky was bright with stars, and the air was fresh and sweet. In the distance, the river bridge twinkled with lights. She took a deep breath, thinking of what had just happened. From where she stood in the parking lot she could see Michael's room, the window covered by slatted shadows. She yearned to be with him.

The moment she got into her car she dialed her cell phone. "Bonnie," she said, her voice bubbling with excitement. "It's me. This is it. I'm in love."

"What are you talking about? You with Trainer?" Bonnie was half asleep.

"Not Trainer — Michael Chessler."

"Wow."

DAY OF RELEASE

"**I** can't believe we're halfway through August, and neither one of us has taken a vacation. We're still locked in this room every single day," Bonnie said, her keyboard clicking mechanically without a missed beat. "And seventy-five grand sitting in the bank. I keep checking my account, staring at the balance. I'm still in shock."

"I know what you mean, but look at what kind of summer it's been. Hectic to say the least." Sienna wasn't working. She sat at an overflowing desk piled with things she should have been doing, but gazed out the window. "I wonder how Michael is."

"I doubt anything's changed since you last spoke to him." Bonnie stopped typing to check her watch. "Let's see, was it thirty minutes ago?"

Sienna laughed. "I can't wait for him to get out of rehab."

"I would never have known."

"Each time I visit him, we get closer."

"How close can you get in a hospital?"

"You'd be surprised." A smile spread across Sienna's face. "If fireworks erupt when I kiss him in a hospital bed, what's it going to be like when we're finally in my bed? I get chills just thinking about it."

"Ain't love grand? You're so hooked."

"I admit it, and it feels so good. Michael was always sweet and masculine, even in a wheelchair, but lately, he's got this kind of independence and confidence. He turns me on even more."

"Handsome in a hospital bed with tousled hair and bedroom eyes doesn't hurt either."

Sienna giggled. "I think his desire's growing along with the strength of his legs."

Bonnie slammed her chair into Sienna's desk. "Okay. Now I want to hear it all."

"You already know everything." She laughed. "I never thought anything like this could happen to me. But I can't get ahead of myself." Her tone changed. "Have you and Mickey decided where you're going on vacation?"

"We're thinking Ireland."

"Sounds wonderful."

"When's Michael getting out? Seems like he's been in rehab forever. But then again, it feels like everything happened only yesterday."

Sienna plucked a red rosebud from a clear glass vase at the edge of her desk. The rose was every bit as sweet as those in full-blown bloom at her mother's house during her visit. As usual, only the best from Trainer. She savored the sweetness, and thought of bringing the rose to Michael, then giggled. She couldn't do that to him. She pushed the long stem back into the vase beside the others, an even dozen love-notes delivered by someone she had decided not to speak to again.

She sighed. "He'll be released sometime today. Not soon enough for me."

"You've got it bad."

"He's amazing. He's everything I thought he'd be, and more. We get along like . . ."

"Have you told him about Rob?" Bonnie's arched eyebrows underscored the question.

"Not yet. And really, Bonnie, why should I? A drug addicted ex-boyfriend is not something you go blabbing about, especially the part where he tries to kill you."

"Maybe you're right." Eyes narrowing, Bonnie shrugged. "How much do you know about him?"

"Enough." Annoyance was obvious in Sienna's face. "I'm trying to forget the past, not relive it. Besides, the rehab center isn't the right place to talk about personal things." She stopped for a breath. Suddenly her eyes sparkled. "We *have* been talking about Michael meeting my mom and Aunt Tessa as soon as he's up to it. I think he's got something up his sleeve too." She wrinkled her nose.

"I hope he's not too good to be true."

"What do you mean?"

"Well, you don't really know that much about him, and you're in love with him."

"To think it almost didn't happen. Look at how many roadblocks there were — like Trainer."

Bonnie pointed to the roses. "Did you tell him?"

"Of course."

"Doesn't look like it had much of an effect." Bonnie plucked out a rose and brought it to her nose. "What did he say?"

She imitated Trainer's voice: "You'd prefer a cripple?"

"What an ass."

"Trainer goes beyond an ass."

"I'm sorry I said that about Michael. It takes me forever to trust people. It's just the way I am. Being exposed to alcoholism during childhood can do more than make you insecure."

"I never thought you were insecure."

"I'm not. I'm the flip-side: arrogant, self-assured, untrusting. Forget what I said. Don't let me ruin this for you. I'm sure Michael's the perfect man."

"Are you being sarcastic?"

"Aren't I always?"

"You're afraid things will change between us, aren't you? We'll still be best friends."

"Stop it. You're gonna make me cry."

"We have such chemistry."

"So, what's the game-plan? Where's it going from here?"

Sienna picked up the phone on the first ring.

"Okay, I'll be right there." She hung up and stared. "I have butterflies at the thought of being with him outside of a hospital room."

"He's ready to roll?" Bonnie stood to meet her in the center of the room. "I guess I should say, walk, huh?"

"Yup. I'm picking him up at Discharge and driving him home."

"So, I guess you won't be back today?"

"Not unless he shoves me out the door."

"Doubtful." Bonnie caught her in a bear hug.

Sienna laughed. "I'll be back tomorrow." She lengthened the space between them. "How do I look?" Without waiting for an answer, she grabbed her handbag and headed for the door.

"Perfect as usual," Bonnie mumbled, settling in her chair. "Think of me when it's all warm and fuzzy."

But Sienna was already hurrying down the corridor.

"First time's always the best," Bonnie grunted.

THINGS HEAT UP BIG TIME

By the time Sienna drove from the parking lot to the Atrium, Michael was outside, sitting in a stream of sunshine. A nurse stood beside his wheelchair. When the Corolla stopped at the curb, she lowered the footrests, then reached for Michael's arm. He shook his head. His feet hit the sidewalk, solid and steady, and he beamed as he stood.

"Let me help," Sienna said, rounding the front of the car. "How do you feel?"

"Great. Better than great." Michael dropped a sketch pad and sack of clothing onto the back seat, then settled in the front.

Sienna carefully snapped his door closed, jogged to the driver's side, and slid behind the wheel. Breathless, she faced him. "You look wonderful. So how does it feel?"

"I can't even begin to tell you." Smiling, he reached across the seat and sifted a lock of her hair between his fingers. "Thanks for the ride." He mouthed a kiss.

"Wouldn't have it any other way." She blew a kiss back. "It's been quite a haul for you, almost six weeks." She looked at him long, savoring everything about him, noticing how his green Henley shirt lightened his eyes. His jeans looked new, the fit showing off his sturdy thighs. "Where'd you get the nice clothes? Those weren't in the closet when I checked."

"Leo stopped by this morning. So you checked on me, huh?" He laughed.

She grinned. "Of course. Have you eaten?" From the hospital

driveway she drove onto the main road. "Want to stop anywhere?"

"Nope, just straight home. And you don't have to treat me like I'll break in half. I'm fine."

Unable to relax, she said, "This traffic is so heavy. Am I driving too fast? Are you in pain?"

"Eh, a little jab now and then, but I'll take pain over numb any day."

"You never told me exactly how the accident happened." Bonnie had planted the seed. Now she had to know.

"I don't remember much." He sounded as if he had not really come to terms with it. "I was on my way home from a meeting. Someone hit me head on. The next thing I knew I woke up in the hospital with a back injury and legs filled with cement."

"What was the surgery like? What did Dr. Pollock do?"

"Actually, it wasn't as long and involved as the first. Dr. Pollock repaired something the first guy missed, something congenital that could have caused a problem even if the accident hadn't set it off. It was just a matter of timing."

"Thank God for Dr. Pollock." She had difficulty concentrating on the road.

"That guy in New York was a pompous ass."

"He was more interested in tennis and rock bands . . ."

"Rock bands?"

"While they were putting me under, I heard them talking as if I wasn't even there." He shook his head. "They blasted the damn radio. The last thing I heard was something like Leo'd listen to. Then I woke up numb."

Sienna imagined the horror; one minute you're driving home, the next you're waking up in a hospital bed, partially paralyzed. "It's over. You can move on now." Reaching across the seat she squeezed his hand.

"I'm already making plans." He pointed to a side road just beyond the Plaza. "Here we are, take a left."

"What an adorable cottage! I didn't even know this road was here."

"One of my little projects, while I was off my feet."

"It's yours?"

"Yup, this is it."

The cottage was rustic with a foundation of stone. A redwood deck clung to the front, its weathered lumber steps leading straight to the front door. Potted geraniums hung from planter hooks along the length of the roofline, and wind chimes on either side of the door pealed like piano keys playing a full range of C notes in the soft afternoon breeze.

"Beautiful," she whispered. "A dream house."

"I'm glad you like it. Pull up here. I've never used the front door. You'll witness a first."

The Suburban was still in front of the cottage. Sienna parked behind it.

Before she had a chance to open her door, step around the Corolla, Michael was out and standing, quickly making his way up to the porch.

"Coming? Sorry I can't carry you over the threshold. Maybe you can carry me," he teased, holding onto the railing. He pulled a keychain from his pocket. "Here, you get the lock."

The door was painted bright red and had a solid brass knocker centered three quarters of the way up, matching the door handle and lock. As soon as Sienna turned the key, Michael swung the door open, ushering her inside.

"Wow," he said, stepping through the doorway. "I feel like I'm walking back into my life." He turned to watch Sienna, who stood at his side, speechless, radiant.

She brought her hands to her face, taking in every uncluttered inch of the interior. The foyer was spacious, tiled in tumbled stone. She looked straight ahead into an oversized, smartly decorated living room that had the same muted stone floor. A brightly colored oriental carpet was laid in the center, and beyond that, a tan sectional sofa with tangerine throw pillows curved around the corner of two walls. The angled sofa faced a cream colored wall with tall, narrow windows flanking either side of a fieldstone fireplace.

"Make yourself at home." Michael gazed around the cottage,

for the first time, standing. He appeared overwhelmed. "These past months have been surreal, but I'm home, in one piece, and you're with me." He smiled. "What more could I ask for?"

"I know what you mean by surreal." She couldn't let herself lapse into the past. Now she had a reason for the present, the future. She looked up at him. "I never realized how tall you are."

"You reach my shoulder." He grinned. "The tables have turned, little one. I can see the top of your head now, instead of the other way around." He wavered.

"You better sit down."

"Yes ma'am. If you look for me, I'll be over there on the sofa. Resting my tall body." He grinned. "I am kinda shot though."

"Of course you are. Are you hungry? I can run and get something for lunch."

"Look in the fridge. I'm sure Leo's been here. For a kid, he thinks of everything. Then again, he did run me over. I guess it's the least he can do."

"Hey, he did you a favor."

"Guess he did."

Michael sank into the comfort of the sofa. Not once did he take his eyes off Sienna as she moved around the kitchen, checking the refrigerator, reaching into cabinets, humming a song whose title he couldn't pinpoint. She was everything a man could want, packed into a small miracle.

She entered carrying a tray.

"I hope you like grilled cheese and tomato on wheat. And is iced tea okay? Or would you prefer coffee?"

"Tea is fine. So are the sandwiches. Were you humming the song from that movie we watched the other night in the rehab solarium?"

"It's a classic. Beautiful isn't it? What I wouldn't give to be on an island like that." She sighed.

Taking in everything she said, Michael nodded.

"You're amazing," she said, sitting beside him on the sofa.

"You are too, but why am I? You first."

"Well, look at this place. You designed everything perfectly.

It's fabulous. I love the way you've decorated. And that kitchen is a chef's dream. You really know what you're doing."

"Is that the only reason I'm amazing?" he teased, tucking a lock of hair behind her ear.

It had been a while since the wild nights that had roared in like an unexpected storm. It was broad daylight, now. And they were in his house. There was an actual bed in the next room. Things seemed different. This was real.

She was coy as she sipped her tea, watching him with lowered lids. "No." She turned her face up to his, motioning to the paisley barrel chair where he had dropped the sketch pad. "So, what are you drawing?"

"Just doodling. So you like the beach?" He moved the tray aside.

"I love the beach. I've always dreamed of living in a lighthouse. What could be better than that?"

"You," he said, gathering her in his arms.

"And why is that?" she whispered. Although she knew the day would eventually lead here, the pace was surprisingly swift. A ripple of excitement raced through her.

"Should I show you?" he breathed into her ear, kissing the sensitive hollow behind it.

"Absolutely," she sighed, pulse quickening.

STILL NO BED

Leaning forward, Sienna placed the tray onto the coffee table. Michael watched the delicacy of her lumbar appear as her knit shirt rode up her back. Her capris slid down to reveal the creamy skin plunging between the cleavage of firm round buttocks. At the thought of what was hidden beneath the pants, he bit back the overpowering urge to jump her. It had been too long.

As she repositioned on the sofa, she allowed her leg to rest against the side of his. They sat shoulder to shoulder.

"Are you thirsty?" she asked, facing him. Her warm breath touched his cheek.

"Only for you," he said, his head angled toward hers.

She watched the movement of his lips, and how he viewed her from the corner of his eye, the way his throat clenched with each swallow, and the rise and fall of his chest.

"Are you tired? Would you like to lie down and rest?" she asked, knowing damn well she'd love to be lying right on top of him — or beneath him.

He shifted, sitting sideways, bending his knee so his thigh rested on the sofa cushion. Gently lifting her leg, he moved it to his lap, then swung an arm across the sofa-back, above her shoulders, and waited. Her eyes looked glazed when he touched her. "I'm not tired. Do *you* want to lie down?"

Lust thickened his words, and the drowsy look in his eyes set her off. Faced with the reality that she was about to live out her most sensual dream, Sienna was coming undone.

Her mouth went dry. With a trembling hand she reached for her glass. An inch of tea remained, and melting ice floated. She moistened her lips.

His lips found hers in an opening kiss, and in a moment their lips pressed savagely, tongues locking. He began to pulse, and shifted her leg so it rested only on his thigh.

He ran his hand across the small of her back to bring it higher where his fingers found the clasp of her bra. A chill ripped through her body as her breasts grazed the fabric of her shirt.

Her back was smooth and cool. He ran his hand up, then down, each caress straying lower until he grasped her hip. On an upsweep, he caressed the side-mound of her breast. It was warm and firm, somehow softer than anything he'd ever touched. Satin — that was it.

For a moment she tensed, closed her eyes, then sank against his chest, sighing. His hand found her entire breast then slid to the other, fingers grasping, kneading, strumming her nipples into tingling peaks. When she shuddered, he whispered, "Tell me what you want."

She sucked in a breath and swung both legs across his thighs, coiled an arm around his neck, and strained against him. Her eyes lost their innocence. "You . . . I want all of you."

Slicing a knife across his chest couldn't have jolted him more. His brown eyes smoldered as he lifted her onto his lap. In the same swift movement, his lips crushed hers again.

After a few moments Sienna broke from him. Holding him at arm's length, her hips rolled.

"Sienna," he whispered. "You're driving me insane." Moaning, he let his head fall to the sofa-back, where he watched her through heavy lids.

"We're just starting." She arched her back and with crossed arms gripped the hem of her shirt, pulling it up and over her head. He caught a glimpse of her breasts, then her hair fell in a blanket of waves.

Michael lifted his head, dark eyes penetrating. He studied every inch of her: finely tapered nose, each high cheekbone sprinkled with threads of honey-colored hair that tumbled down her back, pink lips plump with lust, the neck of a graceful swan set between shoulders browned by the sun. Soft skin poured across her generous chest that flared into luscious breasts, nipple-buds protruding, raspberry and inviting.

"Oh, babe," he moaned. The swipe of his tongue across his lips was an involuntary reaction, as was the thud of his heart. She could be dangerous. He could handle reckless.

He parted the drape of her hair, flinging the long locks over her shoulders then his eyes crawled over her breasts.

She knew she had the upper hand, and almost giggled at the thought: *who ever said you can't have sex with your eyes* . . . His stare was so intense she felt a rush, her panties dampening.

She held her breath as she prepared for an ambush. No one had ever made her feel this way, so hungry, so brazen, so in love . . .

His longing eyes moved to hers, hands caressing her face, fingers trickling down the sides of her neck. Goose bumps rose along with the height of her nipples, and when he cupped her breasts, she sucked in a breath, wondering if he could feel her heart pumping beneath her flesh.

Fingers massaged then squeezed, his thumbs creating friction that shot to her groin, but when his mouth took over she gasped. His lips sucked so hard, she thought her nipples would detach, his wet tongue triggering an orgasm. When his teeth deliberately scraped, nipping and shocking, her panties felt soaked, moisture leaking through the fabric.

She raised her hips. He tugged down her capris, ripped off her panties. She grabbed his hand, guiding his fingers, making sure the pad of his palm rubbed the right spot each time she moved.

"Get on me," he moaned, fumbling for his fly.

"Not yet." Sliding to the floor, she ran a hand across his jeans. He was hot, tight.

"Oh, God," he moaned.

"Lie back, relax," she said, stroking him.

"I don't know how much longer I can hold out," he whispered.

His groaning filled her ears, made her crotch throb. She rocked her hips and reached for his fly, stripping off his jeans. Cool air brushed his skin before her fingers took hold. She heard a faint, "Oh shit, not yet." Then his body went rigid.

Her face hovered inches above him, lips poised. The first strike of her tongue was hot, wet. He gripped the back of her head, grabbing a fistful of her hair.

"It's been so long," he rasped, his fingers weaving through her hair, grazing her face, slipping down the sides of her neck. "God, Sienna. You're making me . . ." he panted.

For a moment, all he heard was the pounding of his heart as blood drummed his ears. Eyes closed, chest heaving, he savored the pleasure. This was better than a dream. His eyes locked on hers.

"You almost killed me," was all he could say as he pulled her onto the sofa, where he sat at the edge, patting the cushion. "Lie down." He slipped to his knees.

Shifting smoothly, she slid onto the sofa. The spot he vacated was warm. She snuggled into position, soles of her feet rubbing the fabric. Why was she tense? Expectant; that had to be it. For a moment she watched him, wide-eyed, then turned her head, bit down on her lip, sucked in a breath and held it.

He ran a hand across her hair, drenching the air with the scent of coconut shampoo. "I've wanted you for so long," he said, lips nibbling her cheek, then neck.

Staring at the spinning fan blades suspended from the cathedral ceiling, she paused then once again faced him. He was irresistible, with damp, dark hair clinging to his neck, the muscles of his broad shoulders rippling across his chest. She ran her fingers along his jaw. "You're all I want." She shivered.

"Baby . . ." Michael's voice was choked with emotion.

He remembered all of the things he'd dreamed of doing to her. The whipped cream chilling in the refrigerator flashed through his mind. Then he saw the ice. He dipped his fingers into the glass, plucking out the largest cube.

His back flexed as he moved, his smooth skin glistened.

When she caught sight of the ice in his hand, goose bumps spread from her chest to her thighs.

"Close your eyes," he whispered as he ran the ice across her lips, then kissed away beads of water. She moaned softly.

"You're gorgeous," he murmured, running the melting cube slowly along the side of her neck, across her chest, chilling each rounded breast.

He traced a path with his lips, savoring, striking each swollen nipple with his tongue which then glided smoothly along the toned indentation of her midsection, stopping long enough to swirl around her navel.

When the ice hit her belly, she screeched, arched her spine and reached for him, first gripping the back of his neck, then digging her nails into his shoulders, followed by her teeth. Her hot breath flooded his ear. "Show me what I've been missing. Taste me."

His chest heaved. He grabbed her hips. Pulled her roughly into his face. His mouth clamped down, tongue lashing, bathing, triggering a screaming orgasm. Her body bucked madly, but his mouth held her to the sofa. When she moaned, "Don't stop," his lips worked harder, his hands greedily kneading her flesh. When she screamed for more, his fingers reached beneath her.

"Oh, God . . . Michael . . . Fuck me — now."

He drew in a sharp breath and dragged her onto his lap. Then with flushed cheeks, he exhaled and shot her a look. "Shit. I don't have any condoms."

"Not a problem." Trembling, she managed to reach her capris, pull out one of several packets. "I figured we'd be needing these," she whispered.

His eyes widened, then he grinned and flipped her onto her back.

He eased in carefully at first, grinding with a gentle rhythm. Within moments she was on top of him, her hips moving with fury. She must have seen the shock on his face, because she stopped abruptly. "I'm too rough . . ."

"I'd call it passionate." He jerked her closer, fingers digging into her buttocks, finding their way inside. "I like a woman in charge," he groaned, his fingers matching her movements.

His face tightened, along with his erection. He plunged with powerful thrusts, almost bouncing her up into the air. She worried he might hurt his back. She worried he'd split her in half.

She counted her orgasms.

One: *Ohhh myyy God.* It began as a wave that mounted and tore through her, peaking, lingering with such intensity, she could barely breath. Her vibrator had never caused such a flood.

Michael pumped harder.

Two: Not as fierce, still every bit as delicious. The passion on his face added to her pleasure. *He must be close because his skin is so damp, almost dripping wet.* Perspiration soaked his hairline, fell onto her cheek.

Three: Getting sore now but, *ohhh*, combined with his groans it was beautiful, sweet, painful ecstasy.

"Oh . . . God," she moaned as he pushed harder.

His face looked pained. He grunted, gasped as he released. Then collapsed beneath her.

"I knew it would be good," he groaned, "but you're a fucking animal." A forced chuckle escaped with a heave.

After catching her breath, Sienna brought herself up and straddled his hips. "Are you okay?" she asked. She lifted her hair from her neck, piling it atop her head. Elbows jutting, she anchored the mass of curls with both hands, taking advantage of the breeze generated by the fan.

Michael's eyes traveled from the sandy patch resting just below his stomach, to where sweat clung to her breasts, throat, hairline. His stare returned to the slick warmth, recalling the feel of her on his tongue, her taste. "I'm great. You did most of the work," he said as if not concentrating on his words. His hands, still strong, clutched her hips as if he were about to once more pull her into motion. Instead, his fingers trailed across her tummy.

At his touch, her back bowed further. She shifted. He hadn't yet gone soft. He appeared flushed and not quite settled, perspiration seeping to his brow. "Be right back," she whispered, peeling off the condom before she left him lying on the cushions, speechless.

Standing naked at the sink she filled a plastic tub with cool water, took a clean cloth from a drawer and slung it over the side. While the tub rested on the counter, she found an elastic band and fastened her hair at the crown; it bunched and spilled like feathery branches of a palm.

Before leaving the room, she soaked a handful of paper towels with ice cold water, dabbed her face, ran it around her neck, mopped between and under her breasts, slid it across nipples that were sore but continued to throb.

With the open floor plan, she had a feeling he'd be watching as she touched herself. At the thought, her nipples tightened. If she'd been alone, she'd have stretched across the bed, letting her hands and vibrator take care of her needs. But he was in the next room. She felt his stare, curious, heated. She ran the damp, wadded towels up the inside of her thighs, and beyond. Useless. The towels simply slipped across her moisture.

A dry paper towel absorbed, but she remained lubricated, hungry, as she tiptoed back into the room. He hadn't moved from the position in which she had left him. She dropped to her knees. Kneeling beside the sofa, she set the plastic basin onto the floor. Their eyes met, fused. His fingers swept her hairline, skimmed her shoulder, then as if in surrender, his arm dropped toward the floor.

She dipped and wrung the cloth, then beginning with his forehead proceeded to wash him. "Close your eyes." Her words were soft. He obeyed. She trickled the cloth over his lids, across his lips, ran it down his neck, lingering on his sculpted chest, her touch light, but sufficient to cool his overheated body.

Her gaze drifted from his abs to the glistening skin the condom had moments before covered. Several times she dipped the cloth, squeezing out just the right amount of water, wiping rhythmically along his blushed flesh, then followed with the fingers of her other hand, concentrating on the heat that once more developed between his thighs.

"You're pretty good at this." His voice, not quite lighthearted, thickened as she stroked. "What, were you a nurse?"

"Nope. But I've had a lot of practice."

"Hmm." His eyes widened.

"Yup. I do this to every new guy I pick up."

He stopped her swabbing hand, held it in place, and stared. "Are you telling me you give sponge baths to every guy you meet?" The muscles of his face tightened, along with his grip.

She gazed up at him, innocent at first, then her face filled with surprise. She burst into laughter.

A slight grin found its way across his grim lips. He raised a brow.

"I do this at the shelter all the time. Give bubble baths to every pet who comes through the door. Then I cuddle 'em without worrying about fleas." She giggled.

A breath whistled through his parted lips while his grin broke into a broad smile. "You had me worried there for a minute."

"There's nothing in this world to worry about."

She covered his mouth with hers, drawing in his tongue, savoring, then eased away and buried her face against his chest.

UNCOVERING SECRETS

Ribbons of daylight that had flooded the windows faded long before their passion subsided. Stretching out across the sofa, Sienna snuggled against the curves of Michael's body. Legs threading through his, she ran a hand over his chest, fingers toying with the soft sprinkling of hair.

He held her tightly. "I don't want to let you go."

"Then don't," she breathed. "Hold me forever."

"I never figured you'd be such a seductress. But come to think of it, those nights in my truck should have been a tip-off." He chuckled, kissed the tip of her nose.

"They weren't?"

"I was too damn nervous to analyze."

"What can I say? You bring out the beast in me." She nibbled his neck, playfully chewing his earlobe.

"This is a hell of a welcome home." He let out a breath. "I'm still trying to get up the energy to move."

"You think we'll ever get to use a bed?" Sienna's words were thick.

Michael drew her close for a lingering kiss, then held her at arm's length. He was grinning. "Maybe one of these days."

She burst out laughing, put a hand over her mouth.

"I'm ready for a shower. And food. I need food." His teeth grazed her shoulder.

"Yes, a shower is a must." She planted a kiss on his cheek. "We better turn on some lights. Where did the afternoon go?"

Michael set her onto the cushion beside him. "Yeah, I never saw an afternoon turn so quickly into evening."

They looked at each other briefly, then turned away, giggling.

"Well? What's for dinner?" he said.

"I could eat a horse, but since I don't eat red meat . . ."

"A vegetarian, huh? We'll have to dine on salad then — and love."

"Love sounds good." She blushed.

"There's plenty to go around." He nuzzled her neck, tickling her.

She giggled. "How about spaghetti? The makings are in the cabinet."

"You really know the way to a man's heart," he said, now nuzzling her hand. "Add a steak to that and I'll be yours forever."

"I saw some in the fridge, with a note attached."

"A note? What did it say?"

"Welcome home, from Leo."

Michael smiled. "That kid never stops amazing me. Let's eat out on the terrace. It's a beautiful evening."

"Showers first?"

"Showers first."

Sienna stared with distaste at her clothing, a crumpled heap on the floor. "I should have thought about bringing a change of clothes."

"But you *did* think about *real* necessities." Michael chuckled, then his face cleared as his eyes enjoyed another sweep of her nakedness.

Her stomach dipped. She stared back, inviting.

His lips crushed hers again, then he abruptly set her aside. "If we don't get off this sofa right now . . ." He let out a breath before saying, "Take something from my closet," which were words lost beneath the pressure of her lips, and her hips as she slid on top of him.

"Christ, Sienna . . ." he murmured before drawing in her tongue.

After showering, Sienna dressed in the smallest pair of sweats she could find in Michael's closet. They hung on her so loosely, she had to roll the elastic waist several times, jacking the legs up above her ankles. The shirt sleeves reached her knees.

When he saw her, Michael laughed. "You look incredibly attractive in my clothing. Then again, you'd look good in anything, or not." He planted a kiss on top of the damp hair curling around her face.

"I have to say the same about you," she replied, admiring him wrapped only in a thick white bath towel.

He touched her hair. "You're starting to look like a poodle."

"Blame my father. Do you have a blow dryer?"

"Under the cabinet. But I like it curly."

"And I like yours long. Don't ever cut it."

"Never. I lit the grill while you were dressing. The steak's on. Water's boiling for the spaghetti. Hey I thought *you* were cooking," he teased. "I guess I should put some clothes on, huh?"

Sienna stood close to Michael, then placed her hands on his smooth shoulders. While on tiptoes she dropped a barrage of kisses around his face. "I'll make the salad. You get dressed. Oh, you taste so good, maybe you shouldn't bother getting dressed." Her arms encircled his neck, pulling his face to hers.

"Mmm, who needs dinner . . ."

The sky, flawless azure when they first arrived at the cottage, was now a black dome speckled with bright stars and half moon. On the terrace, they sat across from one another, talking and laughing. A light breeze whistled through dry leaves in the trees, and crickets replaced the song of birds.

"I like your hot tub." Sienna watched a post lamp sparkle across the swirling water.

"You're welcome to use it." Michael smiled, pushing aside his plate.

She lifted her face to the night. Closed her eyes. "The wind chimes hanging out front sound like church bells. I love it."

His eyes couldn't seem to gaze with sufficient intensity.

"It's a wonderful night." She drew the sweatshirt tighter, almost doubling it around herself. "Too bad summer's just about over."

"We'll have plenty more. Are you cold, sweetheart?"

"It's getting chilly. How about coffee?"

"Sure. We'll have it inside."

"Michael," Sienna said quietly, "I'd like to talk to you first."

He tilted his head. The flames of the candles on the table danced across her face, her hair.

"What's wrong, honey?"

"The night of the carnival, when my aunt called. During the flight up there, all I could do was think about the past while I worried about Mom." She paused, gauging his reaction.

"That's understandable."

"Remember the day I told you something happened that I wasn't comfortable talking about?"

Worry crossed Michael's face. He reached for her hand.

"I met a guy in my senior year of high school. We dated on and off, then during college he expected things to — to go further than I wanted."

"Honey, you don't have to talk about this. I don't want you to be upset. The past is over."

"I know, Michael. But I've had a difficult time dealing with it, and I want you to know. I left Canada to get away from him. Things got out of hand."

Michael's jaw clenched. "Did he abuse you?"

"He tried to kill me." Her voice was as cold as her fear. She trembled and pulled the sweatshirt tighter.

He stood and took her hand, guiding her through the patio door. His arms went around her. "Whatever it is, I'm here for you."

She sighed. "I'm okay. I'm finally okay. A lot has to do with you." She looked up at him. "You gave me courage. That night has been haunting me, but while I was in Canada, I got up the courage to visit the cemetery, and for the first time I'm free of him. He's gone. Out of my life. I don't have to be afraid anymore."

"He's dead?"

Chewing her lip, Sienna nodded.

"How?"

"At his own hands." It was all she could say without dredging up the days of drugs, abuse, his wild eyes, murderous hands around her throat. She would tell Michael everything some day, but not tonight. She had taken the first step, and relief washed over her.

"You've been through hell." Michael's arms tightened around her. "Can you stay the night? I don't like the thought of you being alone, especially after what you just told me — and for my own reasons." He kissed the tip of her nose. "Anyway, it's too late for you to leave, to leave me all alone." He grinned, watching her expression soften.

"I have to work tomorrow, but I guess I could get up early, run home and change. Take care of the cats. Yes, I'd love to stay." The reality of facing the empty condo after such an unforgettable day was disturbing.

"Why don't you try out the hot tub, while I clear off the table. I'll join you in a few minutes."

"You're the best thing that's ever happened to me."

"You took the words right out of my mouth." His fingers slid across her cheek. "By the way, can you get some time off work?"

"I have vacation. Why?"

"You'll see." Michael dropped a kiss on her forehead. "Arrange for at least a week. Let me worry about the rest."

SUMMER AND TRAINER ARE OVER

The August sun changed positions in the sky, rising in a southeast arc as it edged from summer. Since childhood, Sienna gauged seasons by the angle of the sun. As she drove to work, she noted tips of trees were already beginning to burn into colors of fall. It would have saddened her had it not been for Michael. She was happy he had asked her to stay. Making love and leaving would have seemed as cold as the condo, where she had showered and dressed for work after she left him sleeping peacefully at the cottage. She had placed a note on his pillow, followed by a soft kiss.

When she wasn't with him, she felt hollow inside. She hoped this night would be as fulfilling as the last, wondering where their relationship would lead. When she arrived at the office, Bonnie was seated at her desk, doodling while talking on the phone. They exchanged good morning nods, then Sienna slipped behind her desk, not at all ready to begin work.

Bonnie slapped the phone receiver onto the base.

"Everything okay?" said Sienna.

"Oh sure, that was my travel agent." Bonnie said, avoiding Sienna's eyes.

"Making plans for Ireland?"

Bonnie changed the subject. "I've been meaning to ask. How are those dreams?"

"Gone," Sienna grinned, "except for the good ones."

"Well, that's good to hear." Bonnie turned back to work

mumbling. "You look like a different person. Act like one too."

"Don't you want to know what happened yesterday? I thought you'd jump me the minute I got here." Sienna fidgeted with the top button of her blouse.

"Hell yeah. Tell me everything." Bonnie swiveled, rolling her chair close to Sienna's desk, bringing two cups with her. "Just like old times, huh? Coffee-clatching the morning after. But now we have more to talk about than just dreams." She smiled, dimples creasing her cheeks. "Gimme all the details."

While Sienna filled Bonnie in on *almost* all the details, she thought of Michael and his comfortable king size adjustable memory foam bed. She longed to be back beside him, wrapped in his arms, snuggled beneath soft covers, aligned with his body, warm and hard. She loved the hot tub — *and* the adjustable bed. Thinking about last night brought back goose bumps.

"Well, good morning," said Trainer, standing at the doorway. "Where have you been?" He shot an accusing look at Sienna. "I phoned you all night. Why didn't you pick up, or reply to my messages?" He strode into the room, his brown tweed suit befitting of autumn weather, although technically, summer wasn't yet over.

"I wasn't home last night." Sienna's eyes darted from Trainer to Bonnie.

"I understand your *friend* was discharged yesterday." His arms were locked behind his back, his legs stiff in a military stance, although he'd never been in the service.

"As a matter of fact, I drove him home. And that's where I spent the night." Recalling his cruel comments about Michael, she glared at him.

Trainer recoiled, as if she'd struck him.

"I see. And does this mean you will be spending other nights with him?"

"I hope to," she replied and rose from her desk, disliking the feeling of Trainer towering over her, talking down to her.

"I don't understand you, Sienna. You never spent the night at *my* place." He sounded like a whiney little boy whose mother refused to buy him the best toy in the store. "Although I tempted you often enough." His eyes sailed past Bonnie, her dropping jaw, open stare.

Arms at her sides, Sienna stood her ground. "There was never anything between us. Haven't you realized that by now?"

He looked stunned. "After London, I thought . . ."

"I never led you to believe we could be anything other than friends, colleagues."

"I thought we had chemistry."

"There wasn't even a spark."

"What does he have to offer you?"

"Things someone like you would never dream of."

"Well, if you want to settle . . ."

"Stop it." Hands on hips, her words were as strong as her stance. "I'm trying to be civil, but you're testing my patience, and you don't wanna go there with me."

He maintained eye contact a moment longer, then cleared his throat. "I see I can't change your mind, so I will wish you luck, Sienna. I'm sure we'll run into one another . . . at the hospital of course. And yes, it would be best to remain distant acquaintances. By the way, our trip to Paris is cancelled."

With head held high, he left the room.

"You go, girl!" Bonnie rose to hug her. "I see you left that shell of yours in London."

"I guess so. And I refuse to feel guilty."

"Why should you? He might know how to throw his weight around, and his money, but he doesn't know the first thing about love. I'm proud of how you handled yourself."

"What a way to start the day."

The phone on Sienna's desk rang.

"Good morning." Michael's throaty voice flowed into her ear. "Why didn't you wake me?"

"You were sleeping so soundly. I didn't have the heart to. I left you a note." Her soft words carried her smile across the line.

She turned her back so Bonnie wouldn't hear the rest of the conversation. "You're so cute when you sleep . . ."

HER BIRTHDAY BASH

After Sienna left, returning to Michael and the cottage, Bonnie remained in the office, tying up loose ends with her "travel agent".

She dialed the phone. "Michael," she whispered, as if Sienna were still beside her. "She's on her way, so we have to talk fast. I have her mom's phone number. I'll be calling as soon as we hang up. You better give me those details again."

Along with making love as if it were the first time, the next two weeks would be spent keeping Sienna's birthday bash a secret, as Michael, with the help of Gus, conspired to make her dreams come true.

Nights with Sienna were heaven for Michael, who spent every day planning, searching for lush waterfront land on which to build the dream home he had been designing since his hospital stay. He was also busy shopping. He had everything planned.

Fallen leaves surrounded the cottage as September quickly arrived.

"Where are we going?" Sienna asked.

"Dress comfortably, honey, but dress up," Michael said. To him, the clothes she wore didn't matter. She was always stunning, even in his oversized sweats. But Michael knew, when she walked into the middle of an unexpected circle of family and friends, Sienna would definitely want to look her best.

"But where are we *going*?" she repeated.

"We're having dinner on a boat."

"The River Station?"

"Not exactly."

"Michael," appearing exasperated, her hands flew to her hips, her eyes danced, "what do you have up your sleeve?"

"Just get dressed, Sienna." Hands in the pockets of tan dress pants, he grinned, then rolled his eyes at the scowling pout she faked before she headed for the bedroom.

By the time she returned to the living room, he had had time to pace for half an hour, and change into a black pinstriped suit, Persian blue dress shirt, and silk tie. Although he was clean-shaven, his five-o'clock shadow remained. He applied the mousse Sienna left in the vanity drawer, so his wanton waves were now stylishly tamed.

Sienna wore a strapless black sheath, a matching jacket neatly folded over an arm. Her hair, pulled away from her face, formed loose curls at the back of her head.

"Wow." Michael whistled when she stepped through the doorway.

"I'm ready," she said with a glossy-lipped smile.

"You look amazing." His grin was just for her, the special one that told her he thanked God he'd found her and that he'd be lost without her.

"Thank you." Her lush lashes fluttered as she spun around, displaying the view from behind. "And you look very handsome." At the sight of him, her heart melted. She was certain she would never recover from the thrill of looking at the man who had become her world.

"I like those earrings. They match the clip in your hair." He touched her ear and the gold caught the light. "Very stylish . . ."

"They're called chandelier." She kissed the tip of his nose, thrilled with the little things he noticed, and how boyish he sometimes looked.

Arms twined, they stepped into a breezy afternoon filled with sunshine.

Michael lifted the door of his new Mercedes and helped Sienna slide onto the charcoal bucket seat, then he carefully lowered and pressed the gull-wing door closed. The jet black sports car gleamed, pampered and adored by Michael, as was Sienna.

"You're so secretive, you're making my stomach quiver," she said as they drove along I-95 in the direction of the harbor.

Michael laughed, relieved the day of the party had finally arrived. He doubted he'd be able to keep the surprise from her much longer. Sienna had built-in radar where secrets were concerned, specifically his design plans. Gus had the drawings. Michael reminded him several times to bring them to the marina. And when Gus had asked why Michael didn't hold onto them, Michael had appeared astonished, stating, "If Sienna sees me taking plans to dinner, she'll nag the hell out of me till I spill it all in the car."

As they neared the waterfront, the road curved into a two lane thoroughfare. They crossed several small bridges, where the landscape was patched with trees thick as the bristles of a hairbrush. By the time they arrived, the sun was descending into the horizon. Glaring shades of orange and red dominated the skyline like a picture in a travel magazine.

The Mercedes pulled up in front of the vintage hotel from which their party boat would depart. A valet admired the Mercedes, especially the "airplane cockpit" interior vacated by the smiling couple. The hotel was European elegance, wide and towering, spanning six-hundred feet of dock that easily accommodated oversized vessels. While Sienna visited the ladies room, Michael stopped at the hotel desk to check the reservation.

THE MYSTIC

The Mystic stood ready to sail the moment their feet hit the dock. The ocean was calm but for a gentle tide lapping at the trusses. Sienna took a deep breath as she stared at seventy-five feet of pure luxury floating in the bay, fully loaded, like a sleek bullet about to blast off with all the amenities of a five-star hotel at sea. She tightened her hold on Michael's arm. "Wow, this is amazing." *The Mystic? Could this be a sign?* "Persha . . ." she whispered.

"What?"

"Nothing." She smiled up at Michael. "The Mystic is beautiful."

"And so are you. Are you ready to cruise?"

Overwhelmed, she pressed her cheek to his shoulder. "Absolutely!"

"Hungry?"

"Starving. I didn't realize the ride would be so long, but I'm not complaining. This is so exciting."

"We'll be having dinner very soon." He pulled a menu from a pocket. "Take a look. Vegetarian specials."

Rising on tiptoes, she pressed her lips to his. "You think of everything."

As they reached the ramp, Michael looked at her stilettos. "Hold my arm, the steps are steep. I should have told you to wear your flats."

Latching onto him, she chuckled. "What are you getting me into?"

They stepped onto the deck and down eight carpeted stairs into what resembled a Great Room in an exclusive hotel.

Her eyes spread with wonder. "This is incredible, Michael."

"I thought it would be nice to spend your birthday out here, since you love the ocean so much."

"My birthday," she squealed. "I almost forgot, and you remembered. Has anyone ever told you, you're the most wonderful man in the world?" Reaching up she kissed his ear, whispering, "Let's look around."

A sectional sofa pressed against a wall lined with rectangular portals, heavy drapes trimming either side. A bay window, with a shelf intended to hold dinnerware, was recessed behind the sofa. Occasional tables, finished with gleaming burl, were placed in pairs within arm's reach of seating. On the opposite side of the spacious cabin, Sienna spotted a full service wet bar and, when she approached, six heads and smiling faces popped up from behind, shouting, "Happy birthday!"

"Oh my goodness!" she screamed, covering her mouth with her hands. "I'm about to faint."

She turned to Michael, whose eyes sparkled with delight. "You . . . How did you manage to keep this from me?"

"Wasn't easy." He grinned at Gus.

Sienna spun, facing the happy faces that had been hiding behind the bar. "Mom? Aunt Tessa?" She rushed to her mother, pulling her into her arms. "I can't believe you're here!"

Sienna's eyes swam with joy.

"Happy Birthday, honey," her mother said, planting a kiss on Sienna's cheek. "I'm so happy to see you again." She held her daughter at arm's length. "You look absolutely stunning."

Tessa appeared at their side. "I'm here too, you know."

"It's nice to see you, Aunt Tessa."

Sienna reached for Michael's arm, inviting him into the circle. "Michael, have you met my . . ."

"Not yet. But I guess I'm about to." He smiled.

"This is my mother, Margaret, and Aunt Tessa."

"Mrs. Alexander," Michael said softly, shaking her hand. "I'm happy to meet you at last."

"Call me Margaret." She beamed. "Now I know why you're so taken with this guy, Sienna. He's a hunk." Her eyes widened, her cheeks ripening. "And I'm not one to say things like this, not out loud, anyway." She chuckled.

"You're making him blush, Mom."

"Hello, Aunt Tessa." Remembering Sienna's stories, Michael was formal with her aunt. "It's very nice meeting you both." His eyes moved from one to the other before settling on Sienna.

She slid her lips across his cheek. "Isn't he wonderful?"

"He sure is," said Margaret. "Thank you, Michael, for arranging our flight. Tessa and I truly appreciate it. It was very thoughtful of you."

"Seems like a keeper." Tessa nodded, trying to smile.

"It was my pleasure," Michael replied. "I'm glad it all worked out. I have to admit, I had some help."

Bonnie's voice rang out from the bar, where she sat on a stool nursing an exotic cocktail as Mickey played bartender. "Happy Birthday!" They both called out.

Leo and Gina watched from the sofa, where by then, other guests had begun to congregate.

"Think that could be us someday?" he whispered. She nodded, smiled.

After giving Michael the once-over, Tessa said, "You look better than I expected."

Margaret shot her a look. "I think what Tess is trying to say is, we're thrilled to have this opportunity to meet you, Michael. Sienna hasn't told us nearly enough about you."

"She's good at keeping secrets," said Tessa.

Margaret glanced at Sienna, who held her breath, wondering what Tessa's next words might be. Michael just smiled and winked at Sienna, mouthing a kiss.

"I'll have to steal you away later," Tessa added. "When things calm down, we can have a glass of wine and a nice talk, get to know one another."

"I look forward to it," said Michael, glancing at Sienna who moved close to his side.

Beer in a hand, Gus stood by, arm around Tina whom he proudly introduced. "I'd like to borrow him," said Gus, rescuing Michael from the women. "You put together a wonderful affair, and Sienna's one hell of a catch. Her mother seems nice. Her aunt . . . she's a character. Good luck, kid."

Michael grinned. "I guess I'll be needing it. But it's well worth it. Look at them."

He nodded toward the women who were huddled beside the bar, hugging and chattering. "Where are the plans, Gus?"

"Downstairs in the bottom drawer of the cabinet in the master bathroom. That's a helluva setup. Nice Jacuzzi." Gus swigged his beer. "Did you lease this baby for the night?"

"I did. Sienna and I will be spending the night on board. You're all invited to Bonnie's when we get back to the marina," Michael checked his watch, "which should be in a few hours." He grinned. "Have fun."

"Very funny." Gus smirked. "And we're taking Sienna's mom and aunt to the hotel afterward?"

"Yup, and we'll pick them up tomorrow and bring them to the cottage. They're staying for a week."

Gus lifted a brow, and his beer. "Back 'atcha. Have fun."

The captain poked his graying head through the doorway. "If everyone is on board, Mr. Chessler, we're ready to set sail."

"All good here, Captain. Thanks."

The man, whose uniform was immaculate and complexion seasoned, tipped his cap.

The seas were calm as they cruised the Greenwich coastline. The women, enjoying a potpourri of hors d'oeuvres, had moved to the sofa. Perched on barstools, the men shared crackers and dip, beer and liquor, talking sports and work.

After sneaking off to the stateroom, Michael returned with a cylinder containing rolled up sketches which he stowed behind the bar.

HER SURPRISE

Two hours into the cruise, Michael pulled Sienna aside. "It's time to go outside."

"What?" she said, following.

An arm around her, he stood at the stairs, gesturing, "Up to the deck, everyone."

The night was cool, the sky studded with stars. In the distance, the shoreline glistened with lights. The celebrants gathered on the lighted deck as The Mystic headed back from a brief stop at New London.

"What do you have there?" Sienna tugged Michael's arm.

"Happy Birthday, sweetheart." He kissed her cheek and unrolled the plans.

"What's this?"

He smiled. "You said you wanted to live in a lighthouse. This is the best I could do."

"Oh my God, Michael," she screeched, stunned, the plans a blur. She held them up for the others to see. "I'm about to faint. I can't believe you did this. I'm going to cry."

"Don't do that," said Michael. "You'll ruin your makeup." The pad of his thumb slid gently beneath her tearing eye.

"This is the most wonderful surprise ever."

He gathered her in his arms. "This is supposed to be a happy night."

"I *am* happy. I'm crying with joy." She burst into sobbing laughter.

The plans were passed from hand to hand.

When Bonnie saw the floor plan, she muttered, "Holy shit," then looked at Michael and said, "Please don't move her too far away."

"We'll be less than a half hour's drive . . ."

"I'm not leaving the hospital." Sienna grinned. "I guess this is an appropriate time to make my announcement. I got my promotion!"

"You never told me . . ." Bonnie's bottom lip turned down.

"I'll be heading Patient Services, and as soon as there's an opening, you're coming with me."

"I'm speechless."

"That's a first," Tessa snorted at Bonnie, then turned to Margaret. "Our daughter's finally putting her Master's Degree to use."

Margaret held Sienna close. "Congratulations, honey. It's about time your life straightened out. I'm so proud of you."

"She struck gold this time," Tessa shouted. "A great job and a good man."

Margaret shot her a look. "Rein it in, Tess . . ."

"You're eyes aren't blurry, are they?" said Michael, reaching for Sienna's hand.

"No. Why?"

"Because that's where your lighthouse is going." He pointed to the glittering Greenwich shoreline.

"I don't know what to say . . ." Sienna wanted to throw her arms around him, and tell him that she loved him, but for now, she just threw her arms around him.

She studied the drawing. The two-story house was L-shaped and held rows and rows of traditional windows. The front was faced with fieldstone three-quarters high, with dormer peaks covered in white clapboard. Two chimneys rose from a black tiled roof, and a narrow tower resembling a light house was nestled between the angles of the exterior walls. A second floor veranda ran the length of the master bedroom suite, and a patio below trimmed the entire back of the house which stood before the Atlantic.

"We have a lot to celebrate, and drinks down in the lounge," said Gus. "Back to the party, everyone."

HIS SURPRISE

Returning to the main level, Tessa, as promised, pulled Michael aside.

"Come on. Have a glass of wine with me while they're over there doing their thing." She motioned to the tour of the staterooms that was about to begin. "Let's sit and chat, shall we?"

"Nothing I'd like more." Michael poured two glasses of wine and followed.

Sienna shot him a sympathetic look before Bonnie and Margaret pulled her away. She glanced back once more. Michael and Tessa were seated at the far end of the sofa, apparently in pleasant conversation, as Tessa wasn't scowling. She blew him a kiss and followed the others down a flight of stairs.

"When Sienna visited in July, she was a wreck. Between her mother's fall, and trying to get over what that drug addict did to her, she was nearly torn apart. Margaret and I were worried sick about her." Tessa pressed her fingers into Michael's arm and looked directly into his eyes. "She didn't say too much about you, which concerned me, but I'm happy to see you're taking good care of her. She seems like herself again. I think you had a lot to do with it." She dug her fingers tighter into his arm.

The tension on Michael's face eased. "I appreciate you telling me this."

Tessa's gray eyes were uncharacteristically warm, her words gentle, and then a sour look crossed her face. "That Rob Lucas. He was the devil himself. He stalked that poor girl. From the day

Margaret and I met him we knew he was evil, but do kids ever listen to their folks? Of course not. Unfortunately, Sienna had to learn on her own. Worse than the hard way." She shook her head and pursed her mouth into a bitter frown. "Not only did he leave her bleeding on the floor, dead for all he knew, but then he went and killed himself — and almost took some poor soul with him."

"Really . . ." Michael fell silent. Rob Lucas — the name was so familiar. *Rob Lucas.* "Sienna never mentioned him by name." Michael's mouth went dry.

"Too painful, no doubt. It's amazing she's still in one piece. He put her through hell. And right before her birthday no less."

"Her birthday?" Michael counted back months. "So it happened around this time last year?" Stomach churning, he set his wine glass on a table, color draining from his face.

"Robert Lucas from Canada?" The words barely made it through his lips.

Tessa looked at him askance. "That's right. He followed her to New York, broke into her apartment and — well afterward, she moved out of that place to where she lives now. Did you know him?" She stared with disapproval.

In his mind's eye, Michael saw the headlights that appeared out of nowhere that terrible night.

"Interstate 95, pickup truck, head on collision." Michael's voice held the alarm on his face.

"Yes. September one, last year. Sienna told you all about it then?"

"She didn't tell me everything . . ."

The pressure on her neck increases as his fingernails dig into her flesh. She tries to pry loose, but she is losing consciousness. The horror of Rob's face is growing dimmer. His violence begins to fade. Her arms fall limply to her sides, then everything goes black.

Rob stares down at her lying deathly still on the floor. A stream of blood rounds welts that are rising on the soft tissue of her neck, pooling above her clavicle. Realizing what he's done, he begins to sober. Panic sets in, surging through his veins with greater intensity than the drug-fueled euphoria that hyped his central nervous system during the vicious assault.

Without touching her, or checking for a pulse, he flees the apartment, the same way he entered, through the back window, the fire escape. In his haste, he knocks Sienna's potted geraniums and coral tea roses from their place on a slatted shelf.

He jumps to the ground. His boots land in a mound of broken clay planters mixed with dampened potting soil. Trampling severed petals and stems, he runs.

Not once looking back, he hops into his pickup. His high is wearing off fast, and he doesn't like being sober, especially after what he's just done.

He stomps on the accelerator and heads for the highway. He sees a road sign: New England. He'll hide in the forests there, become a hermit if he has to. He just needs to lay low for a while and get his head together. No one will be the wiser when he reenters civilization.

As he drives, the fog in his mind begins to clear, leaving him with a throbbing pain across his forehead, down the side of his skull and into his neck. His heart slams inside his chest, it pains. Although his breath is short, he takes another two bumps, but this time the coke does nothing for him; he's no longer invincible, isn't even angry. Paranoia takes hold as the road begins to crowd. Why are other drivers staring at him? Is he being followed? Will a stranger crossing his path guess he's just committed a murder? Does it show on his face?

He's startled by his reflection in the rearview mirror. Not only is he disheveled, but his eyes are bloodshot, his skin is sallow, lined like an old man's.

What have I done? Why? Why? Damn you, Sienna. He drives recklessly, weaving in and out of rush hour traffic until nightfall, when he turns off the interstate, and roams the roads in search of a motel. The drugs, lack of food, and exhaustion have taken their toll. Vision blurred, he veers back onto I-95 — in the wrong direction.

Michael had been silent for too long, staring off into space, pain on his face telling.

Tessa slammed her palms to her heart. "Dear Lord, it was you. We knew he hurt someone badly, but with Sienna in the hospital and all, we just never — I guess we didn't want to know. She had her own grief to deal with."

For a while they sat in silence. Finally, Michael gathered himself and told Tessa all he could remember of the accident. The midnight ride home from a meeting, exiting off I-95 to stop for gas. The glaring headlights that suddenly appeared out of the rain — the head on collision. Michael had tried to swerve, but the narrow ramp made avoiding the pickup impossible.

As Tessa stared, Michael relived the accident: ear-shattering explosion, breaking glass, odd sensation of abruptness followed by slow motion, then darkness. Memories his mind had resisted for months were now a flash flood.

"Saying it's a small world wouldn't be appropriate in this case. It's plain irony, isn't it?" Tessa's voice held sorrow.

"Yep." Michael sighed. "I'm not sure I ever believed in fate before . . ."

The look of disbelief on Tessa's face turned to fear. "This will be one hell of a shock to Sienna. I'm sorry for what he did to you, but I'm not sure she could handle it. Looking at you every day, remembering Rob . . ." Tessa's pearl eyes turned to slate.

"She doesn't have to know." Michael's jaw set. "We can keep it between us."

Tessa sighed. "Agreed. I'm ready for another, how about you?" She held up her glass.

Michael rose. "Something stronger?"

"Definitely."

JUST WHEN THINGS WERE GOING GOOD

Michael's lips felt tight, but the moment he set eyes on Sienna making her way through the others, his face broke into a smile. He drew her into his arms. "I missed you."

She still had that mind-cleansing influence he had come to rely on. The past was gone, very close to being forgotten. His lips crushed hers with more passion than he would have liked to display in public.

"Wow," she whispered. "What was that about?"

"Aunt Tessa gave me a pep-talk. Did she coach football?"

Sienna laughed.

Beaming, Tessa put herself between them. "You've got yourself one heck of a man here. And by the way, you look lovely. I like that dress."

Margaret didn't seem surprised by their display of emotion, but shocked that Tessa didn't appear the least bit disturbed that Sienna's shoulders were bare.

"Come on, Tess. Let's give the kids a chance to be alone. They've had enough of us for one evening."

Sienna's brows knit. "What did you say to her? She really loves you."

"Is she the only one?" Passion deepened his eyes.

Sienna blinked, her stomach fluttering. Michael seemed different. There was something in the air . . .

"Come on, honey. Let's go outside. There's something I want to talk to you about."

She smiled up at him. "More surprises?"

He kissed the tip of her nose. "Come on. You'll see."

They stepped into the night, Michael leading her onto the deck. For a moment they didn't speak, they simply gazed into each other's eyes.

"Baby . . ." Michael swept her into his arms, burying his face in her hair. "I love you," he whispered. "I want to spend the rest of my life with you." His lips brushed her neck.

His words put her over the edge, and she melted inside. How much stronger could her feelings grow before she exploded with love?

"I love you too." She raised her face for a soft kiss, then looked into his eyes. "I never thought I'd feel this way."

"You wouldn't believe how much I want you. Right here. Right now." He breathed heavily into her ear. "This is crazy. I'm standing right beside you and still can't get close enough."

"I know what you mean." She pressed against him so tightly, nothing could come between them. "I can't get enough of you."

Music from the cabin drifted to the deck. Swaying, they began a slow dance to the music of *TNL: You stepped out of a dream into my life, Oh how easy things seem when I look in your eyes, I see only heaven in a blue sky of love, You stand at the doorway taking my hand, Faces gather like storm clouds, Through the crowds . . . I see only you.*

"The house wasn't your *only* gift," Michael said, reaching into a pocket of his jacket.

With a sweet frown Sienna said, "There's *nothing* that could top that house — other than being with you." She shook her head then added, "You're unbelievable." When she spotted the small brocade box in his hand, she drew in a sharp breath. "What?"

Michael pressed it into her hand and watched her lift the lid.

In moonlight, Sienna's hair was platinum. The moon also caught the fire inside the rose cut diamond solitaire ring.

"Michael," she gasped, lifting her eyes to his. "It's so beautiful."

He slowly slipped six carats of brilliance onto her delicate finger. "Marry me?"

"How many times can I faint in one night. . ." Sienna was trembling. Her eyes flooded with tears, tumbling over her lashes. "I never thought I'd . . . Before we met I . . . Oh, Michael. I want nothing more than to spend the rest of my life with you. I can't believe it. Am I dreaming?"

"If you are, then I am too." He smiled, taking her hand to see how exquisite the ring looked, then gathered her in his arms.

Following a heated kiss that seemed to last longer than the entire cruise, she opened her eyes to the passion in his. "I love you so much," she whispered, then reached for his hand, her voice ringing with excitement. "I can't wait to go down and show them. Tell them we're getting married! Come on."

"Hold on, you. Don't rush off so fast."

Sienna had already turned, and in her excitement, her hand slipped from his at the same time her stiletto caught on the leg of a deck chair positioned against the rear wall. Her body lunged forward, the force hurling her against the side of the vessel. She stumbled into an area where there was nothing more than a rope between her, the shallow wall of the yacht, and the ocean.

Michael reached out for her, but in a second she was up and over the side, her shoe catching in the rope as she plunged head first into hell. The ocean raged like a ravenous demon, so cold, so angry. Waves coiled like a noose around her neck, tightening, squeezing the air from her lungs. Thrashing like snared prey, she tried to stay afloat but the current pulled her under. The ring Michael had just given her was ripped off her finger. Choking, she couldn't scream. She panicked, and for a moment blacked out, then blissful calm swept over her and her mind was clear. The day was distant, the sky aglow. She ran through fields, ran from death, from Rob. Memories fired off, tearing through her mind.

Michael called out to her, and the next moment he was dangling beside her, hoisting her back onto the deck. She thought she heard him cry out in pain, "Oh, God, Sienna!"

The hard, cold surface bit into her tender flesh. She gasped, spitting up salty water. She couldn't see Michael; the night had turned too dark. Still, through burning eyes she witnessed him hovering over her, crying. She had never seen him cry before. Confused, she watched in horror as he wavered. Then his limbs seemed to crumble and he sank to the deck beside her. She saw his legs, twisted grotesquely beneath the weight of his body, and cried out. "Michael!"

The rest was a blur as Sienna heard hysterical voices, felt arms pulling Michael away from where she lay prone, blood trickling from a head wound. She heard the wail of an ambulance that raced the yacht to the pier. The scene on the deck was chaotic, Margaret and Tessa wringing their hands, sobbing. Bonnie stood, speechless, tears streaming down her face. The others, too, watched in horror.

"Michael, move your legs!" Strapped to a gurney Sienna screamed. "Michael," she screamed again. "Your back! I'm sorry. Dear God . . ."

While saving her life, Michael had reinjured his back and would once again lose the precious use of his legs. She would still love him, as she would forever, but she knew the loss was something Michael could never accept. If he never took another step it would be her fault. Michael, and their world that had just begun, would fall apart.

"Honey." Michael's voice sliced through the cloud inside her head. "Sienna." His voice was urgent. "Wake up. Sweetheart, open your eyes, please."

"Michael," she whispered, as his face slowly came into focus. "Your legs," she said weakly. "You're standing. You can move your legs?"

"I'm fine, sweetheart. It's you I'm worried about. You took a hell of a fall on the deck. How do you feel?" He leaned over her, his face a mask of worry.

"Kind of dizzy." She gazed around to find herself dressed in a soft white gown, lying in an E.R. bed at Manchester General. Her fingers fumbled through her hair. It was dry. "Did I fall overboard?" she asked in a childlike voice, her eyes still dazed, watery blue.

"No, honey, you didn't walk the plank," he said softly, almost making her smile. "You tripped over a chair, bumped your head, and it knocked the daylights out of you. You almost gave everyone heart attacks." He nuzzled her hand, whispering, "I should have known something like this would be inevitable. Remember the day we met? You're still an adorable klutz." He stroked her hair from her face. His eyes smiled.

"My ring!" She pulled back her hand to find there was no ring on her finger. "What happened . . ." She struggled to distinguish between reality and dream. "I remember dancing to a beautiful song, and we kissed. I thought you gave me a ring?" Was it in her mind? Were her desires so strong she had actually imagined it all?

Michael pressed his lips to her cheek. "This song?" He breathed the love song into her ear. *"Only you, you placed your kiss on my soul, stood by my side, you made me whole, In a world filled with sorrow, without escape no tomorrow, Faces gathered like storm clouds, My heart the lonely sound, Till through the crowd . . . I see only you."*

He reached into his pocket.

"Is this what you're looking for?" he said, slipping the shimmering pink champagne diamond onto her finger. Beneath the hospital fluorescents the ring glistened brighter than sunlight. "They took everything when they brought you in. Do you remember the ambulance?"

"I heard a siren. I felt the ocean pull the ring off my finger . . . You found it!"

"That was the EMT removing your ring, not the ocean. She gave it to me to hold."

For a moment, Sienna allowed her sleepy eyes to close, her head to slip to the side. "It was all a horrible nightmare, just like one of my old ones, but worse, because you were hurt." She turned to Michael. "I dreamt I was drowning, and you saved me." She reached up, and he took her into his arms. "Thank God you're alright," she whispered. "When can we go home?"

"They want to keep you overnight. Just to make sure

you're okay."

"How's my mom doing? And Aunt Tessa? They must be so worried."

"They're right outside, and holding up fine. I can bring them in if you're up to it."

She shook her head. "Where's Bonnie?"

"Everyone's in the waiting room. They want to make sure *you're* fine before they go. Bonnie will take care of your mom and aunt, and we'll all be together tomorrow."

"I don't want you to leave."

"I'm not going anywhere. I'm staying right here all night." He pointed to a chair-bed in the corner of the room. "We'll go home tomorrow, together. I gave Bonnie my key so she could stop at the cottage and bring back some comfortable clothes for us."

"I'm sorry for ruining the night," she sniffed.

"Hush," he said, kissing her.

THE END

The next morning as they stepped through the hospital doors, Sienna and Michael walked into crisp fresh air. It was almost ten a.m., and for some privileged physicians, rounds were just beginning.

Greg Trainer rolled out of his Porsche, secured his aviator sunglasses, then hurried to open the passenger door. He helped out a willowy blonde.

"Come on, dear," he said, taking her hand.

Arms entwined, Michael and Sienna passed. Trainer nodded, an inquisitive look on his face, eyes following Sienna who wore Michael's hiked-up sweats.

Arms tightening around one another, they exchanged side glances, smiling briefly.

Michael leaned close to Sienna's ear. "He's still at it, I see."

"He gets older, they get younger." Sienna giggled.

Before helping her into the Mercedes, Michael's lips brushed hers. He swept a lock of her hair behind an ear. "I love you, honey," he said softly.

"I love you too, Michael," she whispered, smiling into his sable eyes. Her arms went around his neck. "Forever."

Thunder sounded in the distance, and a passing cloud came out of nowhere, dropping dime sized splatters on the windshield. Michael's brow glistened.

"Let's go home." She sighed against his chest.

"Stop for breakfast first? Looks like our picnic at the beach might have to wait." He wiped rain from his lashes.

"I love the rain . . ." Sienna's heart filled her eyes.

"I know you do." A slow grin spread across Michael's face as he watched her settle into the car. He pulled down the gull-wing door and carefully pressed it closed, while Sienna gazed down at the sparkling ring of love he had placed on her finger — twice.

He slid in beside her, and after a stare that reached into her soul, he took her in his arms. "Forever, my love."

ABOUT THE AUTHOR

January Valentine is the pen name of Victoria Valentine, New York writer and Indie Book Publisher, and founder of *Water Forest Press Books.* www.waterforestpress.com

Other books by Victoria Valentine:

The Cutest Little Duckie children's color storybook. http://www.amazon.com/Cutest-Little-Duckie-Victoria-Valentine/

Desert Noon romance poetry. http://www.amazon.com/Desert-Noon-Passionate-Poetry-ebook/

At the Stroke of Midnight 24 tales of terror & all books: http://www.waterforestpressbooks.miiduu.com

Sweet Dreams: on Amazon and Water Forest Press

Victoria's website: www.victoriavalentine.net

It is my hope that you enjoyed reading *Love Dreams* as much as I enjoyed writing it. I welcome feedback.

I can be reached at: ValentinePress@aol.com

January Valentine

REFERENCES

Chevy Suburban
Toyota Corolla
Dodge Durango
Porsche
Mercedes
Volkswagen Jetta
Volvo
BMW
Cadillac CTS
Honda Motorcycles
Pollywog wheelchair
Pepsi
Juvederm
Febreze
Dom Perignon Rose
Kenny G
Princess Rose Cruise Ship
Bain de Soleil
Corona Extra
Macy's
Nestle Toll House
Wrangler jeans
Converse
Tums
As Seen On TV
TNL: Victoria Valentine
"Night of the Comet": *MGM*. 1984 Written and Directed by Thom Eberhardt. A Thomas Coleman and Michael Rosenblatt Presentation.